Praise for Christine Feehan and Her Carpathian Novels

"The queen of paranormal romance!
The one who started it all!
I love everything she does."

—*New York Times* bestselling
author J. R. Ward

"Feehan has a knack for bringing
vampiric Carpathians to vivid,
virile life in her Dark Carpathian novels."

—*Publishers Weekly*

"After Bram Stoker, Anne Rice, and
Joss Whedon (who created the venerated
Buffy the Vampire Slayer), Feehan is the
person most credited with popularizing
the neck gripper."

—*Time* magazine

By Christine Feehan

Dark Prince • *Dark Desire* • *Dark Gold*
Dark Magic • *Dark Challenge* • *Dark Fire*
Dark Legend • *Dark Guardian*
Dark Symphony • *Dark Melody*
Dark Destiny • *Dark Secret* • *Dark Demon*
Dark Celebration • *Dark Possession*
Dark Hunger • *Dark Curse* • *Dark Slayer*
Dark Peril

Wild Rain • *Burning Wild* • *Wild Fire*

Magic in the Wind • *Twilight Before Christmas*
Oceans of Fire • *Dangerous Tides*
Safe Harbor • *Turbulent Sea*
Hidden Currents

Waterbound

Shadow Game • *Mind Game* • *Night Game*
Conspiracy Game • *Deadly Game*
Predatory Game • *Murder Game* • *Street Game*

Lair of the Lion • *The Scarletti Curse*

CHRISTINE FEEHAN

Dark Magic

A Carpathian Novel

AVONBOOKS

An Imprint of HarperCollinsPublishers

DARK MAGIC. Copyright © 2000 by Christine Feehan. All rights reserved. Printed in the United States of America. No part of this book may be used or reproduced in any manner whatsoever without written permission except in the case of brief quotations embodied in critical articles and reviews. For information, address HarperCollins Publishers, 195 Broadway, New York, NY 10007.

First Avon Books mass market printing: November 2010

Print Edition ISBN: 978-0-06-201951-6
Digital Edition ISBN: 978-0-06-201335-4

Cover art by Patrick King
Cover photograph © Colin D. Young/Shutterstock

This book is for my beloved sister, Renee Jones.
You share every joy and sorrow in my life.
I never have to look for you,
I know you are always there.
If anyone in this world deserves a true lifemate,
it is you....

Chapter One

The night was alive with the heartbeats of countless people. He walked among them, unseen, undetected, moving with the fluid grace of a jungle predator. Their scents were strong in his nostrils. Cloying perfume. Sweat. Shampoos. Soaps. Alcohol. Drugs. AIDS. The sweet, insidious smell of blood. There were so many in this city. Cattle. Sheep. Prey. The city was the perfect hunting ground.

But he had fed well that day, so even though the blood whispered to him, tempting him with the promise of strength, power, the seductive rush of excitement, he refrained from indulging his cravings. After all his centuries of walking the earth, he knew the whispered promises were empty. He already had enormous power and strength, and he knew that the rush, addicting though it might be, was the same illusory high the humans' drugs provided.

The stadium in this modern city was huge, with thousands of people packed inside. He walked past the guards without hesitation, secure in the knowledge that they could not detect his presence.

The magic show—combining feats of escape, disappearance, and mystery—was almost finished, and a hush of breathless anticipation had fallen over the crowd. On stage a column of mist rose eerily from the spot where, a moment before, the magician herself had stood.

He blended into the shadows, his pale silver gaze riveted to the stage. Then she emerged from the mist, every man's fantasy, every man's dream of hot, steamy nights. Of satin and silk. Mystical, mysterious, a mix of innocence and seduction, she moved with the grace of an enchantress. Thick blue-black hair cascaded in waves to her slim hips. A white Victorian lace gown covered her body, cupping high, full breasts and molding her narrow rib cage and tiny, tucked-in waist. Small pearl buttons down the front were open from hem to thigh, revealing enticing glimpses of shapely legs. Her trademark dark glasses concealed her eyes but drew attention to her lush mouth, perfect teeth, and classic cheekbones.

Savannah Dubrinsky, one of the world's greatest magicians.

He had endured nearly a thousand years of black emptiness. No joy, no rage, no desire. No emotion. Nothing but the crouching beast, hungry, insatiable. Nothing but the growing darkness, the stain spreading across his soul. His pale eyes slid over her small, perfect figure, and need slammed into him. Hard. Ugly. Painful. His body swelled, hardened, every muscle taut, hot, aching. His fingers curled slowly around the back of a stadium seat, digging deeply, leaving visible impressions of a man's fingers in the metal. Perspiration beaded on his forehead. He let the pain wash over him, through him. Savored it. *He felt.*

His body didn't just want her. It demanded her, burned for her. The beast raised its head and eyed her, marked her, claimed her. Hunger rose sharply, dangerously, ferociously. On stage, two assistants began chaining her, their hands touching her soft skin, their bodies brushing hers. A low growl rumbled in his throat; his pale eyes glowed a feral red. In that moment one thousand years of self-control went up in flames, setting a dangerous predator free. No one was safe, mortal or immortal, and he knew it.

On stage, Savannah's head came up and swung around as if she were scenting danger, a small fawn caught in a trap, run to ground.

His gut clenched hotly. *Feelings.* Dark desire. Raw lust. A stark, primitive need to possess. He closed his eyes and inhaled sharply. He smelled her fear and was pleased by it. Having thought himself lost for all eternity, he didn't care that his feelings were so intense that they bordered on violence. They were genuine. And there was joy in the ability to feel, no matter how dangerous. It didn't matter to him that he had marked her unfairly, that she did not rightfully belong to him, that he had manipulated the outcome of their union even before her birth, that he had broken the laws of their people in order to have her. None of it mattered. Only that she was his at last.

He felt her mind search; it brushed at him like the wings of a beautiful butterfly. But he was an ancient, powerful and knowledgeable beyond the boundaries of Earth. He was the one his own kind spoke of in whispers, with awe, with fear, with dread. *The Dark One.* Despite her premonition of danger, she had no hope of finding him until he allowed it.

His lips drew back in a silent snarl as the blond assistant bent to trail a hand across Savannah's face and brush her forehead with a kiss before locking her, manacled and chained, inside a steel vault. Fangs exploded into his mouth, and the beast eyed the man with the cold, unblinking stare of a killer. Deliberately he focused on the blond's throat—let him feel, just for one moment, the agony of strangulation. The man grabbed at his throat and stumbled, then recovered, dragging air into his lungs. He took a quick, nervous look around, trying in vain to see into the audience. Still breathing hard in alarm, he turned back to help lower the vault into a chamber flooded with water.

The unseen predator growled his warning softly, a deadly, menacing sound only the blond could hear. The man on stage whitened visibly and muttered something to the other assistant, who shook his head quickly with a slight frown.

While the return of his feelings brought indescribable joy to the ancient, his loss of control was dangerous, even to him. He turned his back on the performance and left the stadium, his every step away from Savannah painful. Still, he accepted the pain, rejoiced in his ability to feel it.

His first hundred years had been a wild orgy of feeling, senses, power, desires—even goodness. But slowly, relentlessly, the darkness that imperiled the soul of a Carpathian male without a lifemate had claimed him. Emotions faded, colors disappeared, until he simply existed. He experimented, found knowledge and power, and paid the price for it. He fed, he hunted, he killed when he deemed it appropriate. And always the darkness thickened, threatening to taint his soul forever, to turn him into one of the damned, the undead.

She was innocent. There was laughter in her, compassion, goodness. She was light to his darkness. A bitter smile curved his sensual mouth, touching it with cruelty. His bulging, sinewy muscles rippled. He tossed back his thick, jet-black, shoulder-length hair. His face became as harsh and merciless as he was. His pale eyes, which easily drew mortals, held them, entranced them, became the eyes of death, the silver slash of cold steel.

Even from a distance he felt thunderous applause shake the ground, the roaring approval that signaled Savannah's escape from the flooded vault. He blended into the night, a sinister shadow impossible for either humans or his kind to detect. His patience was that of the earth itself, his stillness that of the mountains. He stood without moving amid the insanity of the crowds rowdily pouring out of the stadium and into their cars in the parking lot, creating the inevitable traffic jam. He knew where she was at every moment; he had made certain of their link when she was but a child. And not even death could break the bond he had forged between them. She had put an ocean between them, running away to her mother's native country, America, and in her innocence had thought herself safe.

The passage of time meant little to him. Eventually the sounds of cars and people faded away, and the lights blinked out around him, leaving the night to him. He inhaled deeply, drank in her scent. He stretched, a panther stalking prey. He could hear her soft laughter, low, musical, unforgettable. She was talking with the blond assistant, overseeing her props being packed up for loading onto the trucks. Although the two were still in the building and a great distance from him, he could hear their conversation without effort.

"I am so happy this tour is finally over." Savannah meandered wearily after the last of the crew to the loading dock, lowered herself onto the stairs, and watched as the men lifted the steel vault into the huge truck. "Did we make all the money you thought we would?" she teased her assistant gently. Both knew she didn't care about the money and never paid the slightest bit of attention to the financial side of things. Without Peter Sanders to see to all the details, she'd probably be flat broke.

"More than I thought. We can call this one a success." Peter grinned down at her. "San Francisco is supposed to be a fabulous city. Why don't we vacation here? We can do the whole tourist thing—cable cars, the Golden Gate, Alcatraz. We can't pass up this opportunity—we may never come here again."

"Not me," Savannah declined, rousing a little as Peter threw himself onto the step beside her. "I'm catching up on z's. You can tell me all about it."

"Savannah . . ." Peter sighed heavily. "I'm asking you out."

She sat up straight, removed the dark glasses, and looked directly at him. Heavily fringed with long dark lashes, her eyes were deep blue, almost violet, with strange slivers of silver radiating through them like stars. As always, when she looked straight at him, Peter felt a strange disorientation, as if he were falling, drowning, lost in the gleaming stars in her eyes.

"Oh, Peter." Her voice was soft, musical, mesmerizing. It was one of the things that had brought her stardom so quickly. She could hold an audience effortlessly with her voice alone. "All our sexiness and flirting in the show is just an act. We're friends, and we work together, and that means everything to me. When I was growing up, the closest thing I ever had to a best friend was a wolf." She didn't add that she still thought of that wolf every day. "I'm not willing to risk a relationship I value by trying to make something else out of it."

Peter blinked and shook his head to clear it. She always sounded so incredibly logical, so convincing. Whenever she looked at him, it was impossible to disagree with anything she said. She could steal his will as easily as she stole his breath. "A wolf? A real one?"

She nodded. "When I was younger, we lived in a very remote part of the Carpathian Mountains. There were no children to play with. One day a little wolf cub wandered out of the woods near our house. He would play with me whenever I was alone." There was a faint ache in her voice at the thought of her lost animal friend. "He just seemed to know when I needed him, when I was sad or lonely. He was always gentle. Even when he was teething, he only bit me a few times." She rubbed her arm in memory, her fingertips marking the spots in an unconscious caress. "As he grew, he became my constant companion; we were inseparable. I was never afraid in the woods at night because he was always there to protect me. He was enormous, with glossy black fur and intelligent gray eyes that looked at me with such understanding. Sometimes he looked so solemn that he seemed to be carrying the weight of the world on his back. When I made the decision to come to America, it was hard to leave my parents, but heartbreaking to leave my wolf. Before I left, I cried for three nights straight, my arms around his neck. He never moved, not once, as if he understood and was mourning, too. If there had been a way, I would have brought him with me. But he needed to be free."

"You're telling me the truth? A real wolf?" Peter asked incredulously. While he could believe that Savannah could easily tame man or beast, he was puzzled by the animal's behavior. "I thought wolves were shy of people. Not that I've met very many of them—at least not the four-legged variety."

She flashed him a grin. "He was huge and could be ferocious, but my wolf was anything but shy with me. Of course, he was never really around anyone else, not even my parents. He would lope off into the woods if someone came near. Still, he would watch from afar to make certain I was safe. I'd see his eyes shining in the forest, watching, and it made me feel safe."

Realizing he had allowed her to distract him, Peter deliberately looked away from her, knotting his fists in determination. "It isn't natural, the way you live, Savannah. You isolate yourself from any close relationships."

"We're close," she pointed out gently. "I'm very fond of you, Peter, like a brother. I've always wanted a brother."

"Don't, Savannah. You haven't even given us a chance. And who else do you have in your life? I escort you to parties and interviews. I oversee the accountant and arrange the bookings and make certain the bills are paid. The only thing I don't do is sleep with you."

A low growl rumbled warningly through the night, sending a chill spiraling down Peter's spine. Savannah's head went up, and she looked cautiously around. Peter stood, peering toward the trucks pulling away from the loading dock.

"Did you hear that?" He reached a hand down to draw

Savannah to her feet, his eyes frantically searching every shadow. "I didn't tell you, but the oddest thing happened during the show." He was whispering as if the very night had ears. "After I put you in the vault, my throat closed off. It was as if someone had his hands around my throat, someone very powerful. I felt a murderous anger directed at me." He pushed a hand through his hair and laughed nervously. "Silly imagination, I know. But I heard that exact same growl in my head. It's insane, Savannah, but it felt as if I was being warned off you."

"Why didn't you say anything to me?" she demanded, fear in her eyes. Without warning the lights in the docking area blinked out, leaving them in total darkness. Savannah's fingers tightened on Peter's, and he had the distinct feeling they were being watched, even hunted. His car was a distance away, the parking lot shrouded in blackness. Where were the security guards?

"Peter, we have to get out of here. If I tell you to run, do it, and don't look back, no matter what." Her voice was low and compelling, enough so that for a moment he thought he would do anything to please her. But her small body, so close to his, was shaking, and chivalry won.

"Stay behind me, honey. I've got a bad feeling about this," Peter cautioned. Like all celebrities, Savannah suffered her share of threats and stalkers. She was worth a few million, not to mention the steamy, sexy image she exuded. Savannah had a strange, mesmerizing effect on men, as if the memory of her haunted them for eternity.

Savannah cried out in warning a heartbeat before something hit Peter hard in the chest, driving the air from his lungs, tearing her hand from his. He grunted, his chest on fire, feeling as if a ton of bricks had crushed him. His eyes locked with Savannah's and he could see terror there. Something enormously strong caught at him, jerked him thirty feet backward, wrenching his arm from its socket, snapping bones like twigs. He screamed, feeling hot breath on his neck.

Savannah whispered his name, covered the distance between them in a single leap, and flung herself at his attacker. She was struck a blow across her face so hard that she was flung like a rag doll from the loading dock to the asphalt parking lot. Although she twisted agilely in midair and landed on her feet like a cat, her head was ringing, and white dots danced in front of her eyes. Before she could recover, the beast attacking Peter sank its fangs into his throat, ripped and tore, then gulped at the rich blood spurting from the terrible wound. Peter managed to turn his head, expecting a wolf or at least a huge dog. Red eyes glowed at him evilly from a white, skeletal face. Peter died in agony and terror, in fear and guilt for failing to protect Savannah.

With a low, venomous hiss, the creature carelessly tossed away Peter's body, which landed a few feet from Savannah, blood forming a thick pool, spreading slowly across the asphalt. The beast lifted its head and turned toward her, grinning horribly, triumphantly revealing its jagged teeth.

She stepped back, her heart pounding in fear. Grief welled up so sharply for a moment that she couldn't breathe. *Peter.* Her first human friend in her entire twenty-three years. Dead because of her.

She regarded the gaunt stranger who had killed him. Peter's blood smeared his face and teeth. Obscenely, his tongue came out and licked at the red stains on his lips. His eyes burned at her, taunted her. "I found you first. I knew I would."

"Why did you kill him?" There was horror in her voice.

He laughed, launched himself into the air, and landed a few feet from her. "You should try it sometime; all that fear floods the bloodstream with adrenaline. There's nothing like it. I like them looking at me, knowing it's coming."

"What do you want?" She never took her eyes or her mind from him, her body remaining still and ready, perfectly balanced.

"I will be your husband. Your lifemate." There was a threat in his voice. "Your father, the great Mikhail Dubrinsky, will just have to take back the death sentence he pronounced on me. The long arm of his justice doesn't quite reach San Francisco, does it?"

She tilted her chin. "And if I say no?"

"Then I take you the hard way. It might be fun—a change from all those simpering human women, puppets begging to please me."

His depravity sickened her. "They don't beg you. You take their free will. It's the only way you could have a woman." She put all the loathing and contempt she was capable of into her voice.

The ugly smile faded from his hollow features, leaving him an ugly caricature of a man, a creature from the very bowels of hell. His breath escaped in a long hiss. "You will pay for that disrespect." He lunged toward her.

A dark shadow moved out of the night, muscles rippling like steel beneath an elegant silk shirt. The shadow glided in front of Savannah like a shield, forcing her behind him. One large hand brushed her face where her assailant had struck her. The touch was brief yet incredibly tender, and the momentary contact seemed to take the pain with it as the newcomer's fingers slipped away from her skin. His pale, silvery eyes then slashed at the skeletal creature.

"Good evening, Roberto. I see you have dined well." The voice was pleasant, cultured, soothing, even hypnotic.

Savannah choked back a sob. Instantly she felt a stirring in her mind, a flood of warmth, the feeling of arms drawing her into their strong shelter.

"*Gregori*," Roberto growled, his eyes glowing with bloodlust. "I have heard whispers of the dangerous Gregori—the Dark One, the bogey man of the Carpathians. But I do not fear you." It was bravado, and they all knew it; his mind was racing frantically for an escape.

Gregori smiled, a small, humorless quirk of his lips that brought a distinctively cruel gleam to his eyes. "You obviously have never learned table manners. In all your long years, Roberto, what else have you failed to learn?"

Roberto's breath escaped in a long, slow hiss. His head began to undulate slowly from side to side. His fingernails lengthened, becoming razor-sharp claws.

When he attacks, Savannah, you will leave this place. It was an imperious command in her head.

It was my *friend he killed*, me *that he threatened*. It was against her principles to allow anyone else to fight her battles and perhaps be injured or killed in her place. She did not stop to think why it was so easy and natural to speak with Gregori, the most feared of the Carpathian ancients, on a mental path that was not the standard path of communication for their kind.

You will do as I tell you, ma petite. The order was spoken in her mind in the same calm tone that carried undeniable authority. Savannah caught her breath, afraid of defying him. Roberto might think he was up to taking on a Carpathian as powerful as Gregori, but she knew she wasn't. She was young, a novice at her people's arts.

"You have no right to interfere, Gregori," Roberto snapped, sounding like a spoiled, petulant boy. "She is unclaimed."

Gregori's pale eyes narrowed to a slash of cold silver. "She is mine, Roberto. I claimed her many years ago. She is my lifemate."

Roberto took a cautious step to the left. "There has been no official acceptance of your union. I will kill you, and she will belong to me."

"What you have done here is a crime against humanity. What you would do to my woman is crime against our people, our treasured women, and against me personally. Justice *has* followed you to San Francisco, and the sentence our Prince Mikhail pronounced over you will be carried out. The blow you struck to my lifemate alone would earn you your fate." Gregori never raised his voice, never lost his faint, taunting smile. *Go, Savannah. I won't allow him to harm you when it is me he seeks.*

Gregori's soft laughter echoed in her head. *There is no chance of that,* ma petite. *Now do as I say, and go.* He wanted her gone before she witnessed his casual destruction of the abomination who dared to strike a woman. His woman. Savannah already feared him enough.

"I am going to kill you," Roberto said loudly, blustering to pump up his courage.

"Then I can do no other than oblige you by letting you try," Gregori replied pleasantly. His voice dropped an octave lower, became hypnotic. "You are slow, Roberto, slow and clumsy and far too incompetent to take on someone of my skill." His smile was cruel and slightly mocking.

It was impossible to avoid listening to the cadence of Gregori's voice. It worked its way into the brain and clouded the mind. Still, high and powerful from a fresh kill, filled with lust and the need to conquer, Roberto launched himself at Gregori.

Gregori simply was no longer there. He had thrust Savannah as far from them as possible, and with blurring speed he contemptuously marked Roberto's face with four deep furrows, marked it in exactly the spot that was bruised on Savannah's face.

Gregori's soft, taunting laughter sent chills down Savannah's spine. She could hear the sounds of the battle, the whimpers of pain as Gregori coolly, relentlessly, and mercilessly slashed Roberto to pieces. Loss of blood weakened the lesser creature. Compared to Gregori, he was clumsy and slow.

Savannah jammed her knuckles against her mouth and backed up several paces, but she couldn't tear her eyes away from Gregori's harsh face. It was an implacable mask, with its faint, taunting smile and the pale eyes of death. He never changed expression. His assault was the coldest, most merciless thing she had ever witnessed. Every deliberate slash contributed to Roberto's weakness until he was literally covered in a thousand cuts. Never once was Roberto able to lay a hand or a claw on Gregori. It was apparent that Roberto had no chance, that Gregori could deliver the killing blow at any time.

She looked at Peter, lifeless on the asphalt. He had been a great friend to her. She had loved him like a brother, and now he lay senselessly dead. Savannah finally fled in horror across the parking lot, taking refuge in the trees alongside it. She sank down to the ground. *Oh, Peter.* This was her fault. She had thought she had left the world of vampires and Carpathians behind. She bent her head, her stomach heaving in protest at the cold brutality of that world. She was not like these creatures. Tears tangled in her lashes and ran down her face.

Suddenly lightning sizzled and danced, a blue-white whip across the sky. An orange glow soon accompanied a crackle of flames. Savannah covered her face with her hands, knowing that Gregori was destroying Roberto's body completely. His heart and tainted blood had to be reduced to ashes to ensure that the vampire could not rise again. And no Carpathian, not even one turned vampire, should be exposed to autopsy by a human medical examiner. Physical proof of their existence in human hands would be dangerous to their entire race. She squeezed her eyes shut and tried to shut out the smell of burning flesh. Peter, too, would have to be cremated to hide the terrible gaping wound to his throat, evidence of the vampire's presence.

There was a gentle stirring of air beside her. Then Gregori's fingers curled around her arm and drew her to her feet. Up close he looked even more powerful, completely invincible. His arm curved around her shoulders and dragged her against the solid wall of his chest. His thumb touched the tears on her face; his chin brushed the top of her head.

"I am sorry I was too late to save your friend. By the time I was aware of the vampire's presence, he had already struck." He didn't add that he had been too busy rediscovering emotions and getting them under control to sense Roberto immediately. It was his first slip in a thousand years, and he wasn't ready to examine the reason too closely. Guilt, perhaps, for the manipulated chemistry he had with Savannah?

Savannah's mind brushed his and found genuine regret for her sorrow. "How did you find me?"

"I always know where you are, every moment. Five years ago you said you needed time, and I gave it to you. But I've never left you. I never will." There was a gentle finality to his words, an echo of the resolve in his mind.

Savannah's heart lurched. "Don't do this, Gregori. You know how I feel. I've created a new life for myself."

His hand, gentle in her hair, sent butterflies rising in her stomach. "You cannot change what you are. You are my lifemate, and it is time for you to come to me." His voice held velvet-soft compulsion when he whispered *lifemate*, reinforcing his tampering with nature. The more he said it, the more Savannah would believe it. True, he suddenly saw in color and felt emotion because he had found his lifemate. But Gregori also knew he had programmed their chemistry to be compatible before she was born; she had never had a chance.

Her teeth bit at her full lower lip in agitation. "You can't take me against my will, Gregori. It's against our laws."

He bent his dark head, his warm breath sending a shiver of heat coiling in the pit of her stomach. "Savannah, you will accompany me now."

She flung her head up, her blue-black hair cascading in all directions. "No. I'm the closest thing to family Peter had. I will see to the arrangements for him first. Then we will discuss us." She was wringing her hands, betraying her nervousness of him, unaware that she did so.

Gregori's larger hand covered hers and stilled the desperate twisting of her fingers. "You are not thinking straight, *ma petite*. You cannot be found on the scene. You would have no rational way to explain what happened here. I have set things up so that when his body is found and identified, no suspicion can fall upon you or any of our people."

She took a deep breath, hating that he was right. No attention could be drawn to her species. She didn't have to like it. "I won't go with you."

White teeth gleamed at her, a predator's smile. "You may attempt to defy me in this, Savannah, if you feel you must."

She touched her mind to his. Male amusement, implacable resolve, utter calm. Nothing ruffled Gregori. Not death and certainly not her defiance. "I'll call for security," she threatened desperately.

The immaculate white teeth flashed again. The silver eyes glittered. "Do you wish me to release them from the orders I gave them before you do so?"

She closed her eyes, still trembling in shock and fear. "No, no, don't do that," she whispered in defeat.

Gregori studied the misery so transparent on her face. Something tugged at his heart, something unrecognizable to him but nevertheless strong. "The dawn will be upon us in a couple of hours. We need to leave this place."

"I won't go with you," she insisted stubbornly.

"If your pride dictates that you must fight me, you may try to do so." His voice, with its Old World War cadence and formality, was almost tender.

Her eyes deepened to purple. "Stop giving me your permission! I am Mikhail and Raven's daughter, a Carpathian like yourself and not without my own powers. I have the right to my own choices!"

"If it pleases you to think so." His fingers curled easily around her slender wrist. His grip was gentle, but she could feel his enormous strength. Savannah pulled hard, testing his resolve. Gregori appeared not to notice her struggles.

"Do you wish me to make this easier on you? You fear needlessly." His mesmerizing voice was incredibly tender.

"No!" Her heart slammed painfully in her chest. "Don't control my mind. Don't make me a puppet." She knew he was powerful enough to do so, and it terrified her.

Two fingers caught her chin firmly and tipped it up so her gaze was captured by his silver one. "There is no danger of such an atrocity. I am no vampire. I am Carpathian, and you are my lifemate. I will protect you with my life. I will always see to your happiness."

She took a deep breath for control, then let it escape slowly. "We are not lifemates. I did not choose." She held on to that fact, her only hope.

"We can discuss this at a more opportune time."

She nodded warily. "I'll meet you tomorrow then."

His silent laughter filled her mind. Low. Amused. Frustratingly male. "You will come with me now." His voice lowered an octave, became warm honey, compelling, hypnotic, so mesmerizing it was impossible to fight.

Savannah dropped her forehead against the muscles of his chest. Tears were burning in her eyes and throat. "I'm afraid of you, Gregori," she admitted painfully. "I can't live the life of a Carpathian. I'm like my mother. I'm too independent, and I need my own life."

"I know of your fears, *ma petite*. I know your every thought. The bond between us is strong enough to cross oceans. We can deal with your fears together."

"I can't do this. I won't!" Savannah ducked under his arm, blurred her image, and put on a burst of blinding speed.

But no matter which way she twisted or turned, no matter how fast she ran or dodged, Gregori was with her every step of the way. When she finally wore herself out and stopped, she was at the far end of the stadium, tears streaming unchecked down her face. Gregori was beside her, solid, warm, invincible, as if he truly knew her every thought, her every move before she made it.

His arm curved around her waist, lifting her completely from her feet and locking her to him. "By allowing you your freedom, I expose you to the danger of renegades like Roberto." For a moment he dropped his head to bury his face in the thick mass of her silky hair. Then, with no warning, he launched himself into the air, a huge bird of prey with enormous strength, Savannah's small body pressed tightly to him.

She closed her eyes and allowed grief for Peter to consume her, to drive out all awareness of the creature streaking across the sky with her, taking her to his lair. Her fists curled around the thick, steel-like muscles. The wind carried the sound of her sobs up to the stars. Her tears glittered like jewels in the night.

Gregori could feel her pain as if it was his own. Her tears moved him when nothing else could. His mind reached out to the chaos of hers, finding overwhelming grief and a terrible fear of him. Deliberately he surrounded her with warmth and comfort. It brushed her mind, soothing her nerves.

Savannah opened her eyes to find herself out of the city, up in the mountains. Gregori set her gently on the steps of a huge, rambling house. He reached past her to open the door, then stepped back courteously to allow her entry.

Savannah felt small and lost, knowing that if she set

one foot in his lair, she would be placing her life in his hands. Her eyes flashed blue-white fire, as if they had caught a star and trapped it forever in their depths. Tilting her chin defiantly, she stepped backward until the porch railing brought her up short. "I refuse to enter your home."

His laugh came then, low, amused, and maddenly male. "Your body and mine chose for us. There is no other man for you, Savannah. Not now, not ever. I can feel your emotions when men, human or Carpathian, touch you. You are repulsed; you cannot bear their touch." His voice dropped lower still, a black-magic caress that seemed to send heat spreading through her like molten lava. "It is not so with my touch, *ma petite*. We both know that. Do not deny it, or I will be forced to prove my words."

"I am a mere twenty-three," she pointed out desperately. "You are centuries old. I have not lived at all."

He shrugged with casual strength, muscles rippling, his silver eyes on her beautiful, anxious face. "Then you will enjoy the benefits of my experience."

"Gregori, please try to understand. You don't love me. You don't know me. I am not like other Carpathian women. I don't want to be a brood mare for my race. I can't be your prisoner, no matter how petted and indulged I am."

He laughed softly and waved a hand dismissively in the space between them. "You *are* young, child, if you believe what you are saying." There was a gentleness in his voice that turned her heart over in spite of all her fears. "Is your mother a prisoner?"

"My parents are different. My father loves my mother.

Even so, he would sometimes walk on her rights if he could. A gilded cage is still a cage, Gregori."

There was that amusement again, warming the cold steel of his eyes. Savannah felt her temper rise. She had an almost uncontrollable urge to slap his face. His grin widened, a subtle challenge. He indicated the open door.

She forced a laugh. "We can stand out here until dawn, Gregori. I'm willing—are you?"

He leaned one hip lazily against the wall. "You think to dare me?"

"You can't force me against my will without violating our laws."

"In all the centuries I have existed, do you believe I have never broken our laws?" His soft laughter was without humor. "The things I have done render abducting you as petty as the human crime of jaywalking."

"Yet you brought Roberto to justice, even though San Francisco is Aidan Savage's territory to hunt," she pointed out, naming another powerful Carpathian who tracked down and destroyed those among them turned vampire. "Did you do that because of me?"

"You are my lifemate, the only thing that stands between me and the destruction of mortals and immortals alike." He stated it calmly, as an absolute truth. "No one will touch you or try to come between us and live. He struck you, Savannah."

"My father would—"

He was shaking his head. "Do not try to bring your father into this, *chérie*, even if Mikhael is the Prince of our people. This is between you and me. You do not want a war. Roberto struck you; that was reason enough for him to die."

She touched his mind again. No anger. Just resolve. He meant what he said. He wasn't bluffing or trying to frighten her. He wanted truth between them. Savannah pressed the back of her hand against her mouth. She had always known this moment would come. "I'm sorry, Gregori," she whispered hopelessly. "I can't be what you want. I will choose to face the dawn."

His fingers brushed her face with incredible gentleness. "You have no idea what I want from you." His hands cupped her face, thumbs stroking the satin skin over the pulse beating so frantically in her throat. "You know I cannot allow you such a choice, *ma petite*. We can talk through your fears. Come inside with me." His mind was invading hers, a warm, sweet seduction. His eyes, so pale and cold, heated to a flowing mercury that seemed to burn into her mind, threatening her very will.

Savannah's fingers dug into the railing as she felt herself drowning in hot liquid. "Stop it, Gregori!" she cried sharply, determined to break his mental hold. It was sweet torment, rushing heat, seduction so dangerous that she flung herself toward the entrance of the house to flee his dark power over her.

Gregori's arm stopped her headlong flight. His mouth moved against her ear. His body, aggressively male, hard, and ferociously aroused, brushed hers. *Say it, Savannah. Say the words.* Even the whisper in her mind was black velvet. His mouth, perfect and sensuous, so hot and moist, wandered down to her throat. The reality of his flesh was even more erotic than his mental seduction. His teeth grazed her skin lightly. His body clenched, and she could feel the the monster in him awaken, hungry, burning with need—no gentle, thinking lover but a fully aroused Carpathian male.

The words he commanded her to say nearly strangled in her throat and came out so low, it was impossible to tell whether they were spoken aloud or were merely an echo in her mind. "I come to you of my own free will."

He released her instantly, allowing her to stumble across the threshold by herself. Behind her, his large frame filled the doorway. He stood towering over her, silver eyes radiating heat, power, intense satisfaction. Gregori closed the door with his foot and reached for her.

Savannah cried out and tried to evade his touch, but he caught her up with casual strength, cradling her struggling body against his chest. His chin brushed her silky hair. "Be still, *enfante*, or you will end up bruising yourself. There is no way to fight me, and I cannot permit you to harm yourself."

"I hate you."

"You do not hate me, Savannah. You fear me, but most of all, you fear what you are," he replied calmly. He was moving through the house with long strides, carrying her to the basement, then lower still to the chamber hidden so carefully in deep earth.

Her body burned for his, and, so close to his heat, there was no relief. Hunger rose sharply, and something wild in her lifted its head.

Chapter Two

The moment Gregori lowered her to her feet, Savannah sprang away from him. The single leap put the distance of the room between them. Fear was a growing, living thing, mixing with her wild nature.

Gregori could feel her heart beat, and his own tuned itself to match the pounding rhythm of hers. Her blood called to him. He drew the scent into his lungs, into his veins, so his own blood heated and surged with a fierce, burning need. He drew breath for both of them, struggling to control the raging demon in him, struggling for the calm he needed to keep from hurting her, to keep her from hurting herself.

She looked what she was, young, wild, beautiful, her eyes deep violet with fiery stars, enormous with fear. She crouched in the farthest corner from him, her every thought so chaotic that it took him a few moments to sort the whirling emotions. Grief and guilt for her lost friend. Disgust and humiliation that her body could betray her, that she wasn't strong enough to stand up to him. Fear that he could achieve his goal, make her his mate, control her life. Fear that he would hurt her with his strength, with his own burning hunger. The need to escape was paramount; she meant to fight to the death.

Gregori faced her without expression, without moving a muscle. He searched for a way to defuse the situation. He would never allow Savannah to die. He had risked everything for her. Risked his own sanity, his very soul. He would not lose everything now through clumsiness. "I am truly sorry for the loss of your friend, Savannah," Gregori said quietly, gently, his voice low, a whisper of hypnotic music.

Her eyelashes fluttered. She blinked. His words were clearly unexpected.

"I should have been there much more quickly to save him," he admitted softly. "I will not let you down again."

She moistened her lips and dragged in air. He looked invincible, merciless. He looked like a sorcerer, exuding dark temptation from every pore. His sheer sexuality was overpowering. His gentle voice and perfect calm were at odds with the touch of sensual cruelty about his mouth, the intense burning in his pale eyes, and the implacable mask he always wore.

"I am not such a monster that I would attack you while your grief and fear are so sharp. Relax, *enfante*. Your lifemate may be a demon to all others, but you are safe. I want only to comfort you." He felt her tentative mind-touch, seeking the truth of his words. He rarely allowed anyone the intimacy of a mental bond. With her, the melding added to his deep physical ache, the swirling of unfamiliar emotions. But it also gave him pleasure. Intense pleasure.

All Savannah could detect was his need to offer her comfort. His mind seemed serenity itself, a clear, cool pool without a ripple. She felt her body relaxing, his mind calming the chaos of hers. Why was it Gregori she responded to? As he had said, any other male's touch had made her feel revulsion. He just had to be near her, and her mind and body cried out for him.

She rubbed her pounding head. Little hammers seemed to be having a field day in her skull. Gregori moved easily, casually to the nightstand beside the bed. Her gaze stayed glued to him, her face pale, shadows haunting her eyes. He crushed herbs into a crystal bowl, the soothing fragrance instantly filling the room.

"Come here, *ma chérie*." His voice was low and compelling. The sound of it washed over her like clear water. "It's almost dawn."

Her gaze shifted uncomfortably to the bed as Savannah noticed her surroundings for the first time. The room was large, spacious, old-fashioned. Candles lit the interior, making it glow softly. The bed was large, a heavy four-poster carved elaborately with roses and twining leaves. It was beautiful, gothic—and frightening. She cleared her throat and rubbed her forehead uncertainly. "I'd like my own sleeping chamber."

The pale eyes drifted over her possessively. "You will not leave my side."

"No?" All at once she was desperately weary, her head hurting, her legs trembling, and she sat down abruptly on the floor. One hand swept through her heavy blue-black hair, shoving it away from her face in an unconsciously feminine gesture. She blinked, and that fast Gregori was standing over her. She closed her eyes when he reached for her. He was strong, enormously strong, lifting her as if she was no more than a child. She buried her face against his chest, unable to summon the strength to fight him.

Gregori savored the feel of Savannah in his arms, her softness cradled against his heavy muscles, the silk of her hair brushing erotically over his skin. Pain raced through him like molten lava; hunger rose. He lay her on his bed, where she belonged. His primitive nature, the hunter, the predator in him, demanded he take her immediately, bind her irrevocably to him for all time. She belonged to him. He knew exactly what he was, a heartless demon, without Savannah sentenced to an endless, lonely existence. He had walked the earth for centuries, a powerful healer, none greater than he, but completely dead inside. He had been so alone. Always alone. Endlessly alone. But now he had Savannah. And he would destroy anyone who attempted to take her from him, anyone who threatened her.

His hand stroked back her hair, soothingly massaged her scalp. His hypnotic voice took on a low chant of healing, removing the pain from her temples, replacing it with peace. He stretched out beside her, his larger, heavier frame dwarfing hers. Instantly his body reacted to her closeness. He was on fire, his need burning in his blood, his muscles, every fiber of his body. He accepted the pain, grateful he could feel it. As he drew her into his arms, he marveled at the perfection in one so small and fragile. She was trembling so much, he could hear her teeth chatter.

"I know what I am, Savannah, a monster such as the human world cannot conceive. But I have always had honor, integrity, and a talent for healing. I can make you two promises. I will never have untruth between us, and I will protect you with my life. I have said I will not take what is mine this night. We have time to calm your fears."

She burrowed her face into his silk shirt, where she could feel the steady beat of his heart, the heat of his skin. It was impossible for him to hide his fierce arousal, and he didn't bother to try, rather fitting her body to the hard length of his. Savannah was far too drained by the evening's events to continue to struggle. She lay in his arms, exhausted, finding a measure of peace from the very one who threatened her.

"You think I'm like other Carpathian women, Gregori, but I'm not," she said softly, uncertain whether she was offering an apology or an explanation.

His mouth brushed the top of her head, the lightest of caresses; his thumb stroked the spot where Roberto had struck her. "You know what happens to the males of our species, Savannah; your father would not have neglected to educate you in something so important. You cannot run around unclaimed. There are others like Roberto, savage, dangerous, driven to madness by the lack of a lifemate."

"He was half your age. Why would he turn renegade and you not?" She turned her head to meet Gregori's pale eyes. A shiver ran through her at the lack of mercy she saw there, at the stark possession burning in the icy silver depths.

"Have you ever wondered why there are so few of us Carpathians?"

"Of course I have. Just because I don't choose to mate does not mean I don't think about the problems facing our people. Gregori, I don't want to be anyone's lifemate. There's no reason to take it personally."

Gregori smiled at her, his perfect mouth sensual and inviting. "I know you are afraid of me, Savannah."

Determined not to be drawn into an argument she could not win, she went back to a safer topic. "The reason there are so few Carpathians is because there are so few women and no female children. Even the male children rarely survive their first year." Savannah involuntarily moved closer to his warmth. He seemed so strong, making her feel oddly safe and comforted on the worst night of her life.

"What of the men? Do you truly wonder why so few survive without turning vampire?" His hand stroked her hair. "Have you ever felt alone, Savannah, truly alone?"

As a child she had lived in isolation, but her parents, devoted as they were to each other, still spoiled and adored her. Her wolf, too, had been extraordinary, filling every empty place in her life. She had never felt alone until she had put an ocean between herself and the healing soil of her homeland. Away from her parents, the wolf, and even her oppressive obligations as a Carpathian female had left her with a gaping hole in her heart. Being surrounded by people, even the affection she felt toward Peter and the members of her crew, did not alleviate the growing emptiness threatening to consume her. Unwilling to share her secrets with Gregori, however, she didn't answer.

"We males cannot survive the growing darkness without our mates, Savannah. Our nature is aggressive, predatory, possessive, even among our own kind. We are destructive and powerful, and we hunger for blood. We need a balance. Most males begin to decline after several centuries, when they no longer see color, experience no true feeling, and can rely only on the strength of their wills to keep our laws. Some choose to end their existence before it is too late, walking into the dawn, the light of day, and allowing the earth to claim them. A good many others choose to embrace the darkness, giving up their souls, preying on the human race. They abuse women and children, hunt and kill for the momentary high, for the power and rush. It cannot be allowed."

"My father and you are the oldest. How did you survive?"

"Your father and I spent our bloodlust years in the midst of wars across Europe. Our energies could be channeled into saving others from ravaging armies. The vampire hunts provided us with more opponents. Between us, we made a pact to seek the dawn before we turned completely. Your father had the responsibility for our people to keep him sane, and later he found your mother, a human with extraordinary psychic talent and so much courage and compassion that she was able to accept our life."

"What of you?"

"The best I can say of myself is that I never abused a woman or child, and that I spent centuries learning the healing arts. But I have the nature of a predator, Savannah, as do all the males of our race. Because I am centuries old, the beast is strong in me." He sighed softly. "The five years I allotted you your freedom have been hell for me and dangerous to anyone I came into contact with. I am very close to turning, and it is too late for me to seek the dawn. It was necessary for the safety of all concerned that I come for you now." His hands tangled in the silk of her hair, crushing strands to bury his face in, to inhale her fresh scent. "I can wait no longer."

The admission was torn from his soul. He could not afford to give her the one thing she asked of him—her freedom. Although he was Gregori, the Dark One, the most powerful among Carpathians, he was not strong enough to give her up. She must become lifemate to the one Carpathian all others feared. And she was so very young.

"Did you ever wonder what it is like for the women of our race, Gregori? To know that by our eighteenth year we must go from our father's keeping to some stranger's?" This time she did open her mind to him fully, called up the memory of five years ago for both of them.

Like any woman-child of mating age, Savannah had found a heady excitement in knowing that she was beautiful and held power over the male of the species. She was pleased when her father summoned all the available males in to meet her. Ignoring her mother's worry, she had flitted among them, innocent of what havoc she was creating. However, somewhere during the gathering she had become aware of its dangerous atmosphere, the press of male bodies against her, the hunger in their eyes, the smell of their arousal. None of them, she realized, knew her or cared about her or cared to know what she felt or thought. They wanted her, yet it wasn't really her they wanted. She felt suffocated, repulsed, afraid. Not one of them had made her feel the things she was supposed to feel.

Savannah had escaped to her room and bathed her face with cool water, feeling sick and somehow dirty. When she turned around, Gregori, the Dark One, was in her room with her. His power emanated from every pore. He carried it casually, the same way he carried his enormous strength.

He was totally different from the others—much more

frightening, much more powerful. They seemed like callow youths in comparison. His pale eyes moved over her possessively, and her skin burned at the mere brush of his gaze. He took her breath and turned her body to hot liquid, making her want things she had never dreamed of.

Fear had slammed into her at the knowledge that he could easily steal her very will, make her his so irrevocably that she would do anything to be with him.

You belong to me, no other. The words were in her head, the bond so familiar and strong, it was terrifying. The mental path was not the familiar Carpathian one but that of a private, intimate bond. He moved, a single ripple of muscle, and her heart pounded in anticipation. His fingers circled her upper arm so that she was all too aware of his enormous strength. It was nearly impossible to breathe. His fingers slid the length of her arm to encircle her fragile wrist like a bracelet. The skimming contact was like a tongue of fire licking along her skin. Every cell in her body suddenly stilled; she held her breath, waiting. Just waiting. He tugged her to him, close, so close, until her body was imprinted for all time by his. Very gently, he tilted her chin and fastened his mouth to hers.

In that instant her entire life, her very existence changed. The earth rocked, the air sizzled, and her body no longer belonged to her. She needed, burned, ached for him. Body and mind, her very skin, was merged with his. There was no Savannah without Gregori and no Gregori without Savannah. She needed his hands on her; she needed him inside her, her heart, her mind, her body, her very soul.

When he released her, she felt bereft, experiencing a terrible emptiness, as if he had stolen a huge part of her and left her a mere shadow. The idea terrified her. A stranger, someone who didn't love her or know her, was capable of taking over her life. It suddenly seemed far worse than giving herself to one of the others. None of them would ever control her or take over her entire life. If none of them could ever love her, at least they wouldn't own her, body and soul. Terrified, she had pleaded with Gregori to let her go, to let her live her own life. His eyes dark with sorrow and heated with something else, he had released her, had agreed to give her more time. Savannah, however, had planned to flee his power forever.

The worst of it was, after her flight to the United States, Savannah had never felt complete again. Gregori had ripped out a part of her with one small kiss. He was never out of her head. When she closed her eyes at night, all she could see was him. Sometimes, if she concentrated enough, she could even smell his wild, untamed scent. He haunted her dreams and called to her in her sleep. Clearly, the risk he posed to her very soul was far too enormous to allow what he was now demanding.

Gregori's hand cupped the back of her head, then slipped to the nape of her neck. "We can cope with your fears, *ma petite*. They are not insurmountable." His voice, as always, was calm and unruffled.

Savannah's heart sank. Nothing moved him to mercy, not even her sharing one of her most private and frightening memories. "I don't want this," she whispered, tears burning in her throat. She was humiliated that she had admitted so much and that it had meant so little to him.

"Rest now, little one. We will sort it out later."

She was silent, seeming to accept his command quietly. But Savannah had a few tricks up her sleeve; after all, she was considered one of the world's leading magicians.

Gregori might be offering her a temporary reprieve, but when they woke, his appetite would be ferocious. She doubted that even his mammoth self-control would save her then. She would have to make her most daring—and most important—escape ever.

"Savannah?" Gregori's arm drew her tightly, possessively against him. "Do not try to leave me. Fight me, argue, but do not try to leave me. I walk the edge of control. I feel for nothing or no one but you. It would be very dangerous."

"So I am to give up my life so yours can continue." Her tears fell on the back of her hand.

"You cannot exist without me, either, Savannah. It is only a matter of time before the growing emptiness consumes you." He raised her hand to his mouth and touched his tongue to her tears, savoring the taste of her. Then his voice dropped an octave, became purity itself. "Do not deny it. I feel it growing in you. The terrible, aching loneliness."

Savannah's heart jumped at the rough velvet of his tongue rasping across her bare knuckles. She would not allow his natural sensuality to seduce her, no matter how her own body responded to the forbidden call. "How much time do I have before then, Gregori? A century or two? Five? More? You don't know, do you? That's because none of our women were ever allowed to command their own fate. I shouldn't be responsible for your life any more than you should be responsible for mine."

"We are Carpathian, *ma petite*, not human, despite the way your mother raised you. I am responsible for your life, as you are for mine. It is the way of our people, and the only thing protecting humans from our darkness. Our women are cherished, protected, treated with respect, guarded for the treasures we know they are." The dark shadow on his chin rubbed along the top of her head in a curiously soothing gesture. Little strands of her hair caught in the stubble, weaving them together. "Your mother has much to answer for, filling your head with human nonsense when she should have been preparing you for your true destiny."

"Why do you call it nonsense? Because she wanted me to be able to choose for myself what I wanted? To make my own destiny? To savor freedom? I don't want to be owned."

"None of us can choose, Savannah." His arms tightened briefly, and his warm breath found her ear. "Lifemates are born to one another. And *freedom* is a word that can mean many different things." His voice was so beautiful and gentle, at odds with his matter-of-fact words. "Go to sleep, and escape your fear for a time."

She closed her eyes as she felt his lips brush her ear, then slide to her neck. She savored the touch, took it into her body, and hated herself for it. "You go to sleep, Gregori. I want to think."

Teeth grazed her skin, right over her leaping pulse. Then his tongue stroked, easing the sharp sensation. "I do not wish you to think any more, *ma petite*. Do as I say, or I will send you to sleep myself."

She paled. "No!" Like any Carpathian, Savannah knew just how vulnerable she would be when the sun rose and sleep took her body. If Gregori commanded her into the deepest sleep of the Carpathians, she would be completely under his power. "I'll sleep." Deliberately she slowed her breathing, slowed her heart.

Beside her, Gregori concentrated on the entrances to his lair, sealing them with ancient spells. Next he focused on the gates to the wolves' kennels. They swung open, releasing the wolf hybrids to roam and guard the upper stories and grounds of the house. Savannah still thought to escape him. But Savannah had no idea just how powerful he really was. And because he had promised himself he would always give her truth, he could not say the pretty, empty words that might ease her fears. The acquisition of knowledge had helped to keep his mind and body strong in the endless years of empty blackness. He had waited for Savannah, his lifemate, since before her birth. The moment he had touched Mikhail Dubrinsky's woman, Raven, healing the terrible wounds she had suffered at the hands of some misguided vampire slayers, giving his pure, powerful blood to help save her life, he had known she would provide him with his lifemate. That the child growing within her would be his. And he had done everything he could to ensure that outcome.

When the human hunters had tried to kill Raven Dubrinsky, Gregori had saved her and the child within her, sealing the bond between him and the newly conceived female being with his own powerful blood. He had ensured she could not escape him, whispering to her, soothing her, enticing her to stay in his world despite the wounds to her fragile little body. Having gone to such extremes to bind his lifemate to him before she was even born, he would never let her go now.

He pulled Savannah's body as close to him as possible, fitting his larger frame around hers protectively. Roberto traveled with a pack of renegade Carpathians, vampires now, killing, raping, creating mindless human puppets to serve them. If they had all tracked Savannah here to San Francisco, the city would soon become their killing ground. Gregori had to take Savannah to safety, but he knew he would not be leaving the humans of the city to face the threat alone. Aidan Savage, a powerful Carpathian, was in this region, and he would hunt down the renegades and destroy them. Aidan was an able hunter, one feared by the undead.

Gregori stroked Savannah's hair gently. For her sake, he wished he could give her the freedom she so desired, but it was impossible. Instead, she would be chained to his side for eternity. He sighed, then slowed his heart and lungs in preparation for sleep. As an ancient, he had often had to bring Carpathian justice to the renegades, just as he would have expected Mikhail to bring it to him if he had waited too long to claim Savannah and save himself from his own darkness. But he seriously doubted if anyone, even Mikhail, the Prince of their people, could overpower him if he turned vampire. He could not afford the risk. Savannah must remain his. He drew a last breath, taking her scent into his body and holding it there as his heart ceased to beat.

The sun rose above the mountains, rays of light bursting through the windows of the huge, isolated home. Polished oak gleamed. Marble tile glistened. The only sound that could be heard was an occasional soft padding of the wolves as they patrolled the first, second, and basement stories. Outside, too, more wolves moved restlessly throughout the grounds, along the high, heavy fence enclosing them on the property. The fence was more for the protection of any wandering humans than to keep the animals from marauding in the countryside. Their bond with Gregori was strong, the estate and preserve huge. The wolves would never leave of their own accord.

The sun did battle with a thick layer of clouds, valiantly spreading its golden rays throughout the afternoon. The wind began to pick up, swirling leaves in little eddies on the ground. Beneath the earth, the large chamber was silent. Then in that silence a heart began to beat. A rush of air filled lungs. Savannah scanned her surroundings, testing the nature of Gregori's imprisoning protection. Beside her, Gregori lay as still as death, one arm wrapped possessively around her waist.

Savannah allowed relief to flood her body. She had one secret no one other than her wolf knew. Most Carpathian children did not survive their first year. During the critical period when their bodies demanded more than milk but rejected all food and blood, her mother, who had once been fully human and unable to feed on her own kind, had given her diluted animal blood. Although Savannah was small and fragile compared to most Carpathians, she had thrived on her mother's mixture. And, determined to live as normal a life as possible, Savannah had stuck to her unusual diet during her growing years, hoping it might render her different from other Carpathians and able to forge her own future.

At the age of sixteen, Savannah had begun to experiment with the possibility of going out in the sun. Her mother had told her so many stories of life in the sun, across the ocean, stories of freedom and travel. Savannah, in turn, faithfully related each one to her companion, the wolf.

Daringly, she began to wake herself earlier and earlier, slowly exposing her skin to the sun, hoping to build up an immunity Carpathians did not have, forcing them to go to ground in the daylight and come alive only in the night. Sometimes the pain was too much for her to bear, and she would stop her outings for a few days. But Savannah was tenacious when she made up her mind to something, and she wanted to walk in the sun.

Although she was never able to tolerate the sunlight beyond eleven in the morning or before five in the evening in the summer months, her skin had adjusted to the sun's rays. She did have to wear the darkest of sunglasses during the day and in the bright lights on the stage, but otherwise she seemed to escape the terrible Carpathian lethargy the diet of human blood caused. She had sacrificed some of the speed and strength of her race, but she had the freedom of walking in the light, as her mother had described.

Savannah closed her eyes, remembering a time she had sneaked out while her parents slept deep in their underground chamber. The sun was still up, and, feeling particularly pleased with herself, Savannah made her way through the deep forest up to the cliffs.

She began to climb, trying to improve her speed and strength. But she had faltered near the top, slipped, and lost her footing. She'd grasped the rock face, scrambling for a hold, digging deep grooves in the cliff with her nails curved into claws, but she couldn't hold on. She fell but twisted in midair with all the agility of a cat, hoping to land on her feet.

But she had failed to see a broken tree root protruding from the cliff face and pointing up like a sharpened stake. It drove through her thigh, tearing through flesh, muscle, and bone, pinning her in place. Her dark glasses fell from her nose to drop to the forest floor below. Savannah screamed in pain, blood pouring from her wound. For a moment she hung there; then the root gave under her weight, and she landed hard on the rocky ground.

At first she couldn't breathe, the air knocked from her

lungs. Keeping her eyes tightly closed against the terrible light, clenching her teeth, she pressed both hands to her wound and sent out an anguished, desperate call to her wolf. Later, she wondered why she had not hesitated to call him, had not thought to call her parents. He answered immediately, waves of reassurance flooding her mind. The wolf was far away but was coming quickly to her aid.

While she waited, Savannah dug her fingers into the rich soil, mixed it with saliva from her mouth, and packed the wound. It hurt, rivaling the glass splinters of sunlight piercing her skull through her unprotected eyes. *Hurry!* she urged, weak from loss of blood.

The wolf loped out of the forest, his own streaming eyes narrowed to slashing slits. He took two incredible leaps to her side, assessed the situation, and trotted to her glasses. Picking them up carefully in his mouth, he dropped them into her lap. Then his tongue lapped at the wound in a curiously soothing gesture. Savannah's arm slipped around the glossy neck, and she buried her face in the thick pelt of soft fur, seeking strength.

For the first and only time in her life, she asked to feed, knowing she would not survive without blood. She was grateful for the strong bond she had with the wolf, enabling her to explain her need without words. The wolf exposed his throat without hesitation. As gently, as reverently as she was able, Savannah had sunk her teeth deep into the wolf, her mind striving to calm his. Her effort proved unnecessary. If anything, the wolf calmed her, giving of himself freely, without reservation. She was astonished that she felt no revulsion in feeding directly from the animal instead of from a cup her mother handed her. Afterward she lay with her arms around the wolf while it continued to lap gently at her wound. She could have sworn that the wolf had somehow gotten into her body, along with its blood, and somehow soothed the terrible wound in her leg. She felt heat and light and energy spreading through her, healing her. She felt no fear, surrounded by the protective, unconditional caring of the wolf.

Her wound had healed miraculously fast, and she never mentioned the incident to her parents because she knew they would be furious with her experiments, with her going out into the sun. They would have been appalled at the chances she was taking. But she never regretted her decision to refrain from using human blood or to expose her skin to the sun's rays. It led to freedom, the freedom that was going to allow her to escape now.

"I'm sorry, Gregori," she whispered softly. "I cannot put my life into your hands. You are far too powerful for someone like me to try to live with. Please find someone else and be happy." She knew she never would be, but she had no choice if she didn't want this potent Carpathian ancient to take over her life. Her teeth tugged at her lower lip. In spite of her resolve, she found herself strangely reluctant to leave him. And he would take her life over; he couldn't help himself.

It was true she would remain alone. She could not return home or even seek out her wolf. She was doomed to walk the earth alone. But something in her, strong and proud, would not allow this man to dominate her, choose her life for her, dictate to her. He had been right; she knew what emptiness was, to be totally alone in the middle of a crowd. She was different. No matter how hard she tried, Savannah would never be human, and she would never be Carpathian. She knew, although she would never admit it to anyone other than her wolf—she had confided the truth to the animal—that she could not possibly be with any man but Gregori. But she would be alone for an eternity rather than be owned by him. She understood that she would never crave another man as she did Gregori; her soul was already in his possession. And she wanted to explain things to him, to make him understand. But Gregori was not a male to heed anyone's logic other than his own.

Gregori was one of the ancients, the most powerful, the most knowledgeable. The Dark One. He was a deadly killer, a true wild Carpathian male. The centuries had not softened his macho attitudes or changed his beliefs. He believed absolutely in his right to her, believed she belonged to him. He would protect her with his life from all harm, see to her every need and comfort. But he would rule her absolutely.

"I'm sorry," she whispered again and attempted to sit up. A heavy weight in the middle of her chest prevented movement. Her heart lurched uncomfortably. Terrified that she had disturbed Gregori's slumber, Savannah gazed at him. He remained still and silent, without a flicker of life. Savannah took a deep breath and let it out slowly to calm herself. This time she slid cautiously sideways as if scooting out from under something. Instantly a band tightened around each ankle. When Savannah looked down at her feet, there was nothing there, nothing holding her, yet she couldn't move. Something was anchoring her in place.

For a brief moment she considered that some other Carpathian male—or vampire—had tracked them to the lair. But no Carpathian would dare disturb Gregori. Somehow, in his deep sleep, Gregori was controlling her. Easily. Casually. So certain of his own power, so unruffled by her defiance, he could sleep through it. There was no doubt in her mind that it was Gregori preventing her escape. She lay still and allowed her mind to focus on her ankles, looking for a path, anything that could give her a clue to how the invisible manacles worked and how she might escape them.

You will sleep. The command filled her mind, low, compelling, iron in velvet.

Instantly her mind clouded, and her heart slowed. Savannah struggled, alarmed, and fought the desire to do his bidding. It was humiliating that he could control her even while he slept. If he was truly that powerful, what would her life with him be like when he was fully awake and aware?

A low, mocking laugh filled her mind. *Go to sleep*, ma petite. *It is dangerous to test me this way.*

She turned her head. Gregori lay as one dead. How could he be so strong? Even her father, Mikhail, the Prince of Darkness, did not possess such power. Gregori's voice was hypnotic, mesmerizing.

Savannah closed her eyes, exhausted from fighting him. She was overwhelmed with despair. *All right, Gregori, you win—this time.*

All the time, ma petite. There was no bragging, no triumph, just gentle calm.

It was his calm that made her believe Gregori was far more dangerous than she had ever imagined. He didn't threaten or yell or rage. He stated everything quite evenly or, worse, seemed amused by it. A familiar scent filled her lungs as she inhaled one last breath. The wolf, her wolf, filled her mind with comfort, soft fur rubbing against her arm, her cheek. Savannah kept her eyes closed tightly, afraid of destroying the illusion.

I missed you. She merged her mind with the wolf's. *I wish you were really here with me right now.*

I have always been with you.

The wolf's mind accepted her, enfolded her, embraced her with warmth. The mind was so familiar, as if she had walked in it a thousand times. *I wish that were true, that you were here with me for real.* The wild scent was strong in her nostrils. For a moment, Savannah held her breath, not daring to breathe. Then, slowly, she lifted her lashes. Beside her, the wolf stretched out, glossy black fur rubbing her skin. The wolf turned its head, revealing its unusual, intelligent gray eyes. Savannah's heart slammed against her chest. A moan of denial escaped. This was no illusion but the real thing. Gregori, with all his powers, could shape-shift. He was her wolf. How arrogant she had been to assume she was the only one who had perfected the art of going out in the sun. She had thought she was capable of resisting the rays because she fed only on animal blood. If only she had consulted her parents. Why had she kept the wolf her secret?

It had all seemed so innocent and fun, to have a wonderful secret from her parents. But she should have recognized those eyes. Not gray, but piercing, slashing silver. And the wolf had been told her every fear, every desire, her every dream. He knew her secret, innermost thoughts. Worse, they had exchanged blood, she by feeding, he by licking her wound. The exchange was not, perhaps, as the Carpathian mating ritual demanded, but their mental bond was strong, unbreakable.

She had been so stupid! An ordinary wolf would never have been so intelligent, so able to communicate warmth and security, so able to comfort her. Gregori had forged a bond between them from her early childhood.

You were lonely.

I had no chance, did I? Not even as a child.

Not from the moment you were conceived. No remorse, only that calm, implacable resolve.

She shut her mind to him, furious that he had taken such advantage of her, furious that he could have deceived her all those years. She turned her back to him, remembering how the wolf had come to her rescue even with the sun out, nothing protecting his eyes. Gregori might be the most powerful ancient of all, but he was still Carpathian. He must have endured excruciating pain to come to her aid.

She pushed uncomfortably at the heavy fall of her hair, knowing she should acknowledge that long-ago sacrifice. She wanted to be angry with him, furious. She did not want to feel cared for and protected by her jailer. She didn't want the racing of her pulse, the delicious warmth spreading through her at the lengths he had gone to for her all those years, to ensure a bond, to ensure her safety and happiness. His explanation was so stark and matter-of-fact. *You were lonely.* It was that simple to him. She needed, he provided. The code of the Carpathian male.

I'm sorry you were hurt on my account. She chose her thought carefully, not wanting him to read her confused emotions. She immediately felt the sensation of a hand brushing down the length of her hair, the gentlest of caresses.

We have a long night ahead tomorrow. You need healing sleep. This time his command plunged her into the deep sleep Carpathians needed for rejuvenation.

Gregori had sent a sharp, compelling command, not a gentle suggestion but an order she could not refuse. She went under swiftly, mindlessly, without fear or knowledge of what he had done. He had to cut short her adventures and independence. Even now her grief over her human friend and and her terror of him and his kind had taken a heavy toll on her. He could not believe that he had allowed her this rebellion against her true destiny. There was just something in him that melted when he was in her mind, in her presence. He had a terrible feeling that when his body merged with hers, he would be lost to all good sense.

Chapter Three

The sun set slowly, slipping lower and lower in the sky before disappearing behind the mountains to be swallowed by the sea. Red and orange burst across the sky, dramatically replacing its blue with the color of blood. Far below the earth, Gregori's heart and lungs began to function. Automatically he scanned his surroundings to ensure that all safeguards were in place and his lair was undisturbed. He sensed the hunger in his wolves, but no alarm.

Beside him, slender Savannah still rested. His arm curved possessively, protectively, around her waist. His leg was across her thigh, cutting off all possibility of escape. Hunger rose, voracious, ravenous, so sharp and engulfing, it was close to lust. Gregori floated to the basement level, needing to distance himself from temptation.

Savannah was finally here with him in his lair. She might be fighting him—and herself—every inch of the way, but he was in her mind, reading her easily. Much of her fear of him stemmed from her attraction to him. Carpathian desire was all consuming, totally binding, and given solely to one lifemate. One rarely survived the passing of the other. Mind, body, heart, and soul were bound together for all time.

The wolves converged on him eagerly, joyously. He greeted each of them with the same patience and measured enthusiasm. He felt no favoritism. Indeed, he had felt only emptiness until Savannah had come, until he had once more touched her mind with his.

As he fed the wolves, Gregori allowed himself to remember that black moment in the Carpathian Mountains when Savannah had told her wolf that she had to flee from the Dark One, flee to America, her mother's homeland, to escape Gregori and the intensity of her feelings for him. It had taken every ounce of self-control he possessed to allow her to leave him. He had retreated to the highest, most remote mountain he knew. He had traveled the forests of Europe as a lone wolf, had buried himself deep in the bowels of the earth for long periods, coming out only to feed. The darkness within him had grown until Gregori could no longer trust himself. Twice he had nearly killed his prey, and while that should have shaken him, it had caused hardly a ripple of concern. That was when he knew he no longer had a choice. He had to claim her, to possess her. Had to come to America and await her arrival in San Francisco.

Savannah didn't understand that if he did not—if instead he sought the dawn, or his darker nature prevailed and he turned renegade, became the dreaded vampire— he would be condemning *her* to a bleak, unbearable existence of utter aloneness and emptiness. She would not survive. Savannah's mother did not fully grasp the complex relationship between the male and female of their species. Born a human, neither did she completely comprehend the danger a Carpathian as powerful as Gregori represented. Savannah's mother had wanted her daughter to be independent, not realizing that a Carpathian had no choice but to find his or her other half. Raven Dubrinsky had not done her daughter any favors by giving her the illusion of independence.

But for the first time in his life, Gregori was indecisive. Until he officially claimed her, all Carpathian males, including the vampires, would be unsettled, thinking they might usurp his position and claim her for their own. For her own protection, he needed to complete the ritual binding them for all eternity. For the protection of mortals and immortals alike, he had to claim what was rightfully his. He had waited a dangerously long time. Still, he hated to force Savannah to his will when she was so reluctant. Gregori swept a hand through his thick hair, prowling through his home like a caged panther. Hunger was gnawing at him, rising sharply with every passing moment.

He padded across the floor to the balcony and lifted his head to inhale the night. The wind carried the scent of game. Rabbit, deer, a fox, and, faintly, farther away, humans. He sent his call into the night, drawing his prey to him with the casual ease of a master. It was sometimes difficult to remember that humans were beings with intellect and emotions when it was so simple to control them.

Gregori leapt from the second-story balcony, landing softly on the balls of his feet. He moved easily, unhurriedly, his muscles rippling with a subtle hint of the immense power and strength that was so much a part of him. No stone rolled beneath his feet; not a single twig snapped or leaf crackled. He could feel the sounds of the earth, the insects and night creatures, the water running like blood beneath the soil. The sap in the trees called to him; the bats dipped and squeaked in recognition.

Gregori stopped at the high chain-link fence. Bending his knees slightly, he jumped straight up, neatly clearing the eight-foot coils with ease. He landed on the other side, crouching low. No longer an elegant, well-bred man, a dangerous beast lifted his head. Pale eyes began to glow savagely. Hunger gripped and clawed at his insides. Instinct took over, the age-old instinct of a predator need-ing to survive.

He scented the wind, then turned in the direction of his prey. His call had brought forth a young couple. He could hear their hearts beating, the rush of blood in their veins. His body burned for release. The dangerous, in-sidious whispers from the emptiness of his soul reached out to him. A woman. So easy. The man in him, nearly pushed aside by the beast, fought the darkness. In his present state, he could so easily kill her.

The girl was young, in her twenties, the male not much older. They waited for him, their faces eager, as if waiting for a lover. As Gregori approached, the girl held her arms out to him, smiling joyously. Hunger burned red and raw, his body screaming with need. With a low growl, Gregori reached for her, unable to fight the power of the beast.

As Gregori dragged the female roughly to him, he heard a whisper of sound. Light. Rhythmic. Fast. With a throaty growl, he thrust the woman safely away. She was with child. Gregori stretched out a hand and splayed his fingers across the slight bulge of her stomach. It was a male child. So small, so in need of protection. Abruptly he spun around and seized the man. He fought to control himself, to keep the young fellow tranquil and willing. He listened for a moment to the ebb and flow of blood, of life, then lowered his head and drank.

In his state of arousal, the rush hit him hard. The taste of power burst into life, filling him. He needed, burned, craved. He fed hungrily, ravenously, desperate to fill the terrible emptiness. The male's knees buckled, forcing Gregori back to awareness. For a moment he had to fight the beast, happy to feast on rich life, nearly corrupt with the power of life and death. He had to struggle to regain some semblance of control before he drained the man. It was so tempting, so promising. Calling, insistent.

In the midst of the red haze building and growing in him, his body burning and raging, a single thought crept in. *Savannah.* All at once he could smell the night air again, smell her clean, fresh scent. He could feel the breeze on his hot skin like the touch of her fingers. He could see the branches of the trees swaying gently, see her beautiful, knowing eyes staring into his blackened soul.

With an oath, Gregori closed the wound in the man's throat and eased him to the ground, propping him up against a broad tree trunk. Crouching, Gregori felt for a pulse. He did not want to go to Savannah with death on his hands. He had thought to give her time to adjust to him, to their relationship, but he was far too dangerous and unpredictable in the state he was in. He needed her inside him, drawing him back from the edge of madness.

The man sat with ashen skin, his breathing labored. With rest and care, however, he would be fine. Planting a believable accident in the couple's heads to explain the male's weakness, he left them as quickly as he had come, running lightly through the thick stand of trees, easily clearing fallen logs and narrow ribbons of water. Once inside his compound, he slowed to a lazy saunter and once more sent a call into the night. The couple would need aid, so he drew a family out strolling to the spot. He heard their gasps of alarm and concern even with the miles separating them, and his mouth curved in satisfaction.

Just as Gregori leapt for the balcony, he felt the first prickle of unease, of warning. His eyes swung back to the night sky as he faded into the shadows. This place, remote, wild, still savage yet a place of power, would draw the attention of any renegade Carpathian. The vampires would be unable to resist the call of the earth, the draw of the wolves. They might even sense his terrible struggle, one of the hunters so close to turning, so close to becoming one of their kind, damned for all eternity. He had been so caught up in the moment of feeding, he had failed to hide his presence from any of his kind who might be near—another sign of how very close he was to losing his soul.

Gregori touched the minds of his wolves to reassure them and prepare them for a probe. Already he could feel the vampires approach in tight formation, as large bats. They were seeking to touch the minds of humans and animals alike.

Inside the house, the wolves circled, paced, endured the mind search, but Gregori was locked on to them, his calm centering them. The vampires would pick up only the instincts of wild animals roaming, hunting food. Gregori's white teeth gleamed. Had he been the one searching, no one would have felt his presence unless he allowed it. And no mind block would have been strong enough to resist his probe.

Savannah. The renegades were probably searching for her, certain Roberto had found her and secreted her away from them. The rogue had not had the time or strength at the end to send out a warning to his cohorts. They would search all the remote areas as a matter of course.

Gregori shook his head at their stupidity. Savannah was Mikhail's daughter. Mikhail was the Prince of their people, an ancient, his blood powerful. Savannah might have diminished her strength by refusing human blood, but when she chose to feed, she would be dangerous beyond their imaginings.

He turned another humorless smile, cruel and taunting, toward the sky. The searchers were heading away toward the south, toward the teeming city. Gregori spared a thought for the havoc the vampires would create, for the victims they would take before Aidan Savage, the hunter in the area, could track them down. He trusted Aidan with the job and felt justified in leaving the other Carpathian the duty of clearing out the vampires in the Bay area in due time.

Time meant nothing and everything to Gregori. It was limitless, one endless stretch of bleak isolation. For long centuries he had endured the stark, ugly isolation of the solitary male of his species. His emotions had died, leaving him cold-blooded, capable of immeasurable cruelties. But after years of being alone, of being nearly like the undead, he was awakening once again to scents, colors, light, darkness. The way his body burned, so sensitive to the feel of her hair, her body against his, just the sight of her. Was it too much, too late? Would he survive the onslaught, the flood of powerful emotions, or would it all send him careening over the edge into the world of madness?

Gregori had survived for centuries because, like Mikhail, he was meticulous with his plans, never forgetting the minutest detail. His first mistake in hundreds of years had been in failing to keep himself alert to the possible presence of other Carpathians or undead in the stadium parking lot at the magic show. Moments ago he had done the same. All because he was distracted by needing Savannah too much and waiting for her for far too long.

He reentered his house and padded downstairs on bare feet. Once inside the bed chamber, he lit candles and ran a hot bath in the huge sunken marble tub. Then he gave the command for Savannah to wake. His body felt heavy, uncomfortable with his urgent need, but his gluttonous feeding had helped to take the edge from his bloodlust. He watched her face as her heart began to beat and her lungs began to expand with air. He knew the precise moment that she mentally scanned her surroundings and sensed the threat to herself, sensed immediate danger. Sensed his presence.

Savannah surprised him by sitting up slowly, shoving at the silken hair tumbling around her face. Her eyes fastened on his, enormous, beautiful. Her tongue darted out, touching her lips in apprehension.

If it was possible, Gregori's body tightened even more.

He looked powerful, intimidating, his face harshly sensual, Savannah noted in trepidation. His eyes burned with hunger, touched her, devoured her. And in spite of her resolve, in spite of her fears, she could feel her body taking on a life of its own. Heat spread slowly throughout her, bringing a torturous ache and a raging hunger. She could smell his masculine scent. The wild forest clung to him, giving up secrets. Her eyes flashed, sparkling stars in the midst of violet. "How dare you come to me with another woman's perfume clinging to you?"

A faint smile touched his mouth, easing the harshness in his face. "I merely fed, *ma petite*." Savannah was the most beautiful, sensual woman he had ever met. She might think she was in terror of him, but she certainly had no qualms about reprimanding him.

She glared at him, her long hair wild, her small fists clenched. "You call it whatever you like, Gregori, but you stay away from me smelling like her." She was furious with him. He insisted she was his lifemate, tried to force her into an eternity of hell with him, and he dared to come to her smelling of another woman? "Get out and leave me in peace." For some unexplained reason she felt close to tears at the thought of him betraying her.

His silver eyes warmed to caressing mercury and moved possessively over her slender figure. A frown touched his face. "You are weak, Savannah. I can feel it when our minds merge."

"Stay out of my mind. You certainly weren't invited." Her hands went to her hips. "And just for the record, your mind needs to be washed out with soap! Half the things you think we're going to do are never going to happen. I could never look at you again."

He laughed. Aloud. An actual, real laugh. It welled up unexpectedly and emerged low and husky, with genuine amusement. Gregori nearly leapt the distance between them and dragged her into his arms, grateful beyond imagining.

She flung a pillow at his head. "Go ahead and laugh, you arrogant jerk." She wished she had a two-by-four handy.

His eyebrows shot up. Another new experience. He

had been called many things, but *jerk* was not one of them. His concern for her well-being overrode his intrigue, however. It even overrode the crouching beast within him so ready to possess her. "Why are you so weak, *ma petite*? This is not acceptable."

She waved his concern aside. "Is it acceptable for you to play around with other women?" She didn't stop to think why it infuriated her, but it did. "I've been taking care of myself for five years, Gregori, without your assistance. I don't need you, and I don't want you. And if I do have to have you around, a few rules are going to be followed."

His mouth twitched, but his gut clenched hotly, his body so hard, it was painful. Hunger rose, swift and sharp, and the beast inside him roared for release. Five years. He had had to give her those five years. God help them both if he had waited too long. "The bath is ready. You can tell me these rules while we relax in its warmth."

Her eyes widened. "*We?* I don't think so. You may be in the habit of bathing with women, but I can assure you, I don't bathe with men."

"That eases my mind," he replied dryly, amusement curling in his mind, but the urgency of his need building. "I have never bathed with a woman, Savannah, so the new experience should do us both good."

"In your wildest dreams."

"There is no need to be shy. We are both of the earth."

"Spare me the garbage, Gregori. I'm not going to bathe with you, and that's final."

His eyebrows shot up. All at once he looked the predator he was. No lazy amusement, no indulgence, but a hunter with eyes fixed unblinkingly on his prey.

Her heart stopped in alarm, then began to slam uncomfortably in her chest. The worst thing about it was, he could hear it. He knew he had scared her. That made her even more furious. Did he have to be so intimidating? Carpathian males were all enormously strong; they didn't need to look it. There was no need for his huge chest and bulging arms and thighs like oak trees. She had started out with bravado, determined not to be intimidated, but he was power personified.

"I am reading your mind," he mentioned softly.

She hated her traitorous body, the way it dissolved at the sight of him and the sound of his velvet, caressing voice. "I told you to stay out of my mind."

"It is a habit, *ma petite.*"

She flung the other pillow at him. "Don't you dare bring up the wolf. I'm sure our laws forbade such a thing. You're a cad, Gregori, and you're not even sorry."

"Remove your clothes, Savannah."

The soft command had her gaze flying to meet and lock with his. She stepped back, staggered, and would have fallen if he had not moved with his preternatural speed to cover the distance between them. His arms swept her up and pinned her to him, his silver eyes slashing at her. "Why are you so weak?"

She pushed at the wall of his chest in a vain attempt to escape a mind search. He would be able to extract any information he desired quite easily. "You know I never touch human blood. While I was a child, it didn't seem to matter all that much, but over the last couple of years, there have been"—she searched for the word—"repercussions."

He remained silent, his unblinking gaze steady, compelling her to explain. And it *was* compulsion. She could not resist the command in his unwavering eyes.

Savannah sighed. "I'm weak most of the time. I can't

shape-shift without it taking a tremendous toll. That's why my shows are becoming so rare. I can hardly manage mist to escape and then materialize again." She didn't add that she could no longer manage adequate safeguards while she slept, but she could tell by the sudden glint of steel in his eyes that he had caught the echo of her hastily banned thought.

His silver gaze became steel, and his arms tightened, threatening to crush her body against the hard strength of his. "Why have you not remedied the situation?" His voice, a soft menace, sent a shiver through her. She was all too aware of his enormous strength.

"I tried with Peter once, when I was really in a bad way. He was compliant, but I just couldn't bring myself to take his blood." She didn't want to admit that the real reason was that she thought her unusual diet enabled her to walk in the sun.

"This will end. I forbid a continuation of this stupidity." He gave her a little shake, his teeth very white as they snapped together in irritation. "Should there be need, Savannah, I will force your compliance." He wasn't bragging; his voice held no challenge or taunt. He simply stated the fact.

She knew he was threatening her not with physical force but with mental compulsion. "Gregori"—she was striving to sound calm and reasonable—"it would be wrong for you to force your will on me."

He set her on her feet, holding her carefully with one hand, the other going to the buttons of her blouse.

Savannah's breath caught in her throat. Both her hands whipped up to catch his. "What are you doing?"

"Removing your clothes." He didn't seem to be aware of her hands straining to control his. The edges of her blouse parted, revealing her narrow rib cage, the soft swell of her breasts in nearly transparent lace.

The beast surfaced for a moment, wanting to tear, to feed, to claim. It was nearly impossible to control, and for the first time he was truly afraid he had waited too long to come to her. She could be in real danger if he slipped over the edge into madness. Need slammed into him, hard and painful, but he took a deep breath, fought, and won. His hand was steady as he removed the wisp of lace, spilling her full breasts into his view. His fingers brushed satin skin because he couldn't stop himself, his thumb stroking her nipples into hard peaks. He murmured something—Savannah wasn't certain what it was—before he lowered his mouth to taste the creamy offering.

At the first touch of his tongue, the scrape of his teeth, her legs nearly gave out. Her body went liquid with need. He drew her into the moist heat of his mouth, setting both of them on fire.

Savannah's fingers tangled in his thick, midnight-black hair with every intention of jerking his head back, but flames were licking along her skin, igniting a fire deep within her. *Just once, taste the forbidden. Just once.* It was a measure of her pleasure that she didn't know if it was his thought or hers tempting her.

His hand skimmed down her stomach, found the zipper of her jeans. Around her, colors whirled and danced, the air crackled, the earth shifted beneath her feet. A moan of despair, of desire, escaped her throat. The sound of their hearts, the rush of their blood, was music in her ears. It called to something wild in her. The scent of him, masculine and aroused, the scent of his blood, brought hunger, sharp and compelling.

"No! I won't do this!" Savannah, desperate to escape his black-magic spell, flung herself away. She wanted him more than anything, more than her own soul, and the intensity of her need frightened her to death.

Gregori's arms trapped her so that they fell together, floated to the floor, his large body covering hers. Her head was pinned beneath his chest, the scent of his blood strong, his pulse beating, beating at her resistance. His hands hooked in the waistband of her jeans and peeled them from her body with ease, taking with them the lacy scrap that passed for underwear. His hands stroked the length of her, committing every hollow and curve to memory, leaving fire in their wake.

Savannah found his skin hot, salty beneath her lips. Her tongue found his pulse and stroked a caress. His body shuddered with pleasure; his arms tightened into steel bands around her. His breath was warm against her neck, her ear. "Take from me what you need, Savannah," he whispered softly, a black-velvet seduction. "I offer freely as I did in the past. Remember how I tasted?" It was pure temptation, the devil enticing her. *Remember?* He breathed the word into her mind.

Savannah closed her eyes. The scent of blood was overpowering, calling to her, whispering a spell. She was so weak. To feed just once and be strong again . . . It might last for a long time. It would be so easy to let herself taste him. Her body clenched at the thought of it, every instinct crying out for survival.

His hand slid over her thigh, sending a shiver racing through her bloodstream. Her tongue flicked out again, stroked, lingered. Gregori's fingers found moist heat, caressed, lingered. Her teeth grazed his skin, then nipped. He controlled the urge to pin her hips and possess her. She was only half lost, her mind confused, hunger raging and her body burning with need. He fed that heat, his fingers delving deeper, exploring, feeling her muscles clench, her hips thrusting against him, seeking relief. *Hunger*. He thought it, built it, allowed it to consume him. His body was in pain, in need, hot and hard and hurting. Her mind sought his, merging until it was impossible to separate one from the other. *Hunger. Remember. The taste. Just one more time, the taste of him.*

She couldn't think clearly. There was so much need, so much hunger. A part of her could feel his bare skin hot against hers, his body aggressively male, but mostly she was drawn to that steady, strong heartbeat.

Gregori's fingers delved deep into her heat, and flames leapt in response—red fire, white heat, blue lightning. Her will dissolved, and her teeth sank deep. Gregori cried out hoarsely, exploding with pleasure so intense it was ecstasy. It was pure eroticism, her mouth moving, feeding, taking his life-force into her body. He had waited so long. His mind clouded, became a red haze of piercing need, and he pinned her slender hips with bruising force, holding her still for his invasion.

She was a sheath of velvet fire, and he buried himself in her as deeply as he could, ripping past her thin barrier of protection, burning, needing, determined to make her his for all eternity. Her shocked cry of pain was lost against his chest, muffled beneath him. She was so small, so tight and fiery, he was lost in pure sensation. Feeling. Pure feeling. Real feeling. No fantasy he had made up to endure the darkness, the loneliness, but true feeling. The sweet, coppery smell of blood was overwhelming, calling to him with relentless seduction. The smell of her blood, mingled with their combined scents, fed his red haze, sent him careening out of control, and triggered his every predatory, aggressive, bestial instinct.

Savannah automatically closed the wound in his chest with a flick of her tongue, already struggling wildly. He was hurting her with his bruising strength, his body stretching hers, tearing through her innocence so brutally. His hands were everywhere, his teeth following. Low, warning growls rumbled in his throat as she fought him.

Gregori lifted his head, eyes glowing red, dangerous, out of control, no longer human, lost at the edge of madness. The more Savannah fought, the more brutal he became, a wild animal seeking domination, seeking his own pleasure.

White-hot pain sliced through her as his teeth pierced the vulnerable swell of her breast. She cried out a protest, but he held her down easily beneath the weight of his body, kept her pinned and vulnerable while he took his pleasure. As her blood flowed into him, his body buried itself in hers over and over, driving deeper and harder.

Hot blood poured into his mouth. He had never known such a taste, could not possibly get enough. It flowed into his body like nectar, burning yet soothing. He had never felt ecstasy such as her body provided. He wanted it to last forever. Power swept through him, total rapture. His body was wild, seeking more, ever more, to match the frenzied feeding of his mouth.

Gregori no longer existed; the raging animal in his place was draining Savannah of her life's blood, using her body without the care of a tender lifemate. Savannah accepted her oncoming death but worried for her father, who would be pitted against this, the most cunning, the strongest of all Carpathians.

She felt a faint stirring in her mind—not sentences but impressions. Gregori was fighting his way back from madness to help her, his only thought now for her. He felt deep sorrow that he had waited too long and put her in such danger from him. *Kill me*, chérie. *When this thing taking you is done, it will be weak, lazy, sated. Kill it then. I will do my best to aid you in this.*

Guilt washed over her. Gregori had sentenced himself to five years of hell to give her the freedom she had so desired. During that time he had walked very close to madness, yet he had held on—for her. Their minds were merged, and she could touch the suffering he had endured on her behalf. Now he was willing to die to save her. Savannah closed her eyes and willed her body to relax, to become soft and accepting.

Gregori. He thought his soul was lost, that he had become a true vampire with no care for right or wrong. A wild beast with no creed, with enormous power, dangerous beyond belief. He had held out so long against the crushing black emptiness, yet now he was lost, trapped in a vortex of violence and passion, power and pleasure. She had brought him to this evil end. Her fears, her youth, were responsible for reducing his greatness to mindless savagery.

Savannah's fingers found the nape of his neck, and she forced her own pain from her mind, trying not to feel the brutal treatment he was subjecting her to. *Gregori*. The Dark One. Wild. Lawless. Always alone. Never touched, completely isolated. Feared. No Carpathian was comfortable in his presence, yet he had healed many of their race, hunted their assassins, carried out justice when it was the harshest of duties, to keep their people safe.

Who would care now for this wild beast? Who would feel gratitude for what he had sacrificed for them all?

Who would ever attempt to get close enough to reach the man within? Compassion welled up in Savannah, and something else she dared not examine too closely. She could not allow such a fate to befall so great a Carpathian. She would not allow it. Her determination was beyond anything she had ever felt.

Her hands stroked his wild mane of hair and cradled his head to her breast, giving herself up to him freely, her thoughts calm in the eye of the storm, offering him her life without reservation. *Take freely, Gregori. My life for your life.* It was the least she could do, no less than he had done for her, for all of their race. *I am here for you, Gregori. I offer what you need freely.* She meant it. She would not allow him to become the undead. She would not give him up to that soulless world.

Savannah! He seemed a little stronger, or perhaps she simply hoped the man was gaining on the beast. *You must survive. Kill me.* His voice was a fierce, pleading growl in her head.

Her own mind responded. *Feel me, my body joining with yours. I belong to you and you to me. Feel me with you. Reach for me. I will not let you go. Wherever you are, I am with you. Where you go, I follow. I offer my life freely for yours. You cannot take what is given to you. You have committed no wrong in taking.*

His hips continued to surge into her, but with more care, as if he was slowly returning to awareness. Encouraged, Savannah moved her body to meet his, matching his furious rhythm, his heart, his lungs, until they were in perfect synchronization. One body, one heart, one mind. She tried to slow them down, to coax his body to the slower, more gentle rhythm of hers.

Savannah. Her name was a plea this time, still far

away but more determined. The mouth working so ferociously at her breast gentled. *Save yourself.* Gregori was
fighting for her as she was fighting for him.

There is only us. She was calm now, her hands moving
soothingly over the taut, rigid muscles of his back. *No
me, no you.* She was weak, drained, a strange lethargy
overtaking her. *Only us.* Had her voice slurred a bit? *I
will not leave you, nor will I allow the darkness to take
you from me.*

Savannah lay beneath him, almost in a dream world.
Suddenly, as if sensing she was slipping away from
him, the beast raised its head, its eyes red, silver, red,
silver, glaring at her, at once feral, then tender. Warm
blood trickled down the slope of her breast. She blinked
to bring him back into focus. His body was shuddering,
spilling his seed deep within her. A long stroke of his
tongue closed the wound at her breast and followed the
drops of blood to her stomach.

I claim you as my lifemate. The words were husky in
her mind. His voice followed, hoarse, as if the terrible
conflict for his soul had taken its toll. "I belong to you. I
offer my life for you." The voice became stronger, more
Gregori's, a beautiful velvet caress, as he recited the ancient Carpathian vows that would link them for eternity.
"I give you my protection, my allegiance, my heart, my
soul, and my body. I take into my keeping the same that
is yours." He caught the back of her head in his palm,
slashed a wound near his throat, and pressed her mouth
to the gash. She was weak, almost too weak to drink
even under his compulsion. *Drink*, mon amour, *for both
our lives.* He forced her obedience without a qualm.
Without his blood, she would not survive the hour. Yet
all that she had suffered to save him would be for noth-

ing. Because without her he would have no reason or will to survive.

He stroked her hair tenderly, his body moving gently in hers. The ritual had to be completed to prevent a repeat of this terrible danger to her. He needed her residing in him, anchoring his darkness with her light. It would be a long road back, but she was strong, dragging him from the black emptiness of his bestial nature with her trust. He finished the vows softly. "Your life, happiness, and welfare will be placed above my own. You are my lifemate, bound to me for all eternity and always in my care."

His body could feel the ecstasy of the combination of her feeding and the heated velvet of her feminine sheath. He pushed down the pleasure, knowing she was not feeling what he was. The moment he was certain she had enough blood for survival, he allowed himself a second release.

Her head lolled back on her fragile neck, like a flower on a stem. She was so pale, her skin looked nearly translucent. Gregori took her hand and brought it to his mouth, his silver eyes moving over her face, noting shadows and hollows that had not been there before. As he looked at her, something inside him went soft, tender.

He eased himself from her body, glanced down at her slender form, and went perfectly still, shocked, horrified, nearly disbelieving. Bruises, scratches, and bite marks marred her skin. Blood and seed trickled down her leg, and he sought inside himself to remember his taking of her innocence.

A sound, raw and wounded, tore at his throat. How could he have done such a brutal, unforgivable thing? How could there ever be forgiveness? Savannah had managed to guide him back from the black void of the damned. Everything he knew, everything he believed, told him this was a miracle. But she had paid a terrible price.

Gregori carried her limp body to the steaming bath, thankful for the hot water that would help ease her soreness until he could get her into a deep, rejuvenating sleep. In their homeland, the rich soil would have welcomed her, helped mend her. Here, in this strange land, there was only Gregori and his healing powers. He could force her to sleep until her injuries were completely healed. He could take away every memory of his brutality, implant a beautiful tale of their lovemaking. Yet he had told her he would never have untruth between them, and if he changed her memory, their entire relationship from that day forward would become just that—an untruth.

Savannah was lying so still, pale and helpless. Gregori stroked back her ebony hair, his heart in so much pain that it felt as if a hand was squeezing it, ripping it from his chest. The plain truth was, the lie would be for himself, and he didn't deserve it. Her courage had brought him back. If she could face the demon in him, he could do no less.

Chapter Four

Savannah woke slowly, drowsily, from her sleep. Awareness came with her first attempts at movement. The Carpathian gift of exquisite sensitivity, the ability to see and smell and hear and taste so vividly, the phenomenally passionate nature of body and mind that allowed them to mate so wildly, was a curse when it came to pain. Carpathians felt pain as sharply and clearly as they saw and heard, with no chemical agents to numb the sensation. A groan escaped before she could prevent it.

Instantly a soothing hand rested on her forehead, stroking back her hair. "You are not to move, *ma petite*."

A faint smile curved her mouth. "Do you have to make everything you say an order?" Her lashes lifted to reveal her blue-violet eyes.

Gregori expected censure, rage, disgust. Her eyes were cloudy with pain, a little sleepy, and held a hint of fear she tried hard to conceal, but nothing else. He was a shadow in her mind, so she couldn't hide her thoughts. She was concerned mainly for him, for the terrible fight he had endured for his own sanity, the scars on his soul.

She felt guilt and an overwhelming sense of sadness that her youth and inexperience had forced such choices on him. He didn't realize he was frowning until her finger smoothed his lips. Her touch jolted him. The way she looked at him turned his heart over, melting his every jagged edge.

"You took a terrible chance, Savannah. I could have killed you. Next time I give you an order, follow it."

She flashed a wan grin, then hastily sobered when her swollen lips hurt. She was terribly weak, in need of blood. The scent of it rose to taunt her with memories she desperately needed to avoid right now. "I'm actually not very good at following orders. I guess you'll just have to get used to that." Savannah attempted to sit up, but he made it impossible with one large hand splayed over her heart.

She might have gotten away with her attempt at sarcasm except that their minds were so easily accessible to each other, slipping and merging back and forth without thought or effort. He caught the edge of nervousness, the echo of fear. She was very, very aware of his palm resting on the thin sheet over the swell of her breast. Savannah was trying to ignore the sexual tension arcing between them.

He bent, tenderly brushing his mouth across her forehead. "I thank you for your intervention. You saved my life. More importantly, my soul." *Both our lives.* "Do not try to hide your fears from me, *ma petite.* There is no need."

A sigh escaped, and her lashes veiled her eyes. "You can be extremely irritating, Gregori. I'm trying hard to carry this off, and I could use a little help. To be honest, I'm scared to death. Actually, I don't want to think about it right now." She bit her lip, then winced when her mouth stung. She made a subtle movement of retreat, hoping he would move his hand. She was so aware of his touch, his heat. The awareness encompassed both the ache in her body that his touch induced and the terrible fear her mind had no hope of overcoming.

Gregori didn't move a muscle, remaining as still as a statue carved from granite. "You pulled me out of the darkness, from the gates of hell. By all rights, by every law our people have, you should have destroyed me for what I did to you." His voice was low and edged with sorrow. "In all honesty, I had no idea such self-sacrifice, and such a rescue, was possible."

Savannah never wanted to repeat the experience as long as she lived. But somehow, as much as she was frightened, as much as her body hurt, she knew that Gregori was far more tormented than she. "I don't suppose you're so grateful that you would consider living apart from me for a while?" she asked hopefully, closing her eyes for a moment to block out the memory of the fight for his soul. She couldn't face the memory and the very real, very intimidating person at the same time.

For one moment something flickered in the depths of his eyes, rippled in his mind, her mind, then was gone. Pain. Had she hurt him? Savannah wasn't certain she wanted to know.

"The ritual was completed, *ma petite*. It is too late. Neither of us would survive a separation." His fingers tangled in her hair, crushing silky strands as if he couldn't get enough of the feel of her.

Savannah remembered hearing that lifemates could not live apart. But that meant she had to find a way to resolve her inner conflicts and fear of their relationship right away. Was that even possible? "So, what does that mean?" she challenged. "I've heard my father and you both say that. I've heard it all my life. What does it mean?"

"You will need the touch of my mind, my body, the exchange of our blood, and I will need yours. It will happen often, and the need is so powerful, one of us cannot long exist without the other." He kept his voice neutral, low, a soothing cadence.

If it was possible for her to grow more pale, she did. Her heart jumped wildly, her eyes widening in fear. *Never!* She could never, ever, under any circumstances, go through that again. Sex was a nightmare, the exchange of blood painfully overrated. She turned her face away from him in an attempt to spare him her fear. Her mind was working furiously, trying to find a solution. She had brought this on herself. If only . . . But if she had done anything differently, Gregori might be dead—or, worse, a full-fledged vampire, and somehow, even with the threat of a repeat performance, Savannah couldn't bear the thought of that.

She moistened her lips with the tip of her tongue, felt the swollen, cracked evidence of his assault. "But there's no chance of you turning vampire now, right?"

Gregori's heart hitched at the little catch in her voice. "There is no possible chance of my giving up my soul to darkness, Savannah, unless I should lose you. I will not lie to you, *ma petite*. Our life will be difficult at first. I had no idea of the depth of emotion you are capable of creating in me. It will take some time to adjust. If you are asking whether I will hurt you physically again, the answer is no."

"You're certain?" This time there was a distinct quaver in her voice, and her hand trembled when she lifted it to brush back her hair.

The movement caused her to wince, and Gregori felt that wince, that trembling, through his entire body like the blade of a knife. "You are in me, Savannah, a light to guide me through the darkest of times." He wanted to enfold her into the safety of his arms, shelter her for all eternity against his heart. But was he speaking the truth? He felt in his soul that he was, but he had long ago tampered with nature. Would the safeguards against his violence hold?

"I need time." She hated the pleading note in her voice. But her life had changed overnight. And Peter. God help her, she would never forgive herself for Peter's death.

"Roberto was not alone." It was easy to read her thoughts.

Savannah gingerly tested her ability to move. Every muscle seemed to shriek in protest. "What do you mean?"

His hand moved over her shoulder, his touch possessive. A jolt of fear hit her hard. She was naked beneath the sheet. Instantly she felt vulnerable, her blue-violet gaze jumping to his pale one as if she expected him to grow horns.

Gregori sighed softly and eased his weight onto the bed. "I will not hurt you, *mon petit amour.* I cannot with the ritual completed."

"Then why did you say our life will be difficult?" Her fingers were clutching the sheet until her knuckles turned white.

His hand settled gently over hers, tracing a fingertip over each tense knuckle. Every brush of his fingers sent an unexpected jolt of electricity through her. "I cannot lose you after waiting centuries for you. I know I am a hard man, and you will not find me easy to live with. We will both need to make certain adjustments."

"Yeah, like you can lose the macho attitude," she muttered under her breath. Steeling herself, she said aloud, "I want to sit up, Gregori." She felt at a distinct disadvantage, flat on her back and naked beneath the sheet. "If we're going to discuss our future, I'd like to participate."

For a long moment his silver eyes moved over her pale, bruised face, studying her intently, clearly debating whether to allow it. A storm began to gather in her eyes, and reluctantly he shifted back to give her room.

"Easy, *bébé*," he said softly, slipping an arm around her, his breath warm on her neck. The feel of his hair-roughened, iron-hard arm wrapped around her bare skin sent a shiver down her spine and set warmth curling in the pit of her stomach. She detested that warmth, the way her body tuned itself to his, the way her mind struggled to ignore her firm resolution and sought to touch his. It was the ritual. She might tell herself that, but it didn't stop the self-loathing. How could her body want his brutal touch? Was she some kind of masochist?

The trembling started deep inside, progressing through her muscles until her very teeth chattered. Savannah clutched the sheet to her and sat rigidly against the support of his arm. "I think this would go a lot better if you sat over there." She pointed to a chair across the room.

Gregori's hands framed her face, thumbs stroking the delicate line of her jaw. "Look at me, Savannah." His voice was black velvet but an order nevertheless.

Her gaze jumped to his, but hastily she averted her eyes, lashes sweeping down protectively. Beneath the pad of his thumb her pulse raced. "Are you going to fight me at every turn? This is a small thing I ask of you, to look at me, your mate."

"Is it? It is said you can command anyone with one look."

His laughter was soft, playing over her skin like the touch of fingers. "I can do that with my voice alone, *chérie*. Savannah, I have a need for you to look at me."

Reluctantly she locked her gaze to his. Why had she thought his eyes cold? They were pools of molten mercury, warming her, calming her so that the trembling eased and some of her fear dissipated enough to begin to relax her muscles.

"I will never hurt you again. The way I took you was not by choice, and I will carry the shame and guilt of my lack of control for all time." His hands found her hair and brought the crushed silk to his lips. "I know you fear me, Savannah, and I have given you good reason, but I offer my mind freely so that you can see I speak the truth." He was risking everything. His past was murky, at times even black. At her tender age she was incapable of understanding such a history, the bleakness of his existence that had led to this moment. But she would know every fact, every merciless act. She would also know just how far he had gone to ensure that he would have her as his lifemate. It was the only way he knew to reassure her that he meant what he said. If he opened his mind completely, she would know he spoke the truth. She could never love him, but he didn't expect love from her.

Savannah studied his face for a long moment. "It's enough that you made the offer, Gregori. My fears wouldn't go away even knowing you're incapable of hurting me. Fear doesn't work that way." It wasn't necessary for him to sacrifice his pride, to confess every dark, ugly deed. His life had been hard, and he had done the best he could. She had no right to judge his actions. "Maybe we can slow all this down and work at getting to know one another."

He let his breath out slowly, became aware he had been holding it. "You are certain?" At her nod, he released her.

"What did you mean, Roberto was not alone?" Deliberately she changed the subject, tried to ease the tension between them.

"He traveled in a pack. They turned Europe into a killing ground. Your father was hard put to cover up the evidence and protect our people. It hasn't been that long since the assassins swept through our homeland and murdered our people."

"How many are in this pack?"

"Four more."

Her hand went to her throat. She looked so young and defenseless, he wanted to drag her into the protection of his arms. She was doing things to him he didn't understand, but no price was too high to pay for her. "Did they come here because of me? Roberto said he found me first. I thought he meant before you did. Did I bring them here?"

He wanted to lie to her—hadn't he caused her enough pain already?—but he couldn't bring himself to do it, so he said nothing.

Savannah shook her head sadly. "I see." She was still weak and dizzy with the loss of blood from his voracious feeding. "Where are my clothes? I am too weak to manufacture any."

His eyebrows shot up. "Where do you think you are going?"

"I have to make arrangements for Peter's funeral. Everyone's probably looking for me, and the crew must be devastated over Peter's death and worried about me. After I take care of those things, I intend to join you in hunting down the renegades."

"And you think I will allow such a dangerous thing?"

Her eyes grew stormy. "You can't dictate to me, Gregori—we may as well get that straight right now."

Gregori unfolded his long frame from the bed and stretched like a lazy jungle cat. Savannah found her eyes glued to him. He glided soundlessly, muscles rippling beneath his elegant silk shirt. Crushing sweet-smelling herbs into several small pots of water, he lit candles beneath each container. Instantly the room filled with a soothing, beguiling scent that seemed to find its way into her body, her very bloodstream. Picking up a brush from the nightstand, Gregori moved around the bed and returned to her side. "Of course I will be dictating to you, Savannah. But please do not worry. I can assure you, I am quite good at it."

She was shocked. Gregori, the Dark One, teasing her? He sat behind her, careful of her bruises, and began to smooth the tangles from her hair. It felt good, the brush moving over her scalp, down the length of her hair, his hands stroking in long caresses, a kind of magic.

"Very funny. I wasn't born in the fourteenth century or whatever idiotic and *backward* time you were born. I'm a modern woman whether you like it or not. It was your choice to tie yourself to me. Dictating, no matter how good you are at it, is out." There was sorcery, seduction, in the touch of his hands, the velvet of his voice, the little teasing note that she now matched with her own.

His fingers brushed the nape of her neck, sending heat spiraling through her blood. "I am of the Old World, *bébé*." The warmth of his breath was against her ear. "I can do no other than protect my woman."

"Get over it," she suggested sweetly. "We'll get along much better that way."

"We will get along splendidly, *ma petite*, as you will never oppose my will." His voice, pitched low, was temptation itself. The air in the room was thick with the scent of herbs, invading her senses, his voice mesmerizing her.

She turned her head to look at him over one bare shoulder, violet eyes smoldering. His silver eyes gleamed at her, amusement in their depths. "Get a grip, Gregori. You're losing your mind. It did occur to you I would need clothes, didn't it?" She tried to sound tough; it would do her no good to allow him to seduce her into lowering her guard. But she was very drowsy, her head spinning with the scent of the herbs and the feel of his hands in her hair.

"It is not difficult to conjure such items," he reminded her, bending his head to stroke his tongue soothingly across a particularly ugly bruise on her lower back. The healing saliva would work faster mixed with their native soil, but it was all he had.

Savannah jumped as the velvet roughness of his tongue moved erotically along her hip. The heavy scent of the herbs invaded her senses, inducing a languid drowsiness. Gregori's fingers brushed her hair aside, positioning the long length of silk over her shoulder to expose her back to him. He bent his head slowly to her, his own long, dark hair sliding over her sensitive skin.

She made a sound of protest and tried to move away from him, but she landed sprawled on her stomach, her hands trapped beneath her.

"Lie still, Savannah. This must be done." His mouth was against her hip, at the worst of the bruises.

Fear clawed at her, swirled in her brain. He made her feel so completely vulnerable, so helpless. It was going to happen all over again, his brutal possession. Tears burned behind her eyelids, and a moan welled up in her throat.

He found her fear of him intolerable. It shouldn't have mattered to him. He knew he wasn't going to hurt her—just the opposite, he was healing her—but her fear ate at him, turning him inside out. He, who had thought he had no gentleness left in him, touched her with extraordinary tenderness. "If I bring you your wolf, Savannah, will you accept *his* ministrations?" He offered it gently. Glossy black fur rippled along his arms, and bones crackled and stretched to accommodate his changing shape.

Savannah's skin was so unbearably sensitive, even the brush of fur was painful. Through her fear she caught a glimmer of hurt, as if it would bother Gregori that she would prefer the animal to the man. "No, please don't, Gregori. Don't bring the wolf. Let me heal naturally," she pleaded, unable to bear his hurt. She closed her eyes as the roped muscles rippled once more beneath his own skin.

His tongue found the dark mark of his fingers on her rounded bottom, tracing each purple line. "You are not mortal, *ma petite*. This *is* natural to our people." He felt pleasure at her choice, yet wondered that he did so.

Gregori's hands traced her body, finding every scratch, every bruise. His mouth was warm, moist, lapping caresses along her ribs, her waist, her hips and buttocks. Savannah gasped as he inserted a hand between her legs, forcing her to give him access to a long, terrible scratch on her thigh. It wound its way from the back to the inside of her leg. Rough velvet lapped gently, insistently, at the angry red wound, an intimate, erotic touch.

Savannah could barely breathe. His touch was like a drug, invading her body, warming her bloodstream, easing every ache. It was so easy for him to control her mind, her body, as if there were no Savannah without him. She needed his touch every bit as much as she hated it. Even the air in the chamber favored him, the soothing herbs insidious, making her drowsy.

Gregori turned her over gently, his breath catching in his throat. He had never realized just how beautiful the female body really was. *His.* Pride and possession were burning in his pale eyes as his gaze swept her bare skin, then moved to her delicate face. Tears glittered like jewels, caught in her long lashes.

He murmured something she couldn't catch, his fingers brushing the tears from the tips of her lashes so that the teardrops fell into his palm. He closed his hand around them, breathed warm air through his fingers, and opened his hand. Three flawless diamonds lay on his open palm.

Even though she was a mistress of illusion, Savannah's eyes widened in wonder at Gregori's feat, and her fingers curled around the thickness of his wrist. Gregori's heart somersaulted at the touch of her fingers, her mixture of childlike awe at his magic and the stark fear of what his intimate touch was doing to her body. Every Carpathian worth his salt could perform the illusion of tears to diamonds, but Gregori's gems were real, solid. He had used his enormous strength and the tremendous power of his mind to fashion the impossible for her, to make illusion reality.

Taking her hand, his eyes fastened to hers, Gregori allowed the diamonds to fall into her open palm, a shower of gems. Very carefully he closed her fingers around his gift to her. His eyes still holding hers, his tongue stroked along her bruised fist. Once, twice, a third time.

Darts of fire went racing into her bloodstream. Her body stirred, warmed in the cool of the night air. A little sound escaped when he bent his head to find a darkened smudge at the corner of her mouth. Her heart lurched crazily. She wanted to run, but her body was too heavy, the scent of the herbs drugging her senses. In her head, faint, far away, she could hear a chant in his low, smooth voice, the language centuries old. Her lashes drifted down. Fire and ice. Pain and pleasure. Rough velvet lapping at her sore mouth, taking away the sting.

Savannah closed her eyes against the torment of his masculine beauty, the tenderness etched in his sensual features. His tongue moved over her lips, then slipped inside to bathe a cut in her mouth. It felt so good.

He lingered over her neck, her throat, his tongue taking great care over torn flesh. The teeth marks on her shoulder where he had held her pinned beneath him required a slow, lazy swirl of his tongue, long, stroking caresses to remove the pain and replace it with a torturous heat.

Gregori's body responded to every inch of her satin skin, the taste and feel of her, the sight and smell of her, but this time would be all hers. There would be no chance of hurting her; he was determined to replace every bruise, every scratch, every bad memory with healing pleasure.

Enough, Gregori. Her merged mind found his hungry and aroused, matching hers, without the fear clouding hers. Her breath was coming in short gasps somewhere between pleasure and terror.

"Every bruise, *mon petit amour*, no matter how small." Deliberately he whispered the words, his breath warm against the roundness of her breast. He took his time, enjoying his work, tracing the soft fullness, his tongue rasping tenderly over her nipples, soothing the ugly marks marring the perfection of her skin. Each caress lingered, stroked, teased, and healed. He would never get enough of her, never get over the feel and perfection of her. He would never get over the fact that she had refused to condemn him, that she had tried to protect him from the terrible crime he had committed against her. It seemed impossible that she could care enough, that anyone, least of all Savannah, after what he had inflicted upon her, would care enough to do what she had done. Follow him to the depths of hell and drag him back to her.

He groaned at the thought of it, aching inside, weeping silently that he had committed such a horrendous act against his woman, the only woman courageous enough to follow him and drag his soul from hell into her light.

Savannah's fingers tangled in his thick mane, weaving a kind of magic all their own. *Stop tormenting yourself, Gregori. You knew the risk, and yet you still gave me my freedom. Those five years of freedom were precious to me. I thank you for them.*

Gregori closed his eyes. She was turning him inside out, melting his coldness, his frigid existence, with the beauty of her nature. She was all that he was not. Compassion, forgiveness, light, and goodness, now wed to a demon with no knowledge of the things that made her what she was. If it was love for her that was growing in him, it was a powerful, dangerous emotion. *You fear me now.* His torment was in his mind.

She moved slightly so that he could attend the underside of her breast. He felt her shiver in response to the gentle lapping of his tongue, the heat rushing through her body, the pressure building slowly.

I always feared you, Gregori, feared your power over me, feared what you represented, the loss of my freedom. I feared so powerful a being and how you made me feel. Even if this had not happened, I would still fear you.

His mouth moved lower still, over her narrow rib cage, and the small span of her waist. He lingered over four long scratches across her stomach, his body aching, but he so enjoyed his work, it didn't matter. *Now you fear to join with me.*

Her breath caught in her throat, and she stilled beneath him, but the soothing chant went on, and the heavy scent of herbs combined with his gentle touch prevailed. She relaxed beneath him. *I don't want to be hard on your ego—men are so fragile—but sex is definitely overrated. We can refrain from that aspect of things.*

He felt a tinge of amusement at her thoughts. He knew he was bringing a raging fire to her blood, that waves of heat were beating at her. He could easily smell her scent calling to him with her readiness. But she wasn't going to fall into his trap. He had been too big for her small frame, and far too rough. His mouth trailed fire across her stomach to the silken triangle at the junction of her legs. She jumped, her fingers twisting in his hair. "No, Gregori, I mean it."

Her voice was husky, and her small hands were trembling again, the feel against his scalp turning his heart over. His palms moved in gentle caresses over her thighs, and his tongue found the crease of one hip. *I know of only one way to heal you.* He stroked the center of her heat with infinite tenderness.

She cried out, her hips jerking, trying to squirm away from the swirling vortex of flames he was creating. Her muscles clenched. Tremors started in her stomach. Pressure built. There was such need building, heat raging at her innermost core. *Gregori!* It was a helpless plea—of wanting, of fear, of confusion.

The psychic connection between them was so strong, it was easy for him to read her every conflicting emotion, her burning need. His soothing chant never faltered, and he was careful to keep his own raging body under control along with his wild, passionate thoughts. For her sake he merged, created pleasure without fear, a healing to replace the brutal taking of her innocence.

On some level Savannah knew he was in her head, directing her emotions away from fear, heightening her pleasure until she thought she might die with the intensity of it. His touch was so gentle, easing her terrible soreness until the pressure building inside her became nearly unbearable.

Let go, ma petite. *I am here to catch you.* The voice was a spell compelling her compliance. She wanted to obey, to give herself into his care. She wanted him to extinguish the waves of flames beating at her.

Her soft keening, the little whimper escaping her

throat, nearly tore him up. Her release was shattering, shocking her as her body seemed to fragment and dissolve, as the earth moved and colors burst all around her, through her, in her.

Gregori held her while her body rippled with pleasure, while aftershocks shook her. He dragged her close, pulled her into the shelter of his body, desperately needing to be close to her. He was bathed in sweat, his muscles taut and rigid with his own hunger for release. If the cycle of mating heat was anything like the desire clawing at him, he and Savannah were in for either a difficult time or a glorious one.

She could feel the urgency of his need beating at him, tearing at his very soul. "I'm sorry, Gregori." Savannah's voice was soft, filled with guilt, a mere thread of sound, her face buried against his silk-covered ribs.

He lifted strands of ebony hair to his mouth, inhaling her fragrance. "You have no reason to be sorry for anything, *ma petite*."

Her clenched fist lay over his heart, the three diamonds in her palm. "You think I can't read your body? Feel the heaviness in your mind as you try to shield me? I can't change who I am, not even for you. I know I'm failing you, causing you discomfort."

A slow smile curved his mouth. *Discomfort*. Now, there was a word for it. His hand crushed her hair, ran it through his fingers. "I have never asked you to change, nor would I want you to. You seem to forget that I know you better than anyone. I can handle you."

She turned her head so that he could see the silver stars flashing in her blue eyes, a smoldering warning. "You are so arrogant, Gregori, it makes me want to throw things. Do you hear yourself? *Handle* me? Ha! I try to say I'm sorry for failing you, and you act the lord of the manor. Being born centuries ago when women were chattel does not give you an excuse."

"Carpathian women have never been considered chattel," he corrected softly. "Ours is a dwindling race. Our children rarely survive, and there are so few women for lifemates, most of our men are lost to their inner darkness after centuries alone. Our women are our most precious treasure, guarded and protected."

"Gregori." Savannah kept her fist clenched, clutching the diamonds of her tears inside as if they were a symbol. "Let's try to come to some kind of understanding so we can maybe live together in peace." Her body was still rocking with aftershocks, and his looks alone kept warmth curling through her. She had the most surprising desire to touch his dark eyebrows with her fingertip.

His mouth found the silky fragrance of her hair, and his hands ran down the length of her back, finding pleasure in the way her tiny waist tucked into her slender hips. "What kind of understanding?" he murmured almost absently, his mind clearly on other, more provocative things.

The trace of amusement in his voice irritated her, as if he were merely humoring her. Savannah pushed at the solid wall of his chest to put a few inches between them. His large frame didn't budge, and she was locked in by his arm. She pushed at him again. "Forget it."

He bent his head to taste the vulnerable line of her neck, to feel her pulse in the warm, moist cavern of his mouth. His blood surged and pounded. Little jackhammers began to beat at his skull. "I am listening to every word you say, *ma petite*," he murmured, lost in her softness, in the scent of her. He wanted her with every fiber of his being, every cell in his body. "I could repeat each word verbatim, if you desire."

Soon the fire would start, and there would be no choice for either of them. His blood would call to hers with such an urgency that she couldn't ignore the summons. His mind would slip easily in and out of hers, the psychic link so strong it would bind them close even over great distances. She would need it as much he.

Gregori inhaled her into his very body, her scent so feminine, so seductive. She stirred such depths of feelings after such a barren existence, it terrified him. He was used to an emotionless life. She could bring him good, but his potential for evil was enormous. He was a law unto himself. Even the laws of his people, the very laws he defended, had never applied to him.

He could read her feelings quite easily. Savannah had an open, direct nature. She was drawn to him, even prepared to protect him from himself if necessary. But she had no intention of ever allowing him to make love to her again. It cut like a knife that he had been the one to hurt her, to make her fear their natural union.

"You're not listening." Savannah squirmed, trying to get out from under him. "You're trying to seduce me." She said it indignantly.

He lifted his head, pale eyes roaming possessively over her beautiful features. "Yes, I am. Is it working?" His voice—a low, teasing caress—disarmed her where denial would not have. His hand was spanning her throat, his thumb brushing tenderly along her neck, sending flames licking along her skin.

She was smiling at his words in spite of every effort not to. "No, it isn't working at all," she lied. She couldn't look at him without wanting him. Her pulse was racing beneath the pad of his thumb. Her skin was hot satin, inviting his touch, inviting further exploration. There was conflict in her mind, fear uppermost, but there was also desire. Gregori focused on that, fed that spark of need with his own.

He touched his mouth to the corner of hers, brushed a velvet-soft whisper across her lips, and felt her heart jump wildly in response. "Are you certain? I have learned much over the centuries. There is an art to making love." It was blatant sorcery now, all-out seduction.

He was doing something magical to her mouth. Applying hardly a touch, yet with such a mixture of tenderness and possession, her heart turned over. Her fingers tangled in his thick mane of jet-black hair. Long lashes swept her cheeks; then she lifted blue eyes dancing with laughter. "An art? Is that what you call it? I think I could come up with a better name."

He lifted his head, pale eyes glinting silver, warming to liquid mercury. "And you know so much? Your first time was a travesty, an abomination. That was not me, Savannah; it was the beast within. That definitely was not making love. You cannot count that as a lovemaking experience." His voice reflected his deep sorrow even as his eyes were sexy, hungry, intense with a heat that sent flames coursing through her.

She tilted her chin, hating the sorrow in him, the guilt. Wanting his mind on other matters, she deliberately challenged his statement. "You don't know so much about me. There was a man once. He was crazy about me." She tried to look worldly. "Absolutely crazy for me."

His answering laughter was warm against her neck, her throat. His lips touched the skin over her pulse and skimmed lightly up to her ear. "Are you, by any chance, referring to that foppish boy with the orange hair and spiked collar? Dragon something?"

Savannah gasped and pulled away to glare at him. "How could you possibly know about him? I dated him last year."

Gregori nuzzled her neck, inhaling her fragrance, his hand sliding over her shoulder, moving gently over her satin skin to take possession of her breast. "He wore boots and rode a Harley." His breath came out in a rush as his palm cupped the soft weight, his thumb brushing her nipple into a hard peak.

The feel of his large hand—so strong, so warm and possessive on her—sent heat curling through her body. Desire rose sharply. He was seducing her with tenderness. Savannah didn't want it to happen. Her body felt better, but the soreness was there to remind her where this could all lead. Fear was an ugly, living thing she couldn't shake. Her hand caught at his wrist. "How did you find out about Dragon?" she asked, desperate to distract him, to distract herself. How could he make her body burn for his when she was so afraid of him, of having sex with him?

"Making love," he corrected, his voice husky, caressing, betraying the ease with which his mind moved like a shadow through hers. "And to answer your question, I live in you, can touch you whenever I wish. I knew about all of them. Every damn one." He growled the words, and her breath caught in her throat. "He was the only one you thought of kissing." His mouth touched hers. Gently. Lightly. Returned for more. Coaxing, teasing, until she opened to him. He stole her breath, her reason, whirling her into a world of feeling. Bright colors and white-hot heat, the room falling away until there was only his broad shoulders, strong arms, hard body, and perfect, perfect mouth.

When he lifted his head, Savannah nearly pulled him back to her. He watched her face, her eyes cloudy with desire, her lips so beautiful, bereft of his. "Do you have any idea how beautiful you are, Savannah? There is such beauty in your soul, I can see it shining in your eyes."

She touched his face, her palm molding his strong jaw. Why couldn't she resist his hungry eyes? "I think you're casting a spell over me. I can't remember what we were talking about."

Gregori smiled. "Kissing." His teeth nibbled gently at her chin. "Specifically, your wanting to kiss that orange-bearded imbecile."

"I wanted to kiss every one of them," she lied indignantly.

"No, you did not. You were hoping that silly fop would wipe my taste from your mouth for all eternity." His hand stroked back the fall of hair around her face. He feathered kisses along the delicate line of her jaw. "It would not have worked, you know. As I recall, he seemed to have a problem getting close to you."

Her eyes smoldered dangerously. "Did you have anything to do with his allergies?" She *had* wanted someone, anyone, to wipe Gregori's taste from her mouth, her soul.

He raised his voice an octave. "Oh, Savannah, I just have to taste your lips," he mimicked. Then he went into a sneezing fit. "You haven't ridden until you've ridden on a Harley, baby." He sneezed, coughed, and gagged in perfect imitation.

Savannah punched his arm, forgetting for a moment her still-tender fist. When it hurt, she yelped and glared accusingly at him. "It was you doing all that to him! The poor man—you damaged his ego for life. Each time he touched me, he had a sneezing fit."

Gregori raised an eyebrow, completely unrepentant. "Technically, he did not lay a hand on you. He sneezed before he could get that close."

She laid her head back on the pillow, her ebony hair curling around his arm, then her arm, weaving them together. His lips found her throat, then moved lower and found the spot over her breast that burned with need, with invitation. Savannah caught his head firmly in her hands and lifted him determinedly away from her before her treacherous body succumbed completely to his magic. "And the dog episode?"

He tried for innocence, but his laughter was echoing in her mind. "What do you mean?"

"You know very well what I mean," she insisted. "When Dragon walked me home."

"Ah, yes, I seem to recall now. The big bad wolf decked out in chains and spikes, afraid of a little dog."

"Little? A hundred-and-twenty-pound Rottweiler mix? Foaming at the mouth. Roaring. Charging him!"

"He ran like a rabbit." Gregori's soft, caressing voice echoed his satisfaction. He had taken great pleasure in running that particular jackass off. How dare the man try to lay a hand on Savannah?

"No wonder I couldn't touch the dog's mind and call him off. You rotten scoundrel."

"After Dragon left you, I chased him for two blocks, and he went up a tree. I kept him there for several hours, just to make a point. He looked like a rooster with his orange comb."

She laughed in spite of her desire not to. "He never came near me again."

"Of course not. It was unacceptable," he said complacently, with complete satisfaction, the warmth of his breath heating her blood. His mouth touched, skimmed, moved across her nipple, branding her with heat, with flame, before finding the underside of her breast. Savannah closed her eyes against a need so intense that she shook with it. How could she want something that hurt so terribly?

No pain, ma petite, *only pleasure*. His tongue created an aching void in her. *I swear it on my life.* His mouth was hot velvet closing over her breast. Fire danced over her skin, invaded her body, melted her insides so that she was liquid heat, pulsing with need for him, only for him.

Chapter Five

Savannah's fear was being pushed aside by the heated tenderness of Gregori's mouth, by the gentleness in his caressing hands. He carelessly shoved the sheet down, exposing her bare breasts to his hungry gaze. Hot. He was so hot. Savannah could not stand the feel of the thin sheet on her heated hips, twisting around her legs. Her hands were tangled in Gregori's thick hair, crushing it in her fingers like so much silk. His shirt was open to his tapered waist, his hard muscles pressing against her soft breasts. The rough, dark hair on his chest rasped erotically over her nipples.

A wave of heat heralded a storm of fire, through him, through her. Savannah's hands, of their own accord, pushed his shirt from his wide shoulders. She watched with enormous eyes as he slowly shrugged out of it, his silver gaze holding her blue one captive. She was drowning in those pale, mesmerizing eyes. Eyes filled with such intensity, with so much hunger for one woman. Her. Only her.

Afraid of what she was committing herself to, Savannah tentatively, cautiously, touched his mind with hers. She found a hunger so deep, so wild, so urgent, she was instantly lost. How could she deny his fierce need? Even though Gregori knew he was a man without tenderness, that his every instinct was wild and uninhibited, his intent was to be gentle with her, to ensure her pleasure. His every thought was for her, to please her, to worship her body with his.

"I know you are afraid, *mon amour*," he whispered softly, his hands sliding up her rib cage to her breasts. "But I am no longer a beast. You leashed the demon. There is only me, a man who very much wants to make love to his lifemate." She felt his breath against her nipple. "Let me show you how it is supposed to be. Beautiful. Such pleasure. I can bring you so much pleasure, *ma petite*." His mouth closed over her breast, hot and moist. The sound of his voice was mesmerizing, enticing. She could get caught up forever in the mere sound of it. There was no thought in his mind for his own burning body, his own urgent demands; he wanted to show her the beauty and pleasure of true mating.

Flames raced through her blood and licked down her skin at the intensity of the eroticism, the craving his mouth at her breast created. She moaned, low and soft, the note brushing at his soul like the flutter of butterfly wings. Her hands slid over his back, tracing each defined muscle with her fingertips, committing him to memory. Tears filled her eyes. How could a man be so sensual, so perfect? He was stealing her will as easily as he was stealing her body.

"Want me, Savannah," he whispered softly. "Want me the way I want you." His tongue rasped over her skin, traced the underside of her breast, followed each rib even as his hands explored her hips and thighs. His fingers found their goal, the heated, moist entrance, hot and ready, waiting for his body to merge with hers.

She arched into his palm, her body demanding relief. "I feel like I'm burning up, Gregori!" she gasped, shocked at the intensity of her hunger for him. She *needed* him.

"I am the one burning up, going up in flames." His fingers pushed deeper, ensuring her readiness, taking pleasure in her reaction. Her hands on his bare skin were driving him wild, but most of all, it was the trust she was giving to him that moved him so deeply.

Gregori could not conceive of such trust from a woman so brutally used, and it humbled him, the way she was so forgiving. She might never be able to love a monster such as he, but with her understanding, her compassion, she was determined to make something of the imposed sentence of their life together.

The clothes confining his body were tight and painful, so he removed them with a mere thought. He heard her gasp as the hot length of him pressed aggressively against her thigh. She had thought herself safe as long as his clothes were on. She had thought she would have the time to make up her mind, to choose for herself, but her body was making the choice for her. And he was losing himself in the molten heat of her, in her shadowed, secret places.

Savannah's body suddenly went rigid. She caught his face in her hands, exerting pressure so that he had to lift his head from his delicious explorations, his silver eyes molten as they touched on her face. She took a deep breath. "What if I can't do this, Gregori?" She sounded close to tears. "What if I can never do this?"

"No one is making you do anything, *ma petite*," he

replied gently, kissing her stomach. "We are just exploring possibilities."

"But, Gregori," she tried to protest, attempting to bring his head back up so that he could see her very real fear for him, for their life together.

"If I cannot persuade you otherwise, *mon amour*, I am not much of a lifemate, now am I?" The words were muffled in the tight silky curls, the intriguing little triangle at the apex of her thighs.

"You don't understand, Gregori." Savannah closed her eyes against the waves of fire racing through her. "It's me who is no real lifemate. I don't know how to please you, and I'm so afraid of this."

"Relax, *bébé*." He breathed warm air against her, inhaled her scent. "You please me far more than you will ever know." His teeth nipped her thigh, his tongue caressing her shadows and hollows, following the path his fingers had taken.

She cried out at the feelings sweeping through her, tumultuous, turbulent, wild, and untamed. She was no longer on earth but soaring free, spiraling and spinning out of control.

Gregori's body moved over hers, hard and hot, his strength enormous, but his hands were tender as he cupped her head in one palm. His knee inserted itself very gently between hers to give him access to her. Savannah, still rippling with the aftershocks of her climax, was barely aware of the weight of him pinning her down, once more making her vulnerable and open to him.

Gregori took the advantage while he had it, pressing intimately into her entrance. She was slick with need, hot, tight, and velvet soft. He felt her gasp at his invasion, and he paused to allow her body an opportunity to adjust to his size. She was holding her breath, waiting for the terrible, tearing pain. Her fingernails dug into his back, and she made a small sound of protest against the weight of his chest. But she felt only ripples of fire, a storm of intense pleasure washing over her, consuming her.

"Relax, Savannah. Relax for me. You were meant for me, created for me. And I was created for you." He feathered kisses from her temple to her throat, his hips moving in a gentle, coaxing rhythm.

She could feel the sheen of perspiration on his back, evidence of the tremendous effort he was exerting to hold back. His every touch, every movement, was tender, gentle.

He moved into her with exquisite care, astonished at how perfect she was, tight and fiery hot. His thumb brushed her lower lip, the small bruise discoloring the side of her mouth.

At once her lip tingled with warmth, was soothed as if he had laid a mystical balm over it. Her heart slammed against her ribs. He was doing things to her body not only with his body, not only with his hands, but with his mind.

In spite of every fear, in spite of the memory of his earlier attack, Savannah was caught up in the fire, in the tenderness. Her body slowly relaxed, slowly accepted his. Gregori buried himself deeper, a long, sure stroke that had her gasping, her nails digging into his arms, holding tight to keep from soaring away into the night.

He whispered softly to her, a mixture of French and his ancient tongue. She knew very little of either language, had no idea what he was saying, but the words excited her, comforted her. She felt as if she were important to him. Not her body. Her—Savannah.

"How could you doubt such a thing, *chérie?*" he whispered against her breast, his mouth moving back and forth in a subtle rhythm matching the long, slow strokes of his hips.

Her body, of its own accord, followed the tempo of his. They moved together as they were meant to, their hearts beating as one. Gregori's hands gliding over her skin, his soft murmurs of encouragement, added to the beauty of their union. He was incredibly gentle, initiating her as he should have the first time, with care and tenderness.

She wanted to cry. It was unbelievable, the way he made love to her, as if she was the most precious, cherished, beautiful woman in the world. She clutched him, hanging on to the only reality she was certain of as her body tightened, the pressure building and building until she cried out with the need for release. Only then did he allow himself the luxury of burying himself deep and hard, merging himself with her completely. He held them both at the peak, riding the crest until her keening cries and the heated velvet of her body surrounding his drove him over the edge. He took her with him, right over the precipice. Savannah's soft voice was muffled against his chest. She was falling, lights bursting, exploding all around her, but Gregori was there, everywhere, holding her close in strong arms, making certain she was safe.

As they lay locked together, Savannah was unable to take it all in, to believe how he had made her feel. His hands were stroking her hair, his mouth brushing her temple.

Gregori knew he would never get enough of her. Her fingers were twisting absently in his wild mane of hair, and the touch sent a new heat curling through his blood.

Then something invaded the peace and serenity. Suddenly, scenting danger, Gregori lifted his head. On the heels of his own alertness came a warning from the wolves. They called to him, their voices pitched in excited tones. He lowered his head and placed a brief, hard kiss on Savannah's mouth. She looked drowsy, sexy, thoroughly loved.

At that moment the summons came, a soft, muted, but insistent voice, whispering to Savannah. *My darling, I am close. Where are you?* Was it her mother? Savannah attempted to sit up, joy coursing through her. She hadn't seen her mother in five years. Now, when she needed her the most, when she needed guidance and comfort, her mother had unexpectedly appeared.

You will not answer. It was an imperious command, and Gregori expected to be obeyed. He was already pulling away from her, his face an implacable mask, his eyes slivers of steel.

Savannah was already seeking the familiar mental path to her mother. But at once, before she could actually send a message, her body became like lead, and her mind could not converse. Terror gripped her, and she didn't understand.

Helplessly she glanced at Gregori, and when she saw his mask of granite, she knew he had done something to her. Her eyes were eloquent, pleading with him, frightened by his cool, expressionless features. There was something immovable about him, something harsh and unrelenting. Merciless. Why had she ever thought him gentle, tender? He was as cruel as a vampire.

"You cannot call out to your mother. It is not Raven. You are being hunted, Savannah," he said softly, his beautiful voice without inflection. "You will be able to speak only to me on our exclusive path. I want your assurance that you will do as I say."

Savannah was furious. Hurt. More hurt than furious, and that made her all the more furious that she had allowed herself to care enough to let him hurt her in the first place. *You have no right to do this to me. Release me at once, Gregori! I know my own mother when I hear her.*

He stood up and stretched, a lazy ripple of muscles that made her want to claw out his eyes. "It is not your mother. You are mine, Savannah, and it is my duty to protect you in any way I see fit. These vampire friends of Roberto are after something, and I think they are not alone. I believe they have drawn in human butchers. Aidan Savage is here in the city, and he is a good hunter, but I think these renegades are following you." He dressed with fluid efficiency and casual grace. "I am not in the habit of explaining myself. I have made a concession to you in doing so. Choose now how you will proceed."

I refuse your claim on me, she answered in the only way he allowed her to communicate. *I will take my refusal to our people and plead with them for the mercy you evidently don't have in you. I will not be tied to you!*

He bent over her, a dark, imposing figure exuding power. His silver eyes glittered at her. "Hear me, Savannah. If you believe nothing else about me, believe this. You belong to me, with me. No one will ever attempt to take you from me and live. No one." His voice was low, beautiful, and all the more deadly for it.

Her violet gaze was held captive by his pale one. She believed him. And not even her father, the Prince of their people, had a chance of destroying him. Her mind shied away from that thought. Destroy Gregori? She didn't want that. He just couldn't have her. *Let me up, Gregori*, she demanded. The paralysis was beginning to make her crazy. She felt as if she couldn't breathe. She felt smothered, strangled.

"Say you will obey me." He was dressed now, elegant as always. His mind was no longer completely on her; he was tuned to the vibrations in the air, to each note the wolves sang to him.

Savannah knew she was screaming—her entire body was screaming—but no sound emerged. Her body was no longer hers to command. Her mind was screaming in outrage, but Gregori controlled her ability to send out a cry for help.

Stop fighting me. His voice was a soft growl in her mind.

Release me. Her heart was pounding so loud, she was afraid she might explode. This couldn't be happening. Mere moments ago Gregori had been lying with her, holding her in protective arms, gently making love to her. Or so she had thought. But what did she know about making love? Gregori could make anyone feel anything. He didn't need to feel anything for her to make her believe he did. How could he take her body so gently, then turn around like an unfeeling monster and destroy her free will, control her as if she was nothing more than a puppet to him? What kind of person would do such a thing?

Savannah, you will stop fighting me now. We are in danger. You will obey me if you wish to take back control of yourself.

I know my own mother. You don't want anyone else

*around me; that's why you won't allow me to acknowl-
edge her*, she accused him.

So be it. It is your choice. His voice was as unruffled
as always. Nothing seemed to disturb Gregori. Not her
hostility, not her confusion and disillusionment.

Her body jerked into a sitting position; then she was
standing helplessly beside the bed, naked, totally vulnerable, unable to speak or move. Her head was throbbing
as she tried desperately to fight his control of her. She
would not submit her mind to his will, not voluntarily.
He might have her body, but he could fight her to the
death for possession of her mind.

Mocking laughter echoed in her head. *Fight me all
you want*, bébé. *You are only hurting yourself. You will
obey me, Savannah.*

Despair welled up in her. It was true. She was helpless
against his superior power and strength. She hated him
for making her so aware of it, for forcing her to see that
no matter how much she tried to be herself, to maintain
a semblance of pride and dignity, she was stripped to
nothing by a mere thought in his head. Shards of glass
seemed to be piercing her head. The more she resisted,
the worse the pain.

A cotton shirt and jeans suddenly covered her body.
Soft leather shoes wrapped themselves around her feet.
Gregori braided her hair swiftly, efficiently. She detested
the easy, competent way in which he did everything.
One last chance, Savannah. Do you obey me? He leaned
over her, his harsh yet sensual features impassive, an
unreadable mask. His pale eyes were ice cold. He meant
every word he said, and it was obvious he didn't care
which choice she made. There was no give in him, no
gentleness, no remorse.

Inwardly, Savannah shuddered. She was locked to this merciless man for all eternity. There had to be some way to undo the ritual. Even death was better than mindless slavery. She swallowed her pride, unable to stand the leaden weight of her body and mind, unable to allow him such complete control. *I'll obey.* She didn't look at him; she couldn't.

He relinquished control slowly, watching her closely, his mind still in hers. Savannah stood before him, trembling with suppressed anger. Trembling with humiliation and lost dreams. She brought up her closed fist until it was level with his chest, then opened her palm to reveal the three teardrop diamonds. Deliberately she turned her hand over, allowing the gems to fall to the floor and scatter. She didn't look at his face or at the diamonds on the floor, now symbolizing her disposal of their relationship. Staring straight ahead, she awaited his instructions.

"Are you able to shape-shift?" His voice was low and smooth and calm. She hated him for that.

"You know I can't."

"You need blood. You will shield your mind at all times. If you feel a compulsion to send out a call, merge your mind with mine. I will carry you away from this place to one more inaccessible and far easier to defend. Do not make the mistake of attempting to defy me in this, Savannah. With your life at risk, I will not tolerate rebellion."

If he expected her to answer him, he could wait for all eternity. This was an order, the dictator commanding her with his hard authority. It didn't require an answer, and she refused to dignify it with one.

His fingers shackled her wrist and pulled her to him. His body was hard, like the trunk of a tree, completely immovable. She could find no softness or gentleness any-where, not in his body, not in his mind. Had his earlier tenderness all been an illusion, like his trick with the dia-monds? She wanted to cry with shame, but she refused to give him the satisfaction of seeing her weakness.

Gregori launched himself into the air, taking her with him, her weight seeming to him no more than that of a feather. They rose from the bedchamber and proceeded up through the house to the higher levels. An order re-leased the wolves onto the grounds, into the immense preserve. They could hunt for themselves, leave if it be-came necessary. His only obligation, his only concern, was saving Savannah's life. He would send word to Aidan Savage to take proper care of the animals the mo-ment she was safe. The enemy was far stronger, far more organized than Gregori had expected, and Savannah was their target. They had a plan, a scheme they had obvi-ously worked out well in advance of her coming to the city. Gregori would do anything to protect her. Anything.

She lay quietly in his arms, deliberately closing her mind to his. It didn't matter, of course; he had been able to slip in and out of her mind at will since she was an infant. He had always known she could never really love him, would never accept his dominion over her. How could she when she could never really know who he was? He had not expected the terrible wrenching, the knife twisting in his heart, deeper even, right into his soul.

The night was drawing to a close. Two hours, perhaps, before the sun came up. The vampires would need sanc-tuary, and if they were arrogant enough to think his home would provide it to them, they would be in for a nasty surprise. Gregori snarled silently as he burst into the open sky with Savannah.

Gregori tried to block out the hurt of Savannah's rejection. She needed time to understand him. And they had an eternity. She thought herself sentenced to a lifetime with a demon. He believed she was right. She was weak from refusing to take blood because she had mistakenly believed such deprivation would allow her access to the sun. Her health was of paramount importance.

He sent forth a call. Instantly, two men and a woman from a cabin beside the river moved at his bidding to meet him in the shelter of a grove of pine and oak trees. His feet touched earth, but he carried Savannah to the trio.

"You will feed," he told her silkily, expecting her defiance.

"Am I your puppet, too, Gregori?" she asked softly. "Is this going to be the pattern of our life together? Why do you need me as your lifemate when you can have any human woman do as you wish without a fight?"

The contempt in her voice fanned the pain burning his insides. The emotion was totally unfamiliar to him. "I have neither the time nor the inclination to spar with you, Savannah. Feed." He set her on her feet.

"Do you think I will do so only under compulsion?" She tilted her chin at him, a clear challenge. "I do not need your help." Without looking at him again, she turned toward the taller of the two males.

Gregori stepped back, wary of her reaction. His silver eyes glittered. She was baiting a tiger.

Savannah moved forward, a sensual curve to her mouth. Her enormous eyes were so dark, they were violet, mysterious, and sexy. Her gaze was on another man.

Inviting. Enticing. The human smiled, his entire focus on her as he stepped toward her. She lifted her arms to him, her body moving seductively beneath her clothing.

A low growl of warning rumbled deep in Gregori's throat. Unexpectedly he snarled, his white teeth gleaming dangerously. He was fast, his solid frame inserting itself between his lifemate and her prey. It was instinct, not thought. This man could not touch Savannah, not even to supply her with nourishment.

She raised her beautiful eyes, mesmerizing and taunting, to his pale ones. "Isn't this what you want of me?" Her voice, pitched so low, played over his skin like fingers. "To use my voice and body to draw my prey to me and feed?"

"Do not start something you have no hope of winning, Savannah," Gregori warned with dark menace. He yanked the male to him and bent his head to the exposed neck. Her eyes never wavered from his as he drank his fill. When he lifted his head, he dropped the man on the ground, where he lay sprawled between them. "Come here to me," he ordered her softly.

Unexpectedly her heart somersaulted, and butterfly wings fluttered in her stomach. She never should have taunted him. Why had she been so silly? Gregori didn't even bother to pretend to be civilized. Making him jealous wasn't a smart idea. She held up a placating hand. "Gregori."

"Come here to me, Savannah." His voice was brushed with softness, purity. Impossible to ignore.

Reluctantly, she moved around the man on the ground and put herself into reaching distance. Gregori's hand circled her upper arm and drew her against his hard frame. He bent his dark head to hers, his warm breath stirring tendrils of hair by her ear. "You will take what you need from your lifemate." He whispered the order, but the deceptive softness of his voice only increased its impact.

She attempted to pull away from him, frightened that he was so powerful. His hold on her tightened. She could feel the imprint of his body on hers, hard and aroused. "You will do as I say." His thumb was feathering back and forth across her pulse, wreaking havoc with her senses. As always when he touched her, her body softened, became liquid. She didn't want the heat and excitement of his touch.

Her mouth was pressed against his chest, but he bent closer so that she could nestle her face in his shoulder, his neck. He smelled of wood and spice. His skin was hot, and beneath her moving mouth was his pulse, strong and beckoning. His thumb brushed again, insistently, provocatively. Savannah moaned, her breath coming in a little rush. "Why are you forcing me to do this, Gregori?"

"You need, I provide." His hand cradled the back of her head, holding her against him.

She couldn't help herself, couldn't stop herself from stroking her tongue across his pulse once, twice, in a small caress. It was the way his body was against hers, at once protective and sheltering, yet aggressive and demanding. The combination was exhilarating, temptation itself. How could she resist Gregori? He was so powerful. Savannah sighed and closed her eyes, then pierced his neck.

She felt his jolt of pleasure, of pain, the whip of erotic lightning flashing through his bloodstream. His body moved against hers, hard and urgent, only their clothing separating them. Heat curled and pooled low in her body, and the essence of his life poured into her, filling her, strengthening her as it was meant to.

Gregori's arms tightened around Savannah, and he gritted his teeth. The feel of her silky mouth feeding was so erotic, he could barely contain himself. He wanted to drop her to the earth right there and take what was his. He wanted her so badly, his body was going up in flames. It was heaven and hell holding her against him, so much pleasure and so much pain. And, damn her, she was never going to touch another male as long as either of them lived. Never.

He bent his head and brushed her silky hair with his mouth, savoring the feel of her against his jaw, his skin. She was so small and delicate, so curved and soft. All heated satin and silk. He closed his eyes and pretended she loved him. That she could love him. A monster. *Gregori. The Dark One.*

Savannah heard the echo of his thoughts, the taunt of all Carpathian children to their friends. Who would come out of the night and turn them to stone? *Gregori. The Dark One.* The one with the power to heal—or destroy. In that echo she caught from Gregori a deep sorrow, a belief in the rightness of the cruel accusations against him. There was no bitterness, just acceptance.

She felt a stone on her heart, heavy and oppressive. Very carefully, she closed the pinpricks at his throat and rested her head against his chest. She could hear his heart, strong and steady. Dependable. Mysterious. Sexy. Frightening. That was Gregori.

The hand in her hair closed for a moment, bunching long strands together into his fist; then, abruptly, he let go of her. Without looking at her, Gregori hauled the second of the humans to him, bent his dark head, and fed voraciously. When he had replenished himself, he allowed the man to sit down in the tall grass. He lowered the woman to join her companions.

Savannah stepped back uncertainly. Gregori hunkered down to check each human. He stared into their eyes, his hands gentle as he laid them carefully on the ground to recuperate. "They will be fine," he said, unaware of the husky note in his voice. He straightened, then turned his head slowly to look at her with his glinting silver eyes. "You will not touch another male. Not of any species." Each word was distinct and pronounced in a low growl.

"Don't you think you're overreacting, Gregori?" she ventured.

He stepped close and loomed over her so that the heat of his body enfolded her. "I would be unable to prevent myself from harming them." The admission was made in his usual calm manner.

"I thought your claim on me removed all threats."

"Evidently it brought about new ones. Until I am able to assess and control all that is happening to me, what you are causing me to feel, it is best if you do not defy my will."

Her blue eyes darkened to violet and smoldered as she glared at him. "Your will? I should not defy your will? It isn't like I'm given free will around you, Gregori. Don't you always dictate how I should think and feel? I live only to please you." She curtsied.

A growl rumbled in his throat. He reached for her and brought her up close to his body. "How I wish that were true. I think you live only to drive me crazy."

"That could be arranged," she said sweetly. "I have things I have to take care of, Gregori. They're important to me."

"Such as?" Those pale eyes burned over her upturned face.

"Peter. I have to take care of Peter. I'm his only family. He had no one else. And because of me, he's dead. He was trying to protect me." She crushed down the need to sob, to scream, to pound Gregori into the earth.

He was silent for a moment. "The police will want to speak with you. The story is probably already in the newspapers. Are you ready for the repercussions of that?"

She tilted her chin at him. "I loved Peter like a brother. I owe it to him." Her hand swept through her hair in agitation. "I have to do this. I have to. Please, Gregori. Stand with me on this. I know I can't fight you and win. I need this."

Gregori swore eloquently and repeatedly in four languages. What Savannah needed was to be locked away safely, spirited out of this state—better yet, out of the country. The entire Peter Sanders affair was going to be a media circus. The police would already be scouring the city for her. Damn it to hell.

Without answering her, Gregori wrapped an arm around her waist and scooped her up. He went skyward, his normally tranquil thoughts in chaos, a jumble of unfamiliar emotions and a quicksand of indecision. He was always in total control. With his immense power, he had no other choice. But Savannah was turning him inside out. No, he couldn't allow this. He wouldn't. He didn't care if she cried. If her enormous, magnificent eyes were sad and haunted. If her beautiful, perfect mouth drooped. She was not going to sway him from his path. His way was safe and responsible. Safety was the first issue, not her haunting eyes or her soft, satin mouth. Or her terrible sorrow.

He carried her through the night sky, his thoughts roiling and volcanic, spinning around and around in his head until he thought he might go mad. He knew what he had to do. What was wrong with him that he would allow himself to even consider such foolishness? It was too dangerous, too reckless. If the vampire heading the hunt for her was still persisting in his plan, what better chance to spring a trap than when she returned to deal with Peter's funeral?

Savannah was concentrating on the treetops below them. Nowhere could she detect evidence of a dwelling. She felt empty and cold inside. Gregori was everything he had ever been called. Unfeeling. Hard. Cold. Without emotions. Her life was going to be endless hell. He could not possibly grow to love her. He didn't even really want her. He only wanted someone to control. Someone he could use for sex. She swallowed the bile rising in her throat. She was certainly that person.

Each time he touched her or looked at her with his mesmerizing silver eyes, her body went berserk.

Oh, Peter. She had failed to keep him safe, had led a vampire, the scourge of her kind, directly to him. Now, without Gregori's consent, she could not even provide a decent burial for him. She wanted to feel anger—hatred, even—but all she could manage was emptiness. She had known, all those years ago when she had turned to find Gregori in her bedroom, that she was lost for all eternity.

Chapter Six

Savannah never actually saw the outside of the lair. One moment they were soaring through the sky, the next they were plummeting to earth. She closed her eyes as her stomach rolled, and by the time she could pry her lashes up, Gregori was striding into a rock dwelling. The interior walls were thick and cool, smooth to the touch as if they had been polished. The ceiling was high and of the same polished rock as the walls and floor. Gregori had carved the lair from the mountain itself, a miracle of construction. There were three rooms that she could see, and Savannah was certain there was a hidden chamber below the earth, a bolt hole in case they were in deadly peril.

The moment Gregori set her feet on the rock floor, she moved away from him, a quick, feminine retreat. She refused to look at him, keeping her head bent so that she would not have to meet his gaze. She walked slowly through the unusual structure. The furniture looked comfortable, even cozy. "So this is to be my prison?" she said unemotionally.

Gregori didn't answer. There was no expression on his

face, although the lines around his eyes and mouth seemed etched a little deeper than usual. His silver eyes were pale, reflecting images around him, not his own inner thoughts. His hand went to the back of his neck to massage aching muscles tiredly. Then he left the sitting room on silent feet. Glided. Like a panther. In spite of her determination not to, Savannah found herself watching him covertly behind her lashes. There was something mesmerizing about the way he moved. Muscles rippling, powerful, sensuous. She couldn't keep her wayward eyes from following his every movement, or her wayward heart from missing a beat when she saw his hand massaging his neck.

Gregori sat on the edge of the bed, certain she was not paying him any attention. She wanted to be as far from him as possible. But even from a great distance, he was a shadow in her mind. He could read her every thought of him. None of it was good, and he couldn't blame her. He dropped his face into his hands. He was the monster she had named him. She feared him. She would always hate her destiny, always wish the fates had been kinder. And who knew? Maybe they would have been. After all, he had manipulated her future from the moment of her conception. She was light to his darkness, compassion to his cruelty. She could never love such a brutal beast as he. He had taken what was not his, had tampered with nature and taken her for his own.

Savannah's heart turned over when she caught sight of him sitting on the edge of the bed, the picture of utter dejection. Gregori. He was confidence itself. Complete authority. An emotionless robot uncaring that he had taken her life from her forever. What she thought or felt didn't matter to him. She had named him monster, heart-less. A brutal barbarian. Every name she could think of had danced in her head as they had flown through the air to their destination. She had done it deliberately so that he could read what she thought of him, so that he wouldn't know she craved his touch even as she despised his ways.

But it tore at her, the way he sat so alone. Gregori, who had always been alone. She backed up until the coolness of the rock wall was at her back, her blue eyes thoughtful as she watched him. He was giving her pri-vacy, if it could be called that, even withdrawing from her mind. She bit her lower lip, then winced at the slight discomfort and the memory it brought with it. She real-ized she was familiar with his touch, so gentle in her mind. First he had come to her as the wolf, and later, in the terrible moments when her loneliness had been too painful to bear, it had been Gregori's touch that had eased her. Strange, she had never considered that, never once thought *why* she had felt comforted.

Gregori had offered her free exploration of his mind. She knew he was capable of protecting himself, of cov-ering his emotions and memories in layers if he chose, so that she would see only the parts he wished to share with her. She doubted many Carpathians could do such a thing with their lifemate, but Gregori could. Gregori could do anything.

But she was Savannah Dubrinsky. Daughter of Mikhail and Raven. Their blood flowed in her veins, as did Gre-gori's. She had her own power, didn't she? Up to now she had been a child running from herself, from her life with a man of such power. But if her life was intertwined with Gregori's, she had better grow up fast and find out just what she was up against. Mikhail and Raven had raised her to believe in herself.

She took a deep breath and allowed her mind to merge fully with Gregori's. Her touch was feather-light, delicate, a mere shadow, soft in his mind. Even so, had he not been so preoccupied with his own thoughts, she knew he would have felt her presence. She stayed quiet and simply became a sponge.

He believed himself a demon. He believed his soul was black, beyond real redemption. He was absolute in his belief that he had gotten her through his own manipulations, rather than through true chemistry. He had been so close to turning vampire that he had wagered his very soul on tampering with what was not his to do. He had touched the child in Raven's womb, supplied it with blood, even conversed with it. Savannah had a dim memory of his light reaching her when she was in pain, wanting to let go along with the rush of blood from her mother's body. Gregori had prevented her from doing so.

She saw it clearly. His entire life. Finding his mother and father, stakes driven through their hearts, their heads cut off. The terrible years of the vampire killings in Europe. So many women and children lost to the stakes. Then the hunts. The wars. So many friends turning. Gregori hunting them down to destroy their evil power over humans and Carpathians alike. Century after century. Endless. So much blood, so many dying at his hands. Each death took a part of him until it was impossible to face the other Carpathians, until he dared not befriend any of them. He was sentenced to an eternity of isolation. So alone. Always alone. The bleak and empty world of his existence nearly overwhelmed her with sorrow, bringing tears to her eyes. Who could possibly live year after year in such an empty void and survive with his soul intact? It was impossible.

Knowledge had been his only friend. He had always been a rebel. No authority could hope to hold him, only his loyalty to Mikhail. He had his own rigid code of honor, which he was unswerving in following. Honor was his life. Yet he felt he had compromised even that in the way he had acquired Savannah.

When Savannah had refused to examine his mind so that he could prove to her that she had brought him back from the other side, so that she would be unafraid, know he was incapable of ever harming her again, she had refused out of respect for him. Yet he believed she had been rejecting him. He believed she could never really forgive the things in his life he had been chosen to do. He couldn't forgive himself.

She saw it all. Every dark, dangerous deed. Every dark, ugly kill. Every law he had broken. But most of all she saw his greatness. Time and time again, he had given of himself to heal others, draining his great strength, putting himself in danger over and over that others might live. A lifetime of selfless service to a people who grew to fear the very power they relied on. While none of the ugliness of the hunt, none of the danger, touched the others, he lived in constant readiness. He accepted the necessity of his solitary existence, his strict isolation. He had come to believe the Carpathians were right to fear him. And Savannah saw that they were right. He wielded far too much power for one individual, carried far too much weight on his broad shoulders.

For centuries Gregori had no real anchor in their world, no emotions to keep him from turning. There had been only his strength and determination. His will of iron. His strict code of honor. His loyalty to Mikhail and his belief that their race had a place in the world. His resolve to prevent the children of their race from dying, a way to find true lifemates for the men to keep them from turning vampire. Mikhail's finding Raven had given him a measure of relief in the form of hope. Still, once Savannah had been conceived, the world had turned into a long, endless hell for Gregori. Each minute had turned to an hour, each hour into a day, until he was nearly mad with waiting for her.

Upon Savannah's refusal of their union, he had made a vow to himself to give her five years of freedom. He felt that since she would be tied forever to one who would rule her life absolutely, he owed her at least that small amount of time. To Gregori, every moment was an agony of holding out against the darkness so deeply entrenched in him. He had waited until he knew he would succumb, until he knew he would no longer have the wisdom or desire to choose the dawn—self-destruction, the only honorable option for a Carpathian about to turn vampire. He had fulfilled his vow of freedom for her and in doing so nearly lost his soul. After all those centuries of holding out, he had risked the damnation of his soul for her five years of freedom.

Savannah sat very still, absorbing his memories. The only beauty in his barren, lonely existence had been the years she was growing up, when he was free to share her life as the wolf. She was unafraid of the wolf, giving him total, unconditional love, her every confidence, her unqualified acceptance. He had never had that before. He craved it, needed it, and believed she would never give it to him again.

He accepted the fact that she would never love him, that she would always look at him with fear. It was almost as if he believed he deserved not to be loved because he was certain he had acquired her unfairly. He had not been prepared for the gut-wrenching pain it caused him, or the violent emotions she stirred in him. Savannah stayed very, very still, on the verge of a great discovery.

It wasn't any woman he wanted, as she had believed. And he certainly didn't want a puppet, as she had accused him. He wanted Savannah, with her sense of humor, her pride and compassion, and even her nasty temper. No other woman held the slightest interest for him. No other woman would ever do for him.

He was in pain. Terrible pain. He felt her grief over the loss of Peter. He felt her fear of him. He felt the pain of his own loneliness and eternal isolation. It radiated from his very soul. He was resigned to hold that pain for all time. And he would never show it to her.

Savannah moved out of his mind while she was still undetected. He was terribly lonely, so much so that she wanted to cry for him. And he didn't have the faintest idea how to love someone, laugh with someone, or share his life. He only knew that he had to keep her safe at any cost. She had named him monster, and he believed her to be right.

She stared out the window into the forest. Gregori was many things. He had broken just about every law they had without one iota of remorse. He had killed countless times. He had more power in his little finger than most members of her race combined. But he was not a monster. Never that.

Her foot tapped out a light rhythm on the rock floor. The branches of the trees swayed slightly in syncopation. She did have power, far more than she had ever expected. Gregori wanted her. More than that, he needed her. That particular revelation changed everything. It put control back in her hands, gave her back her life. She squared her shoulders. She was no longer a child running from a nameless fear. She was his lifemate, chosen by God to walk with a man of power, of honor. A sensual, strong male who needed her more than anyone else on earth ever could.

Savannah took a deep breath and let it out carefully. "Gregori?" She kept her voice low and neutral.

He lifted his head slowly, but she felt his mind brush hers. The invasion didn't inspire fear this time. She accepted his merge without shying away from it. "This is a very beautiful place. It's amazing that you were able to do this." She heard a slight rustle, a movement behind her, but she didn't turn around. "You're quite an artist."

She could smell him, his woodsy, spicy scent. Masculine, warm, exciting. She touched the rock wall and smiled to herself, thinking the feel of the rock was a lot like the way Gregori's hard body felt beneath her fingertips.

"It took a few months, *chérie*, the months I spent up here alone, waiting for your show to come to San Francisco."

His voice was so beautiful. She allowed herself to listen to it, to feel the purity of it, to let the black velvet brush her mind. "It is really beautiful, Gregori. We can summer here when we're in this country."

He touched her hair because he couldn't help himself, and he was surprised when she didn't flinch away from him. It pleased him to hear her talk as if she accepted that they would be together in the future. He didn't respond, however, afraid that whatever he said would break their fragile truce.

She reached behind her, found his arm with her palm, and touched him. She felt his pulse jump beneath her fingertips and kept her smile to herself. "So, are you going to explain to me how the vampire was able to use my own mother's voice to draw me out? I am presuming it was a vampire. And how come I felt a compulsion to answer? I am Carpathian; a compulsion shouldn't have worked so quickly or easily on me." She continued to stare out the window.

Flames were licking up the length of his arm from where her hand rested. Savannah had somehow worked out for herself that he believed her safety was in jeopardy. "The vampire is an illusionist, much like yourself. He has practiced mimicking voices for centuries. Now he uses the talent for calling others to him. I recognized the brush of compulsion in the tone, and, of course, your mother would have chosen to use your private channel of communication, not the standard." His voice was emotionless, not in any way condemning her blunder.

She blushed anyway. Why hadn't she caught that? Stupid, stupid mistake. A mistake like that could have gotten her, perhaps both of them, killed. She turned to face him. Gregori's sensual features were carefully impassive. His silver eyes merely reflected back her own image. "I guess I owe you an apology for calling you names. I acted childishly, and I'm sorry."

He blinked. She had surprised him. Savannah felt her heart warm, a funny, melting sensation. "I want you to do something for me. I realize I am not very experienced with vampires, but rather than arbitrarily demanding my obedience, perhaps you could tell me what is going on.

I'm going to rely on your judgment, Gregori. I won't try to defy you. I just have this problem with someone telling me what to do. Even as a child I had a hard time with it—don't you remember?" She deliberately referred to her childhood, the one happy bridge they had between them.

His mouth didn't smile, but a hint of warmth crept into the bleakness in his eyes. "I remember. You did your best to do the exact opposite of everything you were told."

Her smile was intriguing. Gregori couldn't stop staring at her mouth.

"You'd think I would have grown out of it by now, but I haven't. Try to work with me on this."

Her enormous blue eyes pleaded with him. He felt as if he was falling into their depths.

"Please."

He wrapped a length of her hair around his wrist. "I will try, *bébé*, but first comes your safety. Always."

She laughed softly. "Gregori, I know you will never let anything happen to me. It isn't something I worry about."

"It is uppermost in my mind." He sounded very stern.

She tilted her chin at him. "Has it occurred to you that I have been all by myself these last five years and that nothing ever happened to me?"

Gregori smiled then, lending a sensuality to the curve of his mouth. "You have never been truly alone, *chérie*, never at any time. When it was too dangerous for me to be near you, I made certain others were close."

Her quick temper flashed in spite of her every resolution not to let it. Her blue eyes scattered sparks. "You had someone watching me?"

There was something about the way the color rose in

her cheeks, the flash of her eyes, the lift of her breasts when she was angry, that made him want to keep her that way. "I was not the only one, *ma petite*. Your father would never have allowed you to be without protection. You should have known that."

"My own father?" How could she not have known? It would be just like Mikhail. Just like Gregori. Here she thought she had acquired such independence, that she had struck a blow for all Carpathian women, and all the time they were having her watched. "I hired a security company to work my tours," she said, wanting him to recognize that she hadn't been careless about her safety.

"Humans." His tone said it all. "You needed one of us."

"Who? Who did you trust enough, Gregori?" she asked, curious. Trust would be alien to his nature. What other male would he have entrusted his lifemate's safety to? It seemed so out of character for him.

Gregori pushed a hand through the shaggy mane of hair falling to his broad shoulders. His neck hurt. Absently, he tried another massage. "Some situations call for extreme measures. I chose the strongest, most powerful man I knew, one with an unwavering code of honor. His name is Julian. Julian Savage."

"Aidan Savage's twin brother. He's here? In the city?" She had never met Aidan Savage, but she had heard of him from her father. He was a vampire hunter for the Carpathian people. Mikhail greatly respected him, and that in itself said a lot for the man. Recently he had found his lifemate. Savannah had hoped to visit them while she was in the city. They were probably as starved for someone from their homeland as she had been. "Did Aidan know his brother was here protecting me?"

"I am certain Aidan would sense his presence in the

area. How could he not? They are twins. Whether Julian will choose to see him, I do not know. He is struggling with the darkness."

Savannah turned away from those bleak, glittering eyes. So cold. So alone. So lost. *Gregori. The Dark One. Her dark one. Her Gregori.* She could hardly bear his pain. It didn't show, not on that expressionless face, the face carved from pure granite, like the rock lair. It wasn't in his pale eyes, so arctic cold they reminded her of death itself. It wasn't in any part of his mind that he was sharing with her. She felt it all the same. His heart, her heart. His soul, her soul. They were one and the same. Two halves of the same whole. He didn't know it yet, didn't really believe it. After all, he thought it wasn't true chemistry, that he had managed to manipulate their joining. She knew better.

She had known it when she shared her life with the wolf. Maybe not in her head, but in her heart and soul. She had known it when she reached into the black void, into the darkness, and pulled him back to her. She had known it when she shared her body with him, as innocent as she was, as inhibited as she had felt. She feared him, but she knew he was the one. Her heart and soul recognized him.

"The dawn approaches, *chérie*," he said softly. "It is best if we get some sleep." It would be best for her. His body was raging at him, wanting the feel of her skin next to his. He needed to hold her in his arms and shelter her close to his heart. For one brief moment, he could pretend he would not be forever alone. She would keep the darkness at bay for him long enough to get him through another day.

Her hand slid down the length of his arm to his hand. Her fingertips brushed the contours of his muscles. Just a skimming sensation, but his entire body clenched with hot desire. It poured into him, raged at him, molten lava surging through his blood and filling his body with piercing heat. In her innocence, she didn't notice what she was doing to him. Her fingers laced in his trustingly.

"What about Peter? What do you think we should do to minimize the risk? Because you're right, the press is going to give me a hard time. They follow me all over, those ratty little tabloids." Her enormous eyes were staring straight into his silver ones.

He couldn't look away, couldn't let go of her hand. He couldn't have moved if his life depended on it. He was lost in those blue-violet eyes, somewhere in their mysterious, haunting, sexy depths. What was it he had decided? Decreed? He was not going to allow her anywhere near Peter's funeral. Why was his resolve fading away to nothing? He had reasons, good reasons. He was certain of it. Yet now, drowning in her huge eyes, his thoughts on the length of her lashes, the curve of her cheek, the feel of her skin, he couldn't think of denying her. After all, she hadn't tried to defy him; she didn't know he had made the decision to keep her away from Peter's funeral. She was including him in the plans, as if they were a unit, a team. She was asking his advice. Would it be so terrible to please her over this? It was important to her.

He blinked to keep from falling into her gaze and found himself staring at the perfection of her mouth. The way her lips parted so expectantly. The way the tip of her tongue darted out to moisten her full lower lip. Almost a caress. He groaned. An invitation. He braced himself to keep from leaning over and tracing the exact path with his own tongue. He was being tortured. Tormented.

Her perfect lips formed a slight frown. He wanted to kiss it right off her mouth. "What is it, Gregori?" She reached up to touch his lips with her fingertip. His heart nearly jumped out of his chest. He caught her wrist and clamped it against his pumping heart.

"Savannah," he whispered. An ache. It came out that way. An ache. He knew it. She knew it. God, he wanted her with every cell in his body. Untamed. Wild. Crazy. He wanted to bury himself so deep inside her that she would never get him out.

Her hand trembled in answer, a slight movement rather like the flutter of butterfly wings. He felt it all the way through his body. "It is all right, *mon amour*," he said softly. "I am not asking for anything."

"I know you're not. I'm not denying you anything. I know we need to have time to become friends, but I'm not going to deny what I feel already. When you're close to me, my body temperature jumps about a thousand degrees." Her blue eyes were dark and beckoning, steady on his.

He touched her mind very gently, almost tenderly, slipped past her guard and knew what courage it took for her to make the admission. She was nervous, even afraid, but willing to meet him halfway. The realization nearly brought him to his knees. A muscle jumped in his jaw, and the silver eyes heated to molten mercury, but his face was as impassive as ever.

"I think you are a witch, Savannah, casting a spell over me." His hand cupped her face, his thumb sliding over her delicate cheekbone.

She moved closer, and he felt her need for comfort, for reassurance. Her arms slid tentatively around his waist. Her head rested on his sternum. Gregori held her tightly, simply held her, waiting for her trembling to cease. Waiting for the warmth of his body to seep into hers.

Gregori's hand came up to stroke the thick length of silken, ebony hair, taking pleasure in the simple act. It brought a measure of peace to both of them. He would never have believed what a small thing like holding a woman could do to a man. She was turning his heart inside out; unfamiliar emotions surged wildly through him and wreaked havoc with his well-ordered life. In his arms, next to his hard strength, she felt fragile, delicate, like an exotic flower that could be easily broken.

"Do not worry about Peter, *ma petite*," he whispered into the silken strands of her hair. "We will see to his resting place tomorrow."

"Thank you, Gregori," Savannah said. "It matters a lot to me."

He lifted her easily into his arms. "I know. It would be simpler if it did not. Come to my bed, *chérie*, where you belong."

His arms were strong, and the wildness in him was beckoning her. Her arms crept around his neck. She moved his hair so that she could burrow close to his skin. "And if the vampire comes?" Her lips drifted against his ear, then lower, her tongue caressing an intriguing little dip. "What do you plan to do with me if the renegades should come again?"

Her breath was heated silk, her mouth hot satin. Her teeth nipped gently. There was no thought in his mind, just a roar of hunger for her body. Mindless, scorching hunger. Her teeth nibbled at his collarbone while her hand slid inside his shirt. Her fingers tangled in the spread of dark hairs across his chest, found each defined muscle and traced it. The roar spread thoughout his body until he shook with it.

He made it to the bed only because it was so close. She lifted her head when he set her feet on the stone floor, a small smile curving her soft mouth. Mysterious. Sexy. His little innocent was seducing him, and doing a damn good job of it. Every muscle in his body was hard and aching. He was on fire, burning with need. Her smile. Her perfect, perfect mouth.

Gregori bent his head and took possession of that mouth. Her lips were warm and satin-smooth. His tongue explored the sweet curve; his teeth tugged insistently, demanding entrance. She complied with his silent command, her mouth moist, hot silk. The world seemed to fall away. He fed voraciously, long, drugging kisses, devouring her sweetness, feeding on sensuality.

His hands framed her face, held her still for his demanding mouth. Colors burst all around him; lightning sizzled and danced, and the roaring in his mind increased. He found her throat, soft and vulnerable. Hands tore at her clothing, needing to get at her creamy skin, needing to feel it soft and supple beneath his palms. Material floated to the floor in strips all around them, a frenzied shower of cloth.

Savannah's breath caught in her throat. She had unleashed something far beyond her control, and despite her good intentions, it frightened her. Gregori was everywhere, his body hard and unyielding, his arms like iron. His enormous strength was intimidating. But the feel of his mouth, hot and masculine, demanding her compliance, was mesmerizing. Her body, of its own accord, seemed to go liquid with heat.

He stripped her white lace panties from her slender form, exposing bare skin to his hungry gaze. She heard his swift intake of breath. His silver eyes moved over her face, her mouth, the line of her throat. Everywhere his eyes touched, she felt a flame dance, then linger, long after he lifted his head to move on to the next spot. Her body was flawless beneath his hungry gaze. Her skin was creamy smooth, her breasts firm and round, her narrow rib cage emphasizing their perfection. He caught her waist and dragged her to him, bending her backward to bring her breasts to his mouth.

She made a soft little sound, like a kitten, her body moving restlessly against his. Her arms cradled his head, holding him to her. His mouth on her breasts was hot and hungry, insistent. Each strong pull bathed her in liquid, so that she moaned and pressed herself against him, loving the feel of his mouth.

His hands moved down her back, finding her hips to urge her closer. He was hard and thick, full with desperate need of her. When he lifted his head, his molten gaze scorching her with heat, Savannah leaned against him to taste the small bead of perspiration running down the tangle of hair on his chest. She followed it, never quite catching up. When her tongue caressed his flat belly, she felt him shudder with anticipation. The tiny little bead raced lower still. Her arms circled his hips, found the firm muscles of his buttocks, and tugged him even closer. As she bent her head nearer, playing catch-up with the rolling bead, her hair brushed across his raging body. Gregori groaned, the sound torn from his throat, raw and aching. His large hands caught at her hair and bunched it tightly in his fists.

"You are playing with fire, *ma petite*." The words were nearly unable to escape his strangled throat.

She glanced up at him, just once. A quick look from under the crescent of her long lashes. Teasing. Sexy. His innocent erotic. "I thought I was playing with *you*," she denied, her attention back on his fierce arousal. Her warm breath bathed him in heat, in temptation.

He threw back his head, his hands tightening in her thick mane of hair. His neck was arched, his eyes closed. "I think it is fair to say it is the same thing," he bit out between clenched teeth.

Her tongue trapped the little racing bead as she cupped his heavy fullness in her hand. "You're the one who started this," she murmured absently.

He was hot and hard, iron wrapped in velvet. He braced himself as she urged him closer, her mouth like hot silk. "*Mon Dieu*, Savannah," he breathed in a rush of air escaping his lungs. "I might not survive this."

Her tongue swirled, the pressure exquisite, the friction almost more than he could bear. His hips moved, a rhythm he had no control over, holding her to him while the world fell away and there was only intense pleasure and lights exploding in his head. For a few precious moments out of his endless empty existence, he could believe someone cared for him, someone loved him enough to bring him out of the darkness and into the light. Into ecstasy.

He caught at her and drew her up so that he could press her backward onto the bed. She was so small, for a moment he was afraid he might hurt her with his strength, but she was moving restlessly, needing him, the hunger in her mind rising to match his own. He caught her hips and dragged her to the edge of the bed so that he could explore her the way he wanted.

She was his alone. Her body his one solace. He was determined to know every inch of her intimately. He knew it was his strength she feared, not what he was doing to her. She stiffened, her body rigid when he pinned her to the blanket. He bent his dark head, his teeth scraping the inside of her thigh. "You trust me, Savannah. I know you do." His breath was warm as he tasted her. "You are part of me. I cannot hurt you. Touch my mind with yours. I want you more than I have ever wanted anything in my entire existence." His tongue caressed her, teased, stroked intimately.

She jerked beneath him, then exhaled sharply. There were no walls, no ceiling, no floor, nothing but space and Gregori. His hands moved over her body, explored, memorized, possessed, even as his mouth drove her wild, took her over and over the edge until she shattered into a million fragments and he put her back together again just to repeat the process. It was endless, forever; it went on and on until she thought she might explode.

She caught his hair and tugged at him, wanting his body, needing him to fill her, to merge completely with her. Gregori reluctantly complied, covering her slender frame with his husky one. He pressed against her and felt her moist heat, ready, enticing him, needing him. He bent to find her throat. Nuzzled. Nipped. His tongue stroked. His hips moved away from her. He surged forward, burying himself deeply just as his teeth sank into her vulnerable throat.

Savannah thought she might die with pleasure. He stretched her, tight and fiery; the friction, as he forged into her over and over in long, deep strokes, nearly drove her insane. She held on to his shoulders, her nails digging deep, to keep from flying away. She could feel his mouth on her throat devouring her life's essence, his mind thrusting into hers, sharing the pleasure, heightening it. She could feel his body swelling, hardening even more, the roaring firestorm threatening to consume her, to consume him.

He was everywhere she turned, in her mind, her body, her heart, her soul. The fire raged in him, in her. His body took hers with aggression, domination, his mouth frenzied with hunger. He seemed insatiable; so was she. She couldn't tell where she left off and he started. He took her harder and faster until her body rippled with life and convulsed with pleasure. It didn't matter to either of them. It wasn't enough; it would never be enough.

Gregori's tongue swept across her throat, closed the pinpricks, but his mouth deliberately left his brand on her. "Feed, Savannah. Hunger for me." His velvet, mesmerizing voice was husky with need.

He didn't have to ask her. She lusted after him. *Lust* was the only word she could think of that came close to describing the intensity of her need. She had to taste him, to have him inside her, not just her body or her heart and mind but her very veins. She craved the taste of him, was addicted to him, hungered for him.

"Do you want me?" he asked, his hips slowing to long, rhythmic strokes.

Savannah smiled against his bare skin. "You know I do. You feel what I feel." Deliberately she bit at his neck, her tongue sweeping the pulse beating so strongly there. "How could I not want you?"

His body clenched in anticipation. Waited. His breath

stopped. His heart, too. Deliberately she prolonged the moment, scraping gently over his pulse, closing her eyes while his body reacted, swelling thickly inside her. When her teeth pierced his skin, he nearly lost his control, the pleasure so intense that he could feel his body gathering, gathering, plunging ever deeper to bury himself in her soul. Around him, she tightened, gripping him with fire and velvet, clenching and rippling until he had no choice but to answer her call. They exploded together, a shattering intensity he would never forget. Her complete surrender, her selfless giving of her body and mind.

Gregori laid his head beside hers, squeezing his eyes shut to prevent her from seeing the moisture there. She fed gently, her mouth soft and sensuous at his neck, her body rippling with aftershocks. He held her tightly, determined never to let her go. Determined he would find a way to make her want to stay with him. Find a way to tie her to him so that if his duplicity was ever discovered, she would still never want to leave him.

Savannah closed the two points of entry on his skin and lay quietly beneath him. He was heavy, his body enveloping hers entirely, nearly crushing her into the blankets. His stillness, the hard possession in the strength of his arms, warned her to stay quiet. He was fighting his demons again. "Gregori?" She tasted his shoulder. "I am your true lifemate. There is no other for me. Your fears are groundless."

His arms tightened even more, nearly strangling her. "I am dangerous, Savannah, more dangerous than you could ever know. I do not trust my emotions. They are new to me and intense. I have killed so often, the pieces of my soul were destroyed a long time ago."

Her hands found his hair, stroked and caressed, attempted to soothe him. "My soul is your other half. It fits perfectly, and there are no pieces missing. It only feels that way to you because after so many centuries of nothingness, of emptiness, you can feel again. It's all just overwhelming to you."

He shifted his weight but did not let her go. He couldn't. He had to touch her, remain inside her, his body locked with hers. "I wish it were true, *mon amour.* I really wish it were so."

"The dawn is here, Gregori," she reminded him softly, all at once aware of their being tangled together, intertwined as one being.

"Are you cold?"

"No." How could she be? His body was hot inside hers, upon hers, his hips moving gently but insistently.

Gregori waved a hand to lock the entrances, placing the safeguards for outside and inside. All the time his attention was centered on his body gliding in and out of hers. The beauty. The mystery. The pleasure. "We will sleep soon, *chérie,* I promise. But not now. Not for a little while." He murmured the words against her breast, then settled closer, his mouth feeding gently on her softness. He wanted to stay there, in the sanctuary of her body, for all time.

Chapter Seven

Detective David Johnson escorted the couple through the crowded squad room to his office. Heads turned, and an eerie silence seemed to follow their progress. He really couldn't blame the men. In all the years of his police work, he had never seen a woman more beautiful or haunting. It was the only word to describe her beauty. *Haunting.* She moved like a song, a whisper, like water moving through space. Flowing. Still, it was embarrassing the way grown policemen were acting like lovesick puppies.

She was a celebrity, the cause of the throngs of unruly newsmen camping on the precinct's doorstep, but he knew it was more than that. Savannah Dubrinsky was the kind of woman who stayed in a man's mind for all time. She was the stuff of dreams. Dreams of hot nights, silk sheets, and lots of steamy sex. A fantasy come alive.

Johnson risked a glance at the man pacing so easily at her side. A dangerous fellow, that one. Dark. Menacing. He moved so silently, no one could possibly detect him unless he wished it. Even his clothes didn't rustle. His hair was long and thick, tied at the nape of his neck with a leather thong. He looked elegant, Old World, like a pirate or a count. His face was arresting, all hard angles and planes, with unusual pale eyes, a slashing silver that gave nothing away. This was a man to be reckoned with. It was in the set of his shoulders, his air of complete authority. Johnson had seen men of power before, men who could make life-and-death decisions every day. This man was a cut above. This man wore power like his own skin. He *was* power. Johnson felt the hard slam of his heart in his chest every time those peculiar cat-like eyes rested on him. Eyes that were unblinking. Disturbing.

The man's posture said it all. God help the person dumb enough to ever lay a finger on Savannah Dubrinsky. Johnson had been worried about some San Francisco nutcase trying to get to the famous magician while she was in town, but now that he had met her husband, he figured anyone trying to touch her would have to be suicidal.

He stepped back to allow Savannah entrance to his office and was not a bit surprised when her husband somehow managed to insert his solid frame between his body and Savannah's. Johnson closed the door firmly and refrained from giving in to the impulse to pull the blinds. The entire squad was staring through the dingy glass, ogling her.

Johnson had never noticed how filthy his office was, the layers of dust and grime, the greasy, leftover, empty boxes of Chinese food and pizza. The pale woman with her haunting beauty made him all too aware of his grim surroundings. He wanted to sweep the debris off his desk into the wastebasket and out of her sight. To his horror, he actually felt faint color stealing up his neck.

He was known throughout the precinct as a cop married to the department, completely cynical, no feelings whatsoever. But his hormones had kicked into high gear and seemed to be working overtime.

Johnson cleared his throat twice, trying not to make an ass of himself. "We appreciate your coming in like this to help us out. Thank you for identifying the body; I know it must have been difficult for you." He waited, but when neither spoke, he went on. "We'd like to clear up a few things concerning that night. We already have statements from security and the drivers who loaded the truck. You both seem to have an airtight alibi, Ms. Dubrinsky. Security saw you leave and saw Peter on the loading dock. Peter never drove out. When was the last time you saw Peter Sanders alive?"

Savannah knew that Gregori had planted the scene in the minds of the security personnel as they had left the stadium that horrible night. "Detective Johnson," she began.

Her voice was every bit as beautiful as she was. "Call me David," he found himself saying to his complete astonishment.

Her husband stirred, a slight rippling of muscles, a suggestion of danger. Those brilliant, slashing eyes settled on Johnson's face, touching him with cold air, the vision of an empty grave, a shiver of death. He swallowed nervously, suddenly glad it was not one of his new detectives assigned to this bizarre case. Johnson could almost believe that this man was perfectly capable of killing someone. What was a woman like Savannah Dubrinsky doing with such a man?

"I picked Savannah up an hour or so after her performance," Gregori informed him softly while Savannah sat with her head bowed, twisting her fingers together. Anguish radiated from her, turning Gregori's heart of stone to mush. He was fully aware of the detective's thoughts and purposely dropped his voice an octave lower. Anyone with half a brain would see he was dangerous; it wasn't easy to hide that kind of thing, and Gregori didn't particularly feel like doing so. "The props were being loaded into the trucks, and most of the workers had already left," he said softly.

Johnson found himself hanging on to every word, listening to the pitch and cadence of the voice. It was like a running brook. This man, this Gregori, was honest, had integrity. Johnson shifted position, leaning across the desk toward the man. He couldn't help himself; it was almost as if he was mesmerized.

"Peter was alive and well at that point," Gregori went on softly. "We talked for a few minutes, perhaps as long as half an hour. The truck with the props was pulling away just as we decided to leave. Peter walked to his car but called back to us that he had left his keys on the loading platform."

Savannah ducked her head, feeling a shudder run through her. She was pale but composed. Inside, she could hear herself screaming in outrage, in sorrow. Gregori appeared not to move, yet his body was touching hers so that his warmth could seep into her skin. It amazed her, the perfectly acceptable tale he wove in his beautiful voice. No one would ever question him. How could they, when he controlled all within hearing of his voice?

"That was the last you saw of him alive?" Johnson asked.

Savannah nodded. Gregori laced his fingers through

hers. "Peter was our friend as well as our business asso-
ciate. He handled everything for Savannah. Without Peter, there is no show. I have many businesses that keep
me extremely busy. Peter took care of every detail of the
magic shows for us. As you can imagine, this is devas-
tating for my wife. For both of us. We should have
waited until he was safe in his car, but I had been away
from Savannah for some time, and we were anxious to
be off together. The security personnel were still within
sight, so we didn't think anything about it."

"You didn't go to the hotel." Johnson made it a statement.

Again it was Gregori who answered smoothly, his
voice soft and hypnotic. "No, we went to property we
own outside of the city. It was not until this evening that
we heard the news."

"Why didn't you check out of the hotel, Savannah?"
Johnson asked her directly. It was difficult not to stare at
her entrancing beauty.

"We thought we would be meeting Peter back there in
a couple of days when we returned to the city, so we kept
the room." Her voice was so low, Johnson could barely
catch her words. She sounded so sad, he felt a stone
weighing on his chest. Johnson pressed a hand to his
heart.

Gregori stirred slightly, stroking Savannah's hair and
neck, his fingers moving in a soothing massage. She was
broadcasting her inner sorrow too loudly, and the detective was becoming affected. *Breathe deeply*, mon amour.
*We cannot afford to have the policeman suffer a heart
attack in our presence. He is very susceptible to you.*

I can't stand lying like this. There were tears in her
voice, in her mind. She was clinging to Gregori's mind

as an anchor, and it made him feel the connection with her was real and solid. Perhaps even unbreakable. *Peter deserved better.*

That is so, bébé, *but we cannot very well tell this man the truth. We would both be locked up as insane.* Gregori leaned forward and stared directly into Johnson's eyes. *You will seek attention for your heart problem after we leave this place. For now you will cease to question Savannah and direct your queries solely to me.*

Johnson blinked, his eyes slightly glazed. Had he fallen asleep? He wasn't feeling very well. He wiped perspiration from his forehead. Perhaps he would make a quick trip to the hospital and have those tests he had been putting off. Meanwhile, Savannah looked so distressed that he focused on Gregori. There was something about the man's voice that enthralled him. He could listen to it forever. "No one seems to know of your marriage. We found no record of it," he ventured.

Gregori nodded. "Savannah's career demanded she appear—how should I put this?—available. A single woman is much more of a draw than a married one. We have been husband and wife for nearly five years. The marriage took place in our country. Savannah's mother is from the United States, but her father's homeland is in the Carpathian Mountains. We were married there."

Johnson refrained from saying she looked far too young and innocent for a man as powerful as Gregori. It was nearly impossible to tell his age. "Mr. Sanders was fine with the marriage?"

The silver eyes slashed like steel. "Of course he was." Gregori could see that that question upset Savannah even more. He leaned close to the detective again. *You will cease this line of inquiry.*

Johnson shook his head. "We're getting off the subject here. Do you know of any enemies Mr. Sanders may have had?"

Gregori took his time answering, looking very thoughtful. Eventually he shook his head. "I wish we could help you more, Detective, but everyone liked Peter. Well, with the exception of the reporters—he was very good at protecting Savannah's privacy and thereby preserving the mystique of the show. I do not think you will find anyone who would speak ill of Peter."

"He handled the finances for the show, didn't he?" Johnson asked shrewdly.

"Yes, he did," Gregori answered easily. "Peter was a full partner with Savannah. He earned it, too."

"Were there any problems with the books?" Johnson slid the question in, watching their faces.

Savannah looked so pale and filled with sorrow, he felt as if he was tormenting her. No emotion showed on Gregori's face, and Johnson knew nothing he said or did would change that. "I am independently wealthy, Detective, with more money than I can possibly use in a lifetime. Savannah did not even need the income from her show. If there was ever a discrepancy, and I certainly do not know of one, I am certain, as is Savannah, that it would be an honest one. Peter made good money from the shows and would have no need to doctor the books. I am sure you can easily check his bank accounts and our books. You are certainly welcome to do so. Peter Sanders was not a thief."

Savannah lifted her chin. "Peter would never have stolen anything. And if he'd ever needed money, all he would have to do is say so. We would have given it to him, and he knew it."

"It was just a thought. There's no evidence pointing in that direction, but we do have to cover every possibility." Johnson raked a hand through his hair. He hated upsetting the woman. "Sanders was in charge of your security arrangements?"

"We had a man for that," Gregori said smoothly. "Peter gave him his orders and kept him informed of the schedule so the man could do his job."

"Could Ms. Dubrinsky have been the target of some psycho fan?"

Savannah made a muffled sound, tearing at Gregori's heart. Beneath his massaging fingers, she was beginning to tremble. "There is always the possibility, Detective. She has at times received some very perverse fan mail. Peter and Roland, the security man, protected her from most of the unpleasantness. But if there had been any threatening mail on this tour, Peter would have informed me immediately."

Johnson had no doubt Gregori was the type of man to be involved in every aspect of his wife's life. "Do you recall any strange incidents that stick in your mind?"

Savannah shook her head.

"What about any odd, unexpected noises that night?"

Instantly Savannah remembered the vampire's hideous laughter. Gregori intervened immediately. "My wife is very shaken up, Detective, and we still have to make the arrangements for Peter. Her crew is waiting for us also."

"So are the reporters."

Gregori's silver eyes glittered a warning. "She will not be talking to reporters. This is difficult enough for her."

Johnson nodded. "We'll try to sneak you out the back. But those folks have been camped out on our stairs ever since we ID'd the body."

Savannah winced visibly.

"Piranhas," Gregori observed.

"They're like vampires," Johnson agreed. He didn't see Savannah shudder. "Once they sink their teeth into a story, they never let go. One in particular, from out of town, has been driving us all crazy. We actually caught him trying to sneak into our files in an attempt to read our reports. He also tried to bribe someone in the coroner's office for information." The detective was aware he was giving out information he should not have been, but he couldn't seem to stop himself. It flowed out of him like water.

Gregori lifted his head, dark hair spilling over his forehead. All at once he looked like a predator, dark and dangerous. Johnson's heart took another hard thud, and for an instant he could have sworn he saw those silver eyes flame a fiery red. Gregori gave the impression of a beast with sheathed claws, waiting, stalking prey. Johnson shivered, then blinked. When he looked again, the man's face was as impassive as ever, the eyes reflecting back his own image. There was a certain masculine beauty to that harsh, cruel face. Johnson shook his head to dispel the image of a stalking wolf from his mind.

"Which reporter was that, Detective?"

"I can't really divulge that information," Johnson said warily. There was something he couldn't quite put his finger on, but he wasn't going to be responsible for some reporter winding up in the hospital. He had no doubt that anyone tangling with Gregori would come out on the short end of the stick.

Gregori smiled at him, a flash of gleaming white teeth. The silver stare fixed on David Johnson's tired eyes. That silver gaze was all at once hot, like molten mercury. Johnson felt himself falling forward, unable to look away. Gregori pushed into the man's mind, past the thin barrier of protection, and searched the memories there. Satisfied he had what he needed, he removed the man's memory of any conversation pertaining to the reporter and implanted the certain knowledge that Savannah and Gregori had cooperated fully and had nothing to do with the Peter Sanders's death.

Johnson blinked and found himself standing, shaking hands with Gregori and smiling sympathetically at Savannah. Gregori's muscular frame dwarfed her slender one as her husband swept her protectively beneath his shoulder. She offered Johnson a wan smile. "I wish we'd had a chance to meet under different circumstances, Detective."

"David," he corrected gently, doing his best not to stare.

Gregori nudged Savannah out of the office. "Thank you for being so careful with Savannah's feelings."

Johnson led the way through a maze of rooms to the back stairs. "If you think it will be necessary, I could have a couple of my men keep an eye on Ms. Dubrinsky for a few days."

"Thank you, Detective, but that will not be necessary," Gregori declined softly, a hint of menace in his velvet voice. His hand found the small of Savannah's back. "I protect my own."

The staircase was narrow and dusty, the carpet worn through in several places. The couple moved down it together in perfect synchronization, like a pair of dancers. Gregori caught at her before she could push open the door. "Someone is outside."

Savannah glanced at the cruel edge to his mouth. "We don't know who it is, Gregori," she cautioned softly.

"Scanning is easy enough," Gregori answered. "That reporter is dangerous, Savannah. He is more than a simple nosy newspaperman."

"You read that detective's mind, his memories, didn't you?" Her fingers curled around his thick wrist, her enormous blue eyes fixed steadily on his face.

Gregori didn't flinch from the accusation. He didn't pretend to look repentant. "Of course I did."

"Gregori," she said softly, "you have that look about you."

His eyebrows shot up. "What look is that?"

"Like you're really hungry and you just discovered lunch."

He smiled in answer, but there was no warmth in his eyes. "Be very careful with this one, Savannah. He is not going to just let it go."

She shrugged carefully. "So let's give him what he wants, and maybe he'll leave us alone." She was afraid she knew what Gregori had in mind. If the reporter couldn't be controlled, if he became a threat to their race, Gregori would have no choice but to destroy him. She couldn't bear the thought of any more needless bloodshed; she wanted a peaceful co-existence with the human race.

"We will try it your way," Gregori conceded, his stomach churning. Why did he give in to her nonsense? Her eyes, large and sad, defeated his good sense every time.

Savannah pressed a fingertip to his lip, tracing the hard edge until it softened, and he took her finger into his mouth in a slow, erotic caress. He needed that connection with her always. She was so young, the ugliness of his life so far removed from her. How could she understand his need to ensure that such ugliness never touched her?

She smiled, a small, secret smile he felt he would never understand. He knew the earth, the wind, the shifting water, fire, air, even space itself. He could command them all, but Savannah eluded him. Completely eluded him. Why did it matter so much that she understand? Wasn't her safety the most important thing in his world?

Savannah shivered at the unexpected heat burning through her body. Gregori had such power over her. When he released her finger from the hot, moist cavern of his mouth, she leaned into him, her hand sliding down his throat to rest on his chest. "I think you should be outlawed, Gregori. You're lethal to women." Her voice feathered over his skin like the touch of fingers.

"Just one woman," he answered, his silver eyes molten mercury. He took possession of her hand; he had to, before his body went up in flames. Bringing her knuckles to his mouth, he sighed as he pressed a kiss against the back of her hand, her fingers, her open palm. "Let us get this over with, *ma petite*, before I change my mind and turn this reporter to stone."

Her breath caught in her throat, her blue eyes enormous. "You can't really do that, can you?" She was looking at him with a mixture of awe and fear, with maybe a hint of pride thrown in.

Gregori's face was completely impassive, the silver gaze reflective. "I can do anything. I thought that was a well-known fact among our people."

She searched his face, trying to determine whether or not he was teasing her. When she couldn't be certain one way or the other, she turned and pushed open the door.

Almost at once a man placed himself solidly in front

of her, and a flash went off. Blinking at the sudden, excruciating pain of the brilliant light in her sensitive eyes, Savannah instinctively put up a hand to cover her face. Gregori turned her into his chest. *You would insist on this.*

Don't even say 'I told you so'!

His soft laugher eased the sting in her eyes, but his face was hard and dangerous as he faced the reporter and his cameraman. "Get out of our way," he warned softly.

The reporter's expression was wary. He stepped back, breath exploding out of his lungs. "Wade Carter, free-lance reporter. I've been following Ms. Dubrinsky for some time. I'd like an interview."

"You will have to go through her press secretary." Gregori kept moving, his arm protectively around Savannah's shoulders.

The reporter had to give way; he dared not challenge the other man. Gregori looked like a predator. A dark, brooding, killing machine. Menacing. He was showing his true nature to the reporter without hesitation. Carter swore to himself, but his excitement showed on his face. "There's a rumor going around that you're her husband. Is that true?"

"I see no reason to deny it." Gregori kept walking, his arm, thick with roped muscles, curling around Savannah's head, successfully hiding her from the other man's scrutiny. He glanced at the cameraman, who was positioning himself for another picture. "One is all you are going to get. Do it again, and I will remove the camera from you. Forcibly. And I will not return it. Do you understand?"

The man instantly lowered the camera, his face going

white. Gregori's voice was low and soft, even gentle, but it held such menace, the veteran of many fracases opted for the better part of valor. "Yes, sir," he muttered, refusing to look at Carter.

"So you don't deny your marriage. Is it true both of you come from the Carpathian Mountains?" Carter sounded eager.

"It is a big region," Gregori said vaguely and signaled their driver to open the door to the limousine.

Carter pushed forward. "Did Peter Sanders know the secrets behind your magic, Savannah?" There was accusation in his voice, belligerence. "No other member of your crew does. Which could make Sanders's death rather convenient, if you have something to hide."

In spite of Gregori's restraining arm, Savannah lifted her head to face the reporter. Her blue eyes smoldered dangerously. "How dare you? Peter Sanders was my friend."

Carter stepped even closer. "You have many secrets, don't you, Savannah, that have nothing to do with your magic show?"

"What is that supposed to mean?"

Gregori's silver eyes flashed. *His mind is protected somehow. I could push past his barrier, but it is complicated, and he would know, and so would whoever has helped him achieve this. This one is very dangerous to you,* mon amour. *Do not cross swords with him. Let us leave this place. I will pay a visit to Wade Carter at a later date.*

He doesn't scare me.

He should. He is one of the human butchers, and he has targeted you. That damn mist you dissolve into. Julian was always uncomfortable with that.

"I think you know very well what I mean. Peter Sanders found out just how some of your illusions were performed, and you killed him."

Savannah shook her head. "I feel sorry for you, Mr. Carter. It must be a horrible way to make a living, accusing people of crimes for a sensational story. You can't have too many friends." She ducked into the limousine and the safety of its shadowy interior.

"You haven't seen the last of me," Carter snarled, leaning down to try to catch a last glimpse of her.

Gregori stepped close, his imposing frame exuding power. He smiled at the reporter, a flash of gleaming white teeth. The silver eyes reflected clearly, vividly, in great detail, Carter's own image. But it was an image of death, of a torn and bloody body falling like a rag doll to the ground. Gregori held the man in his deadly gaze. "Nor have you seen the last of me, Mr. Carter," he said softly, a black-velvet menace.

Wade Carter was suddenly weak with fear. He crossed himself, his right hand finding the silver cross at his neck. Low, taunting laughter echoed in his head. He couldn't seem to get it out, not even when the tall, elegant man slid gracefully into the seat beside Savannah. Carter shook his head repeatedly, trying to dislodge the laughter, the threat, from his mind.

He glared after the fading limo, then clapped both hands against his ears. He had no proof that Savannah Dubrinsky was a vampire, just a gut feeling. The things she did on stage were impossible. No other magician had accomplished the tricks she had perfected. She was so young; how could she have learned to do what no one else in her field could do? He had followed her entire tour, trying unsuccessfully to bribe those working for her. No one admitted to knowing a thing.

Every time he had tried to break in to see her props, to study what she did, something had gone wrong. It was eerie. He didn't believe in coincidence. He might have struck out a time or two, but not on every painstaking attempt. He was a professional; his people were professionals. No road crew or security people were that good. Something smelled, and he meant to get to the bottom of it. Maybe the cops believed the current story, but Peter Sanders's death frankly stunk. All the truck drivers and loaders had the exact same story. No two witnesses ever told precisely the same pat story. Details always differed. And it couldn't be a conspiracy; those questioned didn't all know one another. So it had to be something else. Like memories planted in people's minds—something vampires could do.

Savannah suddenly had a husband no one had known about. And he wasn't just any man, someone who could have been overlooked. Savannah's husband was dark, dangerous. A killer. Wade Carter was certain he was a vampire. Positive. He sat down on the steps, his heart beating like thunder. He had actually met the real thing. And the real thing scared the hell out of him. He would have to wire the others to come. What a break, and he was the one to find them. Or him. He didn't honestly know if Savannah Dubrinsky was a vampire, but his research said it was a possibility. He was going to be famous. Very, very famous. And rich. Very, very rich.

"He knows about us," Gregori said softly. "That reporter is no reporter. He is one of them."

"Who are *they?*" Savannah pushed at her hair, suddenly weary and close to tears. *Peter.* It was all her fault. She never should have allowed him close to her, never put him in danger. She had been so naive. Her world had always been one of boundless love. Her parents protected her, sheltered her. Her wolf—no, her lifemate—had shown her nothing but love during her growing years. None of the ugliness of their lives, none of the dangers, had ever been allowed to touch her.

She glanced at Gregori, the impassive expression, the lines etched deeply into his handsome face. His eyes were so cold and aloof. He had seen far too much horror in his lifetime, knew everything that could happen. He had seen it with his own eyes. "Who are they, Gregori?" she asked again.

His pale eyes moved over her face and brushed her soft mouth, leaving a warmth behind. "There is a dangerous group of humans who believe in vampires and practically make a career out of hunting them down. Despite their obsession with the undead—and over the centuries they have often formed secret societies to pursue their depraved passions—they do not recognize or acknowledge the difference between Carpathians and vampires. To them, we are the same and must be exterminated. Perhaps it is just as well that they do not comprehend they are dealing with two separate entities."

"What drives these people? Have they proof that the vampire exists?" It was nearly impossible to believe; Carpathian renegade hunters were so careful to destroy all evidence of the betrayers.

"Nothing concrete. But the lasting legends and stories and myths keep these humans wondering. And some of the more clever vampires have spent time in society before we were able to hunt them."

"True," Savannah said. She knew her history. In the Middle Ages and just after, the undead had had a field day, living openly among the humans they preyed on. It had taken a huge collective effort to wipe them out before they destroyed any chance at a peaceful co-existence between the two species, Carpathian and human. After the most famous Carpathian vampire hunters, such as Gabriel and Lucien, disappeared, it was Mikhail and Gregori and Aidan and other ancients like them who had hunted down those who turned vampire. Together they had protected their remaining women and had taken measures to ensure that Carpathians and vampires remained figments of human imagination, the stuff of legends, novels, and movies. Their campaign to wipe out all memory, all certain knowledge of their kind had been largely successful, but evidently lapses had occurred.

"A few years ago, before you were born, a society of humans, a secret organization, was formed to investigate and exterminate vampires—the kind of vampires written about in dime novels. We believed these humans posed little real threat to us. None of us expected a repeat of the vampire hunts that swept Europe centuries ago."

There was no sorrow in his expressionless voice, nothing to betray that he was remembering finding his mother's body, but Savannah knew that he was, knew it as surely as if he had confessed it. "The first time they surfaced to do any damage, they murdered your Aunt Noelle. They would have killed another woman, but your own mother, still human, had the courage to save her. The secret society then targeted your mother and father, Raven and the Prince of our people. Once more we thought we stamped out the threat, but they struck again a few years later. They killed several of our people and a few humans. Noelle's son was murdered, and your Uncle Jacques was tortured to the point of madness. Again

Raven was attacked, when she was pregnant with you, and she almost lost you."

Savannah reached out to lay a hand on his arm, but she was otherwise careful to keep her sympathy to herself, not wanting him to realize how easily she had slipped into his mind and taken his memories into her heart. She was becoming quite adept at reading him.

Gregori picked up her hand, marveling that anything that small could bring him such pleasure. Just the simple act of touching his arm, her fingers curling around his wrist, could melt his insides, bring him a measure of comfort, of security. It amazed him. Where certain memories always triggered him to go blank inside, to insulate himself so he could face them without flinching, without the beast roaring in rage, that little hand now tempered his fire and fury. He absently traced a safeguard pattern into her palm, hardly aware he was doing so. Even his subconscious wanted to ensure that she was always safe.

The touch of Gregori's fingers sent darts of fire racing through Savannah's bloodstream. Her teeth bit nervously at her lower lip. "You were saying about this reporter . . . what could he know for certain?" she prompted gently. She didn't want him to stop holding her hand or to stop making that strange, soothing design in the middle of her palm. She wanted the terrible memories holding him in their grip to let him go, to give him back to her. Savannah smiled up at him, her blue eyes clear and steady.

"He does not know anything for certain." A slightly wicked glint appeared in his eyes. "At least not about you."

"What did you do?" she asked softly. "Gregori, you

don't have to protect me by calling attention to yourself. We're a team, aren't we? Whatever happens to you, happens to me."

He looked away from her, out the window. His fingers tightened possessively around her hand. "That may not be so in every case," he answered carefully.

"What are you saying, Gregori? We are lifemates. One can't survive without the other. I may not know everything about lifemates, but I know that."

"That is true, *ma petite*, ordinarily. And ordinarily, a hunter who finds his lifemate ceases to hunt. Yet Aidan Savage must continue because he is in a land where there are few hunters. Hunters are in more danger from the undead than most Carpathians, so to keep from putting his lifemate in jeopardy, the hunter usually allows other males to take over the task. Aidan Savage does not have that luxury." *Nor do I.*

"And you? Do you intend to quit hunting?" she asked softly, already knowing the answer, already in his mind.

"You know I cannot." He said it gently, his voice soft.

"I am your lifemate, Gregori." Her voice trembled just a bit. "You may have to hunt because you're the very best we have, and our people need you. But if something were to happen to you, I would follow you."

Gregori's thumb feathered back and forth across her inner wrist, lingering on her pulse. It was rapid. "It would be dishonest of me to allow you to think I have such a noble motivation. I have hunted for so many centuries, I do not know any other way of life." His face was impassive, but inside he was holding his breath.

A small smile flirted with her perfect mouth. "If it pleases you to think so of yourself, Gregori, that's fine with me. You are arrogant enough for several males; you don't need me to feed you compliments. But perhaps I might be able to do something about teaching you another way of life. In the meantime, I suggest you educate me in the ways of vampires, since it looks as if we'll be hunting them. And you might also remember you are the greatest healer among us. That is unchallenged by anyone."

"I am the greatest killer, also unchallenged." He tried to give her truth again.

She touched his hard mouth. "I will hunt with you then, lifemate."

His heart slammed against his ribs. Her smile was mysterious, secretive, and so beautiful, it broke his heart. "What is behind this smile, *bébé*?" His hand caught and spanned her throat, his thumb brushing her lips in a gentle caress. "What do you know that I do not?" His mind slipped into hers, a sensuous thrust, the ultimate intimacy, not unlike the way his tongue sometimes dueled with her—or his body took possession of hers.

She was familiar with his touch in her mind. She knew he tried to keep its invasiveness to a minimum. He allowed her to set the boundaries and never pushed beyond any barrier she erected, even though he could do so easily. Both of them needed the intimate union of their minds merging, Savannah as much as Gregori. And her newfound knowledge of him was secure behind a miniature barricade she had hastily erected. Wide-eyed and innocent, she looked at him.

His thumb pressed into her lower lip, half mesmerized by the satin perfection of it. "You will never hunt vampires, *ma chérie*, not ever. And if I were ever to catch you attempting such a thing, there would be hell to pay."

She didn't look scared. Rather, amusement crept into

the deep blue of her eyes. "Surely you aren't threatening me, *Dark One*, bogey man of the Carpathians." She laughed softly, a sound that feathered down his spine and somehow took away the sting of that centuries-old designation. "Stop looking so serious, Gregori—you haven't lost your reputation entirely. Everyone else is still terrified of the big bad wolf."

His eyebrows shot up. She was teasing him. About his dark reputation, of all things. Her gaze was clear and sparkling, hinting at mischief. Savannah wasn't railing against her fate, of being tied to him, a monster. She was too filled with life and laughter, with joy. He felt it in her mind, in her heart, in her very soul. He wished it could somehow rub off on him, make him a more compatible lifemate for her. "You are the only one who needs to worry about the big bad wolf, *mon amour*," he threatened with mock gravity.

She leaned over to stare up into his eyes, a smile curving her soft mouth. "You cracked a joke, Gregori. We're making progress. Why, we're practically friends."

"Practically?" he echoed gently.

"Getting there fast," she told him firmly with her chin up, daring him to contradict her.

"Can one be friends with a monster?" he said casually, as if he were simply musing out loud, but there was a shadow in his silver eyes.

"I was being childish, Gregori, when I made such an accusation," she said softly, her eyes meeting his squarely. "I wanted my own life, with no one to answer to. It was thoughtless and wrong of me. And I was afraid. But I'm not now, and I ask your forgiveness—"

"Do not!" he ordered sharply. "*Mon Dieu, chérie*, do not ever apologize to me for your fear. I do not deserve it, and we both know it." His thumb pressed into the heated satin of her lip. "And do not try to be so brave. I am your lifemate. You cannot hide from me something as powerful as fear."

"Trepidation," she corrected, nibbling at the pad of his thumb.

"Is there a difference?" His pale eyes had warmed to molten mercury. Just that fast, her body went liquid in answer.

"You know very well there is." She laughed again, and the sound traveled down from his heart to pool in his groin, a heavy, familiar ache. "Slight, perhaps, but very important."

"I will try to make you happy, Savannah," he promised gravely.

Her fingers went up to brush at the thick mane of hair falling around his face. "You are my lifemate, Gregori. I have no doubt you will make me happy."

He had to look away, out the window into the night. She was so good, with so much beauty in her, while he was so dark, his goodness drained into the ground with the blood of all the lives he had taken while he waited for her. But now, faced with the reality of her, Gregori could not bear her to witness the blackness within him, the hideous stain across his soul.

For beyond his killing and law-breaking, he had committed the gravest crime of all. And he deserved the ultimate penalty, the forfeit of his life. He had deliberately tampered with nature. He knew he was powerful enough, knew his knowledge exceeded the boundaries of Carpathian law. He had taken Savannah's free will, manipulated the chemistry between them so that she would believe he was her true lifemate. And so she was with him—less than a quarter of a century of innocence pitted against his thousand years of hard study. Perhaps that *was* his punishment, he mused—being sentenced to an eternity of knowing Savannah could never really love him, never really accept his black soul. That she would be ever near yet so far away.

If she ever found out the extent of his manipulation, she would despise him. Yet he could never, ever, allow her to leave him. Not if mortals and immortals alike were to be safe. His jaw hardened, and he stared out the window, turning slightly away from her. His mind firmly left hers, not wanting to alert her to the grave crime he had committed. He could bear torture and centuries of isolation, he could bear his own great sins, but he could not endure her loathing him. Unconsciously, he took her hand in his and tightened his grip until it threatened to crush her fragile bones.

Savannah glanced at him, let out a breath slowly to keep from wincing, and kept her hand passively in his. He thought his mind closed to her. Didn't believe she was his true lifemate. He truly believed he had manipulated the outcome of their joining unfairly and that somewhere another Carpathian male with the chemistry to match hers might be waiting. Though he had offered her free access to his mind, had himself given her the power, to meld her mind with his, both as her wolf and as her healer before she was born, he likely didn't think a woman, a fledgling, and one who was not his true lifemate, could possibly have the skill to read his innermost secrets. But Savannah could. And completing the ancient ritual of lifemates had only strengthened the bond.

Chapter Eight

Peter Sanders's ashes were buried on the grounds of a mansion Gregori had built for Savannah while waiting for her to come to San Francisco. Savannah's crew and Detective David Johnson arrived for the memorial service, but they were able to keep the actual location, well outside the city, a secret from the majority of the press. Only Wade Carter showed up, having tailed one of the road crew members to do so, but he wasn't allowed inside the gates. His cameraman had refused to come; something about Savannah Dubrinsky's husband scared the hell out of him. That left Wade with the unwieldy camera around his neck and a very uneasy feeling. The grounds were fenced, and wolves ran loose within the compound.

With Gregori's supporting arm around her, Savannah spoke quietly to her crew, thanked them for their service, and announced her retirement. They were each presented with an envelope containing a sizable bonus as they left. Gregori spent a few minutes talking with Johnson. The police detective, satisfied there was no more information to be gained, left the residence.

Savannah lingered at the memorial site, staring down at the beautiful marble plaque Gregori had designed for Peter. The tears in her eyes were in part for her sorrow at losing such a good friend, and in part for Gregori's thoughtfulness. He had kept Peter close to them, and he had made this day as comforting as it could have been under the circumstances.

She was turning to go back toward the house when the wolves lifted their heads and howled. Gregori whirled around and caught her arm, dragging her close to him. "I believe it is Aidan Savage," he said softly. "We must go inside, where Carter has no chance to catch sight of Aidan. We do not want to lead assassins to Aidan's door." He hissed a command to his wolves and hurried Savannah toward the mansion.

"I thought you had this place safeguarded," she said.

"With your crew and the police coming to the service, it was too dangerous. Someone could have wandered away from the site and been harmed." His hand brushed her hair tenderly. "I know you are tired. You should lie down for another hour or so. It was too soon for our rising."

She leaned against his hard strength and read the remorse in his mind. "This was never your fault, Gregori, never. I never blamed you for Peter."

His hand caressed her hair. "I know you did not." His attention was on the stirring of the wind, heralding one of their kind. "But if I had not been overwhelmed with physical feelings—lust," he condemned himself, "I would have known the vampire was stalking you that night. I had released Julian from his responsibility; you were in my care."

"Do you have to be so hard on yourself?" she asked

with a sigh. "You are not responsible for all Carpathians, nor all humans. If anyone is to blame, it is me for insisting on my freedom. I was thoughtless, not realizing what I was doing to you or even to the unattached males of our kind. I didn't once give a thought to what you would suffer while I was running from myself and our life together. I certainly did not think Peter would be in danger. I should have. I should have known I would be hunted."

His arm swept around her, a tight circle of comfort. "You did nothing wrong, *chérie*," he said fiercely. He was moving her steadily toward the protection of the house.

Rainbow prisms suddenly danced and sparkled through the trees. Gregori shook his head as the light began to shimmer into a substantial shape. "You always were a show-off, Aidan," he greeted his visitor, his voice as expressionless as always. "Let us go inside."

Savannah, touching his mind, felt his affection for the other man. She had heard of Aidan Savage, a hunter of the vampire, but he had left their homeland half a century before her birth to establish residency in the United States. He was one of the few of their kind built like Gregori—tall, like all Carpathian males, but much stockier, with defined, sinewy muscles. Instead of the dark hair of their race, however, he had a long, thick, tawny mane, and his eyes were a peculiar amber flashing with brilliant, glittering gold.

This man's identical twin had guarded her these last five years. Aidan was an imposing figure, so his twin must be also, yet not once had Savannah seen him. Nor had she detected his presence. How had Julian kept himself hidden, with the confidence all males of their race exuded, the power and authority that came with centuries of the hunt, with the acquisition of knowledge?

Gregori's arm moved from around her waist to circle her neck, a male gesture of ownership. Savannah laughed to herself. Carpathian men were not far from the trees.

I caught that, mon amour. Gregori's soft voice brushed at her mind, a low caress that curled warmth in her stomach. He sounded close to teasing, but she noticed he didn't drop his arm from around her neck.

"Aidan, we did not expect you this early. The sun has not yet gone from the sky, and it is uncomfortable to travel in the evening light," he said aloud, once they were indoors.

"I must apologize for missing the service," Aidan replied softly. "But I could not risk it. Still, I wanted you to know you were not entirely alone in this country," he added to Savannah.

"Savannah, this is Aidan Savage. He is loyal to your father and a good friend to me," Gregori introduced them. "Aidan, my lifemate, Savannah."

"You look like your mother," Aidan observed.

"Thank you. I take that as a great compliment," she said, suddenly wishing her mother was there. She missed Raven and Mikhail. "You honor me, to come at this time of the evening to share my grief. I know it's difficult for all of us, but I had to choose a time to accommodate Peter's human friends."

"There is danger for you nearby, Aidan," Gregori warned. "I would have you and your family safe from these butchers. They are human, of the same secret society that hunted in our lands several years ago."

A shadow crossed Aidan's face. He had humans in his family to protect, as well as his lifemate. The amber eyes glowed a deep gold. "The reporter." A soft growl of menace rumbled deep in his throat.

Gregori nodded. "I will find out what I can this night from Mr. Wade Carter. I intend to take Savannah and lead him and whoever his cohorts are far from this city, so that there is no danger to you or yours." They were in the house, free from prying eyes, but Gregori could feel the reporter's evil presence permeating his territory. "I sent a clear warning to you, Aidan." There was a hint of censure in his words, although his voice was soft.

There was a hard edge to Aidan's mouth. "I received your warning. But this is my city, Gregori, and my family. I take care of my own."

Savannah rolled her eyes. "You could just beat on your chests, you know. It probably works just as well."

You will show some respect, Gregori ordered.

Savannah burst out laughing, then reached up to caress his shadowed jaw. "Keep hoping, my love, and perhaps someday someone will obey you."

Aidan's mouth twitched, the golden eyes sliding over Gregori in amusement. "She inherited something besides her mother's good looks, did she not?"

Gregori sighed heavily. "She is impossible."

Aidan laughed, ignoring the warning flash from Gregori's pale eyes. "I believe they all are."

Savannah ducked out from under Gregori's arm and found an overstuffed chair to curl up in. "Of course we're impossible. It's the only way to stay sane."

"I would have brought Alexandria to meet you, but Gregori's warning dictated prudence." Aidan sounded smug, as if he had been able to lay down the law to his woman when Gregori was unable to do so.

Savannah flashed an impish grin up at the man.

"What did you do, leave her sleeping while you ran off to play hero? I'll just bet she has a thing or two to say to you when you wake her."

Aidan had the grace to look sheepish. Then he turned to Gregori. "Your lifemate is a mean little thing, healer. I do not envy you."

Savannah laughed, unrepentant. "He's crazy about me. Don't let him fool you."

"I believe you," Aidan agreed.

"Do not encourage her in her rebellion," Gregori tried to sound severe, but she was turning him inside out. She was everything to him, even with her silliness. Where did she get her outrageous sense of humor? How could she ever be happy with someone who hadn't laughed in centuries? She melted his insides. Melted him. He was careful to keep his face expressionless. It was bad enough that Savannah knew he was practically wrapped around her little finger. Aidan didn't need to know it, too.

"Seriously, Gregori, there is no need for you to lead these butchers from my city. Together we can deal with them," Aidan said. "Julian is somewhere close. I feel him, though he will not answer my call."

"Julian is close to turning. You would not want his help. The more kills, the more the danger increases. You know that. Julian will work out his destiny, Aidan. And if it becomes necessary to hunt him, if he does not come to you before the change, you must call me. Julian has grown very powerful. Very dangerous. Do not take chances because you are his brother. One of Mikhail's brothers turned, and when justice sought him, he tried, like any other vampire, to destroy everyone. He would not have spared even Mikhail." Gregori did not add he had been the one to bring justice to Mikhail's brother. It had been such a difficult deed, he became determined never to get close to another as he had to Mikhail and his family. Gregori glanced at Savannah, found her incredible blue eyes on him, and somehow the painful memory was eased. "Julian has always been a dangerous and knowledgeable man," Gregori concluded.

"Like you, healer." Aidan couldn't help but make the accusation. He hated the talk of his twin turning vampire.

Gregori didn't flinch. "Exactly like me. That is the point. You will call for my aid should there be the need." He was staring directly into the other man's golden gaze. His voice was low and compelling, beautiful and haunting.

Aidan looked away from those silver eyes. Eyes that could see into a man's soul. "I will, Gregori. I know what you say is true, although I do not want to believe Julian could turn."

"Anyone can turn, Aidan. Any one of us without a lifemate." Gregori glided across the room because he could not stand the physical distance Savannah had put between them. Her eyes were once again shadowed and haunted, the memorial service filling her with sadness and guilt. He slipped behind her chair, his hands coming down on her shoulders to begin a gentle massage. He needed the contact as much as she did.

Aidan hid his shock. He had known Gregori for centuries, had learned healing arts from him, had learned to stalk and kill the vampire from him. Nothing ever touched Gregori. Nothing. No one. But those cold silver eyes, as they swept over Savannah, were molten mercury, the man's posture clearly protective, possessive, and the touch on her shoulders was frankly tender. *Are you all right*, chérie? *Perhaps you should lie down for a while.*

Savannah smiled wanly up at him. She was looking

far more pale than he liked. He had hunted that evening despite the early hour, taking enough blood to sustain both of them. But she had refused to feed, as if denying her hunger were some kind of penance for her sins. His hand went to the nape of her neck and massaged gently. Her hunger beat at him, and he knew Aidan could feel it, too.

The Carpathian male was watching him, without obvious censure but with a puzzled expression all the same in his deep golden gaze. Gregori felt it like a knife: he wasn't taking care of his lifemate the way he should.

Don't be silly, Gregori. Savannah's soft voice swirled in his mind. *You take great care of me. Who cares what anyone else thinks?*

"So, healer," Aidan said, "have you made up your mind where you wish to lead these butchers?"

Savannah stirred, twisting to look back at Gregori, her blue eyes suddenly alive. "Do you have somewhere you particularly want to go?"

"You have a place in mind?" he asked. He knew it was a mistake to look into her eyes. He could drown in her eyes. It was like falling over the edge of a cliff.

"Yes. New Orleans. The French Quarter's jazz festival is this week. I've wanted to go for a long time. Now we can go together. Do you like jazz? I love jazz." She flashed a broad smile at him. "I had made plans to go before . . . all this happened. In fact, I got a place there."

She really wanted to go. It was in her eyes, in her mind. This was important to her. Gregori could feel a terrible dread rising. It was almost impossible to deny Savannah anything. Yet he could not take her to New Orleans, vampire capital of the world, city of sin. The butchers probably had their headquarters there. He stifled a groan. "You have a residence in New Orleans?"

"Don't sound so gloomy. You wanted to go somewhere, lead the society away from the Savages, so where better than the next place on my schedule? No one will think our move the least bit odd or suspicious," she pointed out, "since it was already on my agenda."

Gregori glanced at Aidan and shook his head. "Do you hear the logic of that? She has never been to the French Quarter of New Orleans, but no one will think it odd that she suddenly shows up in a home there."

"Very logical," Aidan agreed. "I can see you have your hands full, and I must return to Alexandria. First, though, I would very much like to visit with the reporter with you." For a moment his face was hard, a cruel edge to his mouth. "I remember what was done to our people by this society."

"This fight cannot be yours, Aidan," Gregori said. "I would not put you and your human family in danger."

Aidan inclined his head. "He prowls out there. I can feel him stalking around the compound." There was an eagerness, a need to do battle.

Savannah knew it was the instinctive, predatory nature of the untamed Carpathian male.

"Go now, Aidan," Gregori said firmly.

"It was nice to finally meet you, Aidan," Savannah added. "I hope to meet Alexandria soon. Perhaps when Gregori and I remove the threat of these human butchers, we can get together."

"When Gregori removes the threat," Gregori corrected her, using his implacable, commanding, don't-even-think-of-challenging-my-authority voice.

Aidan nodded his farewell. Then his solid form wavered, began to shimmer, and disappeared out the open window in a kaleidoscope of colors carried on the night breeze.

Savannah reached behind her and took Gregori's hand. "New Orleans. What do you think?"

There was a small silence. "It is dangerous there," he said carefully.

"True, but it will be dangerous anywhere we go, won't it?" she pointed out reasonably. "So what difference does it make where we are? We may as well have some fun."

"I prefer the mountains." He said it quietly, neutrally.

She suddenly grinned at him, that mischievous, impish smile he couldn't resist. "When an old geezer marries a young chick, he has to learn to get back into the swing of things. Party time. Night life. Does it ring a bell, or has it been too long?" she teased.

Gregori bunched her hair in his hand and tugged. "Show some respect, *bébé*, or I might have to turn you over my knee."

"Kinky." One delicate shoulder rose and fell in a sexy little shrug. "I'm willing to try anything once."

He leaned over and kissed her. He had to kiss her; he had no other choice. Once his mouth fastened on hers, he was in trouble. She was heat and light, spice and satin, lace and candlelight. And he was lost. Utterly, completely lost. Gregori jerked himself away from her, swearing in his ancient tongue.

Savannah's eyes were cloudy, dreamy, her lips moist and slightly parted. Her soft mouth curved with that sensuous, mysterious smile he could never quite figure out. "I have a great idea, Gregori," she told him wickedly. "Let's take a commercial flight."

"What?" He was staring at her mouth. She had a great mouth. A perfect mouth. A sexy mouth. *Mon Dieu*, he wanted her mouth.

"Doesn't a commercial flight sound fun? We could take a night flight, mingle with people. It might even throw off the reporter."

"Nothing is going to throw off the reporter. He is tenacious. And there will be no commercial flight. There will be no discussion on this, either. None. If we go to New Orleans, and I am not saying we will, commercial flights are out."

"Oh, Gregori. I was only kidding. Naturally we'll do things your way," she added demurely.

He shook his head, exasperated at himself. Of course she had been teasing. He wasn't used to anyone treating him as Savannah did. *Outrageous woman.* "I need to go out and talk with Wade Carter."

She stood up instantly, expectantly, her blue eyes wide in anticipation. "Tell me what you want me to do. I can probably manage mist. I'm stronger now, using your blood. I can back you up."

Amusement warmed the cool silver of his eyes. "*Mon Dieu*, Savannah, you sound like a cop movie. No, you will not back me up. You are not talking to Carter. You will stay here, safe, where I know he cannot touch you. Am I making myself crystal clear, *bébé*? You are not to leave this dwelling."

"But Gregori," she said softly, "I'm your partner now. I'm supposed to help you. If you insist on tackling this Wade Carter, then I have to help you. I'm your lifemate."

"There is no chance that I will allow such a thing. You may attempt to defy me, but I assure you, it is a waste of your energy." He spoke gently, that mocking male superiority setting her teeth on edge. "I am your lifemate, *chérie*, and I will give any order I deem necessary for your safety."

She thumped his chest hard with her clenched fist. "You make me so mad, Gregori! I'm trying very hard to get along with you and your arrogant orders. You don't even change expression! We could be discussing the weather instead of having a fight."

His eyebrows shot up. "This is no fight, *ma petite*. A fight is where we both are angry and have a contest of wills, a battle. There cannot be such a thing between us. I do not feel anger when I look at you, only the need to care for you and protect you. I am responsible for your health and safety, Savannah. I can do no other than to protect you, even from your own folly. You cannot hope to win. I know this absolutely, so there is no reason to become agitated over the issue."

She thumped him again. He looked startled, then caught her flying fist in his hand and gently pried her fingers open. Very carefully he pressed a kiss into the exact center of her palm. "Savannah? Were you trying to hit me?"

"I did hit you—twice, you scum. You didn't even notice the first time." She sounded very irritated with him.

For some reason it made him want to smile. "I apologize, *mon amour*. Next time, I promise I will notice when you strike me." The hard edge to his mouth softened into a semblance of a smile. "I will even go so far as to pretend that it hurts, if you wish it."

Her blue eyes flashed at him. "Ha, ha, ha, you're so funny, Gregori. Stop being so smug."

"It is not being smug to know my own power, *chérie*. I am trying to care for you as best I know how. You do not make it easy for me. I find myself making poor decisions just to see that smile on your face," he admitted reluctantly.

Savannah laid her head on his chest. "I'm sorry I'm so much trouble, Gregori." She wasn't certain if that was the strict truth. She rather liked stirring him up. "I just want us to be partners. That's how I've always envisioned my relationship with my lifemate. I don't want to be some shrinking violet protected from the real world and used as a brood mare to advance the Carpathian race. I want to be my lifemate's best friend and confidante. Is that so wrong?" She was pleading with him for understanding. "They're humans. We can handle them," she said with more confidence than she felt. If Gregori was concerned, there must be good reason. Still, she was determined to go with him, to share every aspect of his existence. She knew the hunt would always be a huge part of his life.

His arm swept around her, held her close to him; his hands stroked her hair. "Humans have managed to kill our kind throughout the centuries. We have great powers, yes, but we are not invincible. I do not want these people touching you. I will see what Wade Carter and his friends have in mind, just what evidence they actually have, and who is in danger. Then we will discuss where we will be going and how involved I will allow you to become with this situation."

She cringed visibly at the word *allow*, and he wished he could take it back. He tightened his hold possessively and dropped a brief, hard kiss on the top of her head. "You will stay within these walls, Savannah, no matter what happens."

She clung to him for a moment. "Don't let anything

happen to you, Gregori. I mean it—I'll be very angry with you."

A small smile touched his mouth but didn't light his pale eyes. "I will stay in your mind, *chérie*, and you will know I am fine." He hesitated a moment. "You may not like my methods." It was a warning. There was a shadow in the depths of his silver eyes, one he didn't attempt to hide from her.

Her chin lifted. "I may act like a child, Gregori, but I'm not. The preservation of our race always comes first, has to come first. I know it's necessary for you to use whatever means it takes to make that happen."

"I hope you do, Savannah. I hope you are prepared for the reality of my way of life. I can do no other than protect our people. It is not always pretty or clean." He spoke gruffly, his beautiful voice mesmerizing. He stepped away from her abruptly, yet her small fingers retained possession of his hand. "You will stay inside, *ma petite*. I will provide safeguards for you. Do not attempt to defy me."

She rubbed the back of his hand against her cheek. "I'll do as you *request*."

He caught her chin firmly, tipped her face up, and fastened his mouth to hers. At once the electricity arced and sizzled between them. White-hot heat enveloped them both. Then Gregori put her from him and simply disappeared.

He moved through space, unseen, with the ease of long practice, a soft wind blowing through the trees. Wade Carter was attempting to scale the west wall. Three of the wolves were pacing beneath him, fangs gleaming in the gathering dusk. Carter's trousers snagged on a rock outcropping, momentarily holding him prisoner. Gregori shimmered, hanging in the wind, insubstantial, then so-lidified a few feet from the reporter.

Carter's breath exploded out of his lungs. "My God, you really are a vampire! I knew it! I knew I was right."

Gregori could smell the man's fear, his agitation. He perched casually on the wall beside Carter with his easy, lazy grace. "I told you we would meet again soon. I always keep my promises," he replied softly.

The voice seemed to slice right through the reporter's mind. Wade rubbed his pounding temples. He had never been so afraid, never so excited. The real thing was sitting right beside him. He fumbled in his pocket for reassurance, felt for the dart gun. "Why did you decide to show yourself to me?" He tried to keep his voice from shaking.

Gregori smiled at him. There was no humor in that smile, just a white flash of gleaming menace. The cold silver eyes were unblinking, like those of a great jungle cat. Carter found it unnerving. "You disturbed my wife," Gregori answered softly. His voice was beautiful, hyp-notic.

Carter shook his head to banish the sluggishness from his brain. "Do you really think you're so powerful that you can get away with killing me?"

Gregori's muscles rippled, a hint of his enormous strength. "Do you really think I am not?"

"I would never have confronted you without support. I'm not alone," Carter blustered. He was fighting to get the dart gun from his pocket, where it was stuck.

"There is no one else here, Mr. Carter," Gregori corrected. "Just the two of us. I thought I might have a look inside your head." His tone had dropped an octave, was soft and persuasive, impossible to resist.

Sweat broke out on Carter's forehead. "I won't let you," he objected, but he found himself leaning forward to look into the molten silver eyes. He was supposed to be protected against a mind invasion! All in the society were protected. Vampires' voices couldn't affect them; the eyes couldn't put them in a trance. No one could read their minds or take away their memories. All of them in the society had undergone extensive hypnosis to resist such an abomination. And they had worked on a formula for more than thirty years. Scientists, good scientists, who had the benefit of vampire blood to work with.

Gregori pushed through the surprisingly strong barrier to inspect the man's mind. He could see the culmination of the secret society's research, their eagerness to find a new specimen. They had extracted blood from several of the victims they had tortured and mutilated some thirty years earlier. Gregori inhaled sharply. They had a drug they were certain could be used to incapacitate their victim, so that they could imprison what they believed to be vampire and study and dissect it at their leisure. The society was larger than any of his kind had believed.

He released the reporter's mind, deliberately allowing the man to know he had been extracting information. Carter swore obscenely and brought up the dart gun. The needle pierced Gregori's skin right above his heart. He felt the penetration, felt the instant release of poison into his blood.

Gregori! Savannah's distressed cry was in his mind. *Let me come to you.* She was trying to free herself from the invisible wall he'd erected around her, fighting his safeguards.

Be calm, ma petite. *You think I did not deliberately allow this imbecile to inject me with poison? I am the*

healer for our people. If they have something that can
harm us, I must find an antidote.

Savannah pounded on the invisible barrier to get to
Gregori. She could feel the hot tears gathering in her
eyes, the terrible fear threatening to overwhelm her at
her own helplessness. The poison was painful, crawling
through Gregori's system, paralyzing him. Cramps and
sweating, muscles clenching and locking. She felt it with
him and raged at her inability to get to him, to be able to
help him, as was her right.

Gregori remained as calm and impassive as ever,
studying the chemistry of the compound, as interested
as any scientist. He was barely sparing the jubilant reporter any of his attention. He had gone seeking inside
his own body, flowing through his own bloodstream to
follow the path of the spreading poison.

Carter was nearly jumping up and down. If it had not
been for his precarious perch, he would have. Of course,
he had no idea how he was going to get such a big man
into the car and back to the laboratory. He would have to
call for help. But otherwise it had been so easy. The lab
techs were right. The poison was perfect! All those years
of research had finally paid off. And he was the one to
get the glory!

He poked at Gregori's chest with a knife and, drew a
spot of blood. "You don't look so tough now, vampire,"
he gloated. "Not so impressive at all. Are you feeling a
little sick?" He laughed softly. "I've heard the older the
vampire, the greater the sensitivity to pain." He poked
again, slicing downward so that he opened a flowing cut.
"I hope so. I hope you take a long time to die when the
techs get you. Meanwhile, you just remember who will
be playing with Savannah. I have plans for that little

whore." He bent close to peer into Gregori's hooded eyes. "Not that this is personal, you understand. It's all in the name of science."

Savannah's burst of strength, fed by her rage at the reporter taunting Gregori and causing him pain, landed her against the invisible wall. The foundation didn't budge. Whatever Gregori had constructed to contain her was stronger than she thought. She pounded until her fists bled, tears streaming down her face. She could feel every cut, every slice the reporter inflicted. She could hear his taunts and threats. She implored her lifemate to allow her to come to him, but silence was her only answer.

None of it seemed to affect Gregori. He felt the pain but simply put it aside during his self-examination. The poison was thick, moving slowly and painfully throughout his system. He began to break down the chemicals to analyze them so that his people could come up with their own antidote to such a thing. Most of his kind could never do what he was doing. But he was a healer, knowledgeable in herbs and chemicals, poisons both man-made and natural. This was an interesting mixture, fast-acting and dangerous. They had used blood they had taken from their victims for a base. The pain had gone from a dull ache to agony in a few short minutes, enough to incapacitate all but the ancients and their most learned healers. As soon as he had the compounds broken down, he broadcast them to Aidan Savage. The hunter had studied the healing arts under him and would be able to utilize the information.

Within his own body he began the healing process, breaking down each chemical to its natural and separate form and disposing of or absorbing it. Only when the

process was complete did he return to his outside surroundings. He had been aware of the reporter poking at
and cutting him with a knife, presumably to make him
weak from loss of blood. He was bleeding from several
different cuts. He could feel the sting of them as the
wind tugged at his tattered clothing.

His pale eyes rested on the reporter's face. "Are you
finished, Carter, or is there something else you would
like to try before I return you to your laboratory?" he
asked very gently.

The man gasped, realizing the drug was no longer
affecting the vampire. He stabbed wildly for Gregori's
heart. In midair the knife stopped abruptly, as if caught
by someone with enormous strength. Slowly, inexora-
bly, the tip turned to point straight at Carter's throat.

"No, God, no! Don't do it. I can tell you so much.
Don't do it! Make me like you. I can serve you," Wade
Carter pleaded as the knife inched closer to his jugular.

Suddenly the knife clattered harmlessly to the ground
below them. Instantly Wade fumbled to retrieve the dart
gun. But in his hand it lengthened into a hideous scaly
shape that began to coil around his arm. Wade screamed,
the sound filling the night air and setting the wolves
howling in answer.

Gregori regarded him with impassive silver eyes. The
eyes of death. "This is my world, Carter, my domain.
You walked into it and deliberately challenged me. You
tried to hurt what is mine. I cannot allow such a thing."
He bent his dark head so his unblinking eyes could hold
the other man in their thrall, hold him prisoner. "And
understand this, Carter—this is very personal."

He tossed the other man to the ground easily, uncaring
that the drop was dangerously high. The snake coiled it-

self around the reporter's body, effectively tying him so that it was impossible to move. Gregori floated to the ground, snagged the man's shirt, and dragged him through the dirt to his car. "I think we need to pay this laboratory a small visit, do you not, Mr. Carter? You seemed quite anxious for my presence there, and I can do no other than to oblige you and your friends."

No, Gregori, Savannah pleaded. *Let's get out of here. Leave him, and let's go.*

Break off from me, bébé, he ordered and retreated, pulling his mind from hers.

Savannah could feel his implacable resolve. He had made up his mind to destroy the laboratory, what they had of the drug they had used on him, and all the data on it. He also intended to destroy anyone connected to the society that he found. She could find no rage in him such as she herself felt. No need for revenge. He was cool and ruthless, a machine performing a brutal task for the welfare of his race. Gregori had put aside all emotions and was an anonymous robot set on destruction. He was unswerving, relentless. Nothing could stop him.

Savannah, trapped in her cube of protection, slid to the floor and drew up her knees. This was his life. This was who he was, what he had become over the long centuries, a dark angel of death to those who declared war on his race. *Gregori, the Dark One.* He believed himself a monster without equal. She covered her face with her hands. There was no way to stop him. No way at all. Mikhail, her own father, Prince of their people, the only one commanding Gregori's loyalty, could not stop Gregori from doing what he deemed right or necessary.

Her teeth bit into her lower lip. He wielded so much power. There was no other who could have broken down that deadly poison in his own bloodstream. No other who would have deliberately baited a trap using his own body the way Gregori had. She knew the price he paid. She shared intimacy of his mind as well as his body.

He really could turn off his feelings, leave himself an emotionless machine to do the things necessary to protect his people. But inside, deep within his soul, he believed himself an unredeemable monster. The things he had to do for the preservation of their race required enormous pieces of his soul.

Chapter Nine

The night was dark and moonless. Clouds covered the stars and added an air of mystery and menace to the evening. The car pulled up in front of what looked like a deserted warehouse on the bay. There was no one on the docks. The water looked murky, almost oily. Gregori stepped out of the car and listened to the waves slapping at the pier. He scanned the area with the ease of long practice.

Inside the large building three men talked in low tones. Gregori waved a hand at the reporter, and Wade Carter slumped back behind the wheel of the car, his eyes glazed. The wind stirred, and an eddy of leaves and twigs whirled together in a bizarre dance where Gregori's solid form had been. Then the night was silent again. Unnaturally so.

Gregori entered the building through a crack in a yellowed window. He streamed into the room and wound his way through a collection of burners and beakers filled with various chemicals. On the far side of the room were three tables. Bolts of steel held manacles for ankles and wrists. There were three dissecting tables, where the society's "scientists" could leisurely carry out their experiments on their victims. There was a splash of blood on one of the tables. Gregori hovered over it to examine its composition. To his relief, it was not one of his people.

In one corner of the warehouse was a bank of impressive computers, high-tech equipment, and rows of file cabinets. Three desks formed a loose semi-circle closing off the area.

The three men were playing poker, obviously waiting for someone else. He streamed across the table, a cold wind that blew the cards in every direction. The men dived for the flying cards, looking all around for the source of the unexpected disturbance. Uneasily they looked at one another, then back around the large warehouse.

Gregori summoned Wade Carter to the door. The reporter pushed it open and entered, walking with the familiar gait of a zombie, a vampire's human puppet, with heavy, deliberate steps, head down, one foot in front of the other. He jerked to a halt in front of the card table exactly as a marionette would. A puppet on strings.

"So where is he, Wade?" the largest man, in a white coat, demanded. "You'd better have something important to pull Morrison away from his party tonight. It was a big do—he's getting funding for his favorite charity."

The others laughed. "Yeah—us," a dark-haired technician added. "Damn, Wade, I hope you brought us a woman. I'm in the mood for some fun tonight." He cupped himself crudely. "I've been looking forward to getting my hands on that magician you claim is a vampire. She's hot, really hot."

The man in the white coat peered at the reporter. "So where's this vampire?"

"Right behind you," Gregori said softly, gently.

They whirled around, and his shape shimmered, first that of a man, solid and real, then contorting and crackling, bones and sinew popping as his face lengthened into a muzzle, and fangs filled his hungry jaws. Muscles and fur rippled, and the beast lunged forward, straight at the white-coated man's throat.

The man screamed but had no chance to run before the black wolf was on him, tearing at his throat. Splashes of crimson cascaded through the room, a bright arcing fountain. The other two men stood, horrified, frozen in place, unable to look away from the raw, gaping wound that had once been a throat.

Then, galvanized into action by the sight of the thick, red river of blood, they turned as one and ran for the door. The wolf leapt, crossed the distance easily, and brought down the dark-haired technician. Claws tore at the soft stomach, digging into intestines, but the savage muzzle bore in low and mean, ripping deliberately at the prize. Blood spurted, erupting in a volcanic burst. The man howled horribly, clutching himself far too late to save his life, let alone his manhood.

The last victim had reached the door when the wolf leapt onto his back. One quick snap of the powerful jaw and the neck was broken. The wolf backed up and surveyed the dead and dying. Then he trotted over to the bank of computer terminals and slowly regained his own shape.

Gregori's hunger was a living thing, filling him with need. The dark compulsion of the kill was on him. Beast or man, it didn't matter; it was his nature, his destiny.

But he fought back the hunger, even with the smell of blood all around him. The computers had to be destroyed. Every disk. Every document.

Gregori gathered himself and began to summon the energy necessary to send bolts of electricity through the machines. They exploded, bursting from their cases, melting into the desks they were sitting on. Behind him the beakers shattered, spilling their contents onto the floor. Flames began to lick greedily at the dry wood. He waved a hand, and the file cabinets tumbled over, the papers they spilled feeding the fire until it danced high and spread throughout the room.

Wade Carter stood unmoving beside the card table. He didn't seem to notice his fallen companions or the fire rapidly consuming the contents of the warehouse. Gregori assured himself he had destroyed everything in the laboratory before turning his attention to the reporter. Thick smoke was swirling around them as he took hold of the man and dragged him close.

Hunger spread and gnawed, became a living, breathing thing. Gregori bent his dark head and found the pulse in Carter's throat. "You have attempted to condemn my race to death, deliberately tried to bring my lifemate to this place of horror. For that and all your crimes against my people, I sentence you to death." He murmured the ritual words as his teeth pierced the skin and sank deep into the artery.

Hot blood poured into shrunken cells. His body, so hungry, his energy and strength drained from his great effort and from his encounter with the poison, embraced the dark liquid of life. He drank voraciously, insatiably. His prey remained still beneath his hands while he drained away the life.

Gregori, stop! Savannah implored. *You cannot take his life like that. Please, for me, stop.*

Gregori growled, his silver eyes glowing red, reflecting the flames from the fire. Reluctantly he lifted his head, watching impassively as the blood pumped from Carter's wound and the man slumped to the ground. He released Carter's shirt, his gaze still riveted on the steady trickle of blood spilling onto the warehouse floor.

Come home to me. Get out of that awful place.

He could hear the distant wail of sirens, the murmur of a gathering crowd. Still, he remained to ensure that the life force was gone completely from each of those in the laboratory. He had a name now, a place to start hunting. Morrison. Someone who could raise funds. Someone who mingled with society.

Gregori! Come home to me now. Savannah was insistent. He could hear the fear in her voice. She had been taught since birth that only a vampire would kill in the act of feeding. It terrified her to think that Gregori might break that sacred rule. That he had done so at some time in his past. More than once.

Your monster returns, he sent back to her in the emotionless voice he almost always used. He became smoke, the dark whirling wind that blew through the burning laboratory, and rushed out into the night air. He allowed himself to drift upward, watching as the humans on the ground raced around hooking up fire hoses. A stretch limousine arrived and parked a short distance away from the warehouse. A rear window slid down partway, but the occupant remained inside. Morrison.

Gregori drifted higher. He was returning to Savannah his true self, not the fraud he had allowed her to believe in. After his centuries of the hunt, after dispensing dark justice so many endless years, did she really believe he could feel emotion when he killed? Remorse? Vengeance? Mercy? He felt nothing, and he never would. It was simply a job, one he did well, without pride or fear.

He did not want to see the fear in her eyes. The condemnation. But he could not pretend for the rest of eternity. She had to know him for the brutal monster that he was. Her monster. She had to understand that he was far more dangerous than she thought him, that certain things would not be prudent to do. But he did not want to see the fear once more in her eyes. With a soft sigh he began the journey back toward the mountains. He traveled slowly, smoke on the wind, dispersing the air he moved through evenly so as not to alert the vampires to his presence. He felt the weight of his age, the kills, the blood on his hands. Savannah would look at him and finally see her terrible fate.

Once within the compound he waved a hand to dispense with the safeguards, freeing Savannah from her invisible prison. She was sitting, her knees drawn up to her chest, her chin resting on top of her knees. Her large blue eyes fastened on the stream of smoke as he approached her. Gregori took shape at her feet, his tall, masculine frame looming over her.

She stood up slowly, her enormous eyes never leaving his face. It was Savannah who closed the inches separating them, who circled his waist with her slender arms. She laid her head against his chest, over the steady beating of his heart. "I was so afraid for you, Gregori." There were tears in her voice, trails on her face. "Never leave me alone like that again. It's better to be with you, even if I'm in danger." Her hands were moving over him, slipping under his shirt to explore his skin to assure herself he was unharmed. "I could feel how much pain you were in, how the poison he used did so much damage."

Her hands touched his throat. Stroked his thick hair. She touched him everywhere. She had to touch him. She couldn't help herself. She found each raw wound Carter's knife had made. Her breath caught in her throat, and she lowered her head to gently soothe each cut with healing saliva.

Gregori caught both her arms and set her a few inches away from him. "Look at me, *ma chérie*. Really look at me. See me for what I am." He gave her a slight shake. "Really look at me, Savannah."

Her blue-violet eyes searched his pale ones. "What do you think I see, lifemate? You are not the monster I named you. Not the monster you named yourself. You are a great Carpathian, a great healer. You are my other half." Her eyes flashed at him. "Don't think you're going to get away with this nonsense you pulled, leaving me trapped to wait alone within these walls. Never again. I mean it, Gregori. From now on, I go with you."

His hand bunched her hair behind her head tightly. He dragged her closer. "Never into danger. Never." He lowered his head to find her mouth, to claim what was his. His heart was bursting in his chest. Her eyes had been clear—shadowed with worry, perhaps—but free of fear. He held her head pinned perfectly still while his mouth moved over hers, while he devoured her sweetness and made his demands. Savannah held nothing back, accepting his domination, returning his kiss with the same hunger he was communicating to her. He gathered her into his arms, crushing her body to his. "Never, Savannah. Never will I allow you to be in danger."

"How do you think I feel about you?" she demanded.

"Look into my mind, see what I had to go through while you dealt with the poison." She touched his wounds with gentle fingers. "When he was doing this to you."

"The poison would have consumed you, Savannah, had you been injected with it. I relayed the elements of the toxin to Aidan. He will ensure that those in our homeland are aware of this new danger. We can develop an antidote with what we now know." His hands were moving up and down her back, over her hips, cupping her firm bottom, pressing her close. His body was aching and full, and her caressing hands only inflamed him more.

"It could have been lethal for all you knew, Gregori," she said. "You had no idea what was in that poison." She pulled at his clothing, tearing his shirt open to get at his chest, inspecting every inch of him, tasting his skin, the offensive wounds Carter had left behind.

"I am a healer, Savannah. I can neutralize poison." Her hands were inflaming him, pouring fire into his body.

She pushed at his trousers anxiously, her palm sliding around his heavy fullness. The beast in his nature, already so close to the surface, broke free and took her to the floor, ripping the clothes from her body as he did so. He pinned her down, one knee shoving hard between her legs to give him access.

But it was Gregori's silver eyes that captured and held her gaze. It was Gregori who caught her hips in gentle hands and Gregori who tested her readiness with his probing fingers. "You are mine, Savannah. Only mine," he said softly as he surged forward, filling her. He wanted to tell her he loved her, but he couldn't say the words, so he said them with his body. Again and again he buried himself deep within her. Hard and fast. Slow and tender. He took his time, wanting it to be forever, hiding his face so that she couldn't see the unexpected moisture in his eyes.

Her body was made for his. Tight. Hot. Silken. Her skin was satin, her mouth hungry. He wanted her to take away the long, endless centuries, the emptiness. He wanted her to fill that emotionless void in his soul. That black empty spot, utterly bleak and hopeless. And she did. Somehow, with a miracle of total, unconditional acceptance, she did. She gave herself freely, without reservation, accepting his domination, his body taking hers.

He felt her ripple with pleasure again and again, with white heat, velvet gripping him tightly, finally taking him over the edge to soaring into space with her. She clutched him, her nails digging into his back, her mouth pressed against his shoulder, her small cry of satisfaction muffled against the heavy muscles of his chest.

Gregori held her tightly, nearly crushing her. He still did not believe she was actually with him. He couldn't believe she could possibly accept him. He had killed so many times, broken their laws. Felt no remorse. Felt nothing at all. She was so compassionate. So young. So filled with beauty and life. He buried his face against her neck. "You must feed, *bébé*," he reminded her in a neutral voice.

Her stomach lurched. She had been with him, in his mind, when he had fed on the reporter. Blood was a necessity; she accepted that. She even accepted that Wade Carter had to die to preserve their race. But she didn't want his blood. Her tongue touched her lower lip carefully, her heart pounding. Very cautiously, she moved, and immediately she felt the hardness of the marble-tiled floor. She hadn't noticed it before; in fact, it had enhanced their lovemaking, allowing Gregori to drive deeply into her. Now she felt bruised and sore, her hips aching. "This is uncomfortable, Gregori," she ventured.

He rose with one fluid movement and took her with him, cradling her in his arms. "I am sorry, *ma petite*. I should have taken more care with you."

She touched his jaw with gentle fingers. "Promise me you will never leave me like that again. Next time let me go with you."

Her eyes were eloquent, pleading, so much so that he had to look away. "Do not ask me for what I cannot give you. I would give you the moon if you asked, *chérie*, but I cannot allow you to place yourself in danger. Not for any reason. Not even to help me."

Her slender arms wrapped around his neck. Her body pressed tightly against his. "I don't know if I can survive that again," she said softly into his throat. "I was so terrified for you."

"Your hunger beats at me. I want you to feed."

"I can't," she admitted reluctantly, fearful of his reaction. "That man . . ."

He was silent, carrying her down the hall to one of the bedrooms. "Yes, you can, and you will because I wish it." He lowered her to the bed.

She stared up into his pale eyes, eyes that held her captive, commanded her, even as they roved possessively over her body. He cupped one breast, filling his palm with her softness, his thumb feathering across the rosy tip, bringing it to a hard peak. "Gregori." Her voice was a soft plea.

"You will do as I wish, Savannah." He was implacable. His dark features were set, almost cruel.

She tried to look away from him, but he caught her chin in his hand and held her still. "Now, Savannah. Feed now. You did not do so this morning, and we have the night ahead of us. You will feed."

She swallowed hard, her stomach rebelling. "I can't, Gregori. He's dead. I just can't."

"You mean I killed him." He said the words softly.

"No, I know he was a threat to our people. I know he tried to kill you. I know there was no choice. But I can't." She tried to wiggle away from him. She suddenly wanted her clothes on, self-conscious of her nakedness.

"You will feed," he said again. This time his voice was a whisper of sound, so compelling, so hypnotic, she found herself leaning close to him. She could feel the heat from his body, feel the warmth of his breath. *Feed, Savannah. Come to me now.* He dragged her closer to him and pressed her against his chest. "I am your life-mate. I can do no other than to see to your needs."

Savannah could taste him, the salt from his skin. His hunger, her hunger—she couldn't tell where one left off and the other began. He was whispering in her mind, words impossible to understand, the music of them echoing through her body. His grip was impossible to break, the hand on her nape pressing her to him. There was no escaping his iron will. She didn't even want to, her mouth already moving over his skin.

Gregori closed his eyes as her teeth pierced deeply. The pleasure-pain was sensuous, her bare body irresist-ible, but he clamped down on his insatiable hunger. He had already been selfish, taking her on the tile floor, im-patient and needing her in the midst of his own uncer-tainty. Now he cradled her head to him, feeding her until her pale skin was once more glowing and healthy. Then slowly, reluctantly, he allowed her to escape the compulsion.

Her blue eyes blinked, awareness suddenly in their depths. She pulled away abruptly, rolling away from him to scramble for her clothes. "You really are scum, Gregori. You have no right to force me when I've said no."

He watched her look around for her tattered clothes. She sank back down on the bed with a tired sigh. "I seem to have no clothes again."

"Easily fixed, Savannah," he said softly. Fashioning clothes from air and the elements was as old as time, as easy as anything he had ever done. She looked so upset, he wanted to gather her into his arms and hold her, comfort her. She was still disturbed that he had willingly ingested poison. That he had broken their laws by killing while feeding. But mostly she was upset that he had forced her to wait for him while he ventured into danger instead of allowing her to help him. And she was distressed that he had forced her to feed under compulsion.

Gregori handed her soft jeans and a cotton shirt, his silver eyes watching her closely. "I am what I have been shaped to be over these endless centuries, Savannah," he said carefully.

She pushed wearily at her hair. Everything was happening so fast. Her world changing, turning upside down, unfamiliar and out of her control. Peter. The vampire. The human hunter. The poison. Being imprisoned by her own lifemate. She bit her lower lip in agitation, holding up the shirt to cover her breasts. "You can choose to be different, Gregori. Anyone can."

He touched her mind, a slight brush, and knew she

was close to tears. He cupped the side of her face, his thumb brushing her cheekbone. "I do not choose to allow you to place your life in danger, *mon amour*. That is not something that will ever change."

"But I'm to live with you placing yourself in danger," she countered, her blue eyes flashing at him.

His white teeth gleamed, a predatory smirk. "I was never in danger. Wade Carter thought he was protected, but Carpathian children have stronger barriers against predators."

"The point is, you couldn't know that, Gregori. You went out there and let him shoot you with that dart gun without even knowing what it was. And you made sure I couldn't help you."

He took the shirt out of her hands and slipped it over her head. "I was never in danger, Savannah." He said it quietly, patiently, his voice black velvet.

She bent her head, long hair tumbling down to hide her expression. It didn't matter. Gregori was in her mind, easily reading her thoughts. She was confused, afraid, sad. It pressed on her like a terrible weight on her chest.

Gregori lifted her as if she were a baby and tugged on her jeans, encasing her bare, slender legs. He sat on the bed and cradled her in his lap. Very gently he rocked her back and forth. "I am sorry I frightened you, *ma petite*. I would not do so for the world. But you have to realize that you are tied to a man of power. Many things that might endanger our kind do not work on me. I am capable of many things that have never been done by others of our race. I know my own capabilities." He stroked her hair, a gentle, soothing caress.

She turned her face into his throat, hot tears spilling

over. "I don't know your capabilities." Her voice was muffled, the tears clogging her throat. She tightened her fingers in his thick mane of hair, hanging on to him almost desperately.

He dropped his head protectively over hers. "You need to have more faith in my strength, Savannah. Have faith in me. I am not about to throw away my life now that I have found you. Believe in me, in my power and abilities."

She burrowed closer, as if trying to get inside him.

Gregori tightened his arms, sheltering her close. "I know what I can and cannot do, *mon petit amour*. I did not take any unnecessary chances." He held her to him, inhaling her scent, their combined scents, counting himself lucky that she felt so strongly for his safety. "I am very sorry I frightened you," he repeated into the silken strands of her hair.

"Don't do it again," she ordered, nuzzling his throat. Her mouth moved over his skin and left behind a living flame.

Gregori's body reacted, stirring to life. He could feel her discomfort, the sore spots on her hips and back because of his own carelessness. He laid a palm over her hip and sent himself seeking outside his own body. At once, Savannah could feel soothing heat easing sore muscles, speeding to heal bruises. She could hear the ancient healing chant in her mind, Gregori's beautiful voice flowing into her.

She lay passively in his arms, staring up at sensual features etched and carved by time, at masculine Carpathian beauty. He was power and strength. He was her lifemate. She studied him, examining every inch of his face.

Gregori suddenly smiled at her, a genuine smile that warmed the cold steel of his eyes to molten mercury. "What is it you are seeing?"

She touched his chin with a fingertip. It was a nice chin. Stubborn. Determined. Nice all the same. "I'm seeing my lifemate, Gregori. I don't want anything to happen to you." Her hands framed his face. Very slowly she lifted her mouth to his. She kissed him slowly, thoroughly. Completely. Her tongue swept into his mouth, explored, teased, tempted. When she lifted her head, she rested her forehead against his. "Don't ever do that again. Don't leave me alone and helpless without you."

He actually felt the wrenching deep in his heart. She was turning him inside out. She wasn't condemning him as she should have, she was making herself sick with worry. He found her neck and trailed kisses along the slim column. His teeth scraped her shoulder. "So you like jazz."

Savannah raised her head, her blue eyes searching his. "I love jazz," she said softly. He could see the anxiety in her, the sudden hope.

"Then I guess we cannot miss the famous festival in New Orleans," he found himself saying, just to take the shadows from her eyes.

She was silent a moment, her fingers twisting in the blanket. "Do you mean it, Gregori? We can go?"

"You know how much I love crowds of humans," he said, straight-faced. She laughed at him. "They don't bite."

"I do," he said, the words low and soft, his silver gaze at once possessive. Just the heat from her smile wreaked havoc with his body. He had had her only a few minutes before, yet he was hungry all over again. Fiercely hungry. His body reacted urgently, savagely, and he allowed it, making no effort to conceal his great need.

Savannah's breath caught in her throat at the sight of his arousal. This power, at least, she had, and the depth of it amazed her. Her fingers brushed his skin deliberately. He trembled beneath that light touch. She trailed her hand along his flat belly, and she felt him suck in his breath. Her fingers wrapped around the hard length of him, and she felt him shudder with pleasure.

He caught her head in his hands, dragging her closer. He was full with need, hurting with it. "I am going to hate New Orleans," he whispered against her silken hair before she began lowering her head.

Her breath warmed the velvet tip of him, sending fire racing through his blood. "Maybe we can think of something interesting to make it more enjoyable for you," she ventured. Her mouth was satin soft, moist and hot.

Gregori pressed his hips forward, forcing her back on the bed, his knees on the thick blanket above her. She was so beautiful, her flawless skin like cream, her thick hair spilling around her slender shoulders. Sitting up, she slowly peeled off the cotton shirt, baring her full breasts to his silver gaze. She looked lush and sexy in the dark of the night, a mysterious, erotic gift to him.

"You think you might make New Orleans more bearable for me then?" His eyes were saying more than his mouth, touching her here and there, dwelling on every curve of her body.

Her hand spanned his flat stomach and lingered there. "I'm sure I can be inventive enough to make you forget your dread of crowds. Take off my jeans."

"Your jeans?" he echoed.

"You put them on me, and they're definitely in the way. Take them off." Her hand was wandering lower, her fingers walking lightly over his clenching muscles, a deliberate persuasion.

His hands made quick work of unfastening her jeans and tugging them down her legs. She kicked them aside and leaned forward to press a kiss onto his stomach. Her hair slid over his heavy fullness, a silken tangle that nearly drove him out of his mind. "Sometimes your orders are very easy to follow, *ma chérie*," he murmured, his eyes closing as her mouth wandered lower.

He cupped her breasts in his palms, his thumbs caressing the tips into hard, beckoning peaks. His hips thrust forward almost against his own will, his body taking on a life of its own. Her fingers dug into his buttocks, urging him deeper into her, then slid down to caress the thick columns of his thighs. Her fingernails raked his skin gently even as she arched her body to allow him better access to her aching breasts.

He burned for her in his body and his mind. There was a dull roar in his head, a rush of pleasure that washed over him and took with it every vestige of sanity. Outside, the wind began to pick up. It sang at the windows and brushed the thick walls, heralding a storm.

Neither heard or cared. The storm was raging inside as he pushed her down, his mouth finding every inch of her body, every shadow and hollow, caressing and inflaming. Creating fire. Creating a storm. Gregori moved over her, her soft skin against his palms, his mouth hot on her skin. She drove away his demons, the terrible sights and hideous deaths. She took away the loneliness and replaced it with such pleasure, he wasn't certain he would survive it.

Her inarticulate cry was muffled with his own mouth as he entered her, burying himself deep. She was velvet soft, fiery hot, exquisitely tight, surrounding him, gripping him in molten heat. He whispered to her in the ancient language, words she couldn't understand, but he meant every one of them, words he had never said before, never felt before. She might never really know him, yet he was branded by her for all time. He was hers alone. He worshipped her. And the only way he had of showing her was with his body, his strength, his knowledge, his expertise.

His body took hers, a demanding possession that went on and on. A bolt of lighting sizzled and danced across the sky. The earth moved beneath them. None of it mattered. He took his time, over and over, ensuring her pleasure first and foremost. She was clinging to him, with him, as he finally allowed himself release. He never wanted to stop, afraid that if he let her go, she would somehow slip away forever.

Gregori swore softly and rolled over to force his body away from hers. She was making him crazy. Desperate. He was going to kill them both with his insatiable appetite. Already his fingers were curling in her hair, bunching silken strands in his fist.

Savannah heard the soft, hissing words flowing from his mouth, and her heart stood still. He had just shaken her entire world, set it on fire, and now he was angry. She turned her back to him so that he could not see her hurt. "What did I do wrong?" she asked in a small voice.

Gregori tugged on her hair to force her back to him. "You make me feel alive, Savannah."

"Do I? Is that why you're swearing?" She turned onto her stomach, propping herself up on her elbows.

He leaned into her, brushing his mouth across the swell of her breast. "You are managing to tie me up in knots. You take away all my good judgment."

A slight smile curved her mouth. "I never noticed that you had particularly good judgment to begin with."

His white teeth gleamed, a predator's smile, then sank into soft bare flesh. She yelped but moved closer to him when his tongue swirled and caressed, taking away the sting. "I have always had good judgment," he told her firmly, his teeth scraping back and forth in the valley between her breasts.

"So you say. But that doesn't make it so. You let evil idiots shoot you with poisoned darts. You go by yourself into laboratories filled with your enemies. Need I go on?" Her blue eyes were laughing at him.

Her firm, rounded bottom was far too tempting to resist. He brought his open palm down in mock punishment. Savannah jumped, but before she could scoot away, his palm began caressing, producing a far different effect. "Judging from our positions, *ma chérie*, I would say my judgment looks better than yours."

She laughed. "All right, I'm going to let you win this time."

"Would you care for a shower?" he asked solicitously.

When she nodded, Gregori flowed off the bed, lifted her high into his arms, and cradled her against his chest. There was something too innocent about him. She eyed him warily. But in an instant he had already glided across the tiled floor to the balcony door, which flew open at his whim, and carried her, naked, into the cold, glittering downpour.

Savannah tried to squirm away, wiggling and shoving at his chest, laughing in spite of the icy water cascading over her. "Gregori! You're so mean. I can't believe you did this."

"Well, I have poor judgment." He was grinning at her in mocking, male amusement. "Is that not what you said?"

"I take it back!" she moaned, clinging to him, burying her face on his shoulder as the chill rain pelted her bare breasts, making her nipples peak hard and fast.

"Run with me tonight," Gregori whispered against her neck. An enticement. Temptation. Drawing her to him, another tie to his dark world.

She lifted her head, looked into his silver eyes, and was lost. The rain poured over her, drenching her, but as Gregori slowly glided with her to the blanket of pine needles below the balcony, she couldn't look away from those hungry eyes. She nodded, accepting his will for them that night.

Following the desire in his mind, she focused on picturing the necessary image. And her body began to contort. There was a curious wrenching, a strange, disorienting feeling, and then her skin rippled with glossy blue-black fur as her body rapidly changed. Soon a small, blue-eyed wolf stood in the rain, watching as a huge black wolf nudged her, his tongue lapping a rough caress along her muzzle.

Savannah turned and trotted through the dense vegetation, exalting in the freedom of the wolf's body. Gregori glided beside her, close and protective. The wind sang, and the trees rustled. She could hear everything, feel everything, the night itself calling to her. She began to run as her body was meant to, with long, loping strides, her neck stretched forward.

She felt wild. No longer human. Free. She ran fast, swerving in and out through the trees. Gregori kept pace, occasionally touching her sleek body with his muzzle or nudging her flank or shoulder to turn her in the direction he wished to go. Savannah flushed out a rabbit, then chased it for the sheer joy of it before turning along a little-used path through heavy brush.

She scented others of her kind. Wolves running free. Several males, three females. The huge wolf at her side bared his fangs and nudged her away from the scent. Savannah resisted his efforts and trotted around him, lured by the wild call. Gregori growled, fangs exposed, his large body bumping, then blocking hers, effectively stopping her. He pushed her toward home.

She gave him one look that said it all. He had proposed the run, the shape-shifting; now she was demanding that he quit messing with her fun. He began nudging her harder. She would be exhausted with the night's activities. He wanted her to start back.

When she refused, he nipped her small flank, a reminder of who was in charge. She snapped at him but ultimately obeyed, and they loped back together through the forest.

Once at the house, they shimmered back into human form, and Gregori caught her hand and pulled her inside. Water streamed off her naked body and dripped from her hair. She glared at him. "You have to be bossy no matter what you are, don't you?"

He enveloped her in a towel and dried her off until her skin was rosy. "I take your health and safety seriously, Savannah." He was clearly unrepentant.

She shivered a little and pulled the towel around herself, suddenly unnerved by all the changes in herself. She was only twenty-three, not even a quarter of a century old. She had spent the last five years living exclusively in the human world. Now her wild nature was calling to her. Gregori was touching something untamed in her, something to which she had forbidden herself access. Something wild and uninhibited and incredibly sensuous.

Savannah looked up at his dark, handsome face. It was so male. So carnal. So powerful. *Gregori. The Dark One.* Just looking at him made her go weak with need. One glance from his slashing silver eyes could bring a rush of liquid heat, fire racing through her. She became soft and pliant. She became his.

Gregori's palm cupped her face. "Whatever you are thinking is making you fear me, Savannah," he said softly. "Stop it."

"You're making me into something I'm not," she whispered.

"You are Carpathian, my lifemate. You are Savannah Dubrinsky. I cannot take any of those things from you. I do not want a puppet, or a different woman. I want you as you are." His voice was soft and compelling. He lifted her in his arms, carried her to his bed and tucked the covers around her.

The storm lashed at the windows and whistled against the walls. Gregori wove the safeguards in preparation for their sleep. Savannah was exhausted, her eyes already trying to close. Then he slipped into the bed and gathered her into his arms. "I would never change anything about you, *ma petite*, not even your nasty little temper."

She settled against his body as if she was made for it. He felt the brush of her lips against his chest and the last sigh of air as it escaped from her lungs.

Gregori lay awake for a long time, watching as the dawn crept forward, pushing away the night. One wave of his hand closed and locked the heavy shutters over the windows. Still he lay awake, holding Savannah close.

Because he had always known he was dangerous, he had feared for mortals and immortals alike at his hand. But somehow, perhaps naively, he had thought that once he was bound to his lifemate, he would become tamer, more domesticated. His fingers bunched in her hair. But Savannah made him wild. She made him far more dangerous than he had ever been. Before Savannah, he had had no emotions. He had killed when it was necessary because it was necessary. He had feared nothing because he loved nothing and had nothing to lose. Now he had everything to lose. And so he was more dangerous. For no one, nothing, would ever threaten Savannah and live.

Chapter Ten

Gregori stared with dismay at the small, two-story house enclosed in wrought-iron latticework and sandwiched between two smaller, rather rundown properties in the crowded French Quarter of New Orleans. He inserted the key in the lock and turned to look at Savannah's face. It was lit up with expectation, her blue eyes shining.

"I have definitely lost all good sense," he muttered as he pushed open the door.

The interior was dark, but he could see everything easily. The room was layered with dust, old sheets covered the furniture, and the wallpaper was peeling in small curls from the walls.

"Isn't it beautiful?" Savannah flung out her hands and turned in a circle. Jumping into Gregori's arms, she hugged him tightly. "It's so perfect!"

He couldn't help himself; he kissed her inviting mouth. "Perfect for torching. Savannah, did you even look at this place before you bought it?"

She laughed and ruffled his thick mane of hair. "Don't be such a pessimist. Can't you see its potential?"

"It is a firetrap," he groused, but he was studying the heavy draperies and the narrow staircase leading both upstairs and to some lower sanctuary.

"Come with me." Savannah was already hastening toward the stairs. "Let me show you the big surprise, Gregori. This is why I bought it. It isn't just a fantastic house with a great garden."

"Garden?" he echoed. But he followed her. How could he not? She was radiating joy. He found himself just watching her, every movement she made, the way her head turned, the way her eyes danced. She was so beautiful. If she wanted a claustrophobic little house in the middle of the French Quarter, if that made her happy, he would not deny her.

The stairs, very narrow and steep, wound downward in a spiral to an unexpected basement that ran the length of the house. New Orleans was built on water-logged ground below sea level. Even the dead had to be entombed above ground. New Orleans made him edgy. There was no earth to burrow into in an emergency. No easy, natural escape. New Orleans presented problems he didn't want at this time.

Gregori peered at the basement's cement walls, its solid floor. He paced the length of the room, circled the perimeter, moved to the center, and closed his eyes. He inhaled deeply. There were shadows of others in this room, of those who had come before.

"Do you feel it?" Savannah asked softly. She placed a hand on his arm, her fingers curling halfway around his wrist.

He stared down at her small hand. He could feel that touch through his entire body. Yet her fingers couldn't even circle the thickness of his wrist. He found himself aware that she did that often, wrap her fingers around his wrist, connecting them. And that little gesture seemed to melt his heart.

Gregori forced his attention back to the present. So Savannah felt the presence, too. One who had been here before them. *Julian.* Julian Savage had lived in this house. Why? What kind of security had he established here? For Julian must have steered Savannah toward this house when he had become aware of her desire to come to New Orleans.

Gregori slipped an arm around her shoulders. "What do you know about the former owner?"

"Just that he wasn't here for long periods at a time. The real estate agent told me that the house had been in the man's family for nearly two hundred years, that it's actually one of the oldest homes in the Quarter."

"But you never actually met him?" Gregori prompted.

"No," Savannah replied.

"Julian Savage was the former owner, though it is hard to imagine him ever living here. He is a loner, as untamed as the wind." He paced the room again. "If Julian gave up this sanctuary, one he had for nearly two centuries, it can mean only one thing. He is choosing the dawn." He said the words dispassionately, without expression, but inside he felt that curious tearing he was becoming so familiar with. Emotion. Sorrow. So many of his kind gone forever. Julian was stronger than most, more knowledgeable. He hated losing Julian.

Savannah stroked his arm. "We don't know that, Gregori. Maybe he just wanted to give us a wedding present. Don't assume the worst."

Gregori tried to shake off his melancholy, but he felt he would barely be able to breathe in this crowded, closed-in neighborhood. "Other people's houses are right on top of this one," he said. "I think they could take one step and be in our living room."

"You haven't seen the courtyard yet, Gregori. The house opens up to a courtyard in the back, and it's immense and in quite good shape." Savannah began heading up the stairs, ignoring his grousing.

"I hate to think what you would call bad shape," he muttered as he followed her upstairs.

"I wonder why everything is so dusty," Savannah said. "I had the real estate people come in and clean and get things ready for our arrival."

"Do not touch anything," Gregori hissed softly, and very gently he caught her shoulders to put her behind him.

"What is it?" Instinctively she lowered her voice and looked around, trying to see if there was some danger she had been unable to sense.

"If people came and made up the bed and prepared the house for your arrival, then they would have removed the dust too."

"Maybe they're incredibly incompetent," she suggested hopefully.

Gregori glanced at her and found the hard edge of his mouth softening. She was making him want to smile all the time, even in the most serious of situations. "I am certain any company would work overtime trying to make you happy, *ma petite*. I know I do."

She blushed at the memory of how he did so. "So why all the dust?" she asked, deliberately distracting him.

"I think Julian left us a message. You have remained with humans so long, you see only with your eyes."

Savannah rolled her eyes at the reprimand. "And

you've lived in the hills so long, you've forgotten how to have fun."

The pale eyes slid over her, wrapping her in heat. "I have my own ideas of fun, *chérie*. I would be willing to show you if you like," he offered wickedly.

Her chin lifted, blue eyes challenging. "If you think you're scaring me with your big-bad-wolf routine, you're not," she said.

He could hear her heart beat. Smell her scent calling him. "Perhaps I will think of something to change that," he cautioned her. Gregori turned his attention back to the room. Dust was thick on the walls, the fireplace, the tiled floor. He hunkered down, touched the minute specks lightly, and studied the layout from all angles. His eyes glowed red in the darkened interior.

Savannah stepped backward until she was pressed against the wall. Her attention was on the man, not on what he was doing. She watched the way his body moved, the rippling of his muscles beneath the thin silk shirt, the fluid way he seemed to flow from one area to the other. The way he tilted his head, the way he raked a hand impatiently through his thick mane of hair. He was of another world. Elegant. Dangerous. Deadly. Yet when he turned his head and his perfect mouth smiled at her, he looked sensual instead of cruel. His eyes were cold and lethal, seeing everything, missing nothing, but when he turned his gaze on her, the cold steel warmed to molten mercury. Hot. Exciting. Sexy. Almost sinful.

She blinked to bring the room back into focus. There was a subtle change. The dust seemed to shift position under Gregori's hand. He moved his arm gracefully, as if he was conducting an orchestra, and patterns began to emerge on the walls and on the floor. Lines shimmered into ancient letters and symbols. Once Gregori unlocked the secret, the hieroglyphics took shape rapidly, fashioned with the dust particles.

"This is beautiful. It's in the ancient language, isn't it?" Savannah said softly in awe. She moved in a small semi-circle, not wanting to disturb the air. "How did you know to bring it to life?"

"The way the dust had settled was all too arranged. It lay in a design waiting for us. It is an art few are aware of. I had no idea Julian knew it." Gregori sounded pleased. "Your father is quite good at this, but I have seen few others who have mastered it."

"Is my father good at everything?"

Gregori glanced up at the odd note in her voice. "He is the Prince of our people. The oldest of our kind. Yes, he is good at everything he does."

Unlike her, Savannah thought. "And you've known him all your life."

Gregori turned the power of his silver eyes directly on her face. "Your father and I have lived over a thousand years, *bébé*. Why would you think you should have the knowledge of the ancients? You are a beautiful, intelligent fledgling, and you learn quickly."

"Maybe I can never live as you want me to. Maybe I was born too late." There was an ache in her voice, betraying her lack of confidence in herself. The silver stars in the centers of her eyes deepened the blue to a vivid violet. Her anxiety was easy to read.

He went to her immediately and framed her face with his hands. "You have a lifetime to learn the things your father and I have learned. It took us a lifetime. We had none of your responsibilities at such an early age. We were able to wander the world, to live freely. We had no overbearing, dominating lifemate we had to live with." His thumbs caressed her delicate jaw. "Do not, *chérie*, ever think you cannot measure up to my expectations."

"You might get tired of teaching me things."

His hand spanned the slim column of her throat so that her pulse was beating into the center of his palm. "Never. It will never happen. And I have much to learn from you. There has been no laughter in my life. You have brought that to me. There are many things you have brought to my life—feelings and emotions I could never experience without you." He bent to brush her mouth with his. "Can you not feel that I speak the truth?"

Savannah closed her eyes as his mouth took possession of hers, as his mind merged firmly with hers. There was such an intimacy in sharing his thoughts and feelings. Gregori was intense in his hunger and need. There were no doubts in him, no hesitation. He knew they would always be together; he would accept nothing else. If something ever changed that, he would choose to follow her into the dawn.

Gregori released her slowly, almost reluctant. She stood very still, looking up at him, her blue eyes studying his face. "We can do this, Savannah," he encouraged her softly. "Do not get frightened and try to run from your fate. Stay with me and fight."

A small smile touched her mouth. "*Fate.* Interesting word to use. You make it sound like I've been sentenced to prison." She took a deep breath and made herself relax. "You're bad, but not quite that bad," she teased him.

His white teeth gleamed, his predator's smile. "I am very bad, *ma petite*. Do not forget that if you wish to be safe."

She shrugged casually, but her heart leapt in response. "Safety is not a concept I strictly adhere to," she answered, her chin up.

"That is a double-edged sword for me."

Savannah burst out laughing, her natural sense of humor bubbling up. "You bet it is. I don't intend to make things easy for you. You've had your way for far too long. Now teach me how to do this. It's fascinating." She waved an arm to encompass the shimmering script.

Gregori caught her arm to hold her still. "To release the pattern to our eyes is very simple. First study the pattern, then simply reverse it. Hand movements spread the molecules in the first place. Disturbing the air in reverse brings the designs back to where they were originally placed."

"Who taught you such a thing?"

"Many arts have been lost through the ages. Buddhist monks in Tibet had this one at one time to communicate without others knowing. We are one with the earth, with the air, with space. To command and move it is not so difficult." His hands began moving again, and Savannah was fascinated with the beauty and grace of his rhythm. "Do you know the ancient language? Read it? Write it? Speak it?" he asked her.

"A few words only. My mother was just trying to learn it from my father when I left for America. I never had a chance to learn."

"One more thing for me to teach you, *chérie*, and we both will enjoy the experience." His silver eyes were eloquent.

"I can speak the healing chant. I think I was born knowing it. My father drilled it into my mother all the time."

Gregori was moving carefully throughout the room. "The chant is as old as time, as old as our race, and very effective. It is imprinted on us before our birth and has saved many lives. Your mother had to learn it quickly, as every voice is needed." His voice was a whisper, as if his very breath might disturb the ancient message shimmering in the air.

Savannah loved the sound of his voice, the black velvet that slid into her mind, into her heart. "What does it say?" Her voice was as soft as his.

"It is from Julian," he said. "He has brought justice to two vampires that had recently taken up residence in this town, so that you would not be in any danger."

"See? There's no danger at all. We can enjoy the festival." She smiled brightly.

"That is not all he had to say." His voice was neutral.

Savannah's smile faded abruptly. "Somehow I knew you were going to say that. It looks like a lot of work for a simple sentence or two. Over by the window there it looks as if he left us a map."

"He has several safe places scattered around the city, even in the bayou, to ensure our safety. Below, in the basement chamber, is a secret place we can escape to if need be. He left a present for us."

She watched his face, her eyes on his. "And?" she prompted softly.

"There are members of the human vampire-hunting society here. Morrison's name has cropped up again. Apparently, Julian stumbled on evidence of the group some time ago. They set up shop here in New Orleans because so many rumors of vampires persist. They believe there must be activity here to warrant their interest. Julian has given me some places to start looking. Names.

Businesses. A local hangout where the members try to get information."

Savannah let her breath out slowly. "Well, so much for the jazz festival. We wanted them to follow us, but instead we walked into the lion's den. I must have a gift for attracting these weirdos."

"You probably do," Gregori said seriously. "It can be an asset as well as a curse. Your mother was a human psychic. Perhaps she passed on something of her gift to you."

Savannah stood in the center of her house, her long lashes concealing her expression. Gregori made his way back to her. She looked small and vulnerable next to his powerful frame. He tucked a stray strand of her blue-black hair behind her ear. "Savannah," he breathed, "do not look so upset. We wanted them to come after us, did we not? This is not the end of the world. We can still enjoy the jazz festival while we are here."

Savannah shook her head. "Let's just go, Gregori. It sounded good at the time, but now I don't like the idea quite so much."

Gregori regarded her set features for a long moment, examining her pale face. The hard edge to his mouth softened. The silver eyes lost their remote coolness, warming to molten mercury. There was a curious shifting in the region of his heart. "You are trying to protect me again, Savannah." He shook his head. There was no smile on his face, but it was in his heart all the same. No one had ever thought to shield him; no one had ever considered the danger he was in as a hunter. Yet now, this small, fragile woman with her enormous eyes was wrapping herself so tightly around his heart because she genuinely wanted his safety. "I do not need protection from these people. They must be dealt with. If it has to be on their ground, so be it.

Julian has provided me with enough information that I am not walking into this thing blind."

"They already suspect us, Gregori, because Wade Carter told them he was bringing a specimen. And they passed that information on to this Morrison person. They'll be looking for us. For you."

"Then we can do no other than oblige them. I will work on an antidote for their poison. I do not want to chance your being injected without first protecting you."

"Our basement is the perfect place for a Boris Karloff-type laboratory." Her quick smile was already lighting up her eyes. She could take his breath away with that smile.

Gregori lifted a hand and made a small movement to disperse the dust particles. A breeze started, slow and easy, but built into a whirlwind that raced through the building. By the time the wind had died down, there was nothing left of the shimmering message Julian had left them, the room was clean, and the peeling wallpaper was smooth once again. "Come with me, Savannah. We will see what else Julian left for us." He held out a hand to her.

She laced her fingers through his and followed him down the spiral stairs. She did not want to imagine why Julian would give up a house he had had for two hundred years. It couldn't be that he was giving up his life. What if his own twin could not talk him out of it? She swallowed hard, remembering how close she had come to losing Gregori. Where was Julian's lifemate? Did she exist? There were so few women for their men.

"I want you to stay right here by the stairs while I study the room." Gregori made it an order. It was wrapped up in his mesmerizing voice, but it was an order all the same.

"If Julian left us a present, Gregori, there's no need to worry that it would be some kind of trap," she pointed out, slightly annoyed.

He lifted his head, the silver eyes slashing at her. "You are altogether too trusting, *bébé*. You should have learned long ago to use your own senses, never to rely on another. That is the way our race has survived."

"We have to trust each other, Gregori," she protested.

"We are often forced to hunt our own brothers. That is why most males choose not to share blood, even to save lives. It makes them easier to track if and when they turn vampire. Also, remember that vampires are known to be the best deceivers in the world. No, *chérie*, we do not trust any other male without a lifemate."

"What a terrible way you have had to live," she said softly.

"Exist," he corrected. "It is not living to be isolated from and shunned by your own race even while they need you desperately. I shared my blood when necessary, but few were willing to exchange with me."

As always, she could detect no self-pity, no emotion whatsoever. Gregori accepted his way of life. He would never trust anyone all the way. Her teeth tugged at her lower lip. Did that include her? Was a part of Gregori always going to be held away from her? She was so young and inexperienced. She wished she was an ancient woman in full power so she could aid him as he deserved.

He glided through the underground chamber, never touching the floor. Gregori examined every inch of the walls. There are two entrances, one leading to a separate chamber hidden in the thickness of the walls, and the other a tunnel constructed with pipe and cement to keep out the water. "The tunnel most likely leads to the outside."

"A bolt hole," she said. "The courtyard?"

He shook his head. "I doubt it, Savannah. Julian would want to head away from the property and people." It seemed inconceivable to him that Julian would want to be in the city to begin with. The Julian Savage he knew was as solitary as he was. He preferred the high places, the mountains. Solitude.

"So is it booby-trapped?" she asked with a hint of sarcasm.

"I almost wish it was," he said, trying to maintain a straight face. "I do not think I will live it down that you are right in this instance." When she raised her eyebrows and waggled them at him, he gave her satisfaction. "No, it is not." He passed a hand over the smooth wall nearest the courtyard.

A hidden door slid open noiselessly to reveal a chamber large enough for two people to lie in. The interior was beautifully carved with ancient inscriptions. Julian Savage was clearly an artist, the etchings soothing and appealing to the eye. Savannah knew little of the language, but she could tell that what had been wrought was a safeguard of some kind, with healing symbols woven in. The entire effect was one of peace and sanctuary.

Gregori was staring at it, his face impassive but his eyes warm. The real surprise lay beneath a white sheet. Gregori lifted a hand, and the sheet rolled aside.

Savannah's breath caught in her throat, and she stared in astonishment at the richness of the treasure. Soil, lush and dark. The soil from their homeland. The chamber was filled with it, a good six or seven feet deep. Gregori plunged his fingers into the earth. The coolness washed over him, welcomed him. Savannah's hands, too, sank deeply into the earth. It had been five long years since she felt the richness of their soil, felt its healing properties. It whispered to them of comfort, of peace.

"How did he do this?" Savannah smiled up at Gregori, pleased her house had such secrets.

His arm circled her shoulders. "Great patience." A faint smile softened his mouth. "Remember the caskets sent over from Europe when New Orleans was wracked with yellow fever and death? It was rumored for years that they contained vampires, but many obviously contained simply soil from our homeland. Clever of Julian to manage it."

"I wonder how often he stayed here," Savannah ventured softly, letting the soil slide through her fingers. What she really wondered was how much of New Orleans history Julian Savage had been involved in. Humans had long believed that the legendary vampires of their imaginings were rampant in New Orleans. Had Julian's activities over the past two centuries fueled those rumors? "Do you think that human society headquartered themselves here to hunt him?" she asked.

"That society is becoming a pain in the neck. I need to get word to Mikhail that we did not stamp them out as we thought we had. They seem to be back and stronger than ever. Every thirty years or so they crop up to give us problems."

"Julian must have only discovered them quite recently or he would have told you about them when he was reporting in to you about me." There was a bite to her voice. She was still annoyed that Gregori had had someone watching her. Even more than that, she was annoyed with herself for not sensing another of her kind.

"Julian never exactly reported in to me," Gregori said dryly. "He is not the kind of man to answer to anyone. Julian is like the wind, the wolves. Totally free. He goes his own way. He watched over you, but he did not send me reports. That is not his way."

"He sounds interesting," Savannah murmured.

Instantly Gregori could feel his muscles tighten. That black, nameless rage that made him so dangerous boiled in his gut. He would always live with the fear that he had stolen Savannah from another. That some other Carpathian male held the secret to her heart. That he had condemned another to death or, worse, to becoming the undead, because he had stolen Savannah. Since Gregori had manipulated the outcome of their joining, perhaps there was some other whose chemistry matched hers perfectly. His silver eyes were cold and lethal, small red flames leaping in their depths. "You do not need to find Savage interesting. I would never give you up, Savannah."

"Don't be an idiot, Gregori," she said impatiently. "As if I'd even want some other beast just out of the cave when I've almost got you trained." She held out a hand. "Come on, you have to see the courtyard."

His larger hand swallowed hers. She always seemed to know what to say or do to ease the terrible weight crushing his chest. Though he often wanted to shake her, to kiss her into submission, he also wanted her to be as sassy as she was right at that moment. She was turning his world upside down.

He followed her upstairs, helpless to do anything else. Thick double doors opened onto the courtyard. Savannah was right. It was impressive. The garden was bigger than the house itself. Plants grew everywhere, a wild collage of green lace and bright blooms. Spanish tile covered the ground in a patchwork patio. Benches and chairs were scattered among the plants and trees, shaded from the sun. Long lounges were arranged in the open, beneath the stars and moon.

Bats dipped and wheeled, feasting on insects in the air. Fragrance from the flowers muted the oppressive pollution from the narrow streets, but nothing could drown out the noise. Music from all directions clashed with the clatter of horse hooves on cobblestones, car horns blaring, and voices raised in laughter, in merriment.

Gregori sorted out the sounds, listened to snippets of conversation, and got a feel for the rhythm of the neighborhood. It would take a few days for him to become comfortable in this environment. He would have liked a chance to explore it on his own beforehand to ensure Savannah's safety. "We need to take a walk," he said abruptly. "I want to see all the entrances and exits, get to know the faces and voices that belong here."

Savannah pushed open the iron gate and stepped out onto the street. A young couple standing on the porch next door stared at them curiously. Savannah sent them a smile and waved happily. The woman raised an arm in answer.

Do not act so friendly, Savannah. You are a celebrity. We will have enough attention drawn to us.

They are our neighbors. Try not to scare them to death, will you? Savannah took his arm, grinning up at him teasingly. "You look as fierce as a member of the Mafia. No wonder our neighbors are staring. People tend to be curious. Wouldn't you be if someone moved in next door to you?"

"I don't abide next-door neighbors. When humans consider building in the vicinity of one of my homes, the neighborhood is suddenly inundated with wolves. It works every time." He sounded menacing.

Savannah laughed at him. "You're such a baby, Gregori. Scared of a little company."

"*You* scare me to death, woman. Because of you I find myself doing things I know are totally insane. Staying in a house built in a crowded city below sea level. Neighbors on top of us. Human butchers surrounding us."

"Like I'm supposed to believe that would scare you," she said smugly, knowing his only worry was for her safety, not his. They turned a corner and headed toward the famous Bourbon Street.

"Try to look less conspicuous," he instructed.

A dog barked, rushed to the end of its lead, and bared its teeth. Gregori turned his head and hissed, exposing white fangs. The dog stopped its aggression instantly, yelped in alarm, and retreated whining.

"What are you doing?" Savannah demanded, outraged.

"Getting a feel for the place," he said absently, his mind clearly on other matters, his senses tuned to the world around him. "Everyone is crazy here, Savannah. You are going to fit right in." He ruffled her hair affectionately.

She stopped abruptly, her smile fading, her hand slipping from his arm. Gregori's head went up alertly, automatically scanning the area for enemies. "What is it?"

Savannah did an about-face and turned the corner, walking slowly up the street. *Savannah, you will answer me. What is it you sense that I do not?* Gregori caught at her arm, physically stopping her. His fingers shackled her wrist, his body all at once close and protective. *Answer me, or I will force you to go back to the house.*

Shh. I'm trying to concentrate. I've never really done this before. Even in her mind she was very distracted.

Gregori merged with her so that he could feel her thoughts, know whatever it was that she was feeling. It was a compulsion of sorts, not one their race commonly used, a drawing toward some place. Of power? He tried to tune it in. Not power. To evil. Something very evil.

Once more his hand tightened on her wrist and brought her to a halt. There were several homes on the street, but farther down the block the residences gave way to stores. One was a voodoo shop. He concentrated on that, listening intently to the conversation between a tourist and one who worked inside. There was a suggestion of power, of magic, but certainly not the taint of evil.

Two buildings down from the voodoo shop. Savannah's voice brushed at his mind.

It is not on Julian's list, Gregori answered, but he believed her. He felt it through her. Raven Dubrinsky had obviously passed on her psychic talents to her daughter.

They linked hands and strolled casually along the street, seemingly enjoying the night air, mingling with the tourists and those who made their homes there. The majority of the revelers were in the heart of the Quarter, along Bourbon Street, farther down, lining up to get into Preservation Hall. Savannah and Gregori moved along the narrow walkway, pausing to allow a horse-drawn carriage to pass. The occupants of the conveyance were laughing and listening to the sing-song voice of their guide describing points of interest with a few local myths thrown in.

Two young men drinking beer on the steps of a closed

bookstore across the street fixed their eyes on Savannah. Even from that distance Gregori could see their instant fixation, the obsession she so easily produced in men. It was in the way she moved, her flowing hair and enormous eyes, her aura, at once innocent and sexy. There was no hope that they would not recognize her. She embodied magic and fantasy.

Gregori sighed heavily, his gut tightening. She was going to drive him crazy and maybe get some innocent drunk killed. The two men had risen, whispering excitedly, working up their courage to approach her. He could hear them pumping each other up. He fixed his silver eyes on them and concentrated briefly. He wiped their thoughts away and planted in them an urgency to leave the area immediately.

"Do me a favor, *chérie*. Try to look plain and uninteresting."

Savannah laughed softly in spite of her growing sense of dread. "Get over it already," she suggested.

"You are more than disrespectful, woman. I cannot remember a single time in my existence when anyone spoke to me as you do."

She rubbed her cheek along his shoulder in a small caress. Gregori's breath seemed to still in his throat. "That's why I do it. You need someone to give you a little trouble." Her teasing tone slid over him, into him, the tiny threads that tied them together multiplying every moment.

"I would not mind a *little* trouble. You are *big* trouble."

They were in front of the building Savannah had mentally pinpointed as the source of the disturbing emanations. It was closed, the windows dark. Gregori could feel movement inside, sense the presence of several men within the walls.

Savannah clutched at him, her eyes filling with tears. "Something horrible is happening in there, Gregori. There is—" She broke off as his hands closed like a vise around her upper arms.

Gregori gave her a little shake. "Hang on, *ma petite*. I know exactly what is going on. She is not one of us."

"I know that. I'm not entirely incompetent." There was a mixture of anger and tears in her voice. "She's human, but they think she's vampire. Gregori, she's just a child. You can't let them harm her. I can feel her pain."

"She is older than you, *bébé*, and she parades around in a black cloak with her incisors cosmetically altered. She put herself in the hands of these madmen through her own stupidity." Gregori sounded disgusted.

"She doesn't deserve to be tortured because she likes to play at being a vampire. Let's get her out." Savannah's blue eyes flashed fire at him. "We both know you're going to save her, so quit grousing, and let's get to it."

"I will not allow such a thing, Savannah," he said softly. His voice was a beautiful blend of iron in a velvet glove. "Do not try my patience too far, *ma petite*. I assure you, there is no chance of your winning a battle between us."

"Shut up," she snapped rudely, exasperated with his domineering ways. "I know you're not going to leave the girl in there. I can feel her terror, Gregori, and it's making me sick."

"I knew you were going to be trouble the moment I laid eyes on you," he said softly. "I will not risk your safety for some woman who masquerades as a vampire. She chooses to pretend she is like them. I intend to help her, but not with you alone on the street."

Her breath hissed through her teeth. "I am at full strength, Gregori. I can be invisible should I choose to walk among the humans unseen. I don't need to cower in my house because you're afraid for me." Her chin lifted at him belligerently. "I am the daughter of the Prince. I can manage to do a few things others of our kind can do."

His hand caught and spanned her throat. "I will do almost anything for you, Savannah, but how I must complete this task is distasteful." He found himself explaining, as she had requested, when his every aggressive male instinct told him to simply force his will on her. He could not bear for her to believe he thought so little of her abilities. "I do not want you to witness the depravity in these men's minds, nor do I wish you to witness the wind of death whirling through their midst. You cannot have it both ways. You want me to save this woman. I will do so. But not within your sight. Go home and wait for me there."

Savannah shook her head. "When will you get it through your thick skull that I'm your true lifemate? Me. Savannah Dubrinsky, daughter of the Prince. We shared our minds from before my birth. You can't hide from me what you are, who you are. Even in the midst of blood and death, even with the beast at work, I will always see your true self."

"Do as I command you. And know this. If for any reason you choose to disobey my orders, you will be putting the woman's life in jeopardy. I will always see to your safety first. That means if I am distracted by your defiance, I will see to your obedience."

"You are the most stubborn Carpathian male alive," she said, exasperated, but she caught his head between her hands and dragged him down to capture his mouth with hers. "Be safe, lifemate. That is *my* command to you. Be certain *you* do not disobey *my* order."

She turned and glided away, back the way they had come, without so much as a glance over her shoulder. Her hips swayed gently, erotically. The rising wind played with her long hair. Gregori watched her, unable to tear his gaze away.

Chapter Eleven

Finally Gregori turned his head slowly, ferally, and walked purposefully toward the narrow alley beside the building. Brown grass, dried and exhausted with its effort to flourish, was crushed beneath his feet, but there was not a sound to betray his presence, not even the disbursement of air. Once he was hidden from sight, he scanned the area to determine the exact placement of all those in the building and any other humans in the vicinity.

He dissolved instantly, one moment solid, the next invisible. He checked the building: all windows and doors were locked securely. The woman inside screamed, agony, terror, in her voice. The sound brushed at his mind, but he blocked it out, scanning three entry points to the interior. He chose the one beneath the building, through some cracked and crumbling rotted boards.

For a brief moment his image shimmered in the dark, compressing as it did so, shrinking smaller and smaller until a only little mouse nestled in the dried grass. It sat up on its hind legs a moment, whiskers twitching in the air. Then it rushed across the dirt and grass and scampered through a small crack beneath the stairs. The opening was narrow, but the little creature was able to squeeze into a space within the walls.

The insulation was old and thin, most of it long gone, and the mouse scurried quickly through the wall until it found a small knothole leading into a darkened room. The smell of blood and fear made its heart pound, but the predator deep within its tiny body snarled, exposing fangs and a dark, deadly purpose. The mouse hesitated before crossing the yellowed linoleum, its ears twisting this way and that, whiskers high, scenting for danger.

There was no one in the first room, which appeared to be an unused storage area. It smelled musty with mildew. Gregori's form grew, solidified, then shimmered into nothingness once again. He could hear the conversation from the next room clearly. Three men were arguing, one clearly disgusted by what they were doing.

"This girl is no more vampire than I am, Rodney," he snapped. "You just like doing this sick stuff. This one's some kid who likes to hang out with her friends pretending she's got fangs."

"We don't know that for sure," Rodney protested. "And since we have to kill her anyway, it isn't like we can't have a good time with her."

"Forget it." There was disgust in the first man's voice. "No way am I going to let you kill this girl. I thought we were scientists. Even if she really was a vampire, we shouldn't treat her like this. I'm taking her out of here and to a hospital."

"Morrison will kill you," Rodney bit out, all at once angry. "You're not taking her anywhere. We'll all be arrested. You, too—don't forget that. You're a part of this, Gary, you're a big part of this."

"No, I'm not. And if it comes down to that—killing an innocent girl or going to jail—I'll take jail."

Gregori could feel the impending violence, coming not from Rodney but from the third man, the silent one, in the room. He was stalking Gary from behind while Rodney held Gary's attention. The girl was trying desperately to warn Gary, her only hope, that he was in danger.

Gregori felt power in the room. Manipulation. Compulsion. There was more at work here than the society of human butchers. He glided unseen into the room, dispersing cold air in his wake. The third man held an already blood-stained knife out of sight along his right wrist as he came up behind Gary. Gregori inserted his invisible body between the two men. As the knife came up toward Gary's kidney, Gregori caught the attacker's wrist in an unbreakable grip and squeezed, crushing bones to a fine powder.

The attacker screamed, the knife clattering to the floor. Gary whirled around to face the third man. Rodney dove for the knife. The girl was so hysterical, Gregori could feel her heart pounding, hear it slamming at far too fast a pace. He spared her quick attention, shielding her from further thought. She simply slipped into an unconscious state, her eyes open and glazed.

Rodney picked up the knife and scrambled to his feet. "Looks like we're going to have to kill you, too, huh, Gary?"

Gregori sighed. Why did they always have to state the obvious?

Gary was backing away, trying to keep an eye on the third man, who had dropped to his knees, clutching his shattered arm, his face as white as a sheet. He was still screaming, a high-pitched, monotonous cry.

Gary slid the white lab jacket off his shoulders and wrapped it defensively around his upraised arm. "I'm not going to let you hurt her any more, Rodney. I mean it. This was supposed to be a legitimate study. Dissecting anyone alive, vampire or human, is torture, nothing less. I didn't sign on to hurt anyone."

"What do you think that poison you developed was all about?" Rodney snarled, waving the knife.

"I didn't develop a poison. I developed a very potent tranquilizer, designed to sedate nearly any powerful creature. Morrison had you people corrupt the original formula. I came here to talk to him about it. This is murder, Rodney. Any way you look at it, it's murder."

Gregori glided up behind Rodney. The man's mind stank of a vampire influence. He had thought himself protected from vampires by the hypnosis all members of the society were subjected to, but somehow a vampire had infiltrated their ranks and was contaminating the society further with his own depravity. It was the kind of thing vampires over the centuries had done for entertainment. Hiding their true nature, they would befriend humans and slowly bring about moral decay. Often they used the women of the human males they befriended for their own pleasure, later killing them. Sometimes they used the humans to kill each other. Clearly a master vampire was at work here, one that had escaped the net of hunters for some time, probably centuries.

Gregori touched Gary's mind. He found honesty there, integrity. He had never had contact with the vampire and was willing to die to save the girl strapped down on the stainless-steel table. He had interrupted the two other men at work and was sickened by their actions. But Gregori knew Gary would have no chance against a vampire-induced compulsion in the other man to kill. Rodney would win this battle. For a moment Gregori hesitated. If he intervened, he would allow Gary to live, but he would have to destroy Rodney. If he allowed things to take their course, Rodney could lead him back to the vampire's lair.

I know you're not even thinking that. Savannah's outraged whisper was velvet-soft in his mind.

He sighed heavily. *Woman, leave me in peace. I have to do what is best for our people.* But he knew he wouldn't. He knew he could not let Gary die. There was something he liked about the man's courage and integrity, but, damn it, Savannah didn't have to know he had any soft spots. He'd never had them until she came along.

Savannah's laughter brushed along his spine like the touch of her fingers.

Gregori inserted his solid frame between the two men, shimmering in the air, wavering for a moment before materializing. There was instant silence. Even the third man managed to stop screaming, all of them frozen in place. Gregori smiled pleasantly, a show of gleaming white fangs.

"Good evening, gentleman. I heard you were looking for one of my kind. It might be in your best interest, Rodney, to put down the knife." The suggestion was made in a black-velvet drawl.

Gary backed away from the newcomer, instinctively moving toward the stainless steel table. His hands were up in the age-old surrender sign. "Look, I don't know who or what you are, but this girl had nothing to do with anything. Don't hurt her. Do what you have to do to us, but get her an ambulance."

Gregori kept his silver gaze focused on Rodney. The man was looking wild, the dark compulsion of the kill on him. Gregori could see so clearly; now so could Gary. Rodney needed to kill. It was as necessary to him as drawing in his next breath.

"Look out," Gary warned as it occurred to him that the vampire, no matter how dangerous, had stepped between Rodney and himself to save him. He glanced over at the third man. It was clear that the vampire had saved him from Todd Davis also. Steeling himself, he moved around to get in a better position to help the creature.

"Do not," Gregori hissed softly. He waved a hand, and Gary was unable to move, locked into some invisible prison. "Turn your head the other way."

The flash in the room was bright, like a mushroom cloud of lightning. The sound cracked the walls on two sides of the structure, thundering in Gary's ears so that for a moment he was deaf and blind. The house itself shook, rattling the windows like an explosion. When the smoke cleared, Rodney and Davis lay on the floor, lifeless.

Gary stared in horror at the two blackened bodies, then reached out a tentative hand to touch the invisible barricade that had somehow protected him. To his astonishment it was gone. Immediately he went to the girl. She was still breathing, but her pulse was shallow and thready. He tried in vain to undo the manacles locking her to the table.

"You are leaving fingerprints," Gregori informed him softly. He stared at the wide steel bands for a moment, and they simply fell away from her wrists and ankles. "Go now, walk away from this place. I will meet you at the end of the block." The silver eyes stared straight into Gary's eyes. "Be there. I can find you any time I wish it."

"She needs help." The human was determined to stand his ground.

"A crowd gathers while you waste time. I can shield you from their eyes if you go now. Later, there will be too many. The girl will be fine. Do as I say." Already Gregori was turning his attention to finding the damaging prints of the other man, removing all memory of him from the girl, and ensuring that those outside the house would not remember the short, slender man in the gray suit who went out the back way.

Gary Jansen made his way slowly through the people now rushing toward the house. No one even glanced at him, actually knocking into him without seeming to be aware of it. In the distance was the wail of sirens. Fire department. Police. Ambulance. He was shocked, his mind almost numb. Whatever creature had stepped in and saved his life had more power than he had ever conceived a being could have. His brain replayed every movement, every word. He couldn't believe he had been allowed to simply walk away. The creature hadn't even taken his blood. For that matter, he didn't know if the creature drank blood. He got to the end of the block, and weakness hit him. His knees turned to rubber, his legs to jelly, and he had to sit abruptly on the curb.

A hand wrapped around the nape of his neck and held his head down. "Just breathe." It was an order delivered in that same mesmerizing voice from the storehouse.

Gary took in great gulps of air, fighting off the dizziness. He made a poor attempt at humor. "I'm sorry, but it's not every day I meet someone like you." When the hand slowly retreated from his neck, he straightened up to look at the tall, powerful figure looming over him. He had never seen a more dangerous-looking individual. He swallowed his fear. "Are you going to kill me?" The words slipped out unintentionally.

Stop looking like the big, bad wolf, Savannah suggested. *You're going to give the poor man a heart attack.*

Gregori sighed, exasperated. "If I was going to kill you, you would already be dead. What reason would I have for taking your life?"

Gary shrugged. "None, I hope." He stood up carefully and let his breath out slowly. Up close the man looked even more dangerous. Like a hungry jungle cat.

"I have already fed this night," Gregori said dryly.

"You're reading my thoughts, aren't you?" Gary tried to keep the excitement out of his voice. He had always wanted to meet the real thing. Always. From the first vampire movie he had ever seen, he had been fascinated, hooked. He was scared, no question about that, but this was the chance of a lifetime. "I've seen you. Does that mean you have to kill me? You let the girl go because she never saw you."

Gregori nodded toward the street, and they both began walking, slowly putting the chaotic scene behind them. "No one would believe you if you told them. In any case, I could easily remove your memory of our meeting. The girl will not remember you."

"I can hardly believe this myself. You're right, you know. If I told you my own parents, they'd have me locked up. This is awesome, completely awesome." He spun around in a circle, his fists clenched in victory. "Man, this is great."

Bring him home, Gregori, Savannah suggested.

Not a chance, Savannah. This one is crazy, too. I do not need the two of you driving me nuts. Why would anyone with a half a brain want to meet one of us?

"I joined the society to see if they had any real evidence of the existence of"—Gary hesitated—"vampires. You are a vampire, right?"

"You might think so," Gregori said noncommittally.

"They said they had this vampire blood, you know. At first I thought it might be a hoax, but it was unusual, real interesting stuff. I'd never seen anything like it. I'm a biochemist, and this was such an opportunity. The blood made a believer out of me." His words were tumbling over one another in an effort to get out. "Everyone thought I was crazy, even the members of the society, but I thought it might be really cool to establish contact with a real vampire. Unfortunately, they just wanted to capture them and slice them up."

Gregori shook his head over the naiveté of human beings. "Did it occur to you that a vampire might be a very dangerous creature? That maybe to lure one out into the open would cause your own death? Perhaps even the death of your family? Everyone you loved or cared about?"

"Why? Why would a vampire necessarily do that?" Gary challenged. He was clearly a man who thought the best of everyone.

Do you see why I avoid humans, ma chérie? *They are silly, exasperating creatures.*

You like him. You can't hide it from me, even if you try to hide it from yourself. Invite him home.

Not for all the trees on this earth.

I want to meet him.

Savannah. She was up to no good, he was certain of it. Gregori's hand went to the back of his neck, massaging deeply. *What I should do is scare the holy hell out of him so he will get over this nonsense.*

"So, are you?" Gary asked.

"Am I what?" Gregori was distracted. Why had he ever talked to this fool in the first place? Because Savannah was making him crazy. Savannah had made him do something dumb. He had read Gary's mind and found him to be an interesting, likable person.

Don't blame me. She sounded innocent.

"Are you a cold-blooded killer? Would you kill my family and friends?" Gary persisted.

"Yes to the first question," Gregori answered honestly. "And a true vampire is a great deceiver. Surely you have read the legends that vampires often lure humans into their power? A true vampire would destroy you and all you love. That is his sole enjoyment. Do not ever wish an encounter with a vampire upon yourself. As to killing you and your family, were you to threaten mine, I would not hesitate."

Gary stopped walking and stared up at the man beside him. Gregori moved through time and space soundlessly. His unusual silver eyes were mesmerizing, as was his beautiful voice. He moved like a predator, his eyes unblinking and restless. Everything about him screamed danger, yet Gary was strangely drawn to him. He could have listened forever to the sound of that voice. "You aren't kidding me, are you? But are you saying you aren't a vampire?"

"I am a hunter of the undead, a destroyer. There is, however, a true vampire among the members of the society you are in league with. He will destroy them all." The voice was soft and dispassionate, without expression.

Gary pushed a hand through his hair. "You're telling me all this because you're planning to take away my memory of you, aren't you?"

The silver eyes settled on Gary's face with regret. "I

can do no other. I should not have revealed myself to you, but you had great courage, and your one wish that I could grant to you was to allow you to meet something of what you sought."

You're so sweet, Gregori, Savannah purred, her voice strong in his mind.

I am not sweet, he objected strenuously.

"I don't know what I did to deserve this," Gary said, "but I'm really grateful."

"You tried to save both the girl and me. I did not believe one of your kind, from your 'society,' would ever attempt to come to the aid of one of one of my kind." Gregori was truthful because he felt the human warranted it.

"You can trust me, you know. I'm not about to give away your secret. Aren't there any humans who know the truth?"

"They are in constant danger. I would not wish that for you."

You are the sweetest man, Savannah inserted softly, her voice brushing at him. Echoing.

Gregori frowned. *Echoing?* Close. He swung around, cursing in French, an eloquent dissertation that had Gary cringing. Savannah, however, simply took Gregori's arm and smiled up at him, the stars in her eyes dancing. She was like that. Distracting him and then slamming him sideways with her smile. With her blue-violet eyes with their accursed star centers. She didn't even have the decency to look repentant.

Don't be angry, Gregori. I was lonesome in the house all by myself. Are you really, really angry? Or just a little angry? Her voice was soft, a siren's whisper, made of silk sheets and candlelight. Her long lashes were thick and heavy, a sweep of magic that caught his eye and held it there.

It is impossible for you to be lonely when you are always running around in my head.

"You're Savannah Dubrinsky." Gary breathed her name reverently. "My God, I should have guessed."

Gregori's entire demeanor changed, becoming all at once menacing and dangerous. His face was etched in stone, his mouth hard and faintly cruel. The hair on the back of Gary's neck literally stood up. He swallowed hard and instinctively moved a little distance from the woman. Not that he blamed the man, creature, whatever, but his reaction was more that of untamed beast than civilized man. Gary was taking no chances.

Savannah laughed softly. She leaned into the man despite Gregori's restraining arm. "He can read your mind," she reminded Gary softly, her breath swirling with tantalizing warmth over his neck.

He jumped away as if he'd been burned, his face flamed crimson, and he looked guiltily at Gregori.

Gregori's dark features relaxed. The hard edge to his mouth softened. "Do not worry, Gary, she is incorrigible. Even I have trouble with her. I cannot blame you for what I myself cannot control." His arm swept around Savannah's small waist, and he tucked her beneath his shoulder.

Are you angry? The smile was fading from her eyes, her mouth.

Gregori tightened his hold on her when her step faltered. *We can discuss this at home,* chérie. *You are already here; you may as well give the boy a thrill. But I warn you, not too big a thrill.*

She relaxed her body into his. That quickly. That easily. As if she belonged, his other half. He was beginning to believe it might be possible.

Her smile sent a bolt of lightning right through Gary. "Would you like to go to the Café du Monde?" she asked. "It's still open. We can sit there and talk for a while."

Gary glanced at Gregori's impassive face. Who could deny her anything? She was like something mysterious and magical from another world. Gregori looked as merciless and ruthless as ever, his dark, dangerous features granite, his silver eyes cold and glittering with menace. But his posture was protective, the arm circling her waist, tender. Gary turned his face away to hide a smile. Vampires seemed to have women problems, too.

"Would you like to join us at the Café du Monde?" Gregori asked him quietly, already changing direction. They turned down Saint Ann Street toward Decatur and Jackson Square.

As they passed the famous St. Louis Cathedral, Gary cleared his throat. "I always wanted to know, is it true the vampire can't go onto sacred ground? Will a cross help to protect a person, or is that hogwash?"

"The vampire cannot go onto sacred ground. His soul is lost for all time. It is his choice; he made the decision to become vampire," Gregori answered softly. "Do not make the mistake of feeling sorry for the vampire. He is truly evil."

"You're blowing all my theories," Gary said sadly.

"What are your theories?" Savannah asked, her blue eyes steady on his face. It made him feel as if he were the only man in the world, as if whatever he said was terribly important to her.

Gregori stirred restlessly. The cold, merciless eyes swept over Gary, leaving a bad taste in the human's mouth. He wanted to tell the creature he couldn't help himself, that Savannah was just too sexy. But he had the distinct feeling the admission wouldn't win him any favors. Instead, Gary kept his gaze steadfastly away from her haunting beauty and his thoughts centered on his excitement of being with such mythical creatures of the night. His lifelong dream.

"You were going to tell us of your theories," Gregori prompted gently.

They crossed the street with a crowd of wandering tourists. Gregori was all too aware of most of them staring at his lifemate. Heads turned as she stood on the edge of the café's patio, where tables were set close together. One of the waiters waved them toward an empty table, then recognized Savannah, gawking for a brief moment, then hurrying to take their order.

Gregori sat with his back to a thick post, partially hidden in the shadows, his eyes restless, all senses on alert. He couldn't afford to let his guard down. Somewhere in this city was a powerful vampire with a legion of human puppets to do his bidding.

Savannah signed several autographs, chatting briefly with each person who came to their table. Gregori's hand was on the nape of her neck, his fingers moving soothingly, tenderly, against her bare skin. He found himself very proud of her. But by the time their coffee and beignets arrived, even Gary wanted to be rid of the fans pressing close.

Gregori summoned the waiter and leaned close, his voice hypnotic. "Savannah has been happy to provide autographs for your patrons, but she needs to have time for herself to enjoy your superb coffee right now." The suggestion was a clear order, the silver eyes capturing the waiter and giving him no chance to do anything but agree.

Savannah smiled her thanks as the waiters provided her with loose protection from the tourists pressing around them.

"Is it like this everywhere you go?" Gary asked.

"Pretty much." Savannah shrugged calmly. "I don't really mind. Peter always—" She broke off abruptly and brought the steaming cup to her mouth.

Gregori could feel sorrow beating at her, a crushing stone weighing down her heart. His hand slipped down her arm to lace his fingers through hers. At once he poured warmth and comfort into her mind, the sensation of his arms around her body, holding her close. "Peter Sanders always took care of the details surrounding Savannah's shows. He was very good at shielding her. He was murdered after her last show out in San Francisco." He provided the information quietly to Gary.

"I'm sorry," Gary said instantly, meaning it. Her distress was evident in her large blue eyes. They shimmered with sorrow.

Gregori brought Savannah's hand to the warmth of his mouth, his breath heating the pulse beating in her wrist. *The night is especially beautiful*, mon petit amour. *Your hero saved the girl, walks among the humans, and converses with a fool. That alone should bring a smile to your face. Do not weep for what we cannot change. We will make certain that this human with us comes to no harm.*

Are you my hero, then? There were tears in her voice, in her mind, like an iridescent prism. She needed him, his comfort, his support under her terrible weight of guilt and love and loss.

Always, for all eternity, he answered instantly, without hesitation, his eyes hot mercury. He tipped her chin up so that she met the brilliance of his silver gaze. *Always,* mon amour. His molten gaze trapped her blue one and held her enthralled. *Your heart grows lighter. The burden of your sorrow becomes my own.* He held her gaze captive for a few moments to ensure that she was free of the heaviness crushing her.

Savannah blinked and moved a little away from him, wondering what she had been thinking of. What had they been talking about?

"Gary." Gregori drawled the name slowly and sat back in his chair, totally relaxed. He looked like a sprawling tiger, dangerous and untamed. "Tell us about yourself."

"I work a lot. I'm not married. I'm really not much of a people person. I'm basically a nerd."

Gregori shifted, a subtle movement of muscles suggesting great power. "I am not familiar with this term."

"Yeah, well, you wouldn't be," Gary said. "It means I have lots of brains and no brawn. I don't do the athlete thing. I'm into computers and chess and things requiring intellect. Women find me skinny, wimpy, and boring. Not something they would you." There was no bitterness in his voice, just a quiet acceptance of himself, his life.

Gregori's white teeth flashed. "There is only one woman who matters to me, Gary, and she finds me difficult to live with. I cannot imagine why, can you?"

"Maybe because you're jealous, possessive, concerned with every single detail of her life?" Gary plainly took the question literally, offering up his observations without judgment. "You're probably domineering, too. I can see that. Yeah. It might be tough."

Savannah burst out laughing, the sound musical, rivaling the street musicians. People within hearing turned their heads and held their breath, hoping for more. "Very astute, Gary. Very, very astute. I bet you have an enormous IQ."

Gregori stirred again, the movement a ripple of power, of danger. He was suddenly leaning into Gary. "You think you are intelligent? Baiting the wild animal is not too smart."

Gary's laughter joined with Savannah's. "You *are* reading my mind! I knew it. I knew you weren't kidding me. That is so cool. How do you do that? Can humans, do you suppose?" For a moment he had been intimidated, but the laughter in Savannah's eyes eased his tension.

Savannah and Gregori exchanged a smile. It was Gregori who answered. "I know for certain there are a few humans who possess such a talent."

"I wish I had it. What else can you do?"

"I thought we were discussing you," Gregori said softly, somehow unwilling to leave the human with his own unflattering perception of himself. "I have never met a human male with more courage and insight than you displayed tonight, and I have lived a long time. Do not sell yourself so short. Perhaps you bury yourself in your work to avoid the pain of a failed relationship."

Savannah's long lashes swept her cheeks as she hid her expression. This from a man who perceived himself a monster. Who claimed not to feel for anyone or anything.

Gary took a sip of the celebrated coffee and a quick bite of the beignets the Café du Monde was so famous for. He found them delicious. He noticed that the couple across the table from him appeared to be eating, but he wasn't certain they really were. What were they? Why did he feel so comfortable with them? He liked their company. He felt invigorated by it. Soothed by it. Interesting observation, when the man was rather like a dangerous, cornered animal, lethal at any provocation. He had witnessed the power the man possessed.

What if what the man said was true? What if vampires were great deceivers? What if the man sitting so casually across from him was deceiving him? Gary studied the impassive face. It was impossible to tell his age. His was a harsh beauty, with a hint of cruelty, yet he was incredibly handsome. He passed a hand over his face. How did one know?

"That is the problem with the vampire, Gary," Gregori counseled softly. "There is no way a human can tell the difference between what is the hunter and what is the vampire."

Gary noticed he used the word *what* not *who*. What was he?

"To enter our world is very dangerous," Savannah added gently. She went to lay a hand on Gary's arm in her naturally sympathetic way, but a low, fierce growl issuing from Gregori's throat stopped her. She put her hand in her lap.

Gregori ran a fingertip along her knuckles in a kind of apology for his failure to overcome his possessive ways.

Gary took a deep breath. "Maybe that is true, but maybe I'm already compromised. I wasn't supposed to be at the warehouse this evening, but I showed up. My formula didn't look right to me, so I performed a little investigation. I ran a chemical composition test. I was so angry, I went to one of the few society addresses I had. When I found that poor girl there, I went berserk and called the boss—Morrison—at his private number. He wasn't available, but I left word I was going to shut down the society, expose it to the newspapers, to the police. I don't think Rodney was as interested in killing you as he was in killing me. I got the feeling someone ordered him to kill me."

"He was under a vampire's compulsion. Nothing would have stopped him," Gregori admitted.

"So I'm already a target, aren't I?" Gary pointed out triumphantly.

Gregori sighed again. "Try not to sound so happy about it. There are limits to our protection. And you endanger Savannah." *For that alone I could rip out your heart.* The words seemed to shimmer in the air, unspoken but heard.

Gary looked startled. "I'm sorry. I didn't think of that. I guess she would be a target if she's seen with me." He was obviously upset. "I feel terrible that I didn't even consider it."

"Keep your voice down," Gregori reminded him softly. "We need to know more of those involved in this society than we do. Do you have a list of names?"

"Yeah, of the ones who worked in the lab. The legitimate lab, I mean. Not the sick ones you saw tonight." Gary pushed a hand through his hair in agitation. "I want to call the hospital, make certain that girl's all right. You know, I still can't believe they were going to cut her up alive."

"I told you," Gregori reiterated, "the vampire's only source of entertainment is the misery of those around him. He will deliberately corrupt those he believes are the least likely to succumb to his powers. It is a game to him. You are a good man, Gary, but you are no match for a vampire. He could make you kill your own mother.

Anything abhorrent to you, that is what he would force you to do."

"I don't want you to erase my memories," Gary pleaded. "I've waited my whole life for this moment. I know you say I can't tell the difference between a vampire and a hunter, but I think you're wrong. For instance, you scare the hell out of me. You look dangerous, you act dangerous. You don't even try to hide it. You are a very scary man, but you feel like a friend. I would trust you with my life. I'm betting that something evil would appear pleasing but feel foul."

Gregori's glittering silver eyes settled on his face, a glimmer of warmth in them, a hint of humor. "You are already trusting me with your life."

Savannah leaned into Gregori. "I'm so proud of you. You're getting this humor thing down." She looked across the table at Gary, laughter dancing in her enormous blue eyes. "He has a little trouble with the concept of humor."

Gary found himself laughing with her. "I can believe that."

"Watch it, kid. There is no need to be disrespectful. Do not make the mistake of believing you can get away with it the way this one does." Gregori tugged at Savannah's long ebony hair. It hung to her waist, a fall of blue-black silk that moved with a life of its own, that tempted, invited men to touch it.

"So, what are you going to do about me?" Gary ventured painfully.

Savannah resisted the urge to touch him sympathetically. She was naturally demonstrative, naturally affectionate. When someone was upset, she needed to make things better. Gregori inhibited her normal tendency to comfort.

I cannot change what I am, ma petite, he whispered softly in her mind, a slow, soothing black-velvet drawl. His voice wrapped her up and touched her with tenderness. *I can only promise to keep you safe and to try to make you as happy as I can to make up for my deficiencies.*

I didn't say you had deficiencies, she returned softly, her voice a caress, fingers trailing over the back of his neck, down the muscles of his back.

Need slammed into him, low and wicked. His skin crawled with fire. His silver eyes slid slowly, possessively over her, touching her body with tongues of flame. Touching. Caressing. His urgent need exploded in him like a volcano. In his head a dull roar began. Abruptly he wished Gary gone. The café gone. The world gone. He wasn't altogether certain he could wait until he was home with her. The riverbank was suddenly looking very inviting.

Chapter Twelve

Gary raised his hand for the check. There was a deep regret in his eyes. He was going back to his normal life. It wasn't that it was such a bad life, but he felt connected with these people. He had been isolated all his life. Always out of sync with others. The one who always marched to the different drummer. "So, I'm ready. Go ahead. Just promise me you'll visit once in a while."

Gregori's hand, moving on Savannah's neck, suddenly stilled. He inhaled sharply. *Savannah?*

I feel it, too.

Gregori leaned across the table to stare into Gary's eyes. *You will do as Savannah tells you without question, without thought. Instant obedience.* "Gary, I want you to go with Savannah now. We are hunted. She will shield the two of you from all eyes, and I will lead the predators in another direction. Savannah, we will walk together into the shadows. Can you manage to keep the two of you from sight without my assistance? I will need to maintain an image of the two of you with me for some distance, and I would like to provide an unexpected storm. The clouds will be of some aid to you."

"No problem," she answered without hesitation. Nothing in her face betrayed her sudden apprehension. This was Gregori's way of life, not hers. He was the master.

Gregori placed money on the table and smiled into the waiter's eyes. *You will assist us in leaving this place without incident.* His silver eyes held the waiter captive for a brief moment. When he released the man from the hypnotic thrall, the waiter waved the others over, and they formed a loose semi-circle between the table and the rest of the occupants of the patio.

Gregori added a generous tip and nodded to Savannah and Gary to leave. Savannah moved gracefully, going directly across the darkened street, heading for the shadows of the square. She was very much aware of Gregori still close to her, his body protective. For a moment she thought he brushed her shoulder with his hand, the sensation was so real, but when she turned her head, he was several feet behind.

Go, ma petite, *take Gary to the house. Do not allow the neighbors to see either of you. And place the safeguards carefully.*

What about you?

There is no safeguard I cannot unravel. Go now. This time, there was no mistake. He was four feet away, already turning away from her, but she felt his mouth burning possessively on hers, lingering for just a moment, his tongue tracing the curve of her lip. She couldn't believe he could make her want him, burn for him, when he was going off into the night alone to fight their enemies.

The night has always been mine, Savannah. Do not

waste your time worrying about me. The soft, mesmerizing voice exuded confidence. Gregori strode away, walking along the edge of the square, and at his side appeared to be Gary and Savannah, moving at the same casual pace. Leisurely. Tourists out sightseeing.

Clouds began boiling across the sky, fast moving and dark, bringing an unexpected fine mist, steam rising in the heat of the night. Savannah concentrated on her task. It was relatively easy to make herself invisible from those she wished to avoid, but she had never attempted to shield another from prying eyes. Pulling her mind firmly from the issue of Gregori's safety, from the sure knowledge that he would have to kill yet another time, she caught Gary by the shoulder and turned him toward the line of shops leading up the square. "Stay to the inside and keep walking no matter what, even if someone looks as if they are going to bump right into you."

Gary didn't ask any questions, but she could feel his heart pounding in the night air. Fog rose off the river, a thick soup of vapor that drifted with the wind into the square and moved quickly to cover the streets. People laughed loudly to conceal their sudden nervousness. Along with the blanket of fog came an apprehension, a sense of danger. Things moved in the mist, evil things, creatures of the night.

Gregori continued the illusion of Savannah and Gary sauntering with him along the riverbank. They appeared to move as a unit, meandering along, talking quietly to one another. Gregori wanted to put distance between the innocent humans and the illusion he was creating. He could feel those following him, knew they saw only what he wanted them to see. They were ghouls. Macabre puppets sent to do their master's bidding. A slow hiss escaped as he felt the demon inside him lift its head and unsheathe its claws, fighting for freedom.

His body stretched, muscles rippling, welcoming the familiar power surging through him. He laughed softly, a low taunt sent out as a challenge. His mind touched Savannah's, assuring himself that she was nearly to the house. She was doing a good job of concealing herself and the human from all along the streets. Savannah was a mere child, a fledging, with little training in their ways. He was proud of her, weaving in and out of the crush of tourists pouring out of Preservation Hall. It was a difficult task, and she accomplished it like a professional.

He allowed the two illusions he had created to shimmer over the water, then slowly fade and dissolve into the fog. Only he continued across the expanse of water toward the Algiers landing. He made certain the undead could see his challenge. The dark compulsion of the kill was on them, the vampire's minions. A slow, humorless smile deepened the cruel edge to his mouth. The vampire seeking Savannah had had no idea he would be grappling with Gregori, the Dark One, here in New Orleans.

Julian Savage was a great hunter, perhaps second only to himself. If Julian had kept a residence here and had not destroyed the master vampire, it could only mean the vampire left whenever Julian returned to town. The master vampire obviously sacrificed others of his kind without a qualm. Vampires often ran together for strength against the hunter, but there was no bond of loyalty to hold them together.

Gregori waited among the trees along the riverbank. He could hear the dull, zombie-like growls of the two attackers as they made their way through the water after him. Their boat was powered by an engine that sputtered and whined loudly, but they made no attempt to hide their presence. It was typical of the ghoul, the unswerving dedication to carry out the vampire's orders. They had no other purpose, no other life. They were ghouls, servants, puppets, once human but now needing the vampire's tainted blood to continue existing, sleeping in sewers and shallow graves to escape the deadly sun. Vampires usually killed the victims they fed on, but sometimes, when they needed servants to perform tasks for them in daylight, they shared their tainted blood, binding the victims to them, robbing them of their mind and soul.

But these puppets were still very dangerous. They were enormously strong, cunning, and difficult for the ordinary Carpathian male to kill. Nearly impossible for humans. He winced, imagining Savannah trapped by these two abominations. She was a fledgling, incapable of killing these creatures. Maybe he should have killed them from a distance—Gregori had long ago learned every art of killing in his world and that of the humans—but he wanted to ensure that no others were caught in their battle. And he wanted the vampire who had sent them to understand he was picking up the gauntlet. *Gregori. The Dark One*.

The boat had jammed in some tree roots thrusting up out of the dark, murky waters. Gregori made no attempt to hide from the zombies. He waited, his body relaxed, the fog curling around his legs. The light mist fanned his face and spread like a fine blanket across the night.

The two puppets awkwardly climbed from the boat, splashing water in all directions. Gregori inhaled, felt the sudden disturbance in the air. The vampire thought his trap was sprung. All Carpathians could detect one another when they were within a certain range. The vampire must have known the moment Savannah had entered his domain, but he had not detected Gregori's presence. Gregori walked among his own people unseen when he wished it. Cloaking himself had become as natural to him as breathing. The vampire, who had run from Julian, clearly thought he was dealing with a lesser Carpathian. A novice.

The two huge ghouls were clumsily making their way up the embankment. Twice the red-haired man fell into the water, sending droplets spraying while he tried to regain his footing. The two zombies separated, moving in from either side.

Know this, evil one. Gregori sent out the strong mental call. He felt the sudden hesitation in the air as the vampire became aware that the heavy fog, the unusual mist, and the boiling clouds were not a natural phenomenon. The vampire held back, worried. The elements were perfectly recreated and few could produce such a work of art. *You have issued your challenge to me, and I have accepted. Come to me.* Gregori's voice was low and mesmerizing. Beautiful. There was no other like it. And none could resist when he chose to wield its deadly power.

The vampire fought the compulsion, the hypnotic order, but his frame wavered out in the fog above the water. His face was a twisted, evil mask, eyes glowing red, receding gums revealing jagged, sharp teeth. Talons curled on his hands, razor-like and wicked looking. He hissed venom, frightened and furious that one could call such as he forth against his will. There was nowhere to hide from the voice; it whispered, and he was forced to emerge fully into solid form, unable to continue an illusion.

For centuries he had been a bloated spider, weaving his evil web, keeping a low profile and running when it was necessary. "Gregori, I cannot believe one such as you would choose to hunt so meager an opponent as myself," he said, fawning and simpering as if they were old friends.

"Are you calling yourself Morrison these days?" Gregori's pale eyes shifted to the zombie on his left, inching closer, his every moment carefully orchestrated by the vampire. "When we were young, you were Rafael. You disappeared some four hundred years ago."

The jagged teeth, stained brown from centuries of consuming human, adrenaline-based blood, flashed in a grotesque parody of a smile. "I went to ground for nearly a century. When I rose, the world was much changed. You were the Prince's sanctioned killer, feeding on our kind. I left our homeland, driven out by your fever, by your own bloodlust. This is my sanctuary now, my home. I have not asked for more. Why do you come here uninvited to plague me?"

Gregori began to focus on the air itself, to build the charge he needed, gathering it into a ball of crackling, fiery energy just out of sight in the cauldron of clouds. "You do not own this city, Rafael, nor can you dictate to me where I can and cannot go. You put your servants on Savannah's trail. You knew she was my lifemate, yet you deliberately sought her. I can think of no other reason than you wished your centuries of depravity over. You were seeking the dark justice of our people."

The first ghoul lunged at him, bellowing loudly, his movements lumbering. Gregori simply vanished, one sharp nail raking the tainted neck, severing the jugular. The ghoul howled and spun in circles, the spray of red droplets shining black in the night. The noise continued, high-pitched and shrill, echoing across the water, startling wildlife and fowl. Snakes, disturbed by the commotion, plopped from the trees into the water. Far off, in the bayou, alligators slithered down the embankment to slide silently into the murky depths. The screams continued as the vampire's puppet spun this way and that, looking for his intended victim.

Gregori watched dispassionately from where he stood a few yards from the pathetic creature. "Finish him off, Rafael. You created him; you can allow him the dignity of death."

The vampire was feasting his eyes on the spray of blood, saliva dripping down his chin in anticipation. Casually he reached out and caught some of the gushing blood in his palm and licked at it greedily. The creature crawled to him, begging and pleading, imploring the vampire to spare his life. Rafael kicked the creature away from him. The body, still thrashing hopelessly, landed in deeper water and began to sink.

Swearing to himself, Gregori lifted his hand and directed the ball of fire into the man's body. A ghoul could rise again and again and be used by its creator if not properly disposed of. This one would terrify those who lived along the river if Gregori didn't cremate him, rendering him useless to the vampire.

Rafael leapt back, horrified at the sight of the orange ball of flame that passed directly through his work of art and instantly exploded the body into a burning conflagration. He hissed, his head undulating like that of the reptile he was.

Gregori regarded him coolly. "I was mistaken. You are not the master. You are one of his expendable minions, a lower slave to fawn at his knees and curry favor. You cannot be Morrison."

The vampire's eyes glowed red hot, and his lips drew back in a snarl. "You think to ridicule me? You believe the one called Morrison is more powerful than me? I made Morrison. He is *my* servant."

Gregori laughed softly. "Do not attempt to masquerade as one of the ancients, Rafael. As I recall, even as a student you put no effort into learning the necessary guards to keep you safe." He tipped his head to one side. "This was your idea, not Morrison's, correct? You provoked me by sending that ridiculous excuse for a vampire, Roberto, after Savannah, and you put Wade Carter on her trail. The one they call Morrison now is too smart for that. He would want no part of challenging me."

The vampire's eyes glowed with hot fury. His hiss was venomous, his head undulating faster, an enthralling rhythm used to hypnotize a victim. "Morrison is a fool. He is no master." It was difficult to understand the words with the vampire growling and hissing as he said them. Saliva, tainted with his corrupt blood, spewed from his mouth and dribbled down his chin onto the front of his once elegant, faded white silk shirt.

Gregori shook his head slowly. "You wanted me to hunt Morrison. You were using Savannah to draw me out to rid you of your master."

The second ghoul struck from behind, creeping in a stealthy manner up to Gregori, then swinging a huge tree branch at the back of his head. At the last possible second, Gregori spun around, his arm shattering the thick limb, so that splinters and twigs showered down to the muddy banks of the river. He continued on with his smooth motion, a powerful ballet dancer, fluid and strong, his claws ripping out the exposed throat, nearly decapitating the vampire's servant with his casual strength.

The vampire erupted in a howl of rage that carried like thunder through the thick fog. The mist was dense, the tendrils of fog winding tighter and tighter around legs and waists, moving higher to trail in a loose coil around their chests. It seemed almost alive, living and breathing like a crouching beast, gaining strength as it moved.

Gregori smiled pleasantly at the vampire, taking care to step far away from the body now flopping helplessly in the mud. "You are like a peacock, Rafael, raising your feathers and strutting. You must have had centuries to build such a hatred against Morrison." His voice was beautiful, seeping into the vampire's body, turning the strength, built on the deaths of so many others, to water. That voice whispered of power. Real power. Invincible. Merciless. Relentless. "Morrison is the one who allowed you to survive the hunters, sending you from the city. It has been the way he has survived the hunters, leaving when they arrive in the vicinity he occupies."

"Running," Rafael said contemptuously. "He runs even when we are strong. We should own this city. Together we should drive off and kill any hunter who dares to come here. But he runs like the rabbit he is. I despise his weakness."

Gregori pointed to the thrashing ghoul, and a bolt of lightning slammed from the cloud to the ground, driving through the very heart of the puppet and leaving behind only blackened, useless ashes.

"You think you are so powerful," Rafael snickered. "I have killed so many, you are nothing. Nothing compared to one such as me."

Gregori's silver eyes glittered, pale and cold in the black night. Red flames flickered through the silver. He seemed to grow in power and stature. "I am the wind heralding death, the instrument of justice sent by our Prince to carry out the sentence pronounced on you by our people for your crimes against mortals and immortals alike." His voice was purity, beauty, the tones painful to the vampire, like spikes being driven through his head. Yet he had no choice; unwillingly he moved closer, needing to hear the sound of such purity and beauty again.

As the vampire took an involuntary step forward, something tightened around his calves, his thighs, then reached higher to coil around his chest, squeezing slowly. The pressure was steady, relentless. In horror, the vampire looked down to see the tails of fog moving, alive, like a huge, thick python, sliding in an ever-tightening ring to imprison his body. "Fight me!" Rafael screamed, spraying blood and saliva into the mud and water. "You are afraid to fight me."

"I am justice," Gregori said softly, his voice implacable in its resolve. "There can be no fight, no battle, as there can be only one outcome. Mental or physical bout, or simply a match of our wits, there can be only one end. I am justice. That is all."

A rush of wind, and the vampire never saw the Dark One move. The speed was so incredible, the vampire could not follow the blur of motion. But the vampire felt the impact. Hard. The jolt shook his entire body. He stood there, locked in the strange fog's embrace, looking down at the hunter's outstretched hand. Lying in the palm was his own pulsating heart. The vampire threw back his head and howled in rage and horror. The black empty void that was his long-lost soul was gone, rising with his foul stench into the night air like smoke. His teeth snapped and gnashed at the impassive hunter.

Gregori stood his ground, his mind carefully blank. This was his life. His reason for existing. He was the dark justice necessary for his people to survive, to continue their existence in secrecy. He stood there in the night, utterly, completely alone.

Gregori, I am with you always. You are never alone. Look for me in your heart, in your mind, in your very soul.

Look at your hero now. See what I really am. I kill without thought. Without effort. Without remorse. Without mercy. I am the monster you named me, and I am without equal. Someday I will pay the ultimate price.

Savannah's soft laughter whispered over his skin. It was a gentle, cleansing breeze drifting through his mind. *And who is stronger than my lifemate? No one can kill you.*

You think death is the ultimate price? No, Savannah. Someday you will know what I am, and you will look at me in horror and revulsion. When that day comes, I will cease to exist. Gregori watched the vampire begin to fall. He moved then to complete the distasteful task of ensuring that the nosferatu could not rise again. Fiery sparks rained from the sky, the size of golf balls, striking the vampire, coating him in flames. On the muddy bank, at a distance from the burning body, Gregori incinerated the evil one's heart.

It is done, lifemate. Come home to me. Savannah's voice was low and compelling, soft, seductive, not in the least concerned with his insistence that she see that he was a killer. That he would always be a killer. *This is where you belong. Not alone, never alone. Can't you feel me reaching for you? Feel me, Gregori. Feel me reaching for you. Needing you.*

He could feel it, in his mind, in his heart. Her voice touched him in some secret, deep place he kept locked away even from himself. She was everything beautiful in the world, and, God help them both, he could not bring himself to give her up.

I need you, Gregori. The whisper came again. This time there was a new urgency in it. She swamped him with her desire, with rising heat and sudden fear that he would leave her alone. *Gregori? Answer me. Don't leave me. I couldn't bear it if you did.*

There is no chance of such a thing, ma petite. *I am coming home.* It was the only home he had ever known, the only sanctuary he had ever had: Savannah. She whispered to him, soft and sensuous, a dream of his for so long that she was a part of his soul. She whispered to him of unconditional, total acceptance. He launched himself skyward, his body dissolving into the mist, to become part of the moving fog he had manufactured.

Yet a kind of fury seethed in him, raged, consumed him. He had created this impossible situation with Savannah by his tampering with nature. He knew it could not continue. He was more than unstable in this state. She had to know the truth. What had he been thinking? That he could hide it from her and the rest of the Carpathian people for centuries? She was becoming stronger every day. She needed the closeness of a mind meld with him, and he could do no other than allow it.

Gregori had been so certain he could keep part of himself away from her for his own selfish purposes, but her happiness was now of the utmost importance to him. She needed to know the truth, that he was not her true lifemate. He would clean up the society of human butchers, hunt the master vampire, and then choose to meet the dawn. He had no choice. Savannah deserved to be complete.

Scanning automatically some distance from the house, Gregori was already aware of Gary's presence in one of the upstairs bedrooms. The man was under Savannah's hypnotic suggestion to sleep. Gregori could tell she had secured him for the night, but he reinforced the command with one of his own. His safeguards were deadly. If Gary woke before they rose and came looking for them out of curiosity, he would die. He reached through the layers of sleep and penetrated the man's mind. *You will remain as you are until I awaken you. If something goes wrong and you awaken early, you will not try to find us. You would die. I would be unable to save you.* That was not strictly true—he might be able to protect the human—but he wanted to impress the danger into Gary's subconscious mind. Anyone would be curious about where they might be sleeping, and Gary more than most.

The heavy white fog nearly concealed the little house. He paused to examine Savannah's safeguards, carefully working each one backward until he had unraveled them and it was safe to enter the house. Mist streamed inside and collected in the entryway until he was once more real and solid. The house was warm and welcoming, bright and somehow beckoning. The sheets were gone from the furniture, and a fire was dying down in the screened hearth so that red embers danced low and threw shadows on the far wall.

Gregori moved immediately to the spiral staircase. He could feel her, knew unerringly the exact spot where she waited. He didn't need to scan for Savannah; his body would always find her, his mind would always know her location. He went down the stairs slowly, dreading to face her.

The basement was completely transformed. Candles were everywhere, flickering on all levels, lighting the darkened interior of the room. Shadows intertwined intimately from every corner of the room. A variety of herbs were crushed, some lit, filling the air with the scent of woods and flowers. A huge, old-fashioned bathtub stood in the center of the room, wide and deep, with clawed feet. Water shimmered invitingly, steam rising from the surface.

Savannah came to him instantly, her face lit up with some emotion he dared not name. She was in a man's silk shirt and nothing else. The buttons were open so that the edges gaped to reveal her high, full breasts, and narrow rib cage. Another step and her tiny waist and flat stomach, the triangle of tight ebony curls, showed for an intriguing moment before the long tails of the shirt brushed back into place. Her long hair cascaded loose and moved around her like living, breathing silk. With every step she took, he caught glimpses of satin skin.

At once the dull roar started in his head. Heat exploded through his blood, and his body tightened with alarming urgency. Every good and noble intention seemed to go up in flames. She smiled up at him, her slender arms sliding around his neck. "I'm so glad you're home," she whispered softly, her mouth finding the pulse in his throat. He could feel the heat of her body, her soft breasts crushed against him.

Gregori closed his eyes, summoned his iron will, and shackled her wrists in an unbreakable grip. He dragged her arms down and held her away from his raging body. "No, Savannah, I cannot keep up this deception any longer. I cannot."

Her long lashes veiled her blue-violet eyes for a moment, concealing the secrets locked in their depths. "You can't deceive me, Gregori. It is impossible. You of all Carpathians should know that." She twisted her wrists, a small feminine movement that accomplished her release instantly.

Gregori examined her skin for bruises, afraid that in his desperation he had used far too much physical strength. Savannah ignored him, her hands going to the buttons of his shirt. "If you wish to discuss this matter with me, fine, but maintaining the heat in this tub is taking energy I would rather spend otherwise." The soft amusement in her voice was as effective as her fingertips brushing the bare skin of his chest. She pushed the shirt from his broad shoulders and allowed it to float to the floor.

"Savannah." Her name was a groan for mercy. "You have to listen to me this time. I will never find the strength to make this confession again."

"Hmm," she mused, clearly distracted. Her fingers were working on the buttons of his trousers. "Of course I'll listen, but I want you in the bath. Do it for me, Gregori, after all the trouble I went to for you."

Gregori closed his eyes against the flames licking along his skin. His body raged at him, fiercely aroused. Her hands whispered over his hips as she slipped the trousers down his legs, her fingernails lightly raking his thighs. He stepped out of them, all too aware that he could not hide the demands of his body from her.

Savannah smiled that infuriating, secret smile of hers and took his hand to lead him to the tub. He stepped in and sank into the steaming waters. The sensation of heat over his skin increased his sensitivity to pleasure. Savannah stood behind him, her hands loosening the leather thong at the nape of his neck. The light, lingering touch of her hands in his hair was sending waves of fire dancing across his skin.

Savannah poured warm water over his head, soaking his hair thoroughly. She rubbed shampoo between her palms and began a slow, soothing massage of his scalp. With her fingers busy in his hair, she leaned over him, the softness of her breasts whispering against his back. "So, lifemate, what is this terrible secret that tears at you?"

It was easier to say it with her out of his sight, with the comfort of her hands on his scalp. "You are not my true lifemate. I manipulated the outcome with knowledge I had acquired over the centuries."

"I already know you believe this, Gregori," she acknowledged softly. "But I also know you are wrong." There was purity and honesty in her voice.

His throat was raw and burning. "You cannot even see what I am, Savannah. I could never hide what I am from my true lifemate. I try to show you, but you cannot see reality. You have an illusion in your mind, and nothing can replace it."

Her fingertips deepened the massage, never faltering from their purpose. "And you are supposed to be our most learned ancient. My love, you are the one with the illusion of yourself. And, I might add, of me. Yes, I'm young—compared to you, a child—but I am first a Carpathian. And I am your true lifemate." Her hands fell away, and he was instantly bereft. Warm water took their place, rinsing away the shampoo.

"I remember before I was born, a terrible pain, both

my mother's and my own. You came to me when I would have chosen to free myself from the pain, and you surrounded me with your comfort."

"Savannah." He moaned her name again, covering his face with his hands. "With my will, I bound you to me."

"You gave me your blood to save my life, you healed my wounds, and you talked to me of the wonders of the night, of our world. When I was just beginning to crawl, you came to me in the form of a wolf. We shared our minds constantly, nightly. As I grew, we reached for each other and shared all that we were."

"You accept me only because I did these things."

"That is the illusion, Gregori. I have been in your mind. I see what you are, perhaps better than you do. It took me a little time to put things together, because I was afraid of our bond, how strong it was. I was afraid of losing who and what I was to a stronger personality." Her hands began to soap his back. She made small, lazy circles with the suds. "I didn't put it all together at first. My memories from before my birth and my memories of my beautiful wolf, my companion that made me so complete. I didn't think about how easily and naturally we merged our minds. I didn't think about why I never needed or wanted anyone else. It didn't come to me until I realized how completely I merged with you, slipping in and out of your mind. Neither of us noticed it. You didn't even notice it. You failed to notice that in those years of my childhood, you had a semblance of peace in the time you spent with me. But I felt it. I saw it in your mind. It is there now, for you to examine in your memories. That was why it was so hard for you when I fled the Continent and ran away like the child I was. You see colors, Gregori. You have not seen them in centuries. I see how vivid and brilliant they are to you. Only your true life-mate could provide such a thing for you. Your silly guilt is blinding you to reality."

Warm water streamed down his back. Savannah moved around in front of him to kneel beside the tub. As she bent forward, her silky hair framed the perfection of her face. The shirt parted to reveal enticing glimpses of her curves. The rosy tip of one breast tempted him. He found it hard to control the direction of his gaze. She soaped his chest. "I am with you on the hunt. With you on the kill. In your mind, sharing your thoughts. No other could ever do what I do because I am the only life-mate you have. I am a shadow in your mind, so familiar to you, you do not know I am there."

She poured water over his chest, then rubbed the soap between her palms again. Tilting her head to one side, she gazed lovingly at his harshly set face. "You go perfectly blank when you hunt. I know this not because you tell me, but because I am there with you in your mind. What do you want to feel? Sadness? Remorse? You have hunted for nearly a thousand years. You have been forced to kill friends and relatives. You have been isolated and alone for years, without your lifemate. It was impossible in that barren world to feel anything, at all. Only your code and sense of honor and your loyalty to my father kept you going."

Savannah's hands searched below the surface of the water, found the thick, hard length of him, and began a slow, intimate massage. Her fingers were magic, sending waves of pleasure surging through him. "I would not want you to think of anything while you hunt, especially not of me. I would hope that would be too distracting." Her smile was frankly sexy, her hands moving with recently acquired skill. "You can't feel at such times, Gregori. It would slow you down, cause you to make a mistake. Do you really think you can change a thousand years of training? You programmed yourself centuries ago."

His body was raging at him, the beast inside writhing in need. His silver eyes opened wide to look at her. Hot. Hungry. Wild. Untamed. She smiled at him and sat back on her knees, her secret smile turning erotic. Savannah stood up and allowed the shirt to slide from her shoulders to the floor. "I'm with you in your mind, and you don't even know it, because I'm your other half, and I belong there. Who else but a true lifemate could have called you back from the darkness when it spread like a stain across your soul? You would not have answered anyone but me. Who else could go with you on a hunt, when all of your senses are on full alert, and you not be aware of it?"

His breath was audible in the stillness of the room. She moved back, her body a sensuous invitation, blue-black hair caressing her creamy skin. Gregori stood up, ignoring the water streaming off him. He wanted her, and she belonged to him. As he stepped from the tub onto the floor, she inched backward. Her eyes were half closed, desire in her mind, her body calling to his. She moved restlessly, one hand pushing at the silky fall of hair sensitizing her nipples into hard peaks.

"Come here," he growled, his body so heavy with need that he was afraid he would explode into fragments if he took one step.

She shook her head slowly, her tongue deliberately moistening her full lower lip. "I only want my true lifemate. I hunger tonight. My body is hungry." Her hand drifted slowly, enticingly, over her satin skin, and his eyes followed the graceful movement while his body raged at him.

Gregori covered the distance between them in a sudden surge, catching her up, the momentum taking them to the wall. He held her prisoner there, his mouth fastened on hers, commanding her response, feeding, devouring, his hands claiming her body for his own. "No one else will ever touch you and live," he snarled, his mouth burning a trail of fire down her throat to her breast. He fed hungrily, his teeth grazing the creamy fullness. "No other, Savannah."

"Why, Gregori? Why can no other touch my body like this?" she whispered, her mouth on his skin, her tongue lapping at his pulse. "Tell me why my body is only yours and your body is only mine."

His hands cupped her bottom, brought her hard against him. "You know why, Savannah."

"Say it, Gregori. Say it if you believe it. I won't have lies between us. You have to feel it in your heart as I do. You have to feel it in your mind. Your body has to burn for mine. But most of all, in your deepest soul, you have to know I'm your other half."

He lifted her, set her up high on the rim of the sleeping chamber, his hands parting her thighs. "I know I burn for you. Even in my sleep, the sleep of our people where there can be no thought, I burn for you." He bent his head to taste her, his wet hair bathing her inner thighs as he dragged her body closer to him.

Savannah cried out at the first touch of his mouth, the rush of hot desire turning her into a liquid, living flame. She bunched his hair into her fists and held him to her. "Say it, Gregori," she bit out between clenched teeth. "I need to hear you say it."

I am saying it, lifemate. Can you not hear me? He didn't lift his head, wanting to feel her body pleading for his, needing to feel her press harder into him, trying to alleviate the building pressure. She tasted like wild honey and spice. Addicting. Her response was addicting, the way she moaned and writhed, pushing into his assault. She was rippling with life, with fire, and he took her higher and higher until she cried out for mercy. Only then did he lift her into his arms. "Put your legs around my waist." He slid her down his burning body until he held her poised over the hard, burning length of him.

The feel of her, moist and hot and so ready, set the jackhammers tripping in his head and his body clenching with need. Still he held her, poised at her hot, beckoning entrance so vulnerable to his invasion. "Put your mouth on my neck, Savannah," he ordered. "Drink from me as I take you."

"Hurry," she pleaded, a little catch in her voice. Almost blindly she obeyed him, her tongue caressing the pulse beating so strongly. She pushed aside his wet hair, and as he thrust upwards, stabbing into her tight, velvet sheath, her teeth pierced his skin, so that he flowed into her, body and soul and mind.

Gregori cried out hoarsely, already in ecstasy, taking his lifemate as he was meant to, without reservation, without restraint, without barriers between them. Her mind was filled with wild images, and his mind matched and inflamed hers. He didn't have to compartmentalize his thoughts or worry she would find something that would take her from him. He allowed himself to simply feel intense pleasure. Flames, arcing electricity, white-hot lightning, the friction building and building.

She had always been in his soul; this time he took her there, needing the freedom of her total acceptance, her unconditional surrender, her complete faith and trust in him. Savannah swept her tongue across his neck, closing the tiny pinpricks. She arched away from him, offering her perfect breasts to his mouth. "Now you. Feed. Take me into your body the way I take you."

She was small and light in his arms, so little compared to the size of his body, yet when he thrust into her, his hips frenzied, burying himself deep, driving as close to her soul as he could get, her body accommodated his. First he took her mouth, tasting the power of his blood from her lips. Then his teeth scraped along her throat, lower, to find the valley between her breasts.

Savannah was riding him now, her body finding a perfect rhythm with his, urgent, frenzied, her hands catching his head to force his mouth to her. *I need you.* There was such an aching plea echoing in his mind, he waited no longer. He felt his incisors sharpen, lengthen, as they sank deep into her breast.

She cried out, her body clenching around his, rippling with such intensity, with such a firestorm of pleasure that she felt herself exploding into fragments. Savannah dug her nails into his shoulders for an anchor as his hips thrust into her, wild, untamed, uninhibited. Then they were both exploding together, Gregori lifting his head to cry out hoarsely, unable to contain the savage pleasure burning inside him.

Savannah clutched at him, her head on his shoulder. He waited a heartbeat to make certain he was still on earth. Something moved between them, and he saw the thin trickle of blood running down to her stomach to drop on his own body. He bent his head and closed the pinpricks on her breast with his tongue.

"I love you, Gregori," she whispered softly against his throat. "I really love you. The real you. Do you understand?"

He waved a hand to extinguish the candles, plunging the room into complete darkness. With Savannah's body locked around his, they sank into the embrace of the waiting soil, the richness of their homeland. Instantly peace settled into their beating hearts, into the wildness of their minds.

"You are mine for all eternity, Savannah, until we grow weary of this existence and choose to go together to the next." Reluctantly, he freed his body from hers, bent his head to remove the thin trail of red marring her skin. Gregori settled her into him so that his head rested beside her breast.

Her arms crept around his damp hair, cradling him to her, the sleep of their people calling to her. He shifted her slight body so that he could drape one leg over her thighs possessively, so that his hands could shape the length of her body at will, know it was imprinted there in the soil beside his.

The chamber door slid noiselessly shut to seal them inside at his thought. The safeguards were many and all of them deadly. Anyone disturbing their rest would be in mortal peril. Gregori stroked her long hair, contented. At peace. "You are so small, *ma petite*, to bring such pleasure to a man." The warmth of his breath teased her nipple, and his tongue followed in a slow, leisurely caress. "I have made love to you each time I have taken you into my arms. There can be no other for either of us, Savannah."

She stirred with drowsy contentment, the slight movement bringing her breast against his mouth. Her hands stroked his hair gently. "I am not the one who worries, lifemate. I know there is no other."

His tongue made another lazy, contented curl around her creamy skin. "One who has gone centuries in utter darkness takes a long time to believe he will not lose the light. Go to sleep, Savannah, safe in my arms. Let the soil heal both of us and bring us peace, as Julian knew it would."

She was silent for a moment, but his mouth feeding at her breast was causing little aftershocks, rushes of liquid heat. "I will if you behave." There was soft laughter in her voice, an acceptance of anything he wanted.

He wanted her to sleep and silently pushed at her mind, helping her to grow more tired, but he couldn't quite give up her body yet. He spent a few minutes gently, tenderly, nuzzling her breast. She held him while she drifted in a hazy, erotic dream.

"Sleep now," he commanded softly and gave them both up to the healing soil and the rising sun.

Chapter Thirteen

Gary tried not to notice how pale Savannah was as she fixed him a pot of coffee. Her satin skin was almost translucent. He was groggy from the trance-induced sleep and had a hard time waking up, even after a long shower. He had no idea where the change of clothes had come from, but they were lying on the end of the bed when he awakened.

Savannah was beautiful, moving through the house like flowing water, like music in the air. She was dressed in faded blue jeans and a pale turquoise shirt that clung to her curves and emphasized her narrow rib cage and small waist. Her long hair was pulled back in a thick braid that hung below her bottom. Gary tried to keep his eyes to himself. He hadn't seen any evidence of Gregori this evening, but he didn't want to take any chances. He had a feeling the one thing that could change that remote expression fast was to have another man ogling Savannah.

"As soon as Gregori returns, we can go out and get you dinner," Savannah said softly as he accepted the steaming mug of coffee.

It was already dark. Gary had no idea what had happened after he arrived at the house the night before. He cleared his throat nervously. "What exactly happened last night? All I remember is getting to the house with you and then waking up an hour ago. I'm assuming that I slept the day away." There was a wariness in his voice, in his mind, that hadn't been there before. It was a singular experience to realize someone had taken all control away from him.

"I didn't wake you until we were certain it was safe. Last night Gregori had an encounter with two of the undead's servants and a lesser vampire. He defeated them, of course, and destroyed them so they couldn't rise again. It was safer for you to remain here. We weren't holding you prisoner. We simply wanted to keep you safe." Amusement crept into her voice. "I don't think Gregori really knows what to do with you."

Gary's heart jumped. He cleared his throat. "I hope you mean that positively."

Savannah's eyes laughed at him. "Do you really think he'll harm you? He can read your mind. If you were an enemy, he would've killed you back in that warehouse." Wickedly she leaned across the table. "Of course, he really is awfully unpredictable, so you never know what he might do or where he is—" She broke off, laughing, as her arm was flung into the air as if something had shackled her wrist and jerked her backward. Savannah was dragged by something unseen from the kitchen. She was laughing, her blue eyes dancing with mischief.

Gregori tugged at her wrist, taking her out into the sanctuary of the courtyard with its dense, overgrown plants. Flowers tumbled from the overhead arbors and trailed along his shoulders as he emerged fully into the night. "You are deliberately scaring that young man to death," he accused.

She lifted her face to his, stars from the night sky in the centers of her eyes. "Well, really, how could anyone doubt you?" As her palm caressed the hard line of his jaw, one fingertip touched his perfect mouth.

"Stop thinking you have to protect me, Savannah. It is enough that I have you. I do not need anyone else." He bent his head to find her mouth. On rising, he had taken her twice with his insatiable appetite, yet his body was again stirring to life at the thought that she would rally to his defense.

The moment his mouth claimed hers, she felt the earth moving in that peculiar, shifting way, the white streak of fire rushing through her bloodstream to pool low and hot. Her body went liquid, boneless, melting instantly into his. His arms crushed her close. "Feed, *ma petite*. Feed for me."

Her lips burned over his throat in obedience; her tongue stroked his pulse there. It was sensuous. Erotic. His body tightened with alarming need. His pulse jumped beneath the exploring caress. Gregori caught her slender form and held her even tighter to him, enclosing her in the protection of his arms.

Savannah took her time, enticing, teasing, deliberately arousing him further. She reveled in the feel of his body thrusting hard and aggressively, his hips pressed into her. As her teeth pierced deeply, he made a sound, a hoarse, inarticulate cry, as the white lightning sizzled and danced through his body like a whip of pain and ecstasy, until it was impossible to tell where one sensation left off and the other started.

Then he felt the disturbance in the night air, a whisper

of movement, and he knew they were not alone. Holding her protectively, his body sheltering her from prying eyes, Gregori raised slashing silver eyes to the man wandering into the courtyard. Gary hadn't spotted them yet; his gaze was full of wonder at the unexpected beauty of the yard. Gregori sank deeper into the shadows, swirling a cape of invisibility around them. His hand found the nape of her neck, pressing her mouth to his skin.

Her feeding was stirring his body to greater demands. He could not imagine watching her feed from another male when he was burning with fire from the simple act. Slowly, reluctantly, Savannah stroked her tongue across the tiny pinpricks and lifted her head. Her eyes were drowsy, as if they had made love, her lips tempting. A small dot of red clung to the corner of her mouth, and Gregori instantly dipped down to taste it with his tongue.

His mouth shifted so that he could explore hers, at first demanding, then in a slow, careful kiss that seared her with tenderness. Savannah smiled up at him, her heart in her eyes. "We are not alone, *mon amour*," he whispered into her ear.

She laughed softly with regret, throwing her head back so her long braid swayed. "Weren't you the one who invited him to stay?"

"I believe that was you," he corrected through clenched teeth. She was a fever in his blood. A madness he had no hope of curing. He wanted no cure. He bent to find her breast through the thin material of her shirt.

The night air was soft and cool against his skin. The bats dipped and wheeled above them. The scent of blossoms was all around them as their bodies tangled together. Savannah laughed at him, the sound joyful, echoing in his heart. "Be careful, Gregori, we wouldn't want you to lose your illusion of the big bad bogey man." Her fingers laced together behind his neck.

"You are being a little instigator," he accused.

She nibbled at the lobe of his ear, teasing it with the tip of her tongue. The aroma of coffee was drifting nearer. The soles of Gary's tennis shoes swished softly along the tiles of the patio. His clothes brushed against the fronds of huge ferns as he neared the shadows where they were secreted.

Gregori found himself suppressing a groan. Savannah brought his head down to circle his neck with her arms, finding his mouth with hers, taking her time, enjoying herself, a teasing taste of satin fire that burned through his body and threatened to consume him, threatened his control. *You are playing with fire*, ma chérie.

Mmm, and it's so delicious, too, she murmured softly, losing herself in the sheer pleasure of his dominating mouth.

Gary was just on the other side of the arbor, the screen of honeysuckle and trumpet vines heavy between them. Gregori took command of the situation, reluctantly lifting his head, a dark promise in his glittering eyes, a soft groan escaping his throat.

Gary had thought himself completely alone. He looked around the courtyard carefully, his fingers tightening around the coffee mug. He could hear Savannah's soft laughter. Sexy. Tempting. He shook his head. The woman was a menace. He would hate it if she were his. Only a man very strong and able to do without any male friends could have a siren like her. She was more than a handful; she was a disaster waiting to happen.

Are you reading the human's thoughts, ma petite femme? Gregori's satisfied voice whispered in her mind.

Even one such as he knows you are wild like the winds.
With great reluctance he loosened his hold on her. *Go inside the house.*

Her eyes widened in mock surprise. *You mean he might think we were making love? We would have been if he hadn't wandered out and interrupted us.*

Push me further, chérie, *and I may do something you will not like.*

She laughed out loud, totally unafraid as she sashayed through the courtyard. As she passed Gary, she leaned over and blew warm air into his ear.

Savannah! Gregori roared her name, a distinct threat.

I'm going, I'm going, she said, completely unrepentant.

Gregori waited until she was safe within the confines of the walls before he emerged from the shadows. Gary's heart was a loud thunder in Gregori's ears. He smiled, that gleam of a predator's smile. "For all our time together so far, I do not think we have yet been properly introduced. I am Gregori, lifemate to Savannah."

"Gary, Gary Jansen. Your—um, wife, Savannah, said I could wander around."

"Savannah is my wife," Gregori confirmed, sounding stern and menacing in spite of the fact that his voice was velvet-soft.

"So," said Gary, so nervous he was beginning to sweat.

"Come back into the house, and we will decide what to do." Gregori was already gliding past him in that silent way he had.

Gary followed. Savannah was by the fireplace. Once again her skin had a healthy glow. Something burned in the depths of her violet eyes as they rested on Gregori's impassive face. Gary saw those silver eyes flicker over Savannah's face. No longer bleak and cold, they warmed to molten mercury, tender and fiercely protective. When Gregori looked like that, it was impossible to fear him.

"I have considered several alternatives to our problem, Gary," Gregori said softly. "I will lay them out before you, and you will choose which of them you are the most comfortable with."

Gary relaxed visibly. "Yeah, that sounds good."

"You are going to be hunted by vampires and those humans involved in the society alike," Gregori told him. "Any place you usually frequent you must therefore avoid. That includes your family, your home, and your job. Those are the places they will be waiting for you."

"I have to work, Gregori. I don't exactly have a huge savings account."

"You can work for me. I have many businesses and could use someone I trust. Arrangements can be made to move you to any of the cities here in the United States where I have offices, or—and it might be a safer alternative—in Europe. The offer stands whether you decide to keep your memories of us or whether you ask that they be removed."

Savannah leaned against the wall, shocked at Gregori's proposal. Featherlight, she touched his mind. Instantly, Gregori's attention shifted to her. *Be silent, Savannah.* It was a clear command. Although his face was as impassive as ever, she could feel the imperative smoldering in his mind, and for once she fell silent, watching him closely.

"I don't want you to erase my memories," Gary said.

"I've told you that. Besides, I think I have the right to help you with this mess instead of being shipped off to some foreign country like a child."

"You do not know the dangers, Gary. But perhaps that is a good thing. If you insist on keeping your memory, I can do no other than protect Savannah and our people. I would have no choice but to take your blood so that I could monitor you at will."

Gary paled visibly. Slowly he put down the coffee mug, his hand trembling. "I don't understand."

"When I am nearby, I can read your thoughts, but I must be close. If I have taken your blood, I will always know where you are, I can track you easily to anywhere on this earth, and I will know your thoughts. If you ever betrayed us, I would know." Gregori leaned forward, his brilliant silver eyes holding Gary's captive. "Understand this, Gary. If I had to, I would hunt you. I would find you. And I would kill you." There was complete conviction in his voice, in the depths of his eyes.

Gary could not look away. He felt as if that penetrating gaze could see right into his soul.

"It is something you should think about," Gregori continued almost gently. "It has to be your decision alone. Whatever you decide, we will respect it, and we will do our best to protect you. You have my word on that."

"You once told me the vampire was the biggest deceiver of all. How do I know you speak the truth?"

"You do not. You can only feel what is right or wrong. That is why it is necessary that you take your time before deciding. Once the decision is made, we will all have to live with it."

"Does it hurt?" Gary asked, curious, his scientist's brain already seeking data.

Savannah detected the slight smile in Gregori's mind, the sudden admiration for the slightly built human who came to his feet and began to pace the length of the room.

"You do not have to feel a thing," Gregori said quietly, his voice strictly neutral. He didn't want to influence the human in any way.

"I guess it would be too much to ask to let Savannah bite my neck." Gary made an attempt at humor. He was rubbing his neck, every Dracula movie he had ever seen going through his mind.

A low growl rumbling in Gregori's throat was his answer. Savannah burst out laughing. She could sense Gary's growing agitation. He pushed a hand through his hair. "Do I have to answer you now?"

"Before we leave this house," Gregori replied softly.

"That really gives me a long time to think it over," he grumbled. "So, if you remove my memories of you, I would go back to my normal life and not have a clue I was in danger. That's kind of a convenient way to get rid of me, don't you think?" Sarcasm dripped in his voice.

The silver eyes slashed. Gregori stirred, a menacing rippling of muscle, the predator unsheathing his claws. Savannah laid a detaining hand on his arm. Her thumb feathered lightly back and forth across his forearm. Almost at once the tension in the room eased. But those predator's eyes remained unblinking on Gary's face. "If I wanted you dead, Jansen, believe me, you would already be gone. Killing is easy for someone who has lived as long as I have."

"It isn't like I meant to offend you, Gregori," Gary said. "This isn't easy. Nothing like this has ever happened to me before. At least I don't think it has. We haven't met before, have we?"

"No," Savannah answered gravely. "We would have told you. We really are trying to be as honest as we can. This is a tremendous offer, Gary, one I didn't think would even be considered. You have no idea what an honor it—"

"Silence, Savannah. He must make up his own mind without persuasion. It is his decision alone to make," Gregori reprimanded.

He doesn't comprehend the honor you have extended him, she argued. *If he knew, he would be less agitated.*

S'il vous plaît, *Savannah. Let him decide.*

Gary held up a hand. "Don't do that. I know you're talking together. I'm nervous enough. Okay. Okay. Do it. Get it over with. Bite me in the neck. But I'm going to warn you, I've never done this before. It won't be too good for you." He attempted a wan grin.

"Be certain. There can be no doubt. You must know that you trust me. There might be times when I will have to take human life. You cannot change sides in the middle of the fight," Gregori warned.

Gary moistened his lips. "Can I ask a few questions here?"

"Naturally." Gregori was noncommittal.

"Are there any humans that have known of your kind and lived?"

"Of course. There is one family that has lived with one of our people for several centuries, mother to daughter, father to son. One of those closest to Savannah's father was a human priest. They were good friends for nearly fifty years. One couple is raising a human boy."

"So I won't be the only one to know. Because it's a big responsibility to have this knowledge. If you're not vampires, what are you?"

"We are Carpathians, a race of people as old as time itself. We have special powers, some of which you have seen, and we require blood to survive, but we do not kill or enslave those we feed on. We walk in the night and must avoid the sun." Again Gregori's voice was expressionless.

"What is the difference between a vampire and a Carpathian?" Gary asked, excited, interested, feeling a strange elation.

"All vampires were Carpathians at one time. The vampire is a male of our race who has chosen the madness of false power over the rules of our people. When a Carpathian exists too long without a lifemate, he loses all emotion. Colors vanish from his vision. His inner darkness prevails, and he preys on humans and Carpathians alike, not only for blood but for the thrill of the kill. He chooses this evil path rather than facing the dawn and self-destruction. That is why we have the hunters. Hunters rid the world of the vampire and make certain that the existence of our race remains a secret from those who would not understand, those who would perceive us all as vampire and seek out destruction."

Savannah's hand slipped from Gregori's wrist. She took the coffee cup from Gary's hand and refilled it. "It's rather like a B movie, isn't it?"

Gary found himself smiling at her. There was something about her mischievous smile that made anyone near her happy. It was contagious. "So what happens if I let you take my blood and you turn vampire?"

"It is impossible for me to turn now," Gregori said softly, his beautiful voice stating the simple truth. "Savannah is my anchor in the light."

Gary stood there for a few moments, took a swallow of the coffee, and turned to Gregori. "Let's do it." He could believe Savannah was light.

Gregori swept through the man's mind, a slow, gentle touch Gary couldn't detect. He was determined. Convinced. And he was going to help them if he could. *You will come to me, unafraid, unhurt, without any ill effects afterward.* He swamped the human with soothing comfort. Gary moved toward him with the slightly glazed eyes of one under a trance. Gregori bent his head to the prominent vein in Gary's neck and drank. He was careful not to take too much, careful to pass on the blood-clotting agent to ensure fast healing. Before Gregori freed Gary from the hypnotic suggestion, he moved well back into the shadows.

Gary shook his head once, twice. He staggered slightly and felt for the table. He never saw Gregori move, but the larger man was beside him, steadying him, lowering him carefully into a chair. "In a few minutes we should get you something substantial to eat. We arrived last night and have not had time to stock the refrigerator." Gregori glanced at Savannah. *Get him a glass of water to replace his fluid loss,* chérie.

Savannah handed the glass to Gregori, her eyes anxious. Gary touched his neck. He felt a little dizzy, and there was a burning sensation on the side of his neck, but when he touched his pulse, his hand came away free of blood. He glanced at Gregori. "You did it already, didn't you?"

"Drink all of it." Gregori held the glass to his lips. "I saw no reason to prolong the suspense. Your mind was quite made up."

"Welcome to my world, Gary." Savannah was flashing

her mischievous smile. "He considers you family and under his protection now, so he's bound to be impossibly bossy."

Gary groaned. "I didn't consider that. Damn. You're right. He can't help himself; it's his nature."

"Do not start, you two. I did not think what it would be like to have the two of you driving me insane." Gregori sounded disgusted, but Gary was beginning to understand him a little. He never really changed expression, and his eyes gave nothing away, but Gary could almost feel Gregori's silent laughter.

"You do have a sense of humor," he accused him.

"Well, do not blame me. It is Savannah's fault. She insists on it," Gregori replied in disgust. "Let us go and get you something decent to eat."

"Am I going to crave blood, raw steak, that kind of thing?" Gary asked, straight-faced.

"Well, actually . . ." Savannah started.

"I do not have rabies." Gregori silenced her with a look. "I am not contagious."

"All the books say if you drink my blood, I get to drink your blood, and then I'm like you." Gary sounded slightly disappointed.

"Some people grow bat wings," Savannah admitted, her teeth tugging at her lower lip. "That's where Batman came from. And capes, all those swirling capes. A regular epidemic. It's from our blood, a kind of allergic reaction. Don't worry, you would be showing signs already if you were one of those with a problem."

"Is she always like this?" Gary asked Gregori.

"She gets worse," Gregori said truthfully.

The popular restaurant was packed, the line outside long, but Gregori got them a table instantly with a soft whisper in the ear of the hostess. Gary sank gratefully into a waiting chair and immediately drank all three glasses of water provided for them. He had never been so thirsty in his life.

"Where do we start with this mess?" he asked.

"The society you belong to—who got you into it?" Gregori asked.

All around them was the swirl of conversations, some soft and intimate, some loud and obnoxious, others laughing, having a good time. Gregori and Savannah heard it all. It would be all too soon before someone noticed the famous magician in their midst, but Gregori had managed a semi-secluded table and maneuvered Savannah into the darkest corner.

"Everyone at work knew about my obsession with vampires. It was a joke around the laboratory. A few years ago, a man by the name of Dennis Crocket approached me. He was a friend of someone who worked at the lab. He invited me to a meeting. I thought it was pretty hokey, but at least there were others interested in the same subject." Gary was looking around for a waiter, needing more liquid. Waiters were bustling in every direction but his. He gave a little sigh. "At the least, I thought I might find some interesting data. I have quite a collection. In any case, I went."

Gregori glanced at a busboy lounging behind a potted plant, and the kid instantly grabbed a pitcher of water and hurried over to refill all three glasses. "Where was the meeting held?"

"Los Angeles. That's where I work."

"What did you think of the others at the meeting? Were they fanatics? Perverts like those in the storehouse?" Gregori inquired softly, his voice so low that Gary had to lean toward him to catch the words.

He shook his head. "No, not at all. Some people were there for the fun of it. Not really believers, you know, but hoping maybe. It gave them something to do with other people interested in vampire lore. At first the talk was always light—wouldn't it be cool? What kind of powers did they have? Would they be friendly? Then, after I'd been a few times, a couple of men from some other chapter showed up."

Savannah's chin rested in the palm of her hand. She stared with unblinking eyes at Gary, keeping well back in the shadows to protect herself from prying eyes. She was using a simple blurring technique to aid in her camouflage. It didn't really make her invisible to the human eye but caused a strange warp in the air around her so that she was hazy to those glancing her way. "Where was this chapter located?"

Gary wrinkled his forehead in thought. "You know, they have several chapters. In Europe, mostly around the Transylvania area. Romania. Places like that. These guys were Southerners—Florida maybe. I think Florida. In any case, they were much more scientific about everything. They wanted each of us there to provide them with any factual information on anyone who might be a vampire. People we knew who were always pale, who only went out at night. Those who were extremely intelligent, who seemed to be mesmerizing, who were always secretive about their lives and activities."

"Did any names come up?" Gregori asked.

"A few, but none of them really seemed like the real thing. None of us knew anyone remotely resembling what they were describing. We were making jokes and naming friends until we realized they were serious."

The waiter arrived, and Gary hastily scanned the menu

while Savannah and Gregori ordered. Gary found himself ravenously hungry. When he would have ordered everything in sight, it occurred to him that Savannah and Gregori probably wouldn't mind sharing their food. Looking up, he caught Savannah grinning at him, that impish, starry-eyed smile that was making him feel a part of a family unit. Like he belonged with them. He was no longer an outcast, poked fun at by those around him.

She reached out to him, hesitated, then dropped her hand into her lap. "You catch on fast," she praised him.

He felt the flood of acceptance from both of them. It was interesting that he could tell it was from both. Gregori reached over, took Savannah's palm, and pressed a kiss into the exact center. *Je regrette, mon amour, but it seems I cannot overcome certain failings.*

There is no need for you to apologize, lifemate. We both are learning to live in the other's world. I don't find it necessary to touch others to be happy.

Gregori brought her hand to the warmth of his mouth a second time, the molten silver of his eyes caressing her intimately.

Gary cleared his throat. "Enough of that stuff."

A brief smiled softened the edges of Gregori's mouth. "What else did these men have to say?"

"I thought you could read my mind," Gary ventured.

Gregori nodded. "That is so, but if I were to examine your memories, I would know them all. Out of courtesy, respect for you, I do not. All of us have things we would prefer to keep to ourselves, painful or embarrassing moments we need not share."

"Even between the two of you?" Gary was beginning to really like the Carpathian. He also realized that whatever it was the couple shared was unique.

"It is different with lifemates," Savannah answered him. "We are two halves of the same whole. What one feels, so does the other. There can be only truth between us."

"The men from Florida." Gregori brought them back to the discussion at hand. Keeping up a wavering haze between Savannah and the rest of the patrons in the restaurant was energy-draining for her, but every time he went to take it over, she resisted. He could see that her pride was at stake. For some silly reason, she wanted to prove to him she was a capable Carpathian. He would only put up with the nonsense so long. Her care came first. Savannah tossed him a murderous look and withdrew her hand just as the waiter arrived with their dinners.

Gary waited for him to leave before he continued in a low voice. "Two of the men told us to look for certain types. Someone whose family traced their eastern European ancestry back hundreds and hundreds of years, often with an estate that has been in the same family just as long. That kind of thing. They threw out a couple of names and occupations. One was some singer with a huge following who only appears in public at night and won't sign a contract with a recording studio. They say her voice is mesmerizing, haunting. They said if you hear her sing, you can never forget the experience. They seemed very interested in her."

"This woman could be in danger. Who is she?"

Gregori shook his head at Savannah's question. No Carpathian woman would ever be allowed to run around unprotected by the males of their race. It had to be a human target whose eccentric ways had caught the eye of the society.

"She uses two different variations of the same name. Desari or Dara. I think the Dara nickname is supposed to mean from the dark or some such nonsense. She probably needed a show-business name, and her real name is Suzy."

"What specifically did they want the members to do about her?" Savannah asked, still afraid for the unknown woman.

At once Gregori sent her a wave of reassurance. *We will put out the word to all of our kind that she is in danger. They will watch over her when she is near.*

There are so few of us in this country. Most of the time she will be without protection. Savannah passed a hand across her forehead, suddenly tired. She had been involved in the sordid business of vampires and human "vampire" hunters only a short time, and she was already weary of their seemingly endless perversion.

Perhaps this is the very thing we need to keep Julian with us. I will ask him to travel with this performer until the danger to her has passed. Do not worry for the human female. Julian would never allow her to be harmed if he has taken her under his protection. Gregori examined the weariness in her mind. *I will take over the shield now,* ma petite, *and you will not argue with your lifemate.* Gregori took no chances with her stubborn ways. He thrust his will decisively into hers, blocking any attempt to take the control back. She was tired.

She smiled at him, tender, loving, accepting. Gregori slid his arm along the back of her chair protectively.

Oblivious of the interplay between the two Carpathians, Gary continued the conversation. "They wanted us to watch her, to do research on her, find out what we could about her background. And she wasn't the only one. There was a man they seemed very interested in. An Italian, I think. Julian Selvaggio or something close to that."

Selvaggio *is Italian for* Savage. *Aidan and Julian were born* Selvaggio. *It also means* unsociable person, Gregori's voice whispered in her mind.

Savannah felt her heart slam painfully against her ribs. Julian. Of course it was Julian Savage. She looked up at Gregori. The society was setting its members against Julian. She didn't know him personally, but suddenly it all seemed very close to home.

We will send word to him, ma petite. *Who better to guard the woman from those who also wish his death? Julian is a very dangerous hunter. One of our best. Second to your father, he is perhaps the most powerful Carpathian alive.*

I guess we aren't considering you, Savannah said loyally, truthfully.

Gregori turned his attention to Gary. "So the society members from Florida were different from the rest of you. They were serious, and they gave you specific names to get information on. Were there more?"

Gary nodded. "I have a laptop in my hotel room. It lists those they suspect and activities they considered suspicious."

Gregori permitted himself a small smile. His teeth were gleaming white, those of a predator on the prowl. "I think a trip to your hotel room is on the agenda tonight."

Savannah tossed her braid over her shoulder and allowed herself to look around the room. Laughter was erupting from nearly every table. Most of the occupants were tourists, and she enjoyed listening to the various accents and conversations. A group of older locals was four tables away. She found their mixture of French Cajun fascinating. Three of them had grown up together and were telling a fourth, younger man some of the more fanciful tales of their youth.

She found herself tuning in as the young man laughed softly. "Stories about old man alligator have been around since before my grandfather's time. It's just a legend, an old tale to scare the children away from the swamp, nothing more. My mother used to tell me that same story."

An argument broke out instantly among the men. The oldest, the one with the heaviest accent, broke into French, not the elegant French Gregori spoke, but the local dialect. All the same, Savannah was certain he was swearing a blue streak. There was such a soothing cadence to the old man's voice, a rhythm unique to New Orleans.

As she listened, the old alligator grew in stature. He was huge, like the grinning crocodile of the Nile. He had eaten hundreds of hunting dogs, lay in wait along a trail and gulped them as they came running by. He snatched small children from the banks in front of their parents' homes. An entire boatload of partying teens had vanished in his domain. The tales grew with each telling.

At first, Savannah was smiling, enjoying the fascinating old legend, but a slow dread was beginning to seize her. She glanced at Gregori. He was talking quietly with Gary, extracting information with skillful questions even as he gave the illusion of having a pleasant conversation. She knew he was automatically scanning the area, monitoring other conversations, yet he seemed relaxed, unaware of the gathering blackness.

She rubbed her pounding temples, massaged her tight neck. Little beads of sweat broke out on her forehead. Savannah tried to concentrate on the funny tale, the growing exploits of the alligator, but with each passing moment all she could do was feel the black apprehension building like some terrible disease that managed to get inside her mind and cling to her.

Gregori turned his head, the silver eyes slashing her face, at once concerned. *Ma petite, what is it?* His mind was already reaching for hers, merging fully so that he could feel the gathering sense of darkness growing so quickly within her.

Is it possible there is an evil one present? she asked. Her stomach was lurching.

Gregori studied the room. There was always the chance one of the undead had learned to mask himself from other Carpathians. He could do it. It would be egotistical to think another might not learn the trick. The master vampire was very old. He had survived the hunters because he was cunning and perfectly willing to flee the vicinity and leave it to the hunter until such time as it was once again safe to return. Still, Gregori doubted he would deliberately go to the same restaurant as a hunter to secretly gloat, especially if that hunter was Gregori. *The Dark One.* Only those weary of their existence challenged him outright.

Gary was looking from one to the other in alarm. "What is it?"

"Remain calm. Savannah is very sensitive to evil. She can feel it, and I can touch it through her, but I cannot detect it within the room myself."

"Are we in danger?" Gary found the idea more exciting than frightening. He was looking forward to action. *Rambo style.*

Savannah and Gregori exchanged a sudden smile. "Gary." Savannah couldn't help herself. "You've seen too many movies."

"Yeah, well, you don't know what this is like for me.

All my life my classmates and friends made fun of me. The bullies shoved me into walls and tossed me into trash cans. All because I always did my homework and got A's on every paper. This is exciting stuff for me."

"Me, too," Savannah lied. She didn't want any part of it, for herself, for Gary, or for Gregori. She wanted them all to be safe. Whatever horrible thing was waiting for them, crouched just beyond their reach, carried the foul stench of evil. It permeated her mind and left her feeling sick and dizzy. "I have to get out of here, Gregori."

You will be fine, mon amour. *We will leave this place immediately. It seems your mother did pass on her gift to you.* Once more he allowed himself to survey the room. There was nothing but the laughter of the tourists and the good-natured wrangling of those who lived there. Gregori summoned the waiter, paid the check, and took Savannah by the arm as they wound their way among the tables.

Chapter Fourteen

Walking around the French Quarter in the night air helped to clear Savannah's head of the presence of evil. Whatever or whoever it was didn't follow them out of the restaurant. Within a few minutes, she felt better. Gregori kept her under the shelter of his shoulder. He remained silent, but his mind was merged fully with hers, observing the darkness rapidly dispelling.

Gregori guided them without saying a word toward the hotel where Gary was staying. He wanted the list of names, wanted to be able to see how far the society's rot had spread. Gary believed most members of the society were others like him, hoping it might be true that vampires lived and that they were the romantic characters depicted in recent movies and books.

But Gregori had seen what the depraved human mind could do. He had seen the work of the society time and time again. Women butchered and murdered, innocents, children. He laced his fingers through Savannah's, finding a measure of peace and solace in her closeness. The wind blew the dark, ugly memories into the night.

Savannah's fingers tightened around his. "Did you know what it was?"

"No, but it was real, *chérie*. I was in your head. You did not imagine it." They walked along, the silence comfortable between them.

A block from his hotel, Gary cleared his throat. "I thought you said going back to my room might be dangerous."

"Life is dangerous, Gary," Gregori said softly. "You are *Rambo*, remember?"

Savannah's laughter rang out, rivaling the jazz quartet playing on the corner. Heads turned to listen to her, then to watch her, stealing away the attention of the audience gathered in a loose semi-circle around the quartet. She moved in the human world, completely comfortable in it, a part of it. Gregori had walked unseen, and that was how he preferred it. She was dragging him into her world. He could hardly believe he was walking down a crowded street with a mortal with half the block staring openly at them.

"I didn't know you knew who Rambo was," Savannah said, trying not to giggle. She couldn't imagine Gregori in a theater watching a Rambo movie.

"You saw a Rambo flick?" Gary was incredulous.

Gregori made a sound somewhere between contempt and derision. "I read Gary's memories on the subject. Interesting. Silly, but interesting." He glanced at Gary. "This is your hero?"

Gary's grin was as mischievous as Savannah's. "Until I met you, Gregori."

Gregori growled, a low rumble of menace. His two companions just laughed disrespectfully, not in the least intimidated.

"I'll bet he's a secret Rambo fan," Savannah whispered confidentially.

Gary nodded. "He probably sneaks into movie theaters for every old showing."

Savannah was really laughing now, the soft notes dancing in the air, contagious, infectious, beckoning all within hearing to join in.

Gregori shook his head, pretending to ignore the two of them and their shenanigans. But he couldn't help himself; he felt his heart lighten even as he scanned the hotel from the courtyard and knew they would soon be in another confrontation with dark, compulsion-driven members of the society. He stopped them abruptly, drawing them into the shadows of the building. "Someone is in your room waiting, Gary."

"You don't even know which is my room," Gary protested. "There's a lot of people staying here. Let's not make a mistake."

"I do not make mistakes," Gregori said softly, his black-velvet voice very much in evidence. "Would you care to go up alone?"

That was unnecessary, lifemate, Savannah reprimanded. *And beneath you. You like this mortal, and it bothers you that he may be in danger.*

Perhaps it is your easy way with him that bothers me, he suggested silkily. His hand wrapped a length of braid around his fist and gave a tug.

You'd like me to think that, but I am in your head, reading your growing affection for this man.

Gregori didn't want to admit she was right. Savannah was bringing him so far into her world, she was making him feel things uncomfortable for him. Mikhail had had a friendship with a human. Gregori had known he felt great affection for the man, yet Gregori had never understood it. Respected it, perhaps, but he did not understand it. Savannah had genuinely cared for Peter. Gregori didn't dwell on that issue too much, but again, he found it hard to comprehend. Yet now, with Gary, in spite of himself, Gregori actually admired the mortal and didn't want anything to happen to him.

"Tell me what you want me to do," Gary said almost eagerly. He was sick of bullies pushing him around.

"You are going to walk in by yourself and fish for as much information as you can get before they try to kill you," Gregori answered.

"*Try.* I hope that's the operative word," Gary said nervously. "*Try* to kill me."

"You will not have to worry about yourself," Gregori informed him, his voice utterly confident. "But it is necessary that the police do not come looking for you. That means no dead bodies in your room."

"Right, messy. If I have vampires and nut cases from the society hunting me, we don't need the cops, too," Gary admitted. He was sweating now, his palms so wet he kept rubbing them on his jeans.

"Do not worry so much." Gregori flashed a smile meant to reassure, the one that left vivid images of open graves. "I will be with you every step of the way. You might even have fun playing Rambo."

"He had a big gun," Gary pointed out. "I'm going up there with my bare hands. I think it might be pertinent to say I've never won a single fistfight. I've been put in trash cans and toilets and had my face rubbed in the dirt. I'm no good in a fight."

"I am," Gregori said softly, his hand suddenly on

Gary's shoulder. It was the first time Gary could remember the Carpathian voluntarily touching him out of camaraderie. "Gary is saying all these things, *chérie*, yet he intended to go up against a man brandishing a knife with only his lab jacket for protection."

Gary blushed a fiery red. "You know why I was in the lab," he reminded Gregori, ashamed. "I made a tranquilizer that works on your blood, and they turned it into a poison of some kind. We've got to do something about that. If something goes wrong tonight, and they get me, all my notes on the formula are in my laptop, too."

"This is beginning more and more to sound like a bad movie." Gregori sighed. "Come on, you two amateurs." He was impassive on the outside, but he couldn't help laughing on the inside. "Do not worry about the formula. I allowed one of the members to inject me with it, so we know its components and are working on an antidote now."

"It didn't work?" Gary was appalled. He had spent a tremendous amount of time on that formula. Although Morrison and his crew had perverted it, he was still disappointed.

"You cannot have it both ways, Gary." Exasperated, Gregori gave him a little shove toward the entrance to the hotel. "You should not *want* the damn thing to work."

"Hey, my reputation is on the line."

"So was mine. I neutralized the poison." Gregori nudged him again. "Get moving."

Gary concentrated on remembering the code to the door of the small hotel, which was locked when no desk clerk was about. When the lock slid open, he turned around to grin in triumph, but the two Carpathians were gone, dissolved into thin air. He stood a moment, his heart beating fast, half in and half out of the entryway, hoping he hadn't been deserted. *Rambo*. The name swirled in his head like a talisman. Determined, he marched down the hall to his room and inserted the key into the lock.

As Gary pushed open the door, he felt a reassuring brush of something cold along his skin. It had to be Gregori pushing past so that his body was protecting the mortal's—at least, Gary hoped that was what it was. In any case, it gave him added courage.

Two men whirled to face him. The room was a mess. Drawers upended, his clothes scattered, even his books shredded. Gary stopped just inside the doorway. One of the men produced a gun. "Come on in. Shut the door," he ordered tersely.

After facing Gregori, no one could look menacing. Gary found he wasn't nearly as afraid as he would normally have been. He closed the door carefully and faced the two strangers. They exchanged a quick look between them, clearly uneasy that Gary wasn't visibly upset. They had been led to believe this would be an easy job.

"Are you Gary Jansen?" the one with the gun asked.

"This is my room. Perhaps you should introduce yourselves." Gary glanced around at the mess. "Are you thieves, or were you looking for something in particular?"

"We're here to ask the questions. You called Morrison's private number, said something was going on at the warehouse. When we got there, the place was going up in flames, and two of our people were dead. A vampiress was gone, taken to the hospital."

"Then you realize she was not really a vampiress. She

was one of those poor kids who come out at night and play vampire because they like gothic stuff. It's just a game to these kids. An attention-getter. It isn't the real thing. You should know the difference between a kid playing games and the real thing," Gary scolded.

"Do you know the difference?" the one with the gun asked, sudden insight making him suspicious.

Gary looked around and lowered his voice in a conspirator's whisper. "Tell me who you are first."

"I'm Evans, Derek Evans. I know you've heard of me. I work for Morrison. And this is Dan Martin. He's the one you talked to on the phone the other day."

"You should have listened to me," Gary reprimanded Martin. He pushed a hand through his hair and sank into a chair. "That girl was no vampire, and those two idiots had gone crazy. They weren't serious about finding the real thing. They wouldn't know the real thing if it bit them in the neck."

"But you would, wouldn't you," Martin said. "You've seen one." In spite of himself, there was awe in his voice.

"I tried to tell you, but you wouldn't listen," Gary said, shaking his head. "I told you to bring Morrison down to the warehouse. Where is he?"

"He sent us to find you, Gary. He thought you had betrayed us." Evans lowered the gun. "What happened in that warehouse?"

"Before I tell you, I have to know whether Morrison and the society sanctioned killing that poor girl," Gary said, keeping his tone very low.

Martin risked a quick look at Evans. "Of course not, Gary. Morrison would never want an innocent hurt."

"And what of my formula? I developed a tranquilizer

to aid our society members so that we could subdue a vampire, capture him, and study him, not cut one up into pieces. When I was approached about this, I was told that was the society's ultimate objective. But my formula was tainted with poison. Morrison must have ordered it."

"Morrison is the vampire expert. He realized the tranquilizer would never hold anything that strong," Martin supplied quickly.

"It wasn't just any poison," Gary bit out. "It was designed to be painful. Morrison wants to kill the vampires, not study them. The poison is fast-acting, extremely virulent, and agonizing."

"He wants to talk to you. Come with us, Gary. Let him explain all this to you." Martin added, "He sent us here to protect you. He was very worried after what happened in that warehouse."

"Is that why you trashed my room?" Gary asked.

"You didn't come home last night. We waited all day before we decided to look for clues to your disappearance," Evans said reasonably.

"And the gun?" Gary pushed.

"We were worried for our own safety. Morrison thinks maybe a real vampire went to the warehouse. He was afraid maybe the vampire turned you, that's why you weren't around during the day. We couldn't take any chances."

"Have you ever seen Morrison during the day?" Gary asked suddenly.

There was a shocked silence. "Well, sure, yeah," Evans stuttered, frowning, trying to remember. Shards of glass seemed to pierce his skull. He rubbed at his pounding temples. "You have, haven't you, Martin?"

Martin snarled, his face twisted and evil. "Of course. All the time. So have you, Evans. You remember."

He is lying, Gregori said softly in Savannah's head. *He is a servant of the master vampire. He intends to bring Gary somewhere out in the bayou.*

Can you stop him without bringing the police down on Gary?

We must pursue Morrison. He is the one behind the hunt for the proof of the existence of our people. He is using the society in an attempt to destroy our race. We can do no other than stop him. Gregori laid a hand gently on Gary's shoulder and was pleased when the mortal didn't give himself away by jumping. *Go with them. Allow them to lead us to the one who rules them.*

It was a little disconcerting to have Gregori's voice swirling imperiously around in his head, but Gary nodded slowly. "I didn't think Morrison would have anything to do with those idiots at the warehouse. That's why I called him. I thought maybe he could control the situation. Sure, let's go see him. I've got some wild tales to tell. Hell, no one's going to believe what I saw." With studied, casual grace, Gary reached into the mess of papers on the floor and snagged his laptop. Between the two men, he marched confidently out of his room, down the hall, and out into the night.

What are you going to do? Savannah was anxious on Gary's behalf. He had to live in the human world. That meant no suspicion could fall on him if the two men in his company were found dead.

No one will see Gary with the two puppets, Gregori said softly. *I have been at this for a thousand years, chérie. This is the world I live in. I know it well. We will probably not be so lucky this night as to trap our prey, but it is worth the try.*

They plan to kill Gary. Savannah was as adept as Gregori at reading the thoughts of those around her, and she could feel the malevolence seething just beneath the surface of the two men, particularly the one called Martin. He had been close to the vampire for some time, and the stench of evil was strong in him.

They are hoping for more information. Morrison wants to extract it himself, probably because he trusts no one. And he likes to see things in pain and terror. The thought came unbidden before he could censor it. *Go home now, Savannah.*

Don't send me home yet. You might need me to get Gary out. I won't wilt at the first sign of danger, I promise.

The two men were leading Gary toward the river. A boat was waiting, and Gary got in without hesitation. The water was choppy, the wind blowing hard. Gregori moved just above Gary to ensure that the dark compulsion of the kill did not overtake either man until they arrived at their destination. The ride seemed to take forever, and Gary was looking so pale, he was almost green. The ride had made him seasick. As he stepped off the boat into a little inlet in the bayou, he staggered.

Gregori steadied him, his arm, slipping around his shoulders for a brief moment to reassure him. It was evident Gary was aware there was something wrong with the two men. He felt the mortal take a deep breath and let it out slowly. Gary was going to be all right. He trusted Gregori.

Gary noticed immediately that Evans and Martin boxed him in as he walked along the marshy shore. Cypress trees rose out of the water, and a network of roots formed a macabre prison of stakes and weeping limbs. In the darkness they looked sinister. Tendrils of fog began to float toward them off the surface of the water, wisps of white that shrouded the bogs in an eerie iridescence.

There was a peculiar stench that rose off the embankment, a foul odor that permeated the air. Night insects seemed to be in great abundance, stinging bugs that dived and darted. Gary found himself slapping at the annoying things, trying not to hold his nose. The odor was putrefying, disgusting, like decayed meat rotting in the sun. His shoes were sinking into the bog, and he hesitated. Somewhere he had heard a man could sink under the marsh and be lost in the reeds and mud, deep within a sinkhole. Gary coughed and gagged, his body rebelling. Almost at once he could smell a fragrance, a hint of fresh air, a suggestion of wild flowers and forest. He almost believed he could hear the sound of water running over rocks. *Savannah*. He knew it was her touch, aiding him to get through the rotten stench.

The air was suddenly thick, hard to breathe. The wind ceased to blow, and for a moment there was total silence. Even the bugs stopped their incessant noise. The two men escorting Gary stopped, turned their faces toward the bog, and waited. Out in the darkness something moved. Something evil and cunning. A shadow spread over them, engulfed them. Again there was a sudden stillness, as if the shadow had hesitated before moving out into the open. A roar of rage and defiance filled the vacuum of silence with the thunder of a freight train.

Somewhere in the distance, snakes fell with a series of splashes into the water. Alligators slithered in the mud, the sound loud in the silence before they slid into water and disappeared beneath the murky depths. Martin shoved Gary unexpectedly from behind, sending him sprawling into the mud. His knees sank deep, almost to the thigh. Gary swallowed his fear and stood up slowly, facing the two murderous men.

"What is this? I thought I was meeting Morrison." He spoke calmly.

"Morrison decided he didn't need to talk to you," Martin said.

Morrison senses your presence, Gregori said to Savannah. *He is close. I can feel him, but I cannot pinpoint his exact location. This one is powerful; he has learned much in the centuries of his existence.*

He warned his servants, she said, afraid for Gary. Already she was positioning her body in front of the mortal. *He gave the order to kill Gary. You chase the vampire. I'll protect Gary.*

Gregori yanked her to the side, reinforcing the silent command with a hard push at her mind. He was taking no chances with her safety. *It is not going to happen, Savannah*, Gregori snarled, his fangs already exploding in his mouth.

The killing rage was on Martin, the darkness spreading like a stain through the night. He pointed the ugly little revolver at Gary's heart. "Wade out into the river. I'm sure the alligators are hungry tonight."

Gary shook his head sadly. "I feel sorry for you, Martin. You're the pawn the king has sacrificed while he escapes. You never even knew that all this time you were hunting the vampire, he was the one directing every move you ever made."

"I think I'll kill you slowly, Jansen. I don't like you," Martin said.

"Don't you see how he's twisted you? You've become the very thing you despise. Six months ago, would you have even contemplated killing someone? Morrison's done that to you," Gary persisted, trying to save the man's life.

Martin extended his arm, looking down the sights of the gun. Suddenly his expression changed to shock. The evil mask disappeared completely as he stared in horror at his own hand. The gun was swinging around to point at him. He fought the thing, tried to drop it, but it stuck in his palm. "Evans! Help me!" Martin screamed, the sound echoing across the waters.

Gary stepped back, trying to tear his mesmerized gaze from the man who only moments earlier had tried to kill him. Martin's arm was rising slowly toward his own head. "Evans!" He was shrieking it.

Evans lunged at Gary, tackled him, shoving him down into the mud and oozing muck. Pushing Gary's face hard into the mire, Evans tried to suffocate him, scooping filth into the gasping mouth. The sound of the gun was loud in the night, traveling across the bayou and startling wildlife for miles. Evans didn't look up to see the results, determined to kill Gary Jansen and leave his body to the alligators.

Gary thrashed violently, nearly dislodging him, but Evans hung on grimly, his hands finding and clamping around the exposed throat. A low growl warned him. He turned his head to see two red, fiery eyes staring unblinkingly only inches from his face. Startled, Evans released Gary and sank back onto his heels. At once he could make out the huge head of a wolf. Glossy black fur, sinewy muscles. The muzzle. White fangs. He screamed and threw himself backward toward the river, crawling to put distance between himself and the beast.

Gary was gasping for breath, muck in his eyes and mouth, unable to see anything. He could hear the hideous, repetitious screaming, the unearthly growls that raised the hair on the back of his neck, but he was blind, the black goo sealing his eyelids closed. Something huge brushed past him, something muscular, with fur. It smelled wild and dangerous. There was a tremendous splash in the water. The screaming escalated, then was cut off abruptly in mid-cry.

Savannah's arm crept around his shoulders, and she was wiping at the mud with a soft cloth, trying to clear his vision while he used his finger to scoop the stuff from his mouth. "That was too close," she whispered. "I'm sorry. Gregori wouldn't allow me to help."

Gary spat more muck from his mouth. "I'm not surprised." The words were muffled by the goo, but she understood them all the same.

Savannah couldn't look around her and see the death everywhere. Gregori's world was bleak and ugly, filled with violence and destruction. She ached for him, ached for the terrible emptiness that would always have to be a part of his life. She knew that his keeping her away from it was more than a matter of her safety. Gregori might say that to her, even to himself, but deep inside, where it counted, in his heart, in his soul, he didn't want the violence to touch her, to change who she was. It mattered to him that he protect her from such a fate. He was determined that she never would have the death of another on her hands.

Gary managed to pry his eyes open. Savannah was

inspecting him anxiously, dabbing at the mud on his face. He glanced over to where Martin had stood and saw the man's body on the ground, the water from the marsh oozing up around him. The gun was still clutched in his hand, and blood was spreading out from the pool under his head, leeching into the waters of the marsh. Already insects were swarming around the feast. Gary looked away quickly, his stomach lurching. He wasn't cut out to be Rambo.

"Where's Gregori?" he asked, biting the words out between clenched teeth.

Savannah wiped more mud from his mouth. "Leave him alone for a few minutes," she advised softly.

"Where's Evans?" Gary suddenly pushed her aside to look anxiously this way and that, worried that he couldn't protect Savannah.

"He's dead," she said bluntly. "Gregori killed him to save your life." She stood up and wiped ineffectually at her mud-spattered jeans. "I hate this place. I wish we'd never come here."

"Savannah." Gary moved up beside her. There was a catch in her voice he had never heard before. Savannah, always filled with life and laughter, seemed so sad all of a sudden, so lost. "Are you okay? Gregori's right. You shouldn't be here."

She shook her head, fighting down sudden anger. "What neither of you seems to understand is that I *am* here. Whether I'm here physically or not, I'm with him. I feel what he feels, exactly what he feels. It isn't protecting me to wrap me in cotton wool and put me on a shelf." She jerked away from him and walked toward the river.

Gregori materialized behind her, his large, stocky frame dwarfing her smaller one. He bent protectively over her, one hand on her shoulder. Gary watched as she shook it off, not in the least intimidated by his size or power.

"Do not be angry, *mon amour*, I truly sought only to protect you. Had Martin fired the gun, the bullet would have hit you. I could not allow such a thing," Gregori said gently. He could feel the raging conflict in her. She had never been so close to death and violence until Gregori had chosen to force his claim on her. From their first day together as lifemates, she had known nothing else.

"There was no chance that you would have let him shoot me. Instead, because you locked me up with some ancient command, Gary was almost murdered in front of my eyes." Savannah's fists were clenched tightly. She wanted to hit something, and Gregori seemed a solid enough target.

"I will not take chances with your life, *ma petite*," he emphasized, his arms circling her waist from behind. When she would have stepped away from him, he tightened his hold on her. "I will not, Savannah. You should never have been here."

"You lost your chance at the vampire because of me, didn't you?" she demanded, tears in her voice, shimmering in her eyes. "He couldn't sense your presence— you're able to do something to mask it—but he knew I was there, even though I was invisible."

It was the truth. He didn't want it to be, especially with her so confused and upset. Gregori couldn't bear it when she was unhappy. But there was no way to lie, and he wouldn't have done so even if he could have. He remained silent, allowing her to read the answer in his mind.

Savannah shook her head and banged it against the heavy muscles of his chest. "I hate this, Gregori. I feel so useless. I feel like I'm endangering you. We are life-mates. I asked you to meet me halfway in my world, and you've done it. You've done everything I've asked of you. What have I done to live in your world with you?"

Gregori bent his dark head to the slim white column of her neck. "You are my world, *ma petite*, my very existence. You are what makes living bearable. You are my light, the very air I breathe." His mouth brushed her pulse, her earlobe. "You are not meant to walk in death. You never were."

She swung around, her blue eyes darkening to deep violet. "If you walk in death, Gregori, then that is where you will find me. Right beside you. I belong where you are. I am your *lifemate*. There is no other. I am your life-mate." She held up a hand, furious at the situation. "There will be no more discussion on this. You can do no other than to see to my happiness, and the only way I will be happy will be to learn to cloak my presence from vampire, humans, and Carpathians alike."

Savannah stalked away from him, leaving him standing on the water's edge as she went back to Gary. "Come on, let's get out of here."

"What happens when the bodies are found? The cops are going to come looking for the last person seen alive with them," Gary said, reluctantly stepping back into the boat. He was still digging muck out of his nose and mouth.

"No one saw you with them," Gregori answered quietly. "They saw only two men leaving the hotel, two men walking through the Quarter, and two men getting into the boat. That's why we cannot take the boat back."

Gary blinked. "How do you propose we get back? Fly?" he asked sarcastically.

"Exactly," Gregori answered complacently.

Gary shook his head. "This is getting too bizarre for me."

"Do you wish me to blank out your mind from experiencing this?" Gregori asked politely, his thoughts clearly on Savannah.

"No," Gary said decisively. He caught up the laptop from the seat of the boat. "But why don't you take me to another hotel? You and Savannah could use some time alone. And to be honest with you, I wouldn't mind thinking things over a bit. There's a lot to take in."

Gregori found himself liking the mortal even more. He had no idea a human might be so sensitive to another's feelings. Raven, Savannah's mother, had been like that, but she was a special case, a true psychic. His experience with mortals had always been with those hunting him, butchering and murdering his people. He preferred to stay at a distance from mortals. He was not prepared to like Gary Jansen.

Savannah was already dissolving, mist streaming through the tendrils of fog, moving across the water. Gregori caught Gary up and launched himself skyward, streaking after her. Gary squealed, a high-pitched sound suspiciously like that of a piglet. He couldn't help himself as he clutched at Gregori's broad shoulders, his fingers clenching the shirt hard. The wind was whistling past his body so fast, he had to squeeze his eyes closed tight, unable to look down.

Wait for me, Savannah, Gregori ordered, his black-velvet voice edged with iron.

She didn't even hesitate. She continued moving quickly across the river toward the French Quarter.

Savannah! He was imperious now, a flat order delivered in his mesmerizing voice. *You will do what I say.*

No, I won't. There was defiance in her voice, a mixture of belligerence and sorrow. He could feel the tears burning in her throat, in her chest. She was running as much from herself as she was from him.

Gregori swore softly in several languages. *Do not make me force you into obedience*, chérie. *It is not safe for you.*

Maybe I don't want to be safe, she hissed at him, forging ahead into the night. *Maybe I want to do something crazy for a change. I hate this, Gregori. I hate it.*

Mon amour, do not run from what we have together. I know our life has not started out in paradise, that the world we must inhabit is ugly and dangerous, but we do it together.

You hunt. She was crying; he could feel it. *I endanger you.*

Gregori sent her waves of comfort but knew it wasn't enough. The mortal clutching at his shirt stirred. "Um, Gregori?" The wind snatched the words from his mouth and blew them across the water.

Gregori's reply was more of a growl. His body was above the mist now, a protective blanket. "Say what you have to say."

"I think Savannah is upset."

There was no answer. Gregori continued to follow Savannah.

"If you don't mind my saying so, sometimes women just need to cry it out," Gary ventured.

Savannah went straight to their house. Once she was within the safety of the four walls, Gregori broke off to take Gary to a new rooming house. "You know that you cannot leave until we come for you tomorrow," he advised. He was a shadow in Savannah's mind. He could see her clearly, running through the front room to the spiral staircase, toward the precious treasure Julian had left for them.

Savannah tore open the door to the basement, then waved her hand across the hidden door to the chamber. She crawled into the healing soil and sank deep, then curled up and cried as though her heart was breaking. So many deaths. Peter. And what if they had lost Gary tonight? They could have lost him, and she would have been helpless to aid him, because Gregori would not allow it.

After leaving Gary, Gregori came to her in gentleness, with tenderness. His hands were caressing as he undressed her unresisting body. He made no attempt to arouse her, to persuade her to join with him. Instead he crushed herbs, soothing, healing herbs that carried the scents of their homeland to them. He joined her in the sleeping chamber, burrowing deep into the rich soil, taking her slender body into his arms, pulling her close.

Savannah pillowed her head on his broad shoulder, her eyes closed tightly. Her clenched fist was at her mouth, and he could feel the sobs wracking her frame. Gregori murmured to her in French and stroked her hair, his arms protective as he waited for her to cry out the storm of sorrow.

He knew how to hunt and kill the most vicious and cunning of all creatures, the vampire. He could create storms and bring lightning from the sky. He could make the earth move. He had absolutely no idea how to stop a flood of tears. He held her in his arms, and when he could no longer stand it, he issued a sharp command and sent them both to sleep.

Chapter Fifteen

The storm moved in from the sea in the gathering darkness, blowing fast and furious over the canal and into New Orleans. It was wild and uninhibited, slamming rain into the streets with such force that it pooled inches deep immediately, the city's massive pumps unable to keep up with the load. Bolts of lightning streaked and sizzled across the sky and danced in the air, displaying the raw magnificence of nature. Thunder cracked loudly, drums filling the sky, breaking free to shake the very foundations of the buildings.

Gregori padded through the house on bare feet, suddenly worried about Savannah. She was out in the courtyard, alone, quiet, not sharing her thoughts with him. He had merged his mind with hers twice since rising, and both times she was confused, sad, chaotic. He had backed off to allow her space. She wanted the one thing he knew he would never be able to give her: the freedom to join him in his battles. The thought of Savannah in any kind of danger robbed him of the very air he breathed. Gregori was at a loss. For all his knowledge, all his power, he was unable to say the right thing to make it better for her.

Savannah had wandered silently out into the courtyard as the wind had risen, watching the clouds darken, swirl, and boil against the night sky, heralding the coming gale. The sky had opened up, dousing the earth. Savannah simply curled up in a chair and watched with shadowed eyes.

Gregori paused in the open doorway, his eyes molten mercury, watchful and careful. She was staring up at the dancing whips of lightning, uncaring that three inches of water had pooled on the patio, that her long hair was drenched and that the thin shirt she wore clung to her like a second skin. She was so beautiful, she took his breath away. All around her nature was erupting, wild and untamed. In the middle of it all, she sat as if she belonged. The white silk of his shirt, soaked in the rain, was transparent, hugging her high, firm breasts so that she looked like a pagan offering.

She was deep in thought, far away. Gregori touched her mind with his because he needed the contact. She seemed so distant, and he no longer could bear the separation from her. Despite her outward appearance of serenity, her mind was as wild as the storm. She was soaring above the earth, no longer anchored by skin and bone. The fury of the impending gale was in her, turbulent, untamed.

He could find no condemnation in her for his failures, no blame for the sorrow in her. There was only a fierce need to find a way to understand and accept those things she could not change. She felt the shortcomings were her own youth and lack of experience. She was particularly distressed that she had inadvertently placed him in danger because she didn't have the knowledge to shield her presence from their enemies. Gregori nearly groaned aloud. He didn't deserve her; he never would.

Savannah turned her head slowly toward him, her blue eyes dark with the wildness of the storm in their depths. He could feel it then, the heat and hunger. The raging storm. It moved through her blood the way it moved through the night sky. It called to something primitive and savage in him. He felt the beast roar, the hunger swamp him. Silver eyes glowed red in the dark night, ferocious, feral, more animal than man.

Gregori would never forget that moment. Not in a century, not in an eternity. The night was theirs. In spite of everything between them, there was nothing that could keep them apart. They belonged together. They needed each other. Hearts and minds, bodies and souls. Trees swayed in the winds; plants nearly bent double under the onslaught. The humidity was high, the air filled with electricity arcing and snapping. Jagged bolts of white heat slammed into the ground, shaking the earth. Lightning hit the side of a building a few blocks away, charring the walls and sending bricks spilling to the sidewalk and street. It exploded a nearby telephone pole into a shower of fiery sparks.

Savannah stood in the courtyard, the lightning arcing across the sky above her, the wind whipping her hair around her, the rain soaking her body, and she lifted her arms to embrace the raw power of nature. Her skin was creamy, flawless, wet. The silk shirt clung to her rib cage and emphasized the dark rose of her erect, beckoning nipples. Her legs were bare and slender, and the dark triangle of curls at their apex enticed and beckoned, mysteriously summoning him. Her long hair, unbound in the wind, was wet and wild, like the night itself.

Gregori went to her because he had to; he had no other choice. Nothing, no obstacle could have prevented him from getting to her side. His arm snaked out and dragged her to him, his mouth meeting hers with the ferocious intensity of the storm. He couldn't find the words, had no words to give her, only this, his fierce need to show her what she was to him. What she gave to him. Life. Everything.

He wanted her just like that. Wet and wild, with lightning streaking across the sky and scorching their blood. His mouth took hers, feeding voraciously, devouring, claiming her for his own, branding her mouth, her skin with his mark.

Fire raced across her neck as he kissed her, stroked her with his tongue, as his teeth sank deep. The pleasure and pain shook her, reduced her to a wild ecstasy, craving, forever craving more. He took her blood, the sweet, hot fluid filling him as he gorged himself, as he tasted her very essence.

As he fed on her honeyed spice, his hands stripped the edges of the shirt aside so that he could cup the fullness of her breasts, reveling in her body, her softness. So perfect. He could feel what she wanted in her mind—the savage hunger, the need to match the fury of the storm, the need to feel alive in the midst of all the violence surrounding them.

Her need was his. He stroked his tongue across the pinpricks so his mouth could wander down her throat, leaving fire in its wake. He found her breast through the thin, water-soaked transparency of her shirt and suckled wildly, a frantic frenzy of lust and love. His hands found her bare bottom, cupped her buttocks to drag her against his raging body. Need overcame sense; his fangs burst forth, and he pierced the creamy swell of her breast, so that she flowed into him like nectar.

Savannah cradled his head with one arm, her other hand exploring his body, deliberately bringing him to a fever pitch. The storm crashed around them, through them, pooling low in their bodies, demanding relief. He fed as was his right, hands claiming her, sliding down to her wet, hot, pulsing core. His fingers probed, caressed, tempted, teased. The combination of his mouth feeding and fingers stroking drove her wild, so that she moved against his hand, desperate for release.

Savannah's husky cries were lost in the crack of thunder as her body rippled with life and demanded more of him. Gregori lifted his head and watched with hungry eyes the thin trail of red mingling with the rain on her body. He stroked his tongue across her breast, then followed the trickling path of ruby to her belly, then lower, so that he found her hot and ready, crying out as she fragmented under his attack.

Lightning slashed and sizzled, whips of heat that seemed to lash them with their fury, seemed to dance through their bodies, feeding the storm in them, around them. Gregori propelled her backward until she came up against the iron lacework of the arbor. His hands turned her, so that her breasts were between the slats and she caught at the metal for support, her fists clenching as he lifted her lips. His palms caressed and stroked, the softness of her driving him mad with need. He pressed against her bottom with his own raging body, the hard length of him swelling even more. He had never needed anything more.

Savannah made a sound, a little cry torn from her throat. The soft plea shattered his last control, and he surged into her sheath of hot velvet. He heard himself groan with pleasure, the wind taking the sound, wrenched from his deepest being, and sending it off into the turbulent night. His hands held her hips pinned as he buried himself deeper and deeper, hard and fast, as wild as the battering winds.

Her back, so long and flawless, stretched out before him, and he bent his head to lap at the beads of water there. She was small, so delicate, yet strong and as wild as anything nature could conjure up. The insatiable heat of the Carpathian ritual was on them, but his heart was captured for all time, so that as wild as he was, he was equally tender.

He felt her weaken, a momentary dizziness. He knew instantly what was wrong, although she tried to conceal it. He had taken too much blood. Without consent, without comment, he lifted her. Her small cry of bereavement was satisfying to his male ego as he took them across the patio to a lounge chair. Settling himself into the wet cushions, he pulled her onto him, so that she straddled him.

Savannah cried out as she lowered her fiercely aroused body onto his. He filled her completely, white-hot friction, tight and erotic. Gregori caught the nape of her neck, forced her head toward his chest. *You will feed now.*

She was like a wild thing, her body moving frantically over his, taking his iron control and reducing it to ashes. His hands spanned her waist, and he allowed himself the luxury of sheer pleasure, the lightning sizzling through his own body, flames consuming him. His hands moved up the perfect line of her back, found her hair, and forced her head to him. *I need this from you. I need you to take me into your body.* He clenched his teeth against the pleasure threatening to drive him mad.

His command was really a plea, and Savannah leaned forward, her body riding his, her tongue lapping at the beads of water on his chest once, twice. His body clenched as fire streaked through him, pain and pleasure melting into one sensation. Her teeth bound them together as his body did. Body and soul. God, he loved her, felt whole, complete with her. The terrible emptiness, the black void, was pushed aside for all time by the beauty of her spirit, her soul.

He whispered ancient words of love through clenched teeth, surging into her, filling her heart as he filled her body. When the explosion came, it was as turbulent as the slashing whips of lightning, as loud as the cracks of thunder, as wild as the winds ripping through the night.

They clung to each other, exhausted, sated, awed at the beauty of their lovemaking, the beauty of the storm. Even as they sat welded together, her head over his pounding heart, his arms tight around her, the winds began to die down, nature easing its frantic force as their hearts slowly returned to a normal rhythm.

Gregori kissed her temples, the line of her cheekbone, brushed his mouth along the corner of hers, nibbled his way down to her chin. "You are my world, Savannah. You must know it."

She held him, shocked at the intensity, the force of their need for each other. "If this thing between us grows stronger over the years, neither of us will live very long."

Gregori laughed softly. "You could be right, *chérie*. You are a dangerous woman."

He flowed from the lounge chair, still holding her

locked to him, and glided across the courtyard into the house. The shower was hot on their bodies after the cool rain, but they stayed there for some time, too spent to move. Savannah was grateful that he held her in his arms, afraid her legs would never support her again.

Gregori dried her slender body with a towel before waving a hand to clothe himself. Savannah was wandering through the house back to the kitchen, with only another of his shirts to cover her. Her bare skin showed marks that hadn't been there before, and he followed her, cursing his own roughness. He had left his brand on her breast deliberately, the mark of his possession, but the faint smudges elsewhere needed to be healed.

Savannah laughed softly. "I don't hurt anywhere, life-mate. I loved it, and you know it."

"I can make you love it without marking you," he corrected.

She idly picked up a packet of papers and sifted through them, then dropped them onto the counter. "If you ever hurt me, Gregori, I promise you, I'll tell you immediately."

He sensed the return of her restlessness. "What is it?"

"Let's do something, Gregori. Something that has nothing to do with the hunt. Something different. Something touristy."

"The streets are flooded tonight," he pointed out.

She shrugged. "I know. I was just looking at some pamphlets earlier, on all the tourist attractions here," Savannah said nonchalantly.

Gregori looked up alertly at the carefully calculated disinterest in her voice. "Did any of them seem appealing to you?"

She shrugged again very casually. "Most of the more

interesting ones are the day trips. Like the bayous. There's one you can go on with someone who grew up in the bayou." She shrugged again. "I like learning local history. I wouldn't mind a tour of the bayou with some-one who grew up there."

"You have the brochure handy?" he asked.

"It isn't important," Savannah said with a little sigh. Tossing the packet of pamphlets onto the table, she picked up her hairbrush.

Gregori took it out of her hand. "If you want a proper tour of the bayou, Savannah, then we will go."

"I like to do the tourist thing," Savannah admitted with a slight smile. "It's kind of fun to ask questions and learn new things."

"I bet you are very good at it," he answered her, slowly running the brush through the blue-black length of her hair. It crackled with a life of its own, refusing to be tamed. He gathered it into his hands just to feel how soft and silky it was. Over her shoulder, his pale gaze rested on the brochure she had put to one side. If Savannah wanted a tour, he would move heaven and earth to get her one. "We do not always go chasing after vampires and the mortal assassins plaguing our people," he began diplomatically.

"I know. They turn up everywhere we go," she agreed.

He tugged at a tangle in her glossy hair. "When you first proposed to come to New Orleans, we had hoped the society members would follow us and leave Aidan and his people in peace. Is that not what you wanted?"

"Not particularly," she admitted with a flash of her blue eyes. "I was only trying to get you to come here. You know, classic honeymoon. Sweet young wife teaches wizened old grouch how to have fun. That sort of thing."

"Wizened old grouch?" he echoed in astonishment. "The old part I can accept, even the grouch. But I am definitely not wizened." In punishment he tugged her hair.

"Ow!" She swung around and glared indignantly at him. "*Wizened* sort of seemed to fit. You know, *wizard, wizened.*"

Gregori crushed her hair to his face to hide the sudden emotion overwhelming him. The fragrance of flowers and fresh air surrounded him. So this was what he had sought all those long centuries. Fun. Belonging. Someone with whom to share laughter and teasing and to make even the difficult moments in life beautiful. She was so much a part of him, he couldn't return to a barren existence again. He would never choose to stay in the world without her.

"Do you think I am too old, Savannah?" he asked softly, taking strands of her hair into his mouth. So soft. So much like silk but even better.

"Not old, Gregori," she corrected gently. "Just old-fashioned. You have a tendency to believe women should always do as they're told."

He found himself laughing. "Not that you do."

She tilted her head back, a not-so-subtle hint for him to resume brushing. "I wish you would understand that I can't stand by and watch someone get hurt because of me."

He sighed audibly and allowed several heartbeats to go by before replying. "I should never have taken you with me and placed you in such a position, *ma chérie.* For that I apologize."

"I want to discuss this," she insisted, clenching her fist.

He pushed aside the thin shirt, bent his head, and touched his mouth to her bare shoulder. The sensation was as intimate as sin. "There can be no discussion. We put this to rest last night. I will not do this, not even for you. You must understand who I am. You are in me, as I am in you. You know how I feel. I can do no other than to protect you. That is who I am."

"Do you have to be so inflexible about this, Gregori?" Savannah complained. But he was right; she already knew the answer. It was impossible to be in his head and not feel his implacable resolve.

"The storm is passing over us. Do you want to go to the bayou this night?" he asked softly, separating her hair deftly and beginning to weave it into a thick braid.

She loved the feel of his hands in her hair, his fingers massaging her scalp, tugging so gently on the thick length of braid. She reached up to place a palm over her bare shoulder, the exact spot where his lips had touched her. "I would love to go to the bayou with you."

He smiled at her, his silver eyes molten mercury. "We can observe wildlife for a change. No vampires."

"No weird society types," she added.

"No mortals in need of rescuing," Gregori said with intense satisfaction. "Get dressed."

"You're always taking my clothes off, then telling me to get dressed again," Savannah complained with her infuriating smile, that little sexy one that drove him mad.

He turned her around to face him, caught the front of her shirt, and drew the gaping edges together to cover her tempting body. "You cannot expect me to dress you myself, do you?" he asked, leaning down to brush her lips with his. She actually felt her heart jump in response. Or maybe it was his heart. It was nearly impossible to tell the difference anymore.

It took Savannah mere moments to be ready. Hand in

hand, they walked into the courtyard. The rain was now no more than mist, but the water was still inches deep on the tiles. Gregori brought her hand to his mouth. "I will never look at this place in quite the same way, *ma petite*," he said softly. His voice whispered over her skin, black velvet that slipped over her body and seeped into her mind. His voice was purity itself, so beautiful that no one could resist it, least of all her. Savannah found herself blushing, the wild color creeping up her face.

His laughter was soft and husky. His body was already beginning to shape-shift as he launched himself skyward. Savannah watched with pride as his body compacted and iridescent feathers covered the raptor's shape. He was beautiful, with sharp eyes, razor-like beak, talons, a powerful body. She didn't have the expertise to change in mid-air, but she held the image he gave her in her mind and felt the peculiar wrenching of bones and muscles heralding the change.

Sensations were completely different. Like the night she had run free as the wolf, Savannah now had the senses of a bird of prey. Her vision was sharp and clear, her eyes enormously wide. She spread her wings experimentally, then flapped them in the light drizzle. They were much bigger than she had anticipated. It delighted her, and she flapped them harder so she could create a wind, causing waves in the water standing in the patio.

Are you having fun? Gregori's voice held a hint of laughter.

This is so cool, lifemate, she answered. Her rapidly beating wings lifted her into the air. The light mist was already passing overhead. The air was warm and heavy with the promise of moisture, but she soared high, reveling in her ability to do so.

Gregori's larger, stronger body dropped over hers, close and protective, guiding her in the direction of the bayou. As high up as they were, the sharp eyes of the raptor could spot the smallest of movements below. Details were vivid and clear. Even colors were different. Infrared vision, heat sensors—Savannah wasn't certain what it was exactly, but the way she perceived the world was a different and unique experience.

She dipped beneath Gregori and soared away from him, turning sideways and circling high above him. In her mind she could hear him swearing. As always he sounded arrogant, elegant, Old World, completely in command. Laughing, she caught a thermal and rode it up over the river. The male dropped down to cover her with his huge wings, fencing her in. *Spoilsport!* she accused him, her touch in his mind a whisper of lightness, of invitation to join in her fun.

You are in a great deal of trouble, ma femme. He knew the threat was empty when he made it; he would give her the world. But why did she have to be such a little dare-devil all the time?

Anyone choosing to live with you would have to have a sense of adventure, don't you think? Her soft laughter played over his skin like music, like the gentle breeze blowing from the mountains in their homeland.

Even within the bird's body, he stirred to life, need and hunger rising to become a part of him. Relentless. Demanding. Savage in its intensity. It was more than simple lust. More than hunger. More than need. It was all of it merged together with a tenderness he had never conceived he could feel. When she was at her most outrageous, her most defiant, that was when his heart melted. *What I think is, you had better do things the way I want you to do them. Shape-shifting is no simple thing.*

Everybody else does it, she objected, darting out from beneath him.

The male raptor dove at her, coming in fast and as straight as an arrow, plummeting toward her out of the night sky. Savannah, inside the female's body, gave a little shriek of fright, her heart pounding at the unexpectedness of the attack. It came out a strange caw, startling her so that for a moment she forgot what she was doing and nearly shape-shifted back into her own body.

Savannah! His voice was a soft command, hypnotic, impossible to ignore or defy. He held the vision of the bird in her mind, completely merging his mind with hers so that they were one. The male bird of prey once more flew in to cover the female's smaller body, guiding her over the city and canal to the dark bayou.

It was your fault for scaring me, she proclaimed.

Beneath them moss-covered cypress trees stood in the water. Dense reeds rose out of the marsh. The bayou was teeming with life, with sounds of insects and birds and frogs. Turtles shared the fallen, rotting logs with young alligators, and snakes slithered or wound themselves, sated and drowsy, along branches. The male bird prodded the female, and they soared above the beauty of the night for a time, watching the ever-changing scene below them.

Gregori sent a call into the night, seeking the one who would fulfill Savannah's wish. She wanted a guide, one who had been born and raised in the area and who could answer all her questions. A boat moved up through the waters in answer to his summons. He had been particularly strong in his command, urging the man to answer immediately. *Land on the rock below, Savannah, and shape-shift as you do so. I will hold the image with you.*

For a moment she was afraid. The rock was not particularly large, and the marsh was treacherous. *Trust in me*, ma petite. *I would never allow anything to happen to you*, Gregori reassured her gently. She could feel the comfort of his strong arms surrounding her, even in the form of a bird.

The extent of Gregori's powers always astonished Savannah. He certainly was legendary. All Carpathians spoke of him in whispers. She had believed he was powerful, but she had not conceived of the things of which he was capable. She felt unexpected pride in him and an astonishment that he would want someone so inexperienced in Carpathian ways, in the essentials of their training, as she was.

I will teach you all you need to know, chérie, *and I will enjoy the teaching*, he whispered softly in her head. She could feel the fire instantly moving through her blood at the whisper of his voice.

The small bird's talons aimed down and sought purchase on the boulder even while her slender form shimmered in the humid air. As hers solidified, the male bird of prey found a small patch of stable ground nearby to land on. He glided in smoothly on two feet, his muscular frame dwarfing Savannah's. They could hear the steady drone of the boat's engine as it chugged toward them. Laughing, Savannah jumped from her precarious perch on the boulder into the safety of Gregori's arms.

He caught her, crushing her against his chest, sheer elation, exhilaration, rushing through his veins. To feel again was beyond his comprehension, to feel like this, to have such joy in him, was totally unbelievable. He whispered to her in the ancient language, words of love and commitment that he could not find a way to express in any other language. She was more than she could ever know to him; she was his life, the very air he breathed. *You worry about the most ridiculous things*, he said gruffly, burying his face for just a moment against her neck, inhaling her scent.

"Do I?" she asked aloud, her eyes dancing at him. "You're the one always concerned I'm going to do something wild."

"You do wild things," he answered complacently. "I never know what you are going to do next. It is a good thing I reside in your mind, *ma petite*, or I would have to be locked up in the nearest asylum."

Her lips brushed his chin, feathered along his jaw, then nibbled enticingly at the edge of his mouth. "I think you should be locked up. You're positively lethal to women."

"Not to women, only to you." Gregori stopped her teasing mouth with his own, taking possession despite the fact that the boat was almost alongside them. He was helpless in the web of her spell. She was magic, beauty, fascination.

Her laughter was bubbling up again, her fists curling in his shirt. "We have company, lifemate. I presume you sent for him."

"You and your ideas," he growled, gliding across the spongy surface to the boat.

The captain of the vessel didn't appear to notice that Gregori's feet never quite touched the swamp. His eyes were on Savannah in genuine awe. "You're the magician, Savannah Dubrinsky. I've been to three of your shows. I flew all the way to New York City to see you last year, Denver a few months ago, and San Francisco this month. I can't believe it's really you."

"What a compliment." Savannah flashed her famous smile, the one that brought those curious silver stars to the centers of her eyes. "You traveled all that way just to see me? I'm flattered."

"How do you do that? Disappear like you do into mist? I got as close to the stage as I could, and I still couldn't figure it out," he said, leaning forward, extending his hand. "I'm Beau La Rue. I was born and raised right here in the bayou. It's a privilege to meet you, Ms. Dubrinsky."

Savannah slipped her hand into the captain's, a brief touch only as Gregori put her feet firmly on the boat's floor. He was already pulling her back into his arms as he did so, successfully removing her from the captain's grip. "I am Gregori," he said in his soft, gentle way, the voice that enthralled, that captivated. The one that purred with menace. "I am Savannah's husband."

Beau LaRue had met only one other man as dangerous as this in his lifetime. By coincidence it had also been at night in the bayou. Power and danger clung to Gregori like a second skin. His unusual pale eyes were mesmerizing, his voice hypnotic. Beau smiled. He had spent most of his life in these waters, had encountered everything from alligators to smugglers. Life was always good in the bayou, unpredictable and exhilarating.

"You picked an interesting night for your tour," he said happily. The actual storm had passed, but the mood of the water was dangerous tonight. On the banks around them, the alligators, usually so calm and quiet, sunning themselves in the light of day, were bellowing in challenge or sliding silently into the waters to hunt prey.

Gregori's white teeth flashed in answer. He was part of the night, the creatures known to him, the restless, untamed land matching his hungry soul. Beau watched him, observing the utter stillness marking the dangerous predator, the merciless eyes moving constantly, missing nothing. The powerful, well-muscled body was deceptively relaxed but ready for anything. The face, harshly sensual, beautifully cruel, was etched with hardship and knowledge, risk and peril. Gregori stayed in the shadows, but the silver menace of his gaze glowed with a strange iridescent light in the dark of the night.

Beau took the opportunity to study Savannah. She was everything up close that she had been on the stage, even more. Ethereal, mysterious, sexy. The very stuff of men's fantasies. Her face was flawless, lit up with joy, her eyes clear, like beautiful blue star sapphires. Her laughter was musical and infectious. She was small and innocent beside the predator in his boat. She would touch Gregori's arm, point to something on the embankment, her body brushing his lightly, and each time it happened, those pale eyes would warm to molten mercury and caress her face intimately, hungrily.

Beau began to answer her questions, explaining all about his youth, his father trapping for food and fur, how he and his brother collected moss from the trees for his mother and sisters to dry and stuff in their mattresses. He found himself telling her all kinds of childhood memories, things he didn't know he'd even remembered. She hung on his every word, making him feel as though he was the only man on the planet—until Gregori stirred, a mere suggestion of rippling muscle but enough to remind Beau that she was well protected.

He took them to all his favorite spots, to the most

beautiful, exotic places he knew. Gregori asked questions then, about herbs and natural healing arts on the bayou. Beau found the voice impossible to resist, like velvet, a black-magic power he could listen to forever.

"I heard a few men in a restaurant talking about a bayou legend," Savannah said suddenly. She leaned on the side of the boat, presenting him with an intriguing view of her tight jeans. They clung lovingly to every curve.

Gregori moved, a flowing of his body, gliding silently, and his large frame was blanketing Savannah's, blocking out the captain's enticing view. Gregori leaned into her, his arms coming down on either side of the railing to imprison her against him. *You are doing it again.* His words brushed softly in her mind even as his warm breath teased the tendrils of hair at her neck.

Savannah leaned back into him, fitting her bottom into the cradle of his hips. She was happy, free of the oppressive weight of the hunt, of death and violence. There were only the two of them.

Three, he reminded her, his teeth scraping her sensitive pulse. He could feel the answering surge of her blood, the molten lava spreading in his.

My mother thinks my father is a cave man. I'm beginning to think you could give him a run for his money.

Disrespectful little thing.

"Which legend? There are so many," Beau said.

"About an old alligator that lies in wait to eat hunting dogs and little children," Savannah said.

Gregori tugged at her long braid so that she tilted her head back. His mouth brushed the line of her throat. *I could be a hungry alligator,* he offered softly.

"The old man," Beau said. "Everybody loves that

story. It's been handed down for a hundred years or more, and the critter grows with each telling." He paused for a moment, maneuvering his craft along a snag in the canal. Cypress trees bent low, looking like macabre stick figures dressed in long strands of hanging moss. Occasionally splashes could be heard as a snake plopped into the water.

"It's said that old man alligator has lived forever. He's huge now, growing fat with his kills and more wily and cunning than anything else in the bayou. He claims his territory, and the other gators give him wide berth. They say he kills any alligator stupid enough to wander into his territory, young or old alike, male or female. Trappers have disappeared in that area from time to time and old man alligator gets the blame."

Beau allowed the boat to stop, so that they bobbed gently in the water. "It's funny you should ask about that particular tale. The man who gave me the tickets for your concert was very interested in that alligator. We used to come out here at night together, gathering herbs and bark, and we poked around looking for the monster. We never did find it, though."

"Who gave you tickets to Savannah's show?" Gregori asked softly, already knowing the answer.

"A man named Selvaggio, Julian Selvaggio. His family has been in New Orleans almost from the first founding. I met him years ago. We're good friends"—he grinned engagingly—"despite the fact that he's Italian."

Gregori's eyebrows shot up. Julian was born and raised in the Carpathian Mountains. He was no more Italian than Gregori was French. Julian had spent considerable time in Italy, just as Gregori had in France, but both were Carpathian through and through.

"I know Julian," Gregori volunteered, his white teeth gleaming in the darkness. Water lapped at the boat, making a peculiar slapping sound. The rocking was more soothing and peaceful than disturbing.

Beau looked smug. "I thought you might. You both have a connection to Savannah, you both ask the same questions about natural medicine, and you both look as intimidating as hell."

"I am nicer than he is," Gregori said, straight-faced.

Savannah's head brushed his chest. Her laughter was sweet music in the stifling heat of the swamp. "So you never found the alligator. Is it true he eats large dogs?"

"Well, the fact is, a great number of hounds have been lost in the bayou along a particular trail. It's in the old man's supposed territory. A couple of hunters say they saw him lying in wait to bushwhack the dogs. They couldn't nail him, though. No one can. He's been around so long, he knows all the ways of the bayou. One small warning and he's gone." The captain rubbed his forehead as if it was pounding.

"You are talking as if you believe he is real," Gregori pointed out gently. "Yet you say you and Julian did not find him. Julian is a hunter without equal. If there was such a creature, he would find it." He was reading the captain's mind, baiting him. Beside him, Savannah stirred as if to contradict his statement, but Gregori silenced her with an upraised palm.

"Julian knew he was there. He felt him."

"But you saw him." Gregori pushed the man a little harder, suddenly interested in this beast that could survive when so many others had not.

Beau glanced around the canal, uncomfortable in the dark of night. He was superstitious, and he had seen things, unexplainable things, and he didn't like to speak of them without light of the sun. "Maybe. Maybe I have seen the old man," he admitted, his voice low. "But out here, if you admit such a thing, the newcomers think you're loco."

"Tell us about it," Gregori urged, his voice velvet, mesmerizing, impossible to resist.

Chapter Sixteen

For a moment the wind ceased to blow, and the insects in the bayou were silent. A dark shadow seemed to pass overhead. Gregori looked at Savannah. Beau pulled a can of beer out of a cooler, offering drinks to the couple. When they declined, he downed a third of the contents in a single gulp.

"My father was a trapper," Beau told them. "I spent a lot of time in the bayou with him, trapping. When I was about sixteen, we were camped out at the old cabin, the one I pointed out to you earlier. There were some kids partying on a boat, kids from the city. They had a real nice boat, not like the old thing we took to school. I was jealous, you know. The girls were beautiful, and the boys dressed just right. When they saw me and my father, they laughed and pointed at us in our old skiff. I felt ashamed."

Savannah made a soft sound of sympathy, her natural inclination to comfort him. Gregori laced his fingers through hers, clamping her to his side. She was such a compassionate little thing, and she wove such a spell of enchantment around men without even realizing it. He turned her knuckles up to the warmth of his mouth in appreciation of her character.

Beau took another swig of the beer, then wiped at his mouth with the back of his hand. "We watched them go down the fork leading deep into the swamp. Their boat was large and shouldn't have made it that far into the reeds. Roots are thick there, sticking up out of the water every which way. The insects swarm around you, biting until you're covered in blood. It was impossible for that boat, yet somehow they did it, as if the way had been cleared for them. An invitation to death."

Savannah felt a cold chill, a dark, brooding dread that brought a shadow across her heart. "Why would anyone want to go to such a place?" she asked with a shiver.

Gregori's arm circled her shoulders and pulled her into the protection of his body. "There is nothing to fear, *ma petite*. I am with you. Nothing can harm you when you are with me."

Beau believed Gregori's whispered promise to Savannah. Believed it absolutely. He had already noticed the lack of mosquitoes and gnats. It had been so with Julian Selvaggio, too. A strange phenomenon, but then, Beau had witnessed many strange things in the bayou.

The captain's voice dropped even lower, as if the very water beneath the boat could carry his tale to the outside world. "Many go to see if the legend is true. Trappers, poachers hunting a trophy, those hungry, in need of food and money. Those from the outside think it's all voodoo nonsense. They don't understand the power of magic or of the bayou itself. So they hunt what they don't understand. Julian respected nature, respected our ways and the magic here. That is why I told him, why I went on the hunts with him."

"Why would everyone want to kill it?" Savannah's sympathies swung to the alligator. "It just wants to survive."

Beau shook his head soberly and reached down to start the engine. The boat began to chug slowly through the water. "No, Savannah, don't waste your compassion. This is no ordinary gator. The old man is evil. He lies in wait and, hungry or not, kills anything that comes near. Man or beast, it is all the same to him. He pulls them into the water and devours them."

"I thought you liked alligators," Savannah protested. "They're part of nature, part of the bayou. They belong here. We're the ones encroaching on their territory. This poor alligator doesn't ask for anyone to come hunting him. He probably wants to be left alone. But they come anyway."

"Tell us what happened to the kids," Gregori prompted gently.

"They didn't come back. My father was very restless, very worried. He knew of the reputation of the gator, and he didn't like those outsiders going back that far into the swamp. Old man alligator killed for the joy of it. We knew he was evil. Eventually my father insisted we go looking for them. He told me to be very quiet. He took oil lamps and matches, the guns, and a hook—everything we had in camp to protect us."

The stifling air seemed to hang stiffly, waiting in suspense for the rest of the tale. Savannah pressed herself against Gregori's solid form. Suddenly she wasn't certain she wanted to hear the rest. She could feel and hear and smell the picture Beau was describing.

It will be all right, chérie. Gregori's voice brought soothing comfort to her mind and a measure of protection, an insulation between Savannah's sensitivity and whatever she might hear next.

"There was a terrible stench. The air was thick, so much so that we could barely breathe. I remember the sweat pouring off us in rivers, and both of us knew if we continued into the old man's territory, he would have us for dinner. We wanted to turn back. We slowed the boat. My heart was beating so loud, I could hear it. And the insects descended on us. My father was black with them, moving all over him. They stung and bit at us, got in our eyes and nose, even filling our mouths."

Beau was becoming so agitated, Gregori instinctively reached to calm his mind. He matched the man's breathing, brought it under control, then matched the rhythm of his heart and slowed it to normal. He whispered the soothing healing chant of his people and waved his hand gently to create a breeze to blow away the stifling heat and cool the perspiration on Beau's body. At once the terrible pressure building in the captain's chest eased.

Beau smiled thinly. "I've only told this story to one other person. I promised myself I never would, but somehow I felt compelled to share it with Julian, and now you. I'm sorry. It's still like it happened yesterday."

"Sometimes it helps to talk about a bad experience," Savannah said gently, her dark eyes luminous in the night. They glowed like a cat's, strange and beautiful.

The captain shook his head. "As long as I never talked about it, I could pretend it didn't really happen. My father never spoke of it, even to me. I think we both wanted it to be nothing more than a nightmare."

"The city kids were drinking." Gregori picked the information out of his head.

Beau nodded. "We found empty bottles floating in the

water, on the bank. Then we heard them screaming. Not just any kind of screaming, but the kind that stays with you forever. It wakes you up at night in a cold sweat. My father stayed drunk for a month afterward trying to forget those screams. I know it didn't work." He wiped his mouth again. "It's never worked for me."

I don't want to hear this, Gregori. It hurts him too much to remember, Savannah protested, her fingers curling in Gregori's shirt.

Gregori stroked a caressing hand down her hair. *I will ease his pain later. It is interesting; in his mind I sense Julian's presence, as if he, also, soothed this man. Why would the alligator killing humans so upset his father? Why would the terror of it linger in him for so many years? In this place there have been many deaths, few of them pleasant. Perhaps it is necessary that we hear this tale.*

"We were covered in insects, like a blanket, crawling on us. And it was almost impossible to breathe." Beau touched his throat, remembering the feeling of suffocating. "Still, we couldn't leave them. We kept pushing through the reeds and roots. For us, the going was very difficult even though we had a much smaller boat. The water was black and murky near the bank. It formed a pool there, and the water was stagnant. The stench was unbelievable, like a slaughterhouse of dead carcasses left to decay in the sun. My father wanted to leave me in the boat at the mouth of the pool, said he would go on foot, but I knew if I let him, he would die."

"Oh, Beau," Savannah breathed sympathetically. She was almost as distressed as the captain. Automatically Gregori soothed and comforted her, providing a stronger, insulating cushion for her. She was like a sponge, soaking up the terrible trauma.

"I guess we both accepted that we probably wouldn't make it out of there," Beau continued. He skillfully guided the boat around a snag. "But we went in. It was black. Not just like night, but black. My father lit the lamp, and then we could see them. The boat was splintered, huge chunks out of it, as if something enormous had attacked it. It was sinking, nearly under water. One boy was clinging to it, but blood was spraying into the sky. We couldn't get to him. Something came up out of the water, something prehistoric. Its eyes were evil, and its mouth was gaping open. It was no ordinary alligator, and it was enjoying itself, playing with those dying kids."

Beau shoved a hand through his hair in agitation, looking out across the familiar water. Gregori stirred, drawing the captain's attention. Those peculiar silver eyes caught his gaze and held it. Instantly Beau felt calm, centered, protected, disconnected. The tale he was relating became just that, a story that had happened to someone else.

Gregori felt the strange shifting in the captain's mind, like a hazy veil that produced a programmed reaction. He focused and followed the trail, the pattern of evil he was so familiar with. He recognized Julian's healing touch, the safeguards he had set for the mortal to prevent the tainted shadow from spreading. Beau La Rue had been touched by a vampire. He had escaped, but not unscathed.

Savannah's soft little gasp in his mind betrayed her presence. He found himself smiling that she could slip in and out of him, so much a part of him that he could no longer tell where he started and she left off. She had access to his memories and his knowledge. The more time she spent in his mind, the better she was at acquiring the lessons centuries had taught him. *More than you know.* Savannah sounded smug.

Beau was much more relaxed, not the happy captain of earlier, but his tension had definitely eased. "There was nothing we could do for any of them. We had entered the monster's playground, and he was in the mood to play. He didn't try to drown any of them right away, or kill them outright. He tossed them into the air and ripped parts of them away. Pieces of bodies were floating in the water. A girl's head bobbed up and down near the bank. I remember the way her hair was spread out like a fan on the surface of the water."

Gregori touched the man's shoulder. *Enough. There is no need for you to remember the details of this atrocity.*

Beau shook his head, the vivid picture in his mind suddenly dimming to a hazy recollection. "We almost didn't make it out ourselves. It came at us, as big as any of those crocodiles on the Nile. He didn't want food, he wasn't protecting his territory, he just liked to kill. We had penetrated into his lair, his domain, while he was amusing himself, and he was angry. My father threw the oil lamp on the water and set the whole thing on fire. We didn't look back."

"You were very lucky," Gregori said softly, his voice like a fresh, cool breeze. It seeped into La Rue's mind, his pores, and dissipated the sickness gripping him.

You can heal him, Savannah said.

He is mortal.

You can do it, she insisted. *Julian protected him, ensured the poison wouldn't spread, kept the nightmare away, but you can remove it.*

The hard edge to Gregori's mouth softened, almost a smile. She was doing it again. There was no way to convince her he couldn't do what she wanted. She believed it implicitly. He brought her hand to the warmth of his mouth, pressed a kiss into her palm. *Je t'aime, Savannah*, he whispered into her mind like a caress.

Savannah leaned into him. *I love you, too, lifemate.*

Gregori turned his attention to cleansing the mortal's mind, washing away the memory of the encounter with the loathsome creature, the undead. He didn't remove it completely because it was firmly entrenched in the captain's soul; the man had lived with the experience for too many years. But Gregori whitewashed it, toning it down, extracting the remnants of the vampire's tainted touch, the evil punishment for the intrusion, for the ability to escape the snare. The nightmares would be gone, the vivid horror would fade, and the terrible dread and fear Beau had lived with would be gone from his life for all time.

Gregori sighed softly and rubbed the nape of his neck where it tightened after such a mental excursion. Removing the taint of vampire from a mortal, from anyone, was difficult; it took tremendous energy. But looking down into Savannah's shining eyes made it all worthwhile. She was looking at him as if he were the only man on earth.

You are *the only man as far as I'm concerned*, she whispered softly, the words brushing away the weariness in his mind. The sound of the ancient healing chant was soothing, as her voice, beautiful and pure, rinsed away the ugly touch of the vampire's depravity from his own mind. To walk in Beau's mind and heal it, he had had to see every memory in vivid detail. Gregori had to enter the ugliness of the vampire's sick spells to unravel them and heal from the inside out. He found his hand gripping Savannah's, a kind of humbleness sweeping through him. No one had ever done that before—looked after him, worried about his well-being, helped heal him. It was a unique experience for the master healer of their race.

"You took Julian to this place?" Gregori asked the captain.

Beau nodded. "We have gone several times over the years. We never encountered the old man again."

"Did it feel the same to you? His territory? Was it still evil?"

Beau nodded slowly, a faint frown on his face. "But I knew he wasn't there. It was evil, but not quite the same. Of course, with Julian, I always felt different. Everything was different."

"Different?" Savannah echoed. "How?"

Beau shrugged. "He's hard to explain, but you should know. He is like this one." He indicated Gregori. "He's invincible. Man or beast, natural or supernatural, nothing could harm Julian. That's how he makes you feel."

Savannah exchanged a small smile of complete understanding with Beau. She knew exactly what he meant. "Do you think the alligator is still alive after all these years? Surely they die natural deaths."

"He's alive all right," Beau said. "But I don't think he stays in his pool all the time. I think he has a new hideout. Julian really hunted for him. We spent a lot of time on it, but we never uncovered his other lair."

"Have there been any recent sightings of him?" Gregori asked. "Even a rumor, a drunk talking big? Or strange disappearances?"

Beau shrugged, the easy bayou casualness of accepting everyday life. "There are always disappearances in the swamps, unexplained odors, and weird occurrences. No one thinks it unusual. No one believes in the old man anymore. He has become a legend, a scary tale to frighten the tourists. That's all."

"But you know better," Gregori said softly.

Beau sighed. "Yes, I know better. He's out there somewhere in these miles of swamp, and he's hungry. All the time hungry. Not for food, but to kill. That's his hunger, that's what he lives for, just to kill."

The boat was carefully maneuvered into its berth. Gregori thanked La Rue and tried to pay him. When the guide refused, Gregori momentarily blurred his memory of time and placed a quantity of money in the captain's wallet. He had been in the man's mind, knew his financial problems, knew he was worried for his wife's health.

Savannah curled her fingers into Gregori's back pocket as they wandered up the road and back toward civilization. La Rue called to them. "Where's your car? These roads aren't always safe after dark."

Gregori glanced over his shoulder, his pale eyes glittering ominously, picking up a hint of a blood-red moon. His eyes resembled those of a wolf hunting prey. "Do not worry. We will be safe."

Beau La Rue laughed happily. "I wasn't worried about you. I was worried that any who attempted to mug you might be friends of mine. Don't hurt them too badly, eh? Perhaps just give them a little lesson in manners."

"I promise," Gregori assured him. He slipped an arm around Savannah. "Interesting tale about that alligator."

"The vampire is using it to guard him when he's in the swamp?" Savannah ventured.

"Perhaps," Gregori mused. He inhaled sharply, a predator scenting prey. Hunger was gnawing, a sharp edge that persisted, always present, particularly predominant when he had used so much energy. The men grouped together near a large tree up the road were drinking beer and watching their approach. He could feel their eyes on Savannah, could smell their sudden interest.

Savannah dropped a step behind him so that his much larger frame hid her from prying eyes. "So why else would the vampire use the alligator? Why would he safeguard his lair that way?"

"Think what you just said. His lair. The vampire uses the swamp as his lair. If that alligator has been around so long, there is only one explanation. The vampire must shape-shift, must become the alligator. He simply disappears into the swamp and grows fat terrorizing the population while he waits for the hunter to go away."

"But if Julian has lived here for many years—" she started to protest.

He shook his head. "Time means nothing to the undead. And there are swamps beyond this place, other cities to terrorize. He simply goes from one area to another, amusing himself until it is safe for him to return."

Gregori's senses were on the small group of men. He could see them clearly. He could hear their whispers, the swish of beer in the cans, the ebb and flow of blood in their veins. Fangs lengthened ominously. He ran his tongue along the sharp incisors, the ancient call to feed upon him.

Savannah tugged at his pocket, brought him to a halt. "I don't like this, Gregori. Let's get out of here."

"Stay here." He gave the order abruptly, his gaze drifting over her head to his prey.

"They want to fight with you," she protested. "Just leave them."

His hands caught her upper arms, and he bent his dark head to her, his pale eyes capturing her blue gaze. "Know me for what I am, Savannah. They think to threaten us. Perhaps if we leave, another couple will come along, and we will not be here to protect them. They want to test their strength, to intimidate, to rob. They have not worked themselves up to it yet, but the intent is there in their minds. I wish to feed, and your hunger beats at me. This I will do."

"Fine, do it then," she snapped, jerking away from him. "But they give me the creeps. And I want none of their blood."

He pulled her back into his arms and found her throat with his mouth, his teeth scraping, teasing along her creamy skin. "You are so soft inside, *ma petite*, your heart is so gentle. It is good you have me."

"You think," she snapped, but her body was melting of its own accord into his. He was fire and ice, white-hot heat and electric excitement.

Gregori put her from him and turned back toward the cluster of men. They were whispering now, formulating their plan of attack. He moved toward them with his easy stride. They fanned out, thinking to overpower him in a rush.

"Do any of you know Beau La Rue?" he asked softly, startling them.

One man, on his left, cleared his throat. "Yeah, I know him. What of it?" He tried to sound belligerent. To Gregori he sounded young and scared.

"Are you a friend of his?" This time Gregori's voice was pitched low, captivating them, ensnaring them, weaving a black-magic spell.

The man felt compelled to answer, to move forward,

away from the safety of his friends. "Yeah, you have a problem with that?" he snarled, pushing out his chest.

Gregori smiled, a show of gleaming teeth. His eyes glowed hot and strange in the night. *Come to me and allow me to feed.* He sent the call, wrapped them in it, and drew them to him. He drank his fill from four of them, sating his bloodlust and the aching, gnawing hunger. He was not particularly gentle about it, and he allowed them to fall to the ground unaided and dizzy. He planted memories of a fight, one man against so many. They were all in pain, all knocked down and out. The friend of La Rue's he saved for last, for Savannah. When he fed, he was far more careful, making certain the man would feel the need to thank Beau La Rue. He would thank him for saving him from the severe beating the others had received.

He gave Savannah no chance to protest his feeding her. He commanded her obedience, and she was blinking up at him with drowsy eyes before she was aware of what he had done. He saw awareness come, the smoldering heat heralding her temper. She shoved him away. "Imbecile." One word. It should have crushed him, but he wanted to laugh.

Gregori caught her head in his hands and hugged her hard, joy exploding through him. Life was all around him. The night was theirs. He caught her up, and, cradling her in his arms, he launched himself skyward.

Gary nearly fainted when the couple materialized on the balcony outside his room. He slid open the door and gaped at them. "Are you nuts? Anyone can see you out there. Everyone's room looks into the courtyard."

Gregori swept past him and tossed Savannah unceremoniously onto the bed. She took a half-hearted swipe at him, then rolled over to glare at him as he paced across the carpet to Gary's side. "No one can see us when we do not wish it," he explained patiently, averting his gaze from Savannah's perfect bottom. "Did you retrieve the list of names we need? Those under suspicion by the society?"

"The manager here allowed me to use his printer," Gary acknowledged, handing Gregori the list.

"Hey, Gary," Savannah said, "do you want to go on a vampire hunt?"

Gregori swung around to pin her with his brilliant silver gaze. *Do not even start.* He used the beauty of his voice like the weapon it was, compelling and mesmerizing.

Savannah blinked, then smiled sweetly up at him. "Really, Gary. I saw it in one of those tour brochures. Isn't that the perfect place to look for those society types? They must hang out around those kinds of things."

"A vampire hunt?" Gary echoed incredulously. "For real?"

"I have the brochure at home." She studiously avoided Gregori's furious gaze.

She wore the little secret smile again, the one that always drove Gregori crazy, turned him inside out, and melted his heart. She was up to no good. He had no doubt of it. *It has occurred to me that you need a good spanking.*

Her smile grew smug. *I said I was willing to try anything once, lifemate, but I think it best if we wait until we are alone, don't you?*

"Is she putting me on?" Gary demanded of Gregori. "Is there really a vampire hunt for tourists?"

"Believe me, mortal, if there is such a thing, she would

know about it," Gregori admitted. "I fear we are going to be talked into something we will regret."

"You won't regret it," Savannah said quickly, sitting up. Her blue eyes had gone vivid violet, those mysterious silver stars shining in their centers. "We could go tomorrow night. I'll bet it would be fun. It starts out at Lafitte's Blacksmith Shop at eight. They even provide the stakes and garlic. Let's do it, Gregori." Her long eyelashes swept down to cover her expression, and that little infuriating smile brought his attention to her soft mouth. "You might pick up some pointers. After all, these guys are probably professionals."

Gregori felt the laughter welling up from somewhere in his soul. The silver eyes warmed to molten mercury, quicksilver. "You think they might be able help me out?"

Savannah nodded solemnly. "It says right on the brochure, no drunks. That has to mean they know what they're doing, don't you think?"

"What else does it say?" Gary asked, curious.

Savannah grinned at him mischievously. "Actually, it says it's pure fun. You walk around, and they tell you stories. History mixed with myths and legends." *We might actually learn something, Gregori. You never know.* There was a faintly hopeful note in her voice she tried desperately to keep from him.

Gregori instantly crossed the distance between them and cupped the side of her face with his palm, his thumb sliding in a little caress along her jaw. *Why would you ever be insecure, Savannah? I can feel it in you, that you imagine I will consider you silly for wanting to do these tourist things.*

Savannah's laughter was soft and somehow sexy. She put her hand over Gregori's. "I am in you, lifemate," she said gently. "I read you as easily as you read me. You think ninety percent of the things I want to do are silly."

"I think my allowing you to do all these things is silly."

She winced visibly. "We need less of this *allow* stuff. Besides, you owe me a night out without any trouble."

"You had trouble tonight?" Gary asked.

"There was no trouble." Gregori was clearly puzzled.

"You're always getting in fights. Everywhere we go, you just can't help yourself," Savannah accused indignantly. "You picked the one tonight."

"You picked a fight?" Gary was astounded.

"I did not pick a fight," Gregori denied. "A few men were determined to mug us, so I provided them with an interesting experience. There was no fight. Had I actually struck them physical blows, they would be in the hospital." His white teeth gleamed, the silver eyes glittering with more than danger, with a hint of amusement. "As it is, they just think they should be hospitalized. There is nothing wrong with any of them. I was quite gentle for Savannah's sake. Which, I see, she does not appreciate."

"I would appreciate going out and behaving normally."

"I was behaving in my normal fashion, *chérie*," he reminded her gently.

"I take it we're going on a vampire hunt tomorrow night," Gary said, laughter in his voice.

Gregori took the list of names from Gary and glanced at it, committing the contents to memory before handing it back. For a moment his silver gaze rested on Gary's face, a cold, bleak reflection of emptiness. When Gary shivered, Gregori blinked, and the illusion was gone.

Gary wondered just which was the illusion—the warmth Gregori showed on occasion, or the harsh, soulless void in his eyes.

Savannah flounced off the bed, sent Gary a flash of deep blue eyes, then tucked her hand into the crook of Gregori's arm. "We'll meet you at the blacksmith shop— well, bar, tomorrow at eight."

"I've got to get back to work," Gary objected. "I'll lose my job."

"You can't go back," Gregori said softly. "The minute you told Morrison you were going to call the police, the minute you objected to his changing your formula, you sealed your own fate. He will send his people after you, and all of them will be controlled with a compulsion to kill. Morrison is the master vampire—we know that now—and you have crossed him."

"I'm not worth his attention."

"Power is everything to the vampire," Savannah said softly. "He'll come after you with everything he has. It will fester, drive him crazy that you got away. And he knows I was with you in the swamp. By now he knows Gregori was there also. He can't touch us, but he will feel that if he gets to you, he has somehow bested Gregori."

Gregori nodded, astonished that she was so adept at reading the situation. Gary was in far more danger than he could ever conceive. "Have you made any calls from this room? Given your address to anyone, even within your family?"

Gary shook his head. "No, I was going to call the airlines and see if I could use the same ticket on a later flight. And I'll have to call my boss tomorrow. I'll be fired, Gregori, and I don't want that to happen. Even if I did end up working for you, I do have a reputation to look after." The toe of his shoe scuffed at a worn spot in the carpet. "I like research. I don't want to get stuck in a job I hate because of all of this."

Gregori took the laptop from Gary and brought up the word processor with skill. Savannah watched in astonishment as his fingers flew over the keyboard. He typed out a long list of places and businesses. "Take your pick, Gary. I count myself lucky to have you. In the meantime, I will leave you cash. I do not want them tracing you."

"You haven't seen my resume," Gary objected. "I'm not looking for charity."

The silver eyes glinted, a brief, hard humor. "I had your formula inside my body, Gary. That was all the proof of your genius I needed. The society had access to that blood for some time before you did, but none of them were able to come up with anything that worked on us."

"Great, I get that dubious pleasure. Someday you're going to introduce me to one of your friends and you can say, 'By the way, this is the one who invented the poison that is killing our people.'"

Gregori did laugh then, a low, husky sound so pure, it was beautiful to hear. It brought a lightness into Gary's heart, dispelling the gloom that had been gathering. "I never thought of that. We might get a few interesting reactions."

Gary found himself grinning sheepishly. "Yeah, like a lynching party with me as the guest of honor."

"We will have an antidote for all our people soon," Gregori reminded him softly. "There is no need to worry."

"If I had my equipment, I could have one immediately," Gary said. "I always make certain I can reverse whatever reaction I create. It wouldn't be all that hard to find where they perverted the formula. In fact, maybe you still have some lingering aftereffects in your bloodstream."

He looked so hopeful, Savannah burst out laughing. "The mad scientist is going to chase you around with a hypodermic needle, Gregori," she teased.

Gregori lifted an eyebrow, his face an unreadable mask, the pale eyes glittering with more than menace. White teeth flashed, a baring of fangs.

"Maybe not," Gary conceded. "Not the best idea after all."

Savannah was up and moving with her sensuous grace to fit herself beneath Gregori's shoulder. She looked impossibly small next to the big Carpathian, delicate, fragile even. It wasn't so much Gregori's height but the rippling muscles, the thickness of his arms and chest, and the power emanating from him. Her face was turned up toward his, her soft mouth curved with laughter, in no way intimidated by him.

Gregori's arm swept around her and crushed her to him, nearly enveloping her completely. "She thinks I am going to take her on this ridiculous vampire hunt."

"She's right, too, isn't she?" Gary grinned at him.

"Unfortunately," Gregori admitted. "Do you have enough food until tomorrow night? We will have a plan of action by then." He dropped several large bills on the nightstand, hiding his actions from Gary as he did so.

"What plan of action? What can be done? We can't fight the whole society."

"I was thinking we could use you as bait and draw them into a trap," Gregori said, straight-faced.

Gary's eyes widened in alarm. "I'm not sure I like that

plan. Sounds a little risky to me." He looked at Savannah for support.

Gregori shrugged his broad shoulders in a casual shrug. "I do not see a risk."

Savannah's small clenched fist thumped his stomach in retaliation. Gregori glanced down at her with surprise. "Is this when I am supposed to say ouch?"

Savannah and Gary exchanged a long, mournful groan. "Why did I want him to have a sense of humor?" she wondered.

Gary shook his head. "Don't be asking me. You created the monster."

"I know I would be unable to stand the press of human bodies in Preservation Hall," Gregori said suddenly, "but perhaps we could listen to the music from the street. It would get you out of here for a few hours and, with the severity of the storm, hopefully the tourists will have stayed inside."

Gary leapt at the chance to get out of his room. "Let's do it."

Savannah held back, her hand tightening on Gregori's arm. "Is it safe for him?"

Enfante, I cannot believe you would doubt my ability to protect you and the mortal.

The mortal? He has a name. He is easily killed, where we are not.

The silver eyes roamed over her face. His hand came up to caress her cheek, his thumb feathering gently back and forth. "I would not allow Gary to be in any real danger. He cannot live his life in hiding."

I should have protected Peter. He would be alive right now if it wasn't for me. Savannah's voice was husky with grief, the unshed tears clinging to his mind.

I alone am to blame for Peter's death, ma petite. It was my responsibility to detect the vampire's presence. I had not felt any emotion in so long, so many centuries, and when I went into your show and saw you, colors nearly blinded me. Feelings overwhelmed me. I was sorting them out and trying to get myself under control. In all the centuries of my existence, it was the only time I have failed to detect the presence of the undead. Peter's death is something I must live with.

He felt her instant denial of his assessment of the situation, the quick spring to his defense. And it warmed him as nothing else ever could.

As they moved out of the rooming house and through the rain-wet streets, mingling with the unexpected crowds, he thought about the way she made him feel. He was always in control—it was necessary for one of his power and predatory nature—yet she could make him feel as if he was spinning into orbit.

Gregori glanced down at the top of her silky head and allowed the emotion to wash over him, through him. Just watching her brought him a measure of peace and a flood of warmth. He found he could enjoy the upbeat music, even the craziness of the tourists laughing and crushing close in the streets and on the sidewalks. Merged with her, he could feel what she was feeling— carefree, her sense of humor, the quick interest she had in everything and everyone around her. She spoke to people easily, held them in the palm of her hand with the same ease she held him so captivated.

When he took her home after settling Gary back at his room, Gregori turned Savannah into his arms. "You are my world," he whispered softly, meaning it.

She leaned her head into his shoulder, inhaling his

masculine scent. "Thank you for going out tonight. I know it's hard for you to be among humans, but I've spent the last five years living among them. It's been so long since I've had contact with any of our people."

"I have a hard time," he admitted. "I want to supply what you need, Savannah. It is difficult to understand the need in you for their company."

"You've always been so solitary, Gregori," she said softly, "where I've had humans around me since I left home."

His mouth found her temples, then drifted across her eyelids and down to her mouth. He lifted her as his lips teased hers, cradling her in his arms. He took her up the stairs to one of the bedrooms. Gregori made gentle, tender love to her, incredibly reverent, showing her with his body what he never seemed to be able to express adequately in words.

Chapter Seventeen

Lafitte's Blacksmith Shop was dark and mysterious, the perfect setting for the beginning of such a fun adventure. Savannah laughed softly as a couple of locals shook their heads at the pack of crazy tourists crowding into the tavern to join the vampire hunt. She could feel Gregori inwardly wincing, the desire to dissolve and be invisible paramount in his mind, but he hung in there grimly. He turned heads with his impressive stature, the power that sat so easily on his broad shoulders. His expression was stoically impassive, the silver eyes restless, merciless, missing nothing.

Within the bar's darkened interior, the peculiar night vision their species had gave them an advantage. Gary flanked them, astonished at how many tourists actually went on these hunts. Savannah shot him a glare. "We're here to have fun, Gary. Don't start acting like Gregori on me. One grump raining on my parade is enough."

Gary leaned close. "If you wouldn't read people's thoughts all the time, snoop, you might not get so bent out of shape."

"I was not reading your thoughts," Savannah objected with an injured expression, her lush mouth in a frankly sexy pout. "It was written all over your face."

Gregori was definitely having a hard time. Carpathian males rarely allowed other men near their lifemates, certainly not unattached males. He hated the press of bodies. Savannah attracted men the way bees went for honey. Heads turned, and hot gazes followed her progress as they wound their way through the throng toward the back room of the building. Savannah exuded steam. Even in a room filled with bodies, so many that there was really nowhere to sit, Savannah made men feel as if she was the only one there. Dimly lit, with flickering candles, the room held a faint trace of mystery, and she was part of that.

It was inevitable that someone would recognize her; it always happened. Gregori was surprised the press hadn't gotten wind that she was somewhere in the city and had every tourist spot staked out waiting for her. He gave a little sigh as the first wave of fans swarmed them, pressing close to Savannah, wanting to get near her. Gregori instinctively placed his solid frame between her and the crowd. *You are going to start a riot.*

She signed several autographs, a hard enough feat with Gregori acting like her bodyguard. Gary walled her in from the other side, recognizing the menacing glitter in the cold silver of Gregori's eyes. Savannah paid no attention to the two of them; instead, she was sweet and friendly and entered into conversations with people.

When their guide entered, a faint hush followed him. He was impressive, with his long, thick braid, his walking stick, and his dramatic appearance. Gregori raised an eyebrow at Savannah, but her fascinated gaze was on their host. He lit a candle, held his audience for a moment in a theatrical pause, then delivered a warning about the dangerous journey they would be undertaking. He made it clear that drinkers weren't welcome and emphasized that it was not recommended that small children go on the tour.

He's good, this guy, Savannah whispered softly in Gregori's mind. *He grabs everyone right away and holds them. Good showmanship.*

He is a fake.

This isn't meant to be real, Gregori, she scolded. *It is fun. Everyone is here to have a good time. If you prefer not to go, I can meet you later. It isn't as if it's really dangerous. We aren't going to meet any real vampires.*

Like hell I will meet you later. If I left your side, every man in the room would be swarming around you.

Gregori knew the moment the two society members entered Lafitte's Blacksmith Shop. He felt the dark compulsion of the kill, knew they were searching for a likely target. He scanned the darkened interior of the bar. The vampire was alive and well, and his dark army was spreading out to do his bidding. No one else could have known they would be here. He sighed. He had not realized until that moment how important a night out for Savannah was to him. A single night without incident.

He followed the group through the door, dropping money into the outstretched hand as he did so. Savannah was close to him, his hand on the small of her back. Three teenage boys were flirting outrageously with her, and her laughter turned heads and earned her the sudden attention of their host and the two society members.

Gregori watched them shift into position, trying to work their way through the crowd to her side, but it was impossible. He concentrated on them, dulling the compulsion, fogging their thoughts so that they found themselves entering into the spirit of the hunt. Savannah ended up with a sharpened stake and a conspirator's grin from a fellow showman.

They started walking through the streets at a brisk pace, and as they did so, the crowd stretched out into a long line. Their guide stopped at a home, perched on a fence, and began a dramatic tale of love and murder within. He wove the story brilliantly, putting in enough truth mixed with melodrama to make it credible. Savannah's blue eyes were shining. As the crowd moved forward to follow the swirling cape of the fast-paced host, she bent down to fiddle with the strap of her shoe. Gregori felt her slip away from him and turned to wait for her.

Savannah smiled at him, that sexy, mysterious smile that hardened his body and tripped little bombs off in his head. Her hair slid over her shoulder in a fall of cascading silk. The sight of her literally took his breath away. By the time she fixed her shoe, the two society members were right beside her. Savannah straightened, and that infuriating smile curved her soft mouth. "Where are you two from?" Her voice was beautiful and pure, a blend of seduction and music. "I'm Savannah Dubrinsky. Isn't this fun?"

They felt her impact immediately, the mesmerizing snare. Gregori heard their hearts slam unexpectedly, then begin to race. Her blue eyes caught and held their gazes, trapping them in the silver-star centers. "Randall Smith," the shorter of the two answered eagerly. "I moved here several months ago from Florida. This is John Perkins. He's originally from Florida also."

"Did you come here for Mardi Gras and just stay for the fun?" Savannah inquired.

What the hell do you think you are doing? Mon Dieu, ma femme, *you are enough to drive me crazy. I forbid this.*

Savannah fell into step between the two men easily, her enormous eyes wide with interest. Gregori felt the beast lifting its head, roaring for release. The red haze spread, and hunger beat at him.

"We came here to help out a friend of ours," Randall admitted. He began rubbing his suddenly pounding temples. His head was hurting and felt as if it might shatter.

Savannah leaned in closer, her eyes holding his captive. The crowd had once more stopped while their host began his tale of ghosts and unexplained mysteries. His voice cast a spell over the group, adding to the appeal of the story, to the haunting illusion of the night. Randall felt as if he were drowning in her eyes, as if she had trapped him forever in the illuminating starlight. He wanted to give her anything, everything. His head said no, but his wildly beating heart and raging soul needed to confess his every thought to her.

"We belong to a secret society," he whispered softly, his voice so low that only the two Carpathians could possibly hear. He didn't want his partner to know he was betraying the members. There was a curious buzzing in his head, like a swarm of bees. He broke out in a sweat.

Savannah touched him lightly, a brushing of fingers across his arm. Curiously, she brought a refreshing breeze with that touch, one that cleared his head for a moment so that the oppressive pain lightened. Her smile sent a shiver of excitement through him, of such desire and need that he wanted to fall at her feet. "How exciting. Is it dangerous?" She tilted her head, an innocent seductress luring him closer and closer.

Randall was aware of the smallness of her waist, the fullness of her breasts, the sway of her hips. He had never wanted anything more in his life, and her enormous eyes were focused only on him, saw only him. He swallowed hard. "Very dangerous. We hunt vampires. The real thing, not this nonsense."

Her perfect mouth formed a small O. She had beautiful lips, rose-petal soft, moist, pouty, kissable lips.

Savannah, stop now. He is dangerous, whether you think so or not. His mind stinks of the vampire.

I might find out where Morrison is.

I said no. Gregori reached out and shackled her wrist, yanking her from between the two men to the protection of his body. *I will not use you to find the undead. He will trace the path back to you. I have no choice but to destroy this one.*

Her face paled visibly, long lashes sweeping down to conceal her eyes. *Why not heal him as you did the captain?*

I cannot heal what is essentially evil. His thumb feathered gently back and forth across the pulse beating so strongly in her inner wrist. *He is a servant of the vampire, and you know it, Savannah. You knew it the moment you touched his mind. What you can find and trace, so can the vampire. And he is more adept than you. I cannot allow such a risk to you.*

Randall crowded close, wrapped in the thrall of mental compulsion. He perceived the hand on Savannah's wrist as evil, a coiled snake dragging her away from her rightful place at his side.

Gregori focused on the partner, John Perkins. The

man's mind was stronger than Randall Smith's. The vampire's hold on him was much blacker, as if Perkins had been in close contact for a longer period of time. He was staring at Savannah suspiciously. Gregori could easily pick out the dark lust, the jealousy that she chose Randall for her attention instead of him. Perkins was twisted inside, the vampire's compulsion working on his already depraved mind.

Morrison knew how to choose his servants. The vicious, ugly nature of malicious men, those without friends or relatives, those hungry for violence and depravity. He sent them among the curious, those like Gary, people with quick, intelligent minds open to the paranormal. People isolated by their very intelligence and open-mindedness. The vampire was able to use those intelligent men by luring them with false hopes, false promises, using them for research and the legwork needed for his legions of true servants.

Gregori sighed softly. He was what he was. Guilt could not be a part of his existence. He was responsible for the continuation of his race and for Savannah's safety. He thrust into John Perkins's mind, past the vampire's control, and planted the seeds of destruction. His hand on Savannah's wrist tightened, and he quickened their pace to put distance between the society members and his lifemate.

Once again their guide stopped them all and was weaving a tale of debauchery, and murder. The crowd was silent, captivated by the interesting history of the city. Gregori inserted Savannah into the throng, his larger frame protecting her from the impending violence.

Out on the street, John Perkins stared malevolently at

Randall Smith. "You always have to ruin everything, Smith. You always have to be the one to talk to Morrison. I'm closest to him, but you just have to prove you're the big cheese."

"What the hell are you talking about?" Randall demanded, his gaze frantically searching the crowd for Savannah.

Gregori was shielding her, the haze he created making it impossible to detect her in the night. Randall craned his neck, worked to get around his partner, going so far as to shove him out of his way. His heart was beating frantically, his one thought to find Savannah.

"What are you doing, Gregori?" she demanded softly.

Gary inched through the crowd of tourists until he managed to push his way to the Carpathians' side. He was as enthralled by the storyteller as the rest of the crowd. He studied the building with its history of sexual misconduct, fire, and murder with rapt attention.

Gregori bent his dark head down to hers. "I can do no other than eliminate the threat to you. The vampire has a clear trail leading straight to you from this one's mind. It is a trap, *ma petite*, and we cannot afford to fall into it."

"You don't mean *we*," she said, "you mean *me*."

Perkins shoved at Randall hard enough to cause the other man to sprawl in the middle of the street. Randall erupted into obscenities, disturbing the storyteller. Their host paused for the best dramatic effect, heaved a sigh, and strolled toward the two combatants.

Gary had noticed police patrol cars cruising the area often and wondered if it was a courtesy to their tour guide. It was possible he even had some way to signal them if there was trouble.

Before the guide reached the two men, Perkins produced a gun. Everyone froze instantly. "You traitor. You were going to betray us all!" he screamed, his face a twisted mask of fury and hatred.

The dark compulsion of the kill was on him, and on Randall, who retaliated with a gun of his own. The crowd ran in all directions, seeking shelter, hiding behind parked cars, and jumping to the other side of fences. Wild cries rose, and the air was thick with fear. Gregori shoved Savannah into Gary and toward the comparative shelter of a brick wall. He stood tall on the walkway, watching the drama unfolding before him.

The guide, clearly torn between the need for safety and the need to protect his tourists, hesitated in the open. Gregori waved a hand to erect a barrier between the man and any stray bullet. The two society members were raging at one another, then Perkins fired a barrage of bullets to meet the ones Randall sprayed at him.

A dark shadow passed across the sky, blotting out the stars, stilling the wind. Both men fell slowly, shirts splattered with what looked like red paint. They landed like rag dolls in the middle of the street, sprawled out, motionless. Their guns clattered to the pavement to look like harmless toys where they lay. The dark shadow hovered, as alarming as the sudden violence that had erupted. No one moved, no one spoke, no one made a sound. It was as if they knew the dark, sinister shadow clouding the sky was far more deadly than the guns lying so silent in the street.

The large stain spread across the stars, then began to gather itself ominously into a smaller, much blacker and heavier cloud. Dense, compact, it moved slowly, as if surveying the group with an obscene red eye. In its very center a vein of jagged light streaked continually.

Someone gasped. Someone else began a low prayer. After a moment, a few others joined in. The shadow darkened until it blotted out every bit of light above their heads. The lightning veins, jagged and threatening, increased in activity.

Gregori realized the vampire was searching for them. He knew his enemies were near, but Gregori had automatically cloaked his presence, something he did without thought. The undead should have been able to detect Savannah's presence, having followed the faint psychic trail through his servant, but Savannah had been busy, too. Running around so much in Gregori's head, she had utilized the lessons he had learned through hard experience, through trial and error. She was masking her presence every bit as deftly as Gregori was able to do.

It won't make a difference, lifemate. Her words brushed softly in his mind. *He means to attack and destroy all of those here in an effort to get at us.*

He felt a surge of pride at her ability to learn so quickly, to assess their enemy. Gregori stepped away from the huddled mass of tourists, putting distance between himself and the guide. He walked completely erect, his head high, his long hair flowing around him. His hands were loose at his sides, and his body was relaxed, rippling with power.

"Hear me now, ancient one." His voice was soft and musical, filling the silence with beauty and purity. "You have lived long in this world, and you weary of the emptiness. I have come in answer to your call."

"Gregori. The Dark One." The evil voice hissed and growled the words in answer. The ugliness tore at sensitive nerve endings like nails on a chalkboard. Some of the tourists actually covered their ears. "How dare you enter my city and interfere where you have no right?"

"I am justice, evil one. I have come to set you free from the boundaries holding you to this place." Gregori's voice was so soft and hypnotic that those listening edged out from their sanctuaries. It beckoned and pulled, so that none could resist his every desire.

The black shape above their head roiled like a witch's cauldron. A jagged bolt of lightning slammed to earth straight toward the huddled group. Gregori raised a hand and redirected the force of energy away from the tourists and Savannah. A smile edged the cruel set of his mouth. "You think to mock me with this display, ancient one? Do not attempt to anger what you do not understand. You came to me. I did not hunt you. You seek to threaten my lifemate and those I count as my friends. I can do no other than carry the justice of our people to you." Gregori's voice was so reasonable, so perfect and pure, drawing obedience from the most recalcitrant of criminals.

The guide made a sound, somewhere between disbelief and fear. Gregori silenced him with a wave of his hand, needing no distractions. But the noise had been enough for the ancient one to break the spell Gregori's voice was weaving around him. The dark stain above their heads thrashed wildly, as if ridding itself of ever-tightening bonds before slamming a series of lightning strikes at the helpless mortals on the ground.

Screams and moans accompanied the whispered prayers, but Gregori stood his ground, unflinching. He merely redirected the whips of energy and light, sent them streaking back into the black mass above their heads. A hideous snarl, a screech of defiance and hatred, was the only warning before it hailed. Huge golf-ball-sized blocks of bright-red ice rained down toward them. It was thick and horrible to see, the shower of frozen blood from the skies. But it stopped abruptly, as if an unseen force held it hovering inches from their heads.

Gregori remained unchanged, impassive, his face a blank mask as he shielded the tourists and sent the hail hurtling back at their attacker. From out of the cemetery a few blocks from them, an army of the dead rose up. Wolves howled and raced along beside the skeletons as they moved to intercept the Carpathian hunter.

Savannah. He said her name once, a soft brush in her mind.

I've got it, she sent back instantly. Gregori had his hands full dealing with the abominations the vampire was throwing at him; he didn't need to waste his energy protecting the general public from the apparition. She moved out into the open, a small, fragile figure, concentrating on the incoming threat.

To those dwelling in the houses along the block and those driving in their cars, she masked the pack of wolves as dogs racing down the street. The stick-like skeletons, grotesque and bizarre, were merely a fast-moving group of people. She held the illusion until they were within a few feet of Gregori. Dropping the illusion, she fed every ounce of her energy and power to Gregori so he could meet the attack.

The wind rose, whipping at Gregori's solid form, lashing his body, ripping at the waves of black hair so that it streamed around his face. His expression was impassive, the pale silver eyes cold and merciless, unblinking and fixed on his prey. The attack came from sky and ground simultaneously; slivers of sharpened wood shot through the air on the wild winds, aimed directly at Gregori. The wolves leapt for him, eyes glowing hotly in the night. The army of the dead moved relentlessly forward, pressing toward Gregori's lone figure.

His hands moved, a complicated pattern directed at the approaching army; then he was whirling, a flowing wind of motion beautiful to the eye, so fast that he blurred. Yelps and howls accompanied bodies flying through the air. Wolves landed to lie motionless at his feet. His expression never changed. There was no hint of anger or emotion, no sign of fear, no break in concentration. He simply acted as the need arose. The skeletons were mowed down by a wall of flame, an orange-red conflagration that rose in the night sky and danced furiously for a brief moment. The army withered into ashes, leaving only a pile of blackened dust that spewed across the street in the ferocious onslaught of the wind.

Savannah felt Gregori's wince, the pain that sliced through him just before he shut out all sensation. She whirled to face him and saw a sharpened stake protruding from his right shoulder. Even as she saw it, Gregori jerked it free. Blood gushed, spraying the area around him. Just as quickly it stopped, as if cut off in midstream.

The winds rose to a thunderous pitch, a whirling gale of debris above their heads like the funnel cloud of a tornado. The black cloud spun faster and faster, threatening to suck everything and everyone up into its center where the malevolent red eye stared at them with hatred. The tourists screamed in fear, and even the guide grabbed for a lamppost to hang on grimly. Gregori stood alone, the winds assaulting him, tearing at him, reaching for him. As the whirling column threatened him from above, sounding like the roar of a freight train, he merely clapped his hands, then waved to send a backdraft slamming into the dark entity. The vampire screamed his rage.

The thick black cloud sucked in on itself with an audible sound, hovering in the air, waiting, watching, silent. Evil. No one moved. No one dared to breathe. Suddenly the churning black entity gathered itself and streamed across the night sky, racing away from the hunter over the French Quarter and toward the swamp. Gregori launched himself into the air, shape-shifting as he did so, ducking the bolts of white-hot energy and slashing stakes flying in the turbulent air.

On the ground there was a long silence, then a collective sigh of relief. Someone laughed nervously. "No way, man. What a show!"

Savannah latched on to that reaction, fed it quickly, built the idea in their minds, and softened the impact of what they had seen.

"Great special effects," murmured one teenager.

His father laughed a little reluctantly. "How the hell did they do that? The guy just disappeared into the air." He looked over at the carcasses lying a distance away and swore softly under his breath. "Those are real. They can't be part of some show."

"This is crazy." One of the men knelt beside the two men lying in the street. The guide was checking the pulse of the other one. "They're both dead. What the hell happened here?"

Savannah jumped in again, feeding answers to the collective audience, building their memories of what was real and what was illusion. The two tourists from Florida had argued, then fought before pulling their

guns. It was in the middle of an impromptu magic show
the guide had asked Savannah to put on for his clients.
The pack of dogs had come out of nowhere, frightened
by the sound of the guns.

It was the best she could do with so little time. Already the police were swarming around them, taking
statements. She had to work at blurring people's memories of Gregori. All the time she was mentally locked
with him in flight high over the city and bayou, heading
for the most dangerous place of all, the vampire's lair.

Gary stayed close to her side, worried as her face grew
more pale by the moment. The strain of being in two
places at one time was showing on her. The effort to
hold together an elaborate illusion on such a number of
witnesses was tremendous. Small beads of perspiration
dotted her forehead, but her chin was up, and she was as
regal as ever. She captivated the police officer taking her
statement.

Gary was certain she had succeeded with the tourists.
The entire thing was too bizarre to comprehend, and the
memories of Gregori had been eradicated, so the gun-
fight and dogs were their reality. It was only the tour
guide who looked up at the sky with a faint frown and
examined the scorch marks some distance from them.
Several times Gary caught him staring at Savannah in
bewilderment, but the man was far too experienced on
the streets to tell such a wild tale when no one else
seemed to have seen what he had.

Savannah worked at keeping focused on the monu-
mental task on hand. Her mind was really with Gregori,
a part of her merged deep, a haunting shadow in the
corner of his mind.

Gregori could feel her presence, her worry for his injury, the loss of blood. He sent her reassurance even as he approached the heart of the swamp. From La Rue's description, he recognized the area. Insects swarmed to do the master vampire's bidding, rising in black clouds to sting and bite anything that came within his boundaries to disturb him. Gregori threw a protection barrier up and continued downward toward the bogs and the black, murky pool. The putrid smell was in his nostrils, the decay and death of centuries seeping insidiously into the surrounding air.

There was no wind to carry away the stench. Sinkholes gurgled and lay waiting for one wrong step. Patches of vivid emerald-green grass beckoned the unwary into their deadly trap. Wildlife and human alike would be attracted to the spots of brilliant, life-affirming color, lured to a slow death as they sank, trapped in the sucking mud the tufts of green hid so successfully.

Gregori hovered in the air above the murky pool. Layers of rock formed a shelf beneath the surface of the water where the grotesque beast anchored its victims to rot the meat. The water itself was thick with sludge, completely unlike the waterways leading to it. There was no sign of the alligator or the vampire.

Gregori scanned the area carefully, cautiously. This vampire was cunning and vicious. This was his home ground, his lair. It would not be an easy thing to trap him here. Gregori felt the presence of evil, knew the vampire was close. He chose the most solid-looking ground he could find as far from the dark, dead waters as he could get.

He used his powerful voice. Soft. Insistent. Impossible to ignore. "You must come to me. You have waited long to face me, and I have come for you. Come to me." Each word was pure and musical, sifting through the air to reach any and all within hearing and draw them out. Each note was mesmerizing, hypnotic, a sorcerer's spell. Gregori stood with a lazy casualness, his solid frame masculine and invincible despite the blood staining his shirt high on his shoulder.

He began to murmur softly in the ancient tongue, repeating his command for the vampire to show himself. Reeds swayed along the embankment, then bent like a rolling wave. There was no wind to cause the movement. Out of the corner of his eye, Gregori could see a second wave start, and from a third point, another wave. They came at him so that he was surrounded, the unseen enemy converging from all sides. He waited. As patient as the mountains. As still as granite. Merciless. Relentless. *Gregori. The Dark One*. The hunter.

The assault came from above. The sky filled with so many birds, the air groaned at the unexpected migration. Talons extended and razor-sharp beaks ready, the birds came in fast, raking at his face and body. Gregori melted into mist, but droplets of red marring the green reeds gave evidence that the vampire had scored a second hit.

Gregori had no choice but to materialize to stop the blood flow weakening his body. There was a soft hiss of satisfaction, a grating, rumbling bellow of challenge. The ground beneath Gregori's feet was spongy, sucking at his shoes with a greedy sound. While he searched the moving reeds, the enemy attacked from beneath him, erupting out of the ooze with gaping jaws and jagged teeth. The vicious snap grazed his leg as he jumped backward to sink knee-deep into the muck. He slammed a flimsy block between himself and the alligator, the best he could do as he struggled to free himself. A small reptile lunged at him from behind, another from the left. The smallest one ripped his leg open with a vicious slash of teeth.

Gregori went down in the oozing mud with the small creatures rushing to feed on their prey. They drove in, ripping and tearing in a feeding frenzy. The swarm of insects descended on him, biting and stinging. As he fought his way up, there was a sudden eerie silence. The insects veered away, and the small alligators slithered quickly toward the swamp.

Gregori half sat, the muck seeping into his clothes, blood dripping steadily from his leg, arm, and chest. He heard a single sound in the sudden silence of the bog. A rasp as the enormous creature approached him was his only warning. The beast moved quickly, fast and efficient even in the soggy muck. The powerful tail switched back and forth. The eyes glowed a wicked red, evil and cold. The snout was armor-plated and covered with algae and furred streamers of green goo. It lunged toward Gregori, its fetid breath hot with anticipation of the kill.

A streak of white heat, electric energy, slammed down from the sky and sliced through the bony plates and the thick skin and seared the inner organs. The lunge carried the creature forward despite the solid hit by the bolt of lightning. Smoke poured out of the gaping jaws, carrying the smell of burned meat. The beast drove forward, straight at Gregori's chest, determined to rip and tear, the only thought to kill and devour.

Gregori simply disappeared. The powerful jaws closed on empty air. The beast, mortally wounded, roared and shook its massive head from side to side, looking desperately for its enemy. The vampire abandoned the smoking, scorched carcass, rising into the air with a scream of defiance and hatred. Even as he rose, preparing to flee, to leave his centuries-old sanctuary and run for his life, he encountered a barrier. He was struck hard, the blow knocking him from the sky to the ground.

The vampire lay breathless for a moment, shocked at the incredible strength in that blow. Cautiously he got to his feet, sinking a bit into the dark muck of the swamp. *Gregori. The Dark One.* He had always been larger than legend, larger than myth. Now the vampire knew that the whispers, the rumors, were all true. There was no escaping the Dark One. Gregori had used himself as bait to bring the vampire out into the open. What hunter would do such a thing? Believe so much in himself that he would risk his life? The vampire could feel the blow through his entire body. It shook him as nothing else could.

At once he changed tactics, his harsh coldness changing from reptilian to soft warmth. "I do not wish to fight you, Gregori. I acknowledge you are a great hunter. I do not wish to continue this battle. Allow me to leave this place and go to my lair in the Florida Everglades. I will stay hidden for a century—more, if you wish it." His voice was beguiling, fawning.

Gregori materialized a few feet away. Blood dripped steadily from several raw, gaping wounds. His face was impassive, implacable, the pale eyes like steel. "The Prince of our people has sentenced you to death. I can do no other than carry out justice."

The vampire shook his head, a grim parody of a smile on his face. "The Prince does not know of my existence. You do not have to carry out a sentence he has not commanded. I will go to ground."

Gregori sighed softly. "There can be no discussion,

vampire. You know the laws of our people. I am a hunter, a bearer of justice, and I can do no other than to carry out our laws." His eyes never left the vampire, never blinked. The wind was rising, and it blew strands of black hair around his face so that he looked like a warrior of ancient times.

The vampire's eyes went flat and vicious. "Then it begins." Lightning zigzagged across the sky, jumping from cloud to cloud. The wind whipped and roared.

Gregori glided, a fluid motion, gentle, lazy, nonthreatening. His head tilted, the lightning reflected in the silver sheen of his eyes. Blood dripped steadily from his wounds. The vampire caught the scent of fresh blood, and his gaze rested greedily on the powerful, ancient liquid of life. Gregori struck so fast, the vampire never saw him move. Distracted by the sight of the lush feast of an ancient's blood, the vampire comprehended he was in mortal danger only when he felt the impact of a tremendous blow to his chest.

Gregori was already gone, standing tall and motionless some distance away, regarding the vampire with cold, empty eyes. Slowly he extended his arm, turned his palm up, and opened his fist.

The vampire screamed and screamed, the sound high-pitched and ugly in the night. It traveled out over the waterways and canals. The undead slowly, reluctantly, looked from the pulsating object in the hunter's palm, down at his own chest. There was a gaping hole where his heart had been. Stricken, he took two steps forward before his body crumpled and he fell face down into the muck and slime.

Gregori's face paled visibly, and he sat down abruptly. Allowing the poisoned, withered heart to fall from his palm, he examined the burns and blisters on his skin from the contact with the tainted blood. He concentrated on gathering energy from the sky, focused, and sent a fiery ball into the vampire's body. The second strike incinerated the contaminated heart. Gregori sank back into the muck and lay staring up at the night sky. It blurred and faded. A strange lethargy took over, a heavy, drowsy sensation. He was floating on a sea, disconnected, watching the dawn streaking the dark sky gray.

His long lashes swept down, and he relaxed into the soft mud. He felt the disturbance in the air above him. He smelled the fresh scent dispersing the stale stench of the swamp. Savannah. He would know her anywhere. He tried to rouse himself, to warn her the dawn was approaching and it was dangerous to be so far from shelter.

Savannah's gasp was audible. "Oh, Gregori." She touched one of the seeping gouges in his chest. It was a measure of his weariness, the damage to his body, that he could not find the energy to close his wounds. She merged with him and tried to force his obedience in the same way he often did hers. He would close those lacerations, would seek the healing sleep of their people, and leave the rest to her.

She searched in his mind for Gary's mental trail, then reached for their human friend. *Hear me, Gary, we are in trouble. Find LaRue. Beau LaRue. He captains a boat for the bayou tours. Tell him to go to the old man alligator's pool. You must come before the sun gets high and get us to a dark place. Even if we appear dead, take us there. We are counting on you. You are our only hope.*

She searched the area for the most stable stretch of land. Working quickly and hard, Savannah was able to levitate Gregori's body to the small mound, but there was no relief from the sun. As she bent over Gregori, she realized he had not put himself into a healing sleep. Her heart slammed hard against her chest. Her heart stuttered. Gregori was too weak from loss of blood to comply, to heal himself. Quickly she sealed the wounds herself, once more utilizing the information in Gregori's memories. Jerking off her jacket, she lay beside her lifemate, covering both their heads with the material. Slashing her wrist, Savannah laid her arm over Gregori's mouth, allowing the life-giving substance to flow into his depleted body, stroking his throat to coax him to swallow.

Chapter Eighteen

The boat chugged so slowly through the channel, Gary wanted to scream. For the hundredth time he glanced at his watch. The sun was climbing steadily into the sky. He had never been so aware of the heat and light radiating from the sun. It had taken precious time to locate Beau La Rue and convince him Savannah and Gregori were in terrible trouble. With each passing second, he was certain the sun would incinerate them.

"Can't this thing go any faster?" he demanded for the tenth time.

Beau shook his head. "We're close to the old man's pool. It is treacherous in these waters. Snags are everywhere, jagged rocks. It is dangerous. And if we meet the old man, we will not survive."

"Gregori killed him," Gary said coolly, with complete faith in the Carpathian. He was certain the man could not be defeated. Whatever wounds he had sustained would not prevent him from killing his opponent.

"Pray that you are right," the captain said softly, meaning it.

The boat rounded the corner into the thick sludge of the channel leading to the pool. Gary gasped when he saw the blackened ashes and smoldering remains a distance away on the embankment. He couldn't be too late. He couldn't have failed them. "Move this thing," he snapped, rushing to the railing of the boat, prepared to leap over into the murky water.

"Even if the old man is dead," LaRue cautioned, "there are other alligators in this area."

"I thought you said nothing was here but the big one," Gary protested.

"I think you are right. The old one is dead." LaRue's faded eyes searched the landscape. He inhaled sharply. "The stench is fading, and the regular rhythm of the bayou is already restoring itself. See the way that log lies half-buried in the mud? That is no log. Stay in the boat."

Gary paced impatiently until Beau managed to maneuver the craft to the edge of the swamp. Gary, thick blankets in his arms, jumped to ground and sank two inches into the bog. LaRue shook his head. "The land is unstable here. If you sink into the marsh, you're dead." More carefully he tested the land and led the way from spot to spot of firmer ground.

Gary spied the two bodies lying on a mound of rotting vegetation. Swearing, heedless of his own safety, he crossed the distance at a run. A jacket covered their faces. Both appeared dead. He checked their pulses. Neither had one. Gregori's clothes were torn and dirty. The amount of dried blood staining the material in so many places was appalling. Before LaRue could see them clearly, Gary covered them from head to toe with a thick blanket.

"We have to get them into your boat quickly. Is there

a dark room, a cave, anywhere dark we can take them?" Gary asked. He was already lifting Savannah into his arms.

LaRue watched him carry her to his boat. "A hospital would be good." He made the suggestion in a soft, reasonable tone, as if he feared Gary had lost his mind.

Gary made certain that every inch of Savannah's skin was hidden beneath the blanket before hurrying back to Gregori. "I'll need help with him. Don't let the blanket slip. He's very allergic to the sun."

"Is he alive?" LaRue bent to remove the wrapping so that he could check. The wounds were deep and nasty.

Gary caught his wrist. "Gregori said you were someone he trusted. Help me get him into the boat, and find us a place in the dark where they can rest. I'll take care of them. I'm a doctor, and I brought what they need." He picked up Gregori's shoulders and stood waiting for the other man to make up his mind.

Beau hesitated, puzzlement on his face, but then he lifted Gregori's legs and they struggled in silence with the dead weight, inching their way across the unstable, sponge-like ground. Once inside the boat, Gary wrapped Gregori like a mummy in a blanket, pulling both bodies beneath the craft's awning. "Get us out of here and to a dark place fast," he commanded.

Beau shook his head, but he started the boat. He would have liked to examine the pile of smoldering ashes, the scorch marks on the reeds and rocks. Something terrible had taken place there. He knew Gary was right. Old man alligator was dead. The terror of the bayou had finally been reduced to the legend everyone thought he was.

Gary knelt between the bodies, his heart pounding in

dread. He hadn't taken the time to examine them closely; he didn't dare in the sun or with the captain watching. Please God he hadn't failed them, he hadn't been too late. Gregori had lost so much blood. What would happen to him? Why hadn't he asked the couple more questions while he had the opportunity? He dropped his face into his hands and prayed.

"They are good friends of yours?" Beau ventured compassionately.

"Very good friends. Like family. Gregori saved my life on more than one occasion," Gary answered carefully, not wanting to reveal too much.

"I have such a friend. He is like this one. He had a place not too far from here that he often stayed in when we'd spent too much time in the swamp. He didn't like the sun either. I'll take you there. Gregori and Savannah know him. I don't think Julian would mind."

The boat began to pick up speed now that they were out of the root-choked channel and into the clear water. "Thank you," Gary said gratefully.

Beau LaRue knew the bayou like his own backyard. He took the boat to the top safe speed and found every shortcut he could think of. When they approached land, it was a small island with a single hunting cabin on it. The cypress trees were thick, nearly impenetrable. "The ground is very firm here in the center of the island. It doesn't look so, but there is a trail of stepping stones leading through the mire. We can take them to Julian's secret place. He owns this piece of land, and it's always undisturbed. He isn't a man one wants to trifle with."

They took Gregori first because Beau had to lead the way. He picked his way carefully, every step placed on a round stone in the muck. It was difficult going with Gregori so big, his body a dead weight. Beau could not discern the rise and fall of the man's chest, but he refrained from saying so. It seemed insane to him to take someone so mortally wounded to a dark, damp cavern, but he had seen Julian go to this place on more than one occasion when the sun was rising to its peak.

The cave they approached was man-made and very small. There was almost no room to stand. They laid Gregori's body full length on the dirt floor in the darkness and retreated quickly, Gary anxious to get Savannah out of the light. He lifted Savannah into his arms and faced the captain. "Thanks for your help. I'll attend to these two. Leave my bags right here on the stones. I'll see to Savannah and come back for them."

"You want me to stay?" Beau asked, torn between curiosity and his ingrained belief in privacy.

Gary shook his head, already moving across the stones.

Beau cast off, started the engine. "I'll check to see if you need me later tonight."

"Thanks," Gary called over his shoulder, hurrying to get Savannah's body out of the sun.

He sank down beside the two still bodies, breathing hard, worried that they might truly be dead. He was even afraid to bathe Gregori's fearsome wounds, not certain what harm it might do. He passed the time playing solitaire, drinking from his canteen, and going back and forth between being certain they were dead and sure they would rise with the setting of the sun.

Out across the bayou the sky finally became a smoky gray. Gary crawled to the entrance to the cave and stared out at the gathering night. It couldn't happen too fast to suit him. When he turned his head, he saw the rise and fall of Gregori's chest beneath the blanket.

Gregori felt hunger first, then pain. He blocked them both and assessed the damage done to his body. He had lost a good amount of blood, but Savannah had replenished him. It took a short time to focus, to go inside himself and heal the gaping wounds. Even with what Savannah had given him, he was in desperate need of blood. Only after he had closed the lacerations so that there was no further blood loss, he stirred, then sat up. He could hear a heart beating close by, the ebb and flow of life rushing hotly, calling to him so that his fangs began to lengthen in his need.

His mind automatically reached for Savannah. She had saved him. He was getting used to her pulling him back from tight spots. There was no lack of courage in Savannah. He found her life-light huddled in a small corner of his mind. She had brought herself to the brink of death in order to give him life. Swearing, he pushed the blanket from his body and shoved hers aside. He gathered her close and examined every inch of her.

The loud, insistent beat of the heart so close to them, so filled with the rush of life, drew his attention. Slowly Gregori turned his head to see Gary watching him from the entrance to the cave. He had known he was there, knew it was Gary who had taken them from the swamp and found them a dark, safe place to sleep.

"I owe you much," Gregori greeted the human softly. Hunger gnawed again, and he could feel his incisors sharpen in response. His lifemate needed sustenance immediately. "Stay with her while I hunt."

Gary took a deep breath, then let it out slowly. "You can use my blood. I knew you would wake hungry."

The hard edge to Gregori's mouth softened momentarily. "I do not merely hunger, my friend. I need. Savannah needs. I can be dangerous in this state. I would never risk your life."

"I trust you, Gregori," Gary said truthfully, surprised that it was so.

Gregori moved around him. "You are a rare man, Gary Jansen. I feel privileged to know you, to count you as a friend. Please take care of my lifemate while I hunt."

Gregori was already pushing past Gary, a mere brush as he went by, but the contact sent a shiver down Gary's spine. Gregori smelled wild and dangerous, a merciless, predatory animal. Gary didn't know how he knew the difference, but at that moment Gregori was more beast than man. It was only after Gregori was gone, shape-shifting before his eyes into a bird of prey, that Gary realized that the terrible wounds in the Carpathian's body were healed. He watched the raptor rise on the wind until it became a mere speck in the sky.

Gary scrambled across the dirt floor, hunching over to avoid scraping his head on the roof. He sat beside Savannah and waited. It didn't take very long before the bird returned. Gary couldn't take his eyes off the shimmering, iridescent feathers shifting into a solid rock of a man.

Gregori glided through the cypress trees, tall, fit, healthy. Even his clothes were immaculate. His hair was shining clean, tied at his nape with a leather thong. His silver eyes were clear, and once more his face was a mask of sensual beauty. "Gary"—the voice, as always, was purity and strength—"please leave us for a few moments."

"Will she be all right?" Gary asked fearfully. In spite of himself, he had checked her pulse several times.

"She must be all right," Gregori said very softly.

The voice was like velvet, but there was something in it that sent a shiver of apprehension through Gary. If anything happened to Savannah, Gary realized that no one, nothing in the world, would ever be safe again from the Carpathian. He hadn't considered that before, and he had no idea where the knowledge came from, but he knew it absolutely. He crawled from the cramped space and picked his way a small distance from the cave. The night noises bothered him, were strange and a bit daunting.

Gregori gathered Savannah tenderly into his arms. *Come to me, my life and breath. Wake and be with me.* He gave the command, and even as he felt her heart flutter, he pressed her mouth to his throat. *Feed*, ma petite. *Feed and replenish what you selflessly gave to me.*

Savannah turned her head, her first breath a sigh of warmth against his throat. She nuzzled closer, drowsy and weak from lack of blood. Her tongue tasted his skin, caressed his pulse. Gregori's body tightened alarmingly as her teeth sent white-hot pleasure slicing through him. Slowly her skin warmed, went from ashen to a healthy glow. Her arms slipped around his neck, and she held him close, her body fitting into his, a restless ache of need and hunger.

Savannah closed the pinpricks on her lifemate's neck, feathered kisses up his throat to his jaw, then found the corner of his mouth. Gregori caught her head and held her still, his mouth dominating, taking hers with a need as elemental as the wind.

"I thought I lost you," she whispered into his heart, his soul. "I thought I lost you."

"Are you always going to be pulling me out of trouble?" he asked, some strong, unnamed emotion choking him, blocking his throat.

A small smile tugged at her soft mouth. "Back you up, you mean."

He groaned at her terminology. "*Je t'àime*, Savannah. More than I can ever express in words of any language." His arms held her tight, sheltering her against his heart. She was his world, would always be his world. She was his laughter, his light. She showed him how to slip easily between both worlds. She gave him faith in humans that had never been there before.

As if reading his mind, she smiled happily up at him. "Gary really came through for us, didn't he?"

"Absolutely, *ma petite*. And Beau LaRue was not so bad either. Come, we cannot leave the poor man pacing the swamp. He will think we are engaging in something other than conversation."

Wickedly Savannah moved her body against his, her hands sliding provocatively, enticingly, over the rigid thickness straining his trousers. "Aren't we?" she asked with that infuriating sexy smile he could never resist.

"We have a lot of clean-up to do here, Savannah," he said severely. "And we need to get word to our people, spread the society's list through our ranks, warn those in danger."

Her fingers were working at the buttons of his shirt so that she could push the material aside to examine his chest and shoulder, where two of the worst wounds had been. She had to see his body for herself, touch him to assure herself he was completely healed. "I suggest, for now, that your biggest job is to create something for Gary to do so we can have a little privacy." With a smooth movement, she pulled the shirt from over her head so that her full breasts gleamed temptingly at him.

Gregori made a sound somewhere between a sigh and a moan. His hands came up to cup the weight of her in his palms, the feel of her soft, satin skin soothing after the burning torture of the tainted blood. His thumbs caressed the rosy tips into hard peaks. He bent his head slowly to the erotic temptation because he was helpless to do anything else. He needed the merging of their bodies after such a close call as much as she did. He could feel the surge of excitement, the rush of liquid heat through her body at the feel of his mouth pulling strongly at her breast.

Gregori dragged her even closer, his hands wandering over her with a sense of urgency. Her need was feeding his.

"Gary," she whispered. "Don't forget about Gary."

Gregori cursed softly, his hand pinning her hips so that he could strip away the offending clothes on her body. He spared the human a few seconds of his attention, directing him away from the cave. Savannah's soft laughter was taunting, teasing. "I told you, lifemate, you're always taking off my clothes."

"Then stop wearing the damn things," he responded gruffly, his hands at her tiny waist, his mouth finding her flat stomach. "Someday my child will be growing right here," he said softly, kissing her belly. His hands pinned her thighs so that he could explore easily without interruption. "A beautiful little girl with your looks and my disposition."

Savannah laughed softly, her arms cradling his head lovingly. "That should be quite a combination. What's wrong with my disposition?" She was writhing under the onslaught of his hands and mouth, arcing her body more fully into his ministrations.

"You are a wicked woman," he whispered. "I would have to kill any man who treated my daughter the way I am treating you."

She cried out, her body rippling with pleasure. "I happen to love the way you treat me, lifemate," she answered softly and cried out again when he merged their bodies, their minds, their hearts and souls.

The future might be uncertain, with the society dogging the footsteps of their people, but their combined strength was more than enough to see them through. And together they could face any enemy to ensure the continuation of their race.

At Avon Books, we know your passion for romance—once you finish one of our novels, you find yourself wanting more.

May we tempt you with . . .

- **Excerpts** from our upcoming releases.

- Entertaining **extras**, including authors' personal photo albums and book lists.

- Behind-the-scenes **scoop** on your favorite characters and series.

- **Sweepstakes** for the chance to win free books, romantic getaways, and other fun prizes.

- Writing **tips** from our authors and editors.

- **Blog** with our authors and find out why they love to write romance.

- **Exclusive content** that's not contained within the pages of our novels.

Join us at
www.avonbooks.com

AVON

An Imprint of HarperCollinsPublishers
www.avonromance.com

*G*ive in to your Impulses!

These unforgettable stories only take a second to buy and give you hours of reading pleasure!

Go to *www.AvonImpulse.com* and see what we have to offer.

Available wherever e-books are sold.

AVONIMPULSE

IMP 0811